DAUGHTER OF THE STONES

ALEXANDRA WALSH

Boldwood

First published in Great Britain in 2025 by Boldwood Books Ltd.

Cover Design by Alice Moore Design

Cover Images: Shutterstock

A CIP catalogue record for this book is available from the British Library.

Paperback ISBN 978-1-80415-973-6

Large Print ISBN 978-1-80415-974-3

Hardback ISBN 978-1-80415-975-0

Trade Paperback ISBN 978-1-80656-034-9

Ebook ISBN 978-1-80415-971-2

Kindle ISBN 978-1-80415-972-9

Audio CD ISBN 978-1-80415-980-4

MP3 CD ISBN 978-1-80415-979-8

Digital audio download ISBN 978-1-80415-977-4

This book is printed on certified sustainable paper. Boldwood Books is dedicated to putting sustainability at the heart of our business. For more information please visit https://www.boldwoodbooks.com/about-us/sustainability/

Boldwood Books Ltd, 23 Bowerdean Street, London, SW6 3TN

www.boldwoodbooks.com

To Daisy, Joe, Harriet, Nelly and James,
Love you all so much xx

One becomes two; two becomes three; and out of the third comes the fourth, the One.

— THE 'AXIOM OF MARIA' IN *ALCHEMICAL LITERATURE*

DRAMATIS PERSONAE

Laurence 'Larry' King – a patriarch, businessman and the driving force behind the Goldenwych Players

Miranda King née Tempest – (1964–2023) beloved wife of Larry and mother of Gillian, Rachel and Caitlin; she died from lung cancer aged fifty-nine

Gillian Albany (née King) – Larry's eldest daughter, married to Alan

Rachel Cornish (née King) – Larry's middle daughter, married to Pete, mother of Emelia and Porcelain

Caitlin King – the youngest daughter of Larry

Alan Albany – Gillian's husband, who works in the family business

Pete Cornish – Rachel's husband, optician

Stan Beech – local vicar who is engaged to Caitlin

Primrose Cook née King – Larry's older sister. A member of the Players. She and her husband Dale run a successful local shop

Dale Cook – husband of Primrose. Local butcher, which is part of the local shop

Brandon Cook – son of Primrose and Dale

Candy Lightfoot – wife of Brandon Cook. Mother of Jayden and Amber Cook

Kayleigh Cook – daughter of Primrose and Dale

Gail Williams – wife of Kayleigh. Biological mother of Honey Williams-Cook

Dr George Glossop – a long-time friend of Larry's, one of the local GPs. Father of Edward and Lee

Suki Glossop – wife of George, mother of Lee and Edward and adopted auntie to the King girls. Best friend of Miranda King

Edward Glossop – George and Suki's eldest son, works in banking

Lee Glossop – George and Suki's youngest son, also a local GP

Sindy Simmons – best friend of Caitlin King, works with her in the Hill Fort Café. She is divorced from car mechanic, Ricky Mansell, and is single parent to Rosalind

Rosalind (Rosie) Mansell – daughter of Sindy

Vicki Simmons – village hairdresser and mother of Sindy

Martha Orpwood – friend of Caitlin and Sindy, local florist

The Goldenwych Players

Annie Jefferson – a widow. A founder member of the Players and a close friend of Miranda King. Her husband, Paul, died three years ago from cancer

Saul Orchard – old school friend of Larry and George

Barbara Orchard – wife of Saul, a long-time member of the Players

Ted Littleton – a long-time member of the Players, partner of Vicki Simmons

Judy Pelham – dance teacher who also choreographs the Goldenwych Players shows

Daphne Hawthorne – a flamboyant incomer to Goldenwych and a member of the Players, widowed

Iron Age characters

Lear Bladudsunu – King of Britian and leader of the Golden Dobvnni, son of Bladud, father of Goneril, Regan and Cordelia

Estrildis Loegriadohtor – late wife of Lear and mother of Goneril, Regan and Cordelia The Princess of a nearby tribe

Goneril Leardohtor – the eldest daughter of Lear

Regan Leardohtor – the middle daughter of Lear

Cordelia Leardohtor – The youngest daughter of Lear, the tribe's shaman

Aganippus – King of Gallia

Ebraucus – the eldest son of a tribal leader from Brigantes

Maglaurus – heir to the tribe of Albany

Henwinus – heir to the tribe of Dvmnonii

Locrinus – chief healer of the Golden Dobvnni and friends since boyhood with Lear, widower

Lagon – younger son of Locrinus and Saldir. Healer of the Golden Dobvnni with his father

Ivor – elder son of Locrinus and his first wife, Guenlodoe

Gael – betrothed of Ivor

Dardan – Lear's second-in-command

Sadiald – wife of Dardan

Kamber Bladudsunu – younger brother of Lear, chief of Credenhill, a territory bordering Lear's

Buel – friend and first in command for Aganippus

Kerin Goffarsunu – stepfather of Aganippus, leader of the Woolbury Ring Hill Fort in Belgae

Margan Bodloandohtor – mother of Aganippus

Guardid – nursemaid of Nest

The Temple

Angarad – the Mother of the Temple

Becuma – High priestess, the beekeeper and mistress of the hives

Gloigin – twin of Ignogin, the elder by three minutes, handmaiden in the temple

Ignogin – handmaiden in the temple

Oudar – neophyte in the temple

PROLOGUE

Darkness. Overwhelming darkness. The wind howled, tormenting her, snatching her words as she cried out, shouting for her father. Each word was a knife in her chest as she struggled to breathe, to force air into her lungs, but all she could do was gasp in desperation.

'Please, no,' she whispered, her hands floundering as she called again into the raging chaos of the storm-tossed night. 'Help me. Somebody.'

Her knees buckled beneath her and she panted, the breath refusing to enter her body, her chest tight as her heart pounded and tears ran down her cheeks.

'Not like this,' she said, her voice harsh. 'Not alone.'

The ground was sodden, cold, and she floundered in its muddy embrace as she fell.

'No,' she murmured.

Then a soft hand began stroking her face, wiping away the tears and rain.

'Breathe,' the woman said. 'Breathe.'

'How?' she replied.

'You are the one,' the woman said, fading into nothingness. 'Breathe.'

The final word was a whisper on the cold gust of driving rain before the shadows at the edges of her consciousness claimed her and she knew no more.

1

GOLDENWYCH, PRESENT DAY

Caitlin King was early for the meeting with her father. She glanced at her watch as she opened the door of her cherry red SUV. In the distance was the relentless tapping of the junior dance class, the tinny sound drifting through the open window of the small theatre. Shuddering at the noise, Caitlin reached into the back seat and took the circlet of wildflowers from its protective cardboard box.

This was the reason she had arrived with so much time to spare and she was angry her father had not remembered. She shook her long dark hair from her eyes and breathed in the beauty of the golden summer evening. The sun-dappled graveyard would be the balm of peace she craved after her busy day at work in the Hill Fort Café.

Her car pinged as she locked it and in her mind she heard her fiancé Stan's voice. *'You don't need to lock the car, Goldenwych has the lowest crime rate of any area in the UK.'*

His comment, while statistically true, was nevertheless naïve and Caitlin pushed these imaginary admonishments aside. She had grown up in the village, Stan Beech had arrived three years earlier. As the vicar, Stan was at the centre of the community, but he continued to see Goldenwych as a picture-book-perfect, fairy-tale idyll rather than a real place. Although, as she crossed the car park that was shared by the small theatre and the village church, she could understand why Stan was enamoured by the surroundings.

Goldenwych was beautiful. It nestled on the side of a gentle gradient overlooking the Golden Valley and onwards to the Black Mountains and Offa's Dyke; the demarcation line between the English and Welsh borders.

On the edge of the village was a tumbled stone circle which local folklore claimed was connected with the nearby Neolithic chambered tomb called Arthur's Stone. An archaeological dig in the 1980s had found traces of roundhouses and an Iron Age settlement, including graves with a variety of burial goods. During her teens, Caitlin had spent hours in the local libraries searching for more information about the ancient landmarks. There were very few facts, instead the history was a series of surmises and educated guesses, the gaps filled by myth and legend, which in her heart she believed were true.

At the heart of Goldenwych was a large triangular green where cricket was played during the summer. Around this were shops, cafés and the one remaining pub, The Three Sisters. Roads radiated outwards, a few leading towards the new housing estate on the far side of the village, another to rows of cottages and the infant and junior school and another to the tangle of older streets with their mismatched but picturesque cottages and houses of varying eras. The final road meandered up a gentle slope to the church and the small theatre which doubled as a church hall.

Caitlin walked towards the lychgate, admiring the new hand-made terracotta tiles on its roof as they glowed amber in the softening rays of the day. They were a contrast to the wood of the porch, which was black with age and weathering, the posts twisted but sturdy, guarding against evil. Wound around the top of the gate was a garland of flowers from a wedding a few days earlier. Fragrant sprigs of honeysuckle nestled into creamy roses and carnations, all surrounded by an abundance of foliage. Caitlin noticed oak leaves, rosemary, myrtle and maple, each flower and leaf chosen to symbolise love, fertility and prosperity by her friend Martha Orpwood, who was the third generation of women in her family to run the local florist.

'Good work,' Caitlin murmured as she let herself through the gate. 'I bet Stan hasn't a clue you've put a pagan protection spell on his church.'

She loved her fiancé, but his refusal to embrace the village's more unusual traditions grated on her. For her, the quirks of Goldenwych, the place she had been born and raised, were part of her soul. When Martha had arrived with the garland the day before the wedding, Stan and Caitlin had been in the vicarage and, upon seeing it, he had hurried outside and queried its suitability.

'Won't it be damaged when people open the gate?' he had asked.

'No,' Martha had replied, her florist's wire and pliers in hand, 'it's a village tradition and everyone knows not to touch the flowers.'

'They're beautiful,' said Caitlin, who had followed Stan, 'and the bride requested them especially.'

Stan had slipped his arm around her waist. 'Who am I to stand in the way of tradition?' he had said, but his smile had not quite reached his eyes.

Caitlin breathed in the heady scent of the freshly cut grass as she followed the path through the graveyard. She took the fork leading away from the twelfth-century church towards a tranquil corner where a bench rested under the welcome shade of a linden tree. Graves of contrasting styles and ages stood sentinel around the quiet space, but Caitlin had eyes for only one. A green slate monolith, its colour striking but natural, and the mark of a local stone. It was almost one metre high and it sat alone under the tree. At its base was an engraved plaque in the same colour slate with words picked out in gold:

Miranda King (31 October 1964 – 21 June 2023)
Beloved wife of Larry and mother of Gillian, Rachel and Caitlin
'Love comforteth like sunshine after rain'

Two circlets of flowers, one made of blush pink roses and honeysuckle, the other white gerbera and carnations, lay in a line down the centre of the grave, joined by purple ribbons. Caitlin's eyes filled with tears as she stared at them before adding her own wildflower ring at the bottom, tying it to the flowers above with the ribbons woven through the design.

She knelt on the grass, enjoying the cool, soft dampness of the earth on her skin, gazing at the flowers. Was this a sign of forgiveness? It had been two years since their mother had died, were they ready to move forward?

'Hello, Mum,' said Caitlin. 'Have you had a good day? It's looks as though you've been busy, you have flowers from both Bean and Rabbit, as well as from me. Has Dad visited?'

She bent forward to clear a few weeds from the grave, breathing in the familiar scents of the graveyard: the summer stocks, lavender and the sweet scent of the linden tree.

'It's your favourite time of year, Mum,' she said, 'the summer solstice, the longest day and shortest night. What was it you used to say? "A turning point in the year, the Earth begins to tilt away from the sun as it travels back to the darkness of winter." If you were here, Mum, we'd all be wearing the wreaths of flowers in our hair as we danced around the bonfire with you and Auntie Suki.'

Her voice cracked and Caitlin flicked away the tears welling in the corner of her eyes.

'The café was manic today and your brownie recipe is as popular as ever,' she continued, forcing brightness into her words. 'There's a meeting of the Players tomorrow. Dad's thoroughly overexcited, he's announcing the new Christmas play, but he asked to meet me here this evening to help make the theatre ready and probably to discuss refreshments for tomorrow.'

There was a rustle above her and a rook landed in the linden tree. It stared down at her with bright black intelligent eyes. Caitlin watched as it ruffled its feathers before opening its beak – pale, curved, majestic, wicked – and cawing.

'Hello,' said Caitlin and the rook cried again in response.

They stared at each other and Caitlin felt as though the bird could see inside her, reading her troubled thoughts, encouraging her to share them.

Before she could stop herself, she blurted out, 'Why is Stan annoying me, Mum? I love him, but in the past few weeks, he's been different, challenging me on stupid things, arguing for the sake of it.' She glanced around, ensuring she was alone as she continued, 'He's away for a few days, but rather than missing him, I'm overwhelmed by the sheer joy of having the bed to myself. When I realised it was the solstice and your day while he was gone, I knew I'd be able to have a fire and celebrate like we used to, all without Stan tutting in the background. He doesn't really understand that side of me.'

She gave a sad laugh.

'Don't worry, though,' she finished, 'we'll work it out before the wedding.'

The church clock struck seven and Caitlin stood up, brushing a fallen leaf from the soft folds of her summer dress.

'I'd better go, Mum.'

She placed her hand on the monolith again and breathed in, as though trying to capture a hint of her mother's perfume, but all she could smell was the grass.

'Love you,' she whispered before walking back along the path.

In the light and shade of the summer evening with its dazzling show of shifting shadows of bright and dark, she did not see the man at the fork in the path until she was upon him.

'Lee,' she exclaimed. He smiled down at her before she leaned into his hug. 'What are you doing here?'

Lee Glossop and his elder brother Edward had grown up with Caitlin and her two elder sisters, Gillian and Rachel. He was the son of Dr George Glossop, her father's best friend since boyhood, while their mums, Miranda and Suki, had become good friends through their husbands. Lee had followed in his father's footsteps and was a doctor, too, recently joining George as a GP at the Goldenwych Surgery.

Lee opened the lychgate for her.

'A summons from Mum and Dad,' he said. 'Dad, in particular – he insisted I help, apparently he and your dad will be too busy backstage tomorrow to do anything as mundane as arrange the chairs.'

'They're both as bad as each other at the beginning of a show,' she said. 'Thank goodness your mum can usually bring them back to reality.'

'How was your mum?' he asked as they ambled across the car park.

'She was fine,' said Caitlin. 'It's hard to believe it's two years since she died.'

'You must miss her,' he said.

'Yes, but it was a relief for her; she was in such pain by the end.'

'Summer solstice isn't the same without our mums lighting a bonfire and telling us lurid tales of pagan rites,' he said.

'And the tales becoming more outrageous as they worked their way down a bottle of wine,' said Caitlin.

'Do you have any plans for later?'

'When we've finished setting out the chairs, Martha's coming over. We're going to recreate the ritual of the bonfire,' she said. 'Although, I'm using my firepit rather than a huge out-of-control stack of wood, leaves and newspapers like our parents used to build.'

'What will Stan say?' said Lee. 'He doesn't approve of your pagan ways.'

'He won't know, he's away at a conference,' she replied. 'Fancy joining us?'

'Are you sure?' he asked and she nodded. 'Then I'd love to come, although I'm on call, so I might have to dash away.'

His phone pinged and he pulled a face, making Caitlin laugh. She walked back towards her car where there was a cool box with snacks for the helpers, but as she took her car keys from her pocket and turned back to Lee, she halted. He was hurrying towards her, his phone clamped to his ear, his face ashen.

'What...?' she mouthed, but he shook his head, reaching out to take her arm.

'She's here, Dad,' Lee said into his phone. 'Could you call Gilly and Rachel? I'll take her there now.'

'What's happened?' said Caitlin as Lee hung up.

'It's your dad,' said Lee. 'He collapsed while he and my dad were rehearsing for tomorrow. Dad says it could be a stroke, but we don't know yet.'

Caitlin stared at him in horror.

'Which hospital?' she asked, wrenching herself away from him.

'I'll drive,' said Lee, removing the keys from her hand. 'Come on.'

As he hurried her into his car, Caitlin heard a harsh caw and turned to see the rook from earlier. It landed briefly on the roof of the lychgate before flying away into the burning summer sky.

2

GOLDEN VALLEY, DOBVNNI, 862 BCE

Cordelia danced. The rhythmic thud of the drums kept pace with her heartbeat as she spun through the shadows. Firelight filled the gloaming, its brilliance challenging the fading beauty of the clear summer sky. All around her were shouts of triumph and shrieks of delight as the straw figure at the centre of the flames buckled, collapsing inwards, its limbs flailing as it surrendered to its inevitable fate. A cacophony of exultation swept through the hill fort and, caught in the moment, she added her voice to the screams as the sacrifice succumbed.

It was the festival of Litha, the summer solstice, and the straw man was a central part of the celebrations. Its destruction in fire presented a warning to the Dark Twin of winter, the opposing force of the Light Twin of summer. The ritual was to acknowledge the approaching darkness and to warn the winter it was not yet time for its icy grip to envelop the land. There were days of sunshine and abundance still to come. At sunrise the following day, Cordelia would take her place with the other high priestesses to enact the rites of summer with the symbolic crowning of the sun god and goddess to ensure the harmony of their settlement.

With a flourish, the drummer brought the music to an end and there were cheers and clapping from dancers and watchers alike. Cordelia hugged her friend and fellow priestess Becuma who had danced beside her before hurrying to the raised dais where her family awaited.

'My child, you danced as well as your mother and I can give you no higher praise,' said her father, Lear Bladudsunu, the King of Britain and the respected leader of their tribe, as he hugged her.

'Thank you, Fa,' she said. 'You know this is my favourite time of year. I love these celebrations because they're based in joy and laughter.'

There were eight festivals, each marking the passing of time and carrying their own rituals for the fruitful continuation of their tribe.

'Come, my sweet,' said her father, 'take a seat beside your sisters. Tonight, you aren't a high priestess, you're my youngest daughter, a princess of our people.'

They hugged again, squeezing each other, an unspoken show of the fierceness of their love and respect for each other.

When her father released her, they smiled, eyes full of love, before Cordelia sat in the space made for her by her middle sister, Regan.

'Don't listen to him,' Regan said, pulling a grotesque face as she poured mead into Cordelia's goblet. 'You dance like a goose.'

'At least I stay upright, you always trip over your big feet,' she replied as they giggled.

'Grow up,' whispered Goneril, the eldest of the three. 'We're supposed to be on our best behaviour for Fa's guests.'

Goneril angled her head towards a number of well-dressed men of varying ages seated on the other side of their father. Most of the older men were members of their community, advisors and friends to Lear, but the remainder were visitors. They ranged in age from barely entering manhood to the mature features of Aganippus, King of Gallia. Beside him sat men of twenty winters or more, similar to the age of the sisters, all from nearby tribes: Maglaurus, heir to the tribe of Albany, Henwinus, heir to the tribe of Dvmnonii and Ebraucus, the eldest son of a tribal leader from Brigantes. Each of the assembled guests were suitors hoping to wed one of the great man's daughters.

Regan and Cordelia exchanged a mischievous look and leaned over to tickle Goneril until she laughed.

One of the older men, Locrinus, their father's friend and the tribe's chief healer, glanced over and winked. He was like a brother to Lear and an adopted uncle to the three sisters. Seated either side of him were his sons, Lagon and Ivor, both of whom were conversing with the guests.

Lear, ever alert to the smooth running of the festivities, followed Locrinus's look to ensure there were no disturbances.

Cordelia saw her father turn towards them and, without thinking, she blew him a kiss. He pretended to catch it and placed his hand on his heart, then returned her kiss with one of his own. It was game they had played since childhood and it always made Cordelia realise how lucky she was to have such a wise and honourable father.

Goneril scowled as Regan and Cordelia laughed at the action.

'Stop being so grumpy, Goneril,' said Regan. 'It's Litha, a time for joy.'

'She's right. If we can't share laughter on this night, during the solstice celebrations, then things would be amiss,' said Cordelia.

'Are you jealous? Did you want Fa to blow you a kiss?' Regan teased Goneril. 'Shall I blow you one instead, or would you prefer it if it came from Maglaurus?'

A smile twitched at Goneril's lips and she flicked a tiny honey cake from the platter in front of her at her sisters.

'Who's childish now?' Cordelia said as she caught the cake and ate it in one bite.

Goneril shot a look towards Henwinus, Maglaurus, Aganippus and Ebraucus.

'We are in the presence of our future husbands, don't let them think we're a bunch of savages,' she muttered.

The summer solstice was considered an auspicious time for the arrangement of marriages and, despite Goneril's declaration upon seeing the potential husbands – 'They are lowly specimens, far below what I expect from a spouse' – she had been flirting with Maglaurus ever since. Cordelia and Regan had shared amused grins as they watched the fair-haired and bearded young man trail around behind Goneril whenever he was allowed.

'We are the daughters of Lear Bladudsunu,' Goneril continued. 'The granddaughters of Bladud Hudibrassunu, the founder of the great town of Kaerbadum in Atrebates. Everyone knows the tale of how his leprosy was cured by its healing springs. When he was well and whole again, he dedicated the waters to the goddess Sulis.'

'Quite right,' Regan added in the same lofty tone her sister had adopted, 'and, don't forget, our father is revered for creating peace among the tribes all the way from Atrebates through Belgae and the Cornovii to here, our home of Dobvnni.'

'It was a feat of strategy, diplomacy and unflinching warcraft, and has given us this home overlooking our beautiful Golden Valley,' Cordelia concluded, her voice low and serious.

'Shut up, you two,' Goneril replied, but she was working hard to suppress her laughter. 'Tonight is important, Father is choosing mine and Regan's husbands and we want to ensure they're strong and powerful.'

'And rich,' said Cordelia.

'Why would you care?' Regan said. 'You're a shamanic high priestess, you'll be able to stay at home forever.'

Regan's voice cracked and Cordelia hugged her. Marriage might mean a rise in status for women, but it would also entail leaving the hill fort where they had grown up, probably never to return. Cordelia thanked the goddesses every day for the talents she had inherited from their mother, Estrildis Loegriadohtor, which meant she would remain here for life. It was a comforting thought as she had no desire to travel to the far reaches of the land with a stranger.

'The feast!' her father shouted, bringing her attention back to the celebrations, his excitement bubbling through his words. 'Let us thank the gods and goddesses for this marvellous bounty.'

Cordelia touched her forehead, the position of her psychic third eye, and watched as, all around, others followed her lead. It was the sign they made for gratitude and was always shared at their festivals.

As the food was carried to the gathering, Lear stood.

'Let us praise the goddesses for their fruitful bounty,' he declared as a roast pig was deposited on a wooden bench beside the seated guests, followed by an array of large platters overflowing with food.

As he rose, Cordelia and her sisters followed. She suppressed a giggle as Regan shook back her long white-blonde hair, ignoring the glance from Henwinus, the man beside the dazzled Maglaurus, who could not take his eyes from her.

Regan was the beauty of the trio, the smallest in stature, her hair thick and wavy, shimmering with light despite the hidden shadows in its curls. Her eyes were green and her skin of a rich creaminess, decorated with a sprinkling of golden freckles. Goneril was taller, her hair chestnut-red with eyes of amber, her complexion pale with hints of pink, while Cordelia, as the youngest, was different again: tall and slender, her dark hair held the depth of velvet night, her face as pale as the moon and eyes as blue as the summer sky. The trio were the inspiration for many bards' poems.

'My daughters will guide you,' Lear boomed to his guests. 'There may be dishes here with which you are unfamiliar.'

He beamed with pride as he ushered the three young women forward.

'Here, let me help,' said Cordelia as Aganippus, the King of Gallia, reached towards the dish of fresh salmon. She served him using an iron-bladed knife, cutting through the pink flesh and placing it in a bowl decorated with a bright red haematite glaze and swirls of amber. 'The boiled samphire and blaanda bread will complement the fish, as will the nettle purée. Are these dishes familiar?'

'The salmon is and the samphire, but I have never tasted blaanda bread,' he said and Cordelia liked the way his eyes sparkled when he smiled.

His accent was unfamiliar but attractive and ever since his arrival, whenever he had spoken, Cordelia knew she had heard his voice before. She wondered whether they had met in the Everywhen, the spiritual plane she roamed as the tribe's shaman. She knew the answer would present itself at the most auspicious time and, when it did, she would understand.

'It's very good,' she said, 'especially when served dripping in butter as it is this evening.'

'Thank you,' he said and returned to his seat.

Cordelia watched him as he sampled the bread, smiling as he looked at her and pretended to swoon at its deliciousness.

You're a priestess, she reminded herself. *You were born to serve your people, not flirt with potential suitors.*

Yet, for the first time, she felt a small pang of disappointment and as this unexpected feeling washed over her, she heard the distant caw of a rook. A shiver ran down her spine and she turned to look at the small copse of hazel trees nearby. A rook was watching her from a high branch, its black eyes narrowed, its white beak shimmering in the first rays of moonlight. As their eyes locked, the rook bowed its head before taking flight into the summer evening. Cordelia watched as it disappeared into the shadows and whispered a blessing.

A rook accompanied her when she undertook her shamanic journeys. It was her spirit guide and offered her safe flight home from the Everywhen should her journey become too dangerous or disturbing. She was used to the corporeal birds acknowledging her too.

* * *

By the time the food was finished, diamond-bright stars hung in the clear sky. Even without the glowing embers of the dying fire, the air was warm and groups of people milled around, chatting, laughing, enjoying the festivities. The musicians played gentle tunes, their drums, pipes and harps blending together in a magical conjunction.

Cordelia sat between Aganippus and Ebraucus, listening with interest to the different methods of worshipping the solstice in the provinces of Gallia and Brigantes, the homes of the two men. Both were similar, but she winced when Ebraucus boasted of sacrificing a young deer.

'Is this not a waste?' asked Cordelia. 'If left to mature, these animals could bring greater prosperity to the tribe with their offspring.'

'It's a sign we believe the gods will provide,' said Ebraucus, his words slurred from a surfeit of mead, spittle on his chin which he did not wipe away. 'The gods are pleased by our humility, they provide us with excellent hunting.'

Cordelia did not believe in sacrificing any living creature. Her worship was goddess-led and they had never once craved fresh blood, preferring a symbolic offering, like the straw man.

'The Brigantes tribe decided to make do with deer after their elders banned human sacrifice,' said Aganippus, who was watching Ebraucus in disgust.

'They practised human sacrifice?' said Cordelia, horrified.

'Until a few years ago,' replied Aganippus.

'Do you not do the same here?' said Ebraucus.

'No, we're not savages,' said Cordelia, revolted by the idea. 'The Druids and other wise leaders have long since made it known these practices are frowned upon—'

Before she could continue, her father came striding towards them.

'Come, my daughters,' he said, taking her by the hand and beckoning Goneril and Regan, 'it is time for you to dance.'

Goneril opened her mouth, about to protest, then she saw Lagon and Ivor walking towards them holding three batons made from bronze, the ends wrapped in rags which were soaked in vegetable oil from the previous year's press.

'The fire dance?' she exclaimed.

'It would please me to see my daughters dance together one more time,' Lear beamed. 'I believe change is in the air and this might be the last time I am afforded the joy of having my trio, my triskele of daughters, by my side.'

He glanced over at Maglaurus before winking at Goneril, who blushed.

'Come, Goneril,' said Regan, taking her sister's hand. 'Let us indulge our loving father.'

Cordelia stood between her sisters, a sudden wave of sadness washing over her. *Would this be their last dance?* she wondered. They had always been together, but the stark realisation she might never see them again once they were married engulfed her and she felt their bond of love tighten. They might bicker and tease each other, but they were the best of friends, as well as sisters.

She looked at Regan, who was plaiting her hair to keep it from her face. Regan was an elegant dancer and Cordelia knew her sister saw this performance as another chance to impress Henwinus. He was an orphan but had been raised by his uncle and would inherit his vast tracts of land in Dvmnonii. Cordelia waited for a flash of insight as to whether Regan and Henwinus would be married, but nothing materialised.

Decisions are yet to be made, she thought, *something else must happen first.*

Perhaps, it was the dance. A chance for Henwinus to fall in love with Regan as she swirled in the firelight.

Lagon handed Cordelia her baton.

'Be careful,' he said. 'The rags are smouldering. As soon as they receive a rush of air, they'll burst into flame.'

'Thank you,' she said, smiling up at him.

Lagon was a constant presence in her life, a best friend, perhaps a brother to replace the one she and her sisters had lost so many years earlier. Although, her feelings towards Lagon were not always sisterly. As they had grown, she had often experienced sparks of attraction towards him.

Ivor, older than Lagon by two winters, handed the remaining two poles to Goneril and Regan. 'Dance with care, my beautiful princesses,' he said and bowed low from the waist as he backed away from them.

'Fool,' laughed Goneril, but Cordelia noticed the flush on her sister's cheek.

Ivor, too, was handsome but in a different way to Lagon. The men were half-brothers, sharing the same father but being born from Locrinus's two marriages. Ivor favoured his late mother's sandy-coloured hair and brown eyes, while Lagon followed their shared father's look, with dark hair and blue eyes.

The three sisters took their positions in a line. Around them, the inhabitants of the hill fort gathered, the air heavy with expectation. The fire dance was one for which they were famed and, as such, they practised the routine at least twice a week. Cordelia always took the lead and when both her sisters had whispered, 'Ready,' she nodded towards the band, giving them the cue to begin.

Music filled the air, ancient in its beauty, the harp and the drum weaving the tale of the goddesses of old when they walked in the land of Albion. The three sisters, their feet slow at first, quickly found their way into the well-worn groove of their story-telling. As each twirled their baton, the soaked rags burst into flame, causing a wave of noise and excitement from the onlookers. The intensity of the tune increased, the steps became more complex, but still the sisters' feet were deft and skilful as they spun and weaved, their hair flying in the summer night, the moon bathing them with silver.

Out of the corner of her eye, Cordelia saw Becuma dart forward and throw a handful of tiny wax disks into the flames. She knew what would happen next; it was a trick they used when wishing to impress during their rituals. There was an exclamation as the flames flashed blue, then green, before returning to their normal hue, but as they did, Cordelia felt the earth shift.

'No,' she gasped, 'not here.'

'Cordelia, what's wrong?' Regan's voice was urgent.

Cordelia's knees buckled, causing her to stumble, but she managed to regain her balance, her eyes closed as lights swirled in an arc. The vision was vivid: all around her was devastation, destruction and despair, pouring rain and shouts of anguish. A man, her father, his face streaked with blood, his teeth bared and one eye covered in a bloodied patch, stood over a lifeless body, his sword raised, his mouth open in a silent scream.

'No,' she gasped, but the vision had passed and she was back in the present.

Regan and Goneril danced around her, their batons twirling, affording her a chance to recover. She nodded to her concerned sisters, indicating she was able to continue and threw her flaming stick in the air, catching it deftly as her sisters followed suit. They slipped easily back into their dance with few noticing the unexpected changes.

The song reached a crescendo and the three women tossed their sticks to each other in a blur of speed and expertise, criss-crossing in and out, the flames creating the burning image of the triskele, the symbol of the triple goddess.

A roar of wonder raised from the crowd as the music reached its dramatic climax and the three daughters of Lear finished in a triangle, their backs to each other, their right hands raised as the flames on their batons flared against the night sky.

Above them, three rooks circled, their caws filling the night sky, and Cordelia collapsed in a dead faint at her sisters' feet.

3

GOLDEN VALLEY, DOBVNNI, 862 BCE

'My daughter is our shaman.' Her father's voice was faint as he explained her fall to their guests, but there was a note of pride. 'She has the clear sight – inherited, not learned.'

Becuma and Angarad helped lift her, but Cordelia gasped as though in pain.

'What's wrong with her?' said Regan, her voice tense, worried. 'Be careful, she might still be in the Everywhen.'

'No,' reassured Cordelia, her voice hoarse. 'The rook returned me home, I am here.'

She felt Regan's hand squeezing hers.

'Take her to our roundhouse,' ordered Goneril. 'We'll care for her.'

The four women guided Cordelia away from the gathering. As she passed her father, he smiled reassuringly, but she could not look at him, speak to him. The image of his other-worldly violence was scorched on her mind. His conversation with Aganippus floated to her through the night sky.

'I had no idea she possessed the gift,' said Aganippus, his voice full of concern. 'Will she recover?'

'Of course,' Lear said. 'This must have been a powerful message for it to have taken her by surprise.'

'Please send her my regards,' said Aganippus.

Cordelia felt a strange pang of loneliness as she heard his footsteps retreating.

'Come,' said Becuma, 'you must rest, and tomorrow, we will decide what your journey shows us.'

'Yes,' whispered Cordelia.

She allowed herself to be led to her quarters, unable to believe what she had seen: the violence, the brutality. The pale body on the ground. In her trance, she had seen her father raise his sword and bring it down with swift, brutal blows. She had felt the icy slice of metal, the cold fingers of death, before she was flying, lifted by the rook, leaving behind the horror of her vision.

Goneril lit the oil lamp, guiding Cordelia to the bed, helping her to take off her shoes. Regan, Becuma and Angarad moved around the room on silent feet, sprinkling herbs and tinctures across the entrances and around the bed.

'These will keep you safe,' said Angarad.

She was the Mother of the Temple, the most senior woman of rank in the hill fort and revered for her wisdom.

'Thank you,' murmured Cordelia, her eyes heavy.

'She must sleep,' said Angarad to Goneril, Regan and Becuma. 'I'll stay with her.'

The tone of her voice was firm, the other women knew not to challenge her and, with whispered 'goodnights', they left.

'What did you see?' asked Angarad as soon as they were alone.

'Fa,' said Cordelia, her voice faint, dream-like, as though the trance lingered in her blood. 'He was injured.'

'Badly?'

'No, he was angry, full of violence, there was a battle,' she said.

Angarad closed her eyes.

'I see nothing,' she said. 'Tomorrow, after the ceremony for Litha, the crowning of the god and goddess, you must travel back there—'

'No,' gasped Cordelia, 'please, don't make me.'

'You must visit it again before it travels too far from you. If there is to be an attack, we must be forewarned. We might be able to heal whatever has caused this rift in the Everywhen and prevent the bloodshed from happening.'

'It can't be done.'

'Yes, it can,' replied Angarad. 'Your mother achieved it on several occasions and you are more powerful than her.'

'Mother averted wars?'

'She went deep into the Everywhen and changed our destiny, it's how we became so prosperous,' said Angarad. 'She guided your father and helped him to achieve his status of king. It's why he's so proud you inherited the gift, he feels he has another advisor, one who will steer him through troubled times.'

The image of her father, his teeth bared in rage, made Cordelia shudder.

'Sleep now,' advised Angarad. 'Tomorrow, we will know.'

Angarad turned away, busying herself with the guttering oil lamp, and as she did, Cordelia felt a streak of pain down her arm. When she raised it in the dim light, she saw a silver line on her skin, like a thin scar that had healed, even though it had not been there before her vision. She stared at it, wondering if the trance lingered and this was a dream, but when she touched it, she knew it was real.

* * *

The candlelight flickered, casting grotesque shadows on the walls as Cordelia adjusted her ceremonial headdress. The two antlers, taken from the body of a young deer who had succumbed to the bite of an adder, made her silhouette monstrous.

Becuma, wearing the flowing white robes of the priestesses, dipped a soft brush of rabbit fur into the blue woad and with a well-practised hand painted the swirls and patterns of the dreaming spells across Cordelia's face, finishing with a triskele in the centre of her forehead, the position of the psychic third eye.

Behind her waited the three handmaidens of the temple, twin sisters Gloigin and Ignogin, and Oudar, the neophyte, the youngest member of the sisterhood. Gloigin stepped forward and took the bowl and brush from Becuma before retreating to the shadows.

'The girdle,' said Angarad.

She stood behind Cordelia wearing robes dyed brilliant blue and embroidered with leaves of green, red, orange, brown and white, falling in a graduation of colour from her shoulders to her feet, embodying the changing seasons and the turning of the year. Ignogin presented a heavily embroidered fabric belt, which Angarad tied around Cordelia's waist, fastening the silken cords with an intricate series of knots.

'The jewel.'

Oudar stepped forward and held a cushion aloft. On it nestled a pendant of deepest purple attached to a woven cord that matched the girdle. Angarad reached around Cordelia's neck and fastened the necklace with a small but perfect clasp of a gleaming copper hook and eye, then she and Becuma stepped away. Behind her, the other women echoed their movements.

'May the Goddess hear your words,' Angarad said, bowing low.

'Your wishes have been heard,' replied Cordelia, inclining her head.

'The wax tablets have been prepared as you requested,' Becuma said. 'We shall keep vigil until you return.'

'Thank you, my friend,' murmured Cordelia to Becuma.

The women straightened, their eyes averted from Cordelia as though she were too bright to allow them to look directly at her, the embodiment of the sun. They filed out in silence.

Upon the altar, a fire burned in a shallow metal cauldron. Beside it, in a basket of white willow, were five small, round wax tablets, nestled among bunches of herbs. Next to this stood a golden flask engraved with images of bees and a matching goblet. They glinted in the firelight, giving the impression the bees were moving.

'Matronae, mother goddess, I invoke thee for protection,' Cordelia said as she poured wine from the flask into her goblet, before adding a libation to the flames. 'Hecate, sister moon, I invoke thee for my safe return. Aine, sister of the sun, I invoke thee to shine a light on my path as I heal our past and future.'

The fire spluttered as the tiny drops evaporated. She dropped two of the small round wax tablets into the flames. As they melted, the sweet scent of the honey from the beeswax floated on the air, before, with a hiss, the flames flared purple.

'Corycia, Kleodora, Melaina, the Bee Maidens Three, show me the path to the truth,' she continued crumbling herbs into her drink. 'Help me to repair our wounds and return our strength and compassion. Show me the path as I follow your wisdom.'

Cordelia swallowed the wine in one gulp and winced as the bitterness of the herbs hit the back of her throat. Breathing deeply, she waited until a woozy feeling began to creep over her, the hallucinogenic properties of the henbane were steeling through her blood; as it took her hold, she groaned, the world around her blurred, her eyes widening and rolling uncontrollably. She sank to her knees, her arms outstretched as she flew into the Every-when, where a wolf howled and on her shoulder she felt the claws of her spirit guide, her rook. Her connection to the mortal plane was kept safe by the rhythmic drumming and the low chanting of invocations to the goddesses by her sister priestesses.

In the distance, another rook cawed and she flew into the blinding white of the Everywhen until the image formed around her and she was standing in the centre of the hill fort.

'No,' she said as she gazed at the horrifying vision. 'This cannot be...'

The once prosperous and welcoming community was in tatters. The straw roofs of the roundhouses sagged with neglect, one had been half burned and the entire structure abandoned. People she did not recognise scurried about their business, their heads bowed, faces white and pinched with hunger and cold, skinny dogs worried mangy chickens and the central meeting space, which was usually filled with energy and laughter, even on the coldest of winter days, was desolate and bare. In the distance, the temple was in ruins and a goat wandered through the entrance to what had once been the inner sanctum.

A woman stumbled past her. Tripping on one of the ruts, she fell to her knees and the covering on her head slipped into the mud. Cordelia gasped, it was her sister Regan, but her hair had been shorn almost to her scalp and her skin was blotchy and scarred. From the nearest roundhouse, another woman hurried to her aid and Cordelia felt her stomach clench. Goneril was gaunt, her face angular from lack of food, one eye was swollen shut and there were bruises around her neck. Cordelia could see the finger marks on her sister's skin from where an assailant must have throttled her but had released her before she choked to death.

'Where are my useless daughters?'

The voice was low, angry, full of menace, and the two women clung to each other in fear.

A man, his left eye covered in a leather patch, emerged from the round-house. He was stooped and skinny, leaning on a heavy walking stick, his lips bared in fury.

'How many more beatings must I give you before you two useless wretches prove yourself worthy of calling yourselves my daughters?' he shouted.

'Sorry, Fa,' whispered Goneril, helping Regan to her feet.

'You dare to answer me back,' he said and Cordelia ran forward to try to halt the violence, but her father brought his stick down on Goneril's arm. She screamed in pain and the two women crumpled once more into the cold, icy slush of mud and dung on the ground.

The rook cawed and the scene changed. Cordelia stared around in alarm, this place was like nowhere she had ever seen before in her dream-walking. She was standing in a long narrow room, it glowed with an unearthly, harsh white light and there were doors at points along the walls. There was no trace of the roundhouses or the settlement, but as she looked around, a path of golden light opened before her and Cordelia knew she was safe. The glowing footprints on the floor buzzed like the sacred bees from the temple's hive and, even in her trance state, she understood this sound indicated she was being shown a message of life-changing importance.

One of the doors shone silver before swinging open. She stepped forward, following the lights, but the room she entered confused her. The space was the size of a small roundhouse, but the walls were straight, it was square with no softening curves. A bed dominated the centre of the room, where an old man lay asleep. She did not understand the vision, this man was attached by what she could only think of as cords, clear and flexible, to strange black boxes which flashed and beeped.

A woman sat beside the bed, holding the man's hand, and she was crying. Cordelia watched as the woman wiped away her tears and reached forward to stroke the man's face. When she spoke, her accent was strange, her words both familiar and unusual, a language similar to her own tongue but with different inflections and intonations.

'Dad,' the woman said in a quiet voice, 'I love you, please don't leave me.

You're strong; Uncle George says you can make a full recovery. Please, Dad, fight to stay with me.'

Cordelia moved forward, drawn to the sorrow of the woman's heart. She wanted to offer comfort by standing nearby. During these visions, she knew she could move through any obstacle – doors, walls, none held any substance for her and she could pass freely through them like a spirit – but when she moved towards the bed, expecting to skim through its solidity, she felt the coldness of metal and the smoothness of the sheets as she bumped into the bed, making it tremble.

The woman looked up.

'Who are you?' she said in horror.

For a fleeting second, their eyes met and Cordelia gasped, then the rook cawed and all went black.

4

THE TALE OF THE THREE SISTERS

There were once three women: The Queen, The Baroness and The Princess. They were sisters, bound by blood and, although they did not know it, an ancient prophecy from the mists of time.

They travelled far and wide, stating they were the emissaries of their husbands, who were busy waging war for reasons no one – least of all the men – understood. Each path the women travelled, every problem they solved, their fame grew and they became a respected trio, loved and adored by the good, honest and pure of heart, but reviled and feared by the sly, evil and conniving of character. Wherever they journeyed, they righted wrongs and calmed quarrels, ended feuds and reunited families. The bards told tales of the adventures of The Queen, The Baroness and The Princess.

One evening, tired from a day on the road, the women followed a path lined with pure white stones, hoping for the hospitality of a goodfellow at its end. The road wound around a hill, a gentle slope leading through dark woodlands, past fallow farmland and into a deserted town, where the gates of a magnificent castle were opened wide. As the three women rode into the gleaming quadrangle at the heart of this ancient stronghold, silver trumpets pealed through the silent air, announcing their arrival.

Livery-clad servants and grooms scurried forward, taking charge of the horses and beckoning the women through the great golden doors into the sumptuous hall within. Courtiers, lords and ladies, nobles and ladies-in-waiting smiled in welcome. The senior Lord Chamberlain swept them to comfortable state rooms, where legions of servants were on hand to help them bathe, relax and dress in the exquisitely crafted silken gowns that awaited.

The armourer arrived and asked permission of The Queen, The Baroness and The Princess to repair and polish their armour. The blacksmith requested their approval to sharpen their weapons and fire them additional, superior swords, to tend their horses' hooves and saddles. The Lord Chamberlain invited them to stay for as long as they desired.

The Queen, The Baroness and The Princess had been on the weary road of adventure for a long time and this was the most hospitable and generous welcome they had ever received.

'My good people, the honour is ours,' said The Queen, allowing the servants to carry away their armour and swords.

'This is a remarkable place,' added The Baroness with a grateful smile. 'Such kindness is exemplary.'

'A welcome that is unprecedented,' said The Princess, who alone was concerned that with the removal of their armour and weapons, they were vulnerable. As a form of protection, she held back a slender dagger and secreted it in her boot.

'My good people,' said The Queen, as the servants prepared to leave. 'It is remiss of us not to have asked sooner but please would you share the name of your lord and master to enable my sisters and I to thank him personally?'

But as she asked the question, the servants vanished.

5

GOLDENWYCH, PRESENT DAY

'Caitlin, wake up.' Lee's voice was urgent.

She could feel him crouched beside her, but her body was heavy, she was unable to move, everything around her felt uncertain as though the edges were blurred.

His fingers felt for her pulse.

'What's wrong with her?' said Gillian, her voice sounded distant, far away, but underneath the harshness, Caitlin detected hints of concern.

'Is she breathing? Check her bag for her inhalers.' Rachel's voice reached her through the lifting fog.

There was a rustle as her sister pulled the handbag from beside Caitlin's chair and rummaged through it, ignoring any thoughts of privacy in the way only a sibling would.

'Her pulse is steady,' said Lee.

'I'm fine,' Caitlin murmured, but her voice was weak and it was a struggle to open her eyes.

'Should we call a doctor?' said Pete, Rachel's husband.

'I am a doctor,' replied Lee. He squeezed her hand and she felt the heaviness lift, opening her eyes to see her sisters staring at her.

'What happened?' snapped Gillian. Her face was ashen, her eyes angry and fearful.

'I don't know,' Caitlin replied.

'Was it your asthma?' said Lee, taking an inhaler from Rachel and passing it to Caitlin.

'No,' she said, trying to remember. 'I was talking to Dad, then the woman came in, the one in fancy dress, there was the forest and the castle...'

Even to her own ears, she sounded demented and, with an effort, forced herself to breathe deeply, to focus.

'I must have fallen asleep,' she said, looking up at the ring of faces.

For an instant, the distress on the faces of her two elder sisters felt like a comforting balm, then their masks of dislike slipped back into place.

'Trust you to make it about yourself, Moon,' snapped Rachel, shoving Caitlin's handbag, which she had been hugging like a lifebelt, back into Caitlin's arms.

'About—?' Caitlin swallowed the end of the sentence, clenching her fists. She glanced at Lee, who raised his eyebrows as though telling her not to bother responding to such a ridiculous statement. She took a long calming breath. 'I'm sorry,' she murmured, but Dr George Glossop, Lee's father, stepped forward and hugged her.

'No apology needed,' he said, forcing an end to the conversation before it could escalate into an argument. 'We're relieved you're all right. We shouldn't have left you alone, we should have gone to feed the meters in the car park in shifts, not at the same time.'

'Except we needed a break from this oppressive room,' Caitlin heard Rachel mutter and she understood her sister's comment. The room was depressing and claustrophobic.

* * *

When the sisters had arrived at the hospital four hours earlier, George had told them in no uncertain terms their father's health was the most pressing concern.

'He needs peace and quiet,' George had stated. 'Whatever feud is going on between the three of you is to be left at the hospital door. As godfather to all of you, I insist you behave like the sensible, caring, loving women I know you are inside.'

Gillian, Rachel and Caitlin had glared at each other but were chagrined into silence. Gillian was with her husband, Alan Albany, and a few moments later, Pete Cornish, Rachel's husband had arrived grumbling about the cost of parking. Lee had driven Caitlin to the hospital and on the way she had rung Stan, but his phone had gone straight to voicemail and she had heard nothing since.

'How serious is Dad's condition?' Caitlin had asked as they had hurried along the corridor, its pale walls lit by harsh white lights, to her father's room.

'Luckily, we were together checking the final details for the announcement of the play before we set out for the theatre,' George had said. 'It's very hard seeing your friend collapse, but that's why a doctor's training is rigorous, all other emotions leave you and you focus on the event. As I was with him, his medical care began instantly and it's helped a great deal. The consultant believes your dad has had a transient ischaemic attack, or TIA. It's also known as a mini stroke and is caused by a temporary disruption in the blood supply to part of the brain.'

'Will he survive?' Gillian had asked.

'Yes, these are usually quite minor, although they're often a warning, an indication that a more serious health issue, such as a full-blown stroke, might be imminent if the situation isn't monitored. He's been talking lucidly and the consultant is confident he'll make a full recovery,' George had said. 'However, he was very tired and fell asleep a few minutes ago, so let's try not to disturb him.'

When they had entered her father's private room, tears had welled in Caitlin's eyes. He had looked so small and fragile in the hospital bed Caitlin could hardly believe this was her dynamic father. She always thought of him as larger than life. He was the owner of a huge factory complex, inherited from his father and grandfather, and he relished the day-to-day challenges of running his business empire. He was never still, always exclaiming with joy and delight over his newest favourite hobby, of which there were many, but his true passion was amateur dramatics.

It was common to find him reciting lines or rehearsing sword fights in his office in the middle of the day or scribbling possible dialogue during meetings. On one memorable occasion, he had asked his board members to read a new scene he had written for the evening's rehearsal as he wanted to judge whether it worked or not. To see him brought to this frail, white-faced old man hooked up to banks of machines was heartbreaking.

* * *

'It's late,' George continued, bringing Caitlin back to the present. 'And we shouldn't have left you alone—'

'Don't even suggest I should go home,' Caitlin interrupted before he could say any more.

'Nor me,' said Rachel and Gillian together.

There was a tense silence, broken by the arrival of a nurse, who smiled at them vaguely before checking Larry's monitors and doing his observations.

'How is he?' asked George.

'He's fine,' said the nurse, replacing his chart on the bedside table. 'Fast asleep, perhaps you should all go home and do the same – have a good night's rest. There's nothing you can do here and you're more likely to disturb him. We'll call you if anything changes.'

The nurse left but no one moved.

'What do you think, Lee?' asked George as the silence grew.

Lee walked to the end of the bed and picked up the blue folder containing the notes. He flicked through them, pausing to check a few details, then passed them to his father. George read the sections Lee pointed to, then returned the file to his son. The two men were GPs in the village, but this was a relatively new position for Lee. He had taken over the role six months earlier after years of working his way up to the level of consultant in neurology in a busy London hospital.

'He's not my patient, of course, so I can't comment officially but from his notes, he appears stable,' said Lee, then he turned to Caitlin and her sisters. 'I think the nurse is right. You'll be more use to your dad alert and rested tomorrow when he wakes up, rather than staying here all night and exhausting yourselves out of a sense of duty.'

He slotted the folder back into its holder and smiled at them all.

'His doctor has said it was a mild TIA, and with rest and recuperation, he should make a full recovery,' Lee said, trying to offer some reassurance. 'It's nearly midnight, perhaps we should follow the nurse's advice and allow the staff to do their jobs.'

'Wise words, sir,' said Alan, scooping his jacket from the chair and draping it over his arm. 'Come on, Gilly-Bean, let's head off. We'll need to pop into the factory first thing tomorrow to give everyone an update, then we can come back and assess the situation.'

'But—' Gillian began, then was silenced by an unexpected and enormous yawn. Alan raised his eyebrows at her affectionately and stretched out his hand to take hers.

'See you all on the morrow, blessèd family,' he said, blew a kiss to Caitlin and ushered his wife towards the door.

Gillian was her father's second-in-command at the family business, King's Enterprises, while Alan bore the title Managing Director. However, the trio worked together in a seamless dance to ensure the smooth running of the many subsidiaries which made up the company. The largest was the ball bearing factory, followed by the haulage section, but the divisions were many and varied, with Larry often investing in small companies and giving them office, warehouse or other business space.

'We're a family business,' he liked to say, 'and we help many other families along the way.'

'I'll need to inform the board members...' Caitlin heard Alan say as they left the room.

'Why does he have to speak like a Shakespearean character all the time?' grumbled Pete. 'The way he talks, you'd think he was an eighty-year-old retired colonel, but he's only seven years older than me.'

'On his birth certificate,' sneered Rachel, 'but in his mind he's about 200.'

They shared a spiteful laugh as Rachel gathered her Mulberry handbag and checked her iPhone – the latest model – for messages.

'See you tomorrow, Uncle George,' said Rachel, hugging him. She smiled at Lee, then glanced at Caitlin and said, 'Don't be a martyr and stay all night, Moon. We all know you're Daddy's Little Princess, you don't have to make yourself ill by proving it.'

She stalked from the room, leaving Pete looking embarrassed. He nodded hasty farewells to everyone and hurried out.

'Rachel's been sleeping in the knife drawer again,' murmured Lee and Caitlin forced a smile as though Rachel's comment had been irritating and faintly amusing rather than hurtful.

'When does she sleep anywhere else?' she said.

The machines bleeped and, in his sleep, Larry sighed. Caitlin squeezed his hand, but there was no response.

'Are you sure we're safe to leave?' she asked Lee.

'Yes,' replied Lee. 'Uncle Larry needs sleep and if his condition changes, I'll drive you straight back.'

'I can drive myself,' she said.

'True, but I want to help,' Lee replied and Caitlin smiled. He had looked after her since they were children, she knew the habit was a hard one for him to break even if she would soon be married to another man.

'He's well cared for here,' said George.

It was with great reluctance that Caitlin allowed herself to be led away. She hugged George goodbye in the car park and she and Lee waited for him to pull away, before climbing into Lee's car.

'Do you want me to take you to collect your car from the church?' he asked as they drove back through the deserted streets towards Goldenwych.

'No, I'll walk down in the morning and fetch it. It's perfectly safe in the church car park,' she replied, checking her messages.

'Any word from Stan?' asked Lee.

'Nothing,' she said. 'He's probably turned his phone off.'

She stared out of the window at the summer night. The shortest of the year, the turning point where the Earth began its slow descent into darker days. An image of a bonfire and people dancing flashed across her mind.

'We missed the solstice celebrations,' she said. 'No dancing around the firepit for us.'

'Not necessarily,' said Lee. 'There's a full moon out and the sun will rise again soon. We could drive to the stone circle and wait?'

'We haven't done that since we were teenagers,' she laughed, but her heart quickened with excitement at the idea.

It had been a long and stressful evening, the sensible thing was to return home. She knew she should sleep, shower, then return to her father when she was rested, but suddenly, every cell in her body longed for the coolness of the stones in the tumbled circle on the edge of the village. Her body ached to lay on the grass at its centre, to watch the stars on their journey across the sky, to catch her breath as the moon set and they waited for the glorious sunrise.

'Do you mean it?' asked Caitlin and Lee grinned.

'We both know we should do the right thing and go home.'

'But...' She let the word hang in the air.

'There are blankets and a hamper in the boot,' said Lee.

'What?' said Caitlin. 'Why?'

'Once I'd finished setting out the chairs for Dad, I was going to go up there myself,' he said. 'It's my first solstice since I moved home and I fancied a night communing with the ancients. I guessed you might be at the theatre too and I was going to invite you and Martha, but then the emergency call came and things changed.'

'What about Stan?' she asked. 'It was quite a bold move to think he would be fine with me spending the night with another man.' She batted her eyelashes in an exaggerated fashion.

'Hardly,' said Lee. 'We've grown up together and Martha would have been there, too. Anyway, Dad told me Stan was away and I know you love the solstice, so I was going to surprise you.'

'Lee, you're amazing.' She reached over to squeeze his leg. 'My favourite big brother.'

She did not notice the look of sadness flitter across his eyes at her words.

'Come on then,' she said. 'Let's go.'

Lee revved the engine as he had always done when they were teenagers and they burst out laughing. She did not understand the rush of delight coursing through her. Was it the intense shock of hearing her father had collapsed, followed by the relief of being told he was going to make a good recovery? These were heady emotions to process. Or was it the excitement of watching the sun rise with Lee? Caitlin had no idea, but as they drove past her cottage and out through the village, she could not stop smiling.

6

GOLDENWYCH, PRESENT DAY

The stone circle was deserted. The monoliths loomed dense and black against the starry sky, darker than the velvet night, enigmatic in their beauty and splendour. Each was an individual, as though the original builders had tried to deliberately mismatch them, to vary the heights, the shapes, the sizes. A few had fallen during the millennia, but of the remainder, a number stood at waist level, others towered into the night sky, while the rest rose and fell like a solidified wave. On the far side of the circle which faced the Golden Valley were three stones placed together, known locally as the Three Sisters. A trio of huge green slate sentinels with sparkling quartz embedded deep in their hearts, they had been carved by unknown and ancient hands and were inscrutable in the golden light of the solstice moon.

Caitlin took the torch Lee proffered and ran ahead, her desire to be within the stones driving her with a wildness she felt was not entirely her own. She hurried through a gap made from two fallen stones and plunged forward to the centre of the ancient space, breathing in the scents of the night air: the musky aroma of foxes, the damp earth, the chalky smell of the stones, it was the perfume of nature and as old as time. She stopped, revelling in the silence, in the intensity of the landscape and the glory of the balmy night. Laughter bubbled up within her and, throwing her arms wide, she tilted her head back and stared at the magnificence of the starry night.

'Look at me, Mum,' she called skywards, her voice somewhere between singing and sighing. 'Can you see me? I love you, Mum.'

And she began to spin, slowly at first, then faster and faster until the stars blurred above her in a mystical dance across the cosmos. As dizziness overwhelmed her, she dropped to her knees before collapsing flat on her back, her eyes squeezed shut, riding the rolling, pitching sensation of her giddiness as her senses returned to normal. She felt Lee stretch out beside her.

'I thought there would be people here,' he said.

'Perhaps we're too early,' Caitlin replied, opening one eye to look at him. 'Most visitors want to watch the sunrise.'

'True,' he said, grinning at her. 'Are you back to normal yet or is the ground still moving?'

Caitlin opened both eyes.

'Normal.'

Lee laughed.

'Never,' he said. 'Your nickname is Moon, you'll never be normal.'

'Shut up, Woody,' she giggled in response, using his own sobriquet as she continued to gaze up at the stars and the setting full moon.

When they were young, she had decided to look all their names up in a name dictionary she had bought at the Goldenwych summer fete. To her surprise, Lee's name was rooted in the Old English word, *leah*, which meant 'wood clearing'.

'Perhaps we should call you Woody,' Rachel had suggested with a sneer when Caitlin had finished reading the description aloud to her sisters and the two Glossop boys.

'It sounds a bit rude,' Gillian had said primly, causing the others to roll around laughing, and it had been his nickname ever since.

'Honestly, what's wrong with the teenagers of today?' Lee sighed. 'We used to sneak up here every summer solstice.'

'Our sordid past,' Caitlin said with a grin, warmth in her voice. 'Until you went off to become a doctor, Slick disappeared to do business studies, then Bean joined Dad's company and Rabbit met Pete, who was above such things as pagan rites at midsummer.'

'Remind me, why did you and your sisters call Edward, Slick?'

'Don't you remember he went through a stage of slicking his hair back?'

she said, rolling over to look at Lee as they discussed his older brother. 'It looked terrible, but he thought he looked like James Dean. He was having that real thing about 1950s cinema.'

'Of course,' said Lee as remembrance dawned. 'He watched *Rebel Without A Cause* at least once a day.'

'Didn't Rachel call him, *Rebel Without a Clue*?'

'Harsh...'

'But fair,' said Caitlin and Lee grinned in acknowledgement of his elder brother's teenage foolishness.

'After Dad called Rachel "Snow Rabbit" she wanted to ensure everyone had a ridiculous nickname,' said Caitlin.

'Of course, from that white, fake-fur coat and matching hat she had when she was little,' said Lee.

'Dad claimed she was as cute as a snow rabbit he'd seen on a documentary and, much to her disgust, it stuck.'

'It has, hasn't it?' said Lee with a laugh. 'It's so ingrained, these days I have to work hard to call her Rachel.'

'Don't try too hard,' replied Caitlin. 'She might protest, but she likes it really, although I think Gilly is a bit over being called Bean.'

'From your mum's favourite film and book, *Practical Magic*?' said Lee with a slight inflection, as though questioning his memory of the reason.

'Well remembered, it was because of her auburn hair. Gillian in the book has red hair and is known as Gilly-Bean.'

'And then there's you,' said Lee. 'Moon.'

'That's my name, don't wear it out,' she remarked – another throwback comment to their youth.

In the distance, a firework sparked in the sky, distracting them from their conversation.

'At last, some proper teenage behaviour,' said Lee. 'Come on, let's fetch the picnic.'

He stood up and put his hand out to help Caitlin. They flicked the torches on and followed the wide yellow paths of light back to Lee's estate car.

'You're very well prepared,' commented Caitlin as she peered into the boot, where there was an old-fashioned picnic hamper, a medium-sized rucksack, two folding chairs and two rolled-up picnic blankets.

'Chairs or blankets?' Lee asked.

'Blankets,' said Caitlin in disgust. 'Unless your knees won't take it, Granddad, and you need the chair.'

'I'm only three years older than you and I was the one who helped you up just now.'

Caitlin picked up the blankets and gave Lee a look of mock sternness.

'I'll take the hamper,' said Caitlin and set off with her treasures to the centre of the circle again. 'Here; with a view through the Three Sisters. Mum always said it was the best place to see the first rays of sun glimmer.'

When they were very young, Caitlin, Gillian and Rachel had asked their mother if the Three Sisters were named after them. Miranda had laughed kindly and explained the vast age of the stones. Intrigued, the girls had insisted on having their photograph taken with them, a ritual that was repeated every summer solstice until their mother's death.

The stones were positioned more closely together than the other remaining monoliths in the circle and were carved with dozens of patterns of concentric circles, which overlapped with straight or wavy lines extending from the middle outwards, while the other grey stones remained unadorned. As a teenager, Caitlin had bought herself a book about ancient British rock art and discovered the circular pattern was known as a cup design and the long marks as tails. They were a common neolithic motif on stone circles across the country, but what made the Three Sisters special were the intricate, three-part triskele, the classic Celtic swirl, surrounded by what appeared to be flames. When she discovered the green slate was not local but more commonly found in Cumbria over 250 miles away, Caitlin had been even more intrigued. Once she had learned to drive, she would often visit the circle and meditate beside the stones. It gave her an immense sense of peace and was where she had come to mourn after her mother had died.

Caitlin unrolled the first blanket and laid it on the ground, anchoring the corners with stones, while Lee did the same with the second.

'There are two warmer blankets in here in case we're cold,' he said, opening the rucksack, 'a flask of coffee and a bottle of red wine, depending on your preference.'

'Wine,' said Caitlin, unsure why she felt so carefree while her father lay in a hospital bed.

'Good choice,' he said and delved further into the bag, retrieving two melamine wine glasses decorated with lurid swirling purple patterns.

'Are they the glasses our mums used every solstice?' Caitlin asked in surprise.

'The very same. I thought it would be a fitting tribute to your mum.'

'Thank you,' she said, gazing at Lee in gratitude. 'For all of this, for staying with me and being so wonderful. Earlier, when you told me Dad was ill, I didn't really take it in. All I could think was, "No, not tonight, not the day before Mum's anniversary," then I realised how perfect it would be for them. They were inseparable, always, which was why his behaviour on the night Mum died was so unfathomable. I wondered if this was him making it up to her, joining her on the same night...'

Caitlin's words disappeared into a sob as the impact of the night's events finally hit her. Lee wrapped his arms around her.

'He's going to be all right,' he said. 'The readings in his chart show it was a mild attack. There's no reason why he won't make a full recovery.'

'You're telling the truth?'

'Of course,' he replied, hugging her again before releasing her and opening the bottle of wine. 'The other reason I prepared the picnic was because I thought this might be a good way for you to remember your mum.'

He poured her a glass of wine and she took it, balancing it on a flat piece of grass before sitting on the blanket and opening the buckle on the wicker picnic hamper.

'It's hard to believe she's been gone for two years from tonight,' said Caitlin.

'True, although she'd be appalled to know Gilly and Rachel have been angry with you the entire time. It isn't your fault she left you her café.'

'She gave them a lump sum each,' said Caitlin. 'Neither of them was interested in the Hill Fort Café, they hated working there when we were younger.'

'I've often wondered if there's more to their anger,' said Lee.

'What do you mean?' asked Caitlin sharply.

'It's so intense,' he replied. 'I don't know if it's really aimed at you, or even your mum. I think the person who should bear the responsibility for the rift between you all is your dad. He behaved oddly the night your mum died, as you said, and—'

Caitlin held up her hand to halt his words. 'Dad knows he was in the wrong, he apologised to all three of us after Mum's funeral, individually and together. Gilly and Rachel have said they forgive him,' she explained, but when Lee did not respond, instead busying himself with unpacking the beautifully wrapped parcels of food, she continued, 'You think they lied and they haven't forgiven him?'

'Not deliberately,' he said. 'Grief and anger and love and families are complicated, messy things. Do Bean and Rabbit even know what they're angry about any more?'

Caitlin smiled at the way he reverted to their childhood nicknames when he was upset.

'Yes, they do,' said Caitlin, but her tone had softened. When he raised his eyebrows enquiringly, she shook her head. 'If I told you, they'd hate me even more than they do now.'

'Hate is a big word,' he said.

'True, perhaps anger or resentment might be better,' she replied, then she looked at the picnic properly and laughed. 'Did you buy this food at my café?'

'Maybe some of it,' he said as she held up the distinctive purple packaging she used patterned with the golden Celtic triskele pattern. 'Sindy helped with my subterfuge.'

'I'll be having a word with her.' Caitlin pretended to be stern.

Sindy Simmons had been her best friend since childhood, even though Sindy was closer in age to Gillian than Caitlin. Sindy and Caitlin had become friends when they were both members of the Junior Players and Signets, the name given to the younger students in Judy Pelham's dance classes, where they learned ballet, tap, modern, beginners' ballroom and country dancing.

Sindy had worked with Caitlin at the Hill Fort Café ever since she had inherited it from Miranda. Caitlin was not a natural baker, unable to deviate from her mother's recipes without the cake mutating into disaster, whereas Sindy could create mouth-watering bakes seemingly out of thin air. Caitlin preferred creating the savoury dishes and mixing the herbal teas for which the café was famous.

They placed the two torches so they shone on the picnic and as Lee finished unwrapping the food, Caitlin realised she was ravenous. When he handed her a pasty made with crisp saffron-gold pastry and decorated with tiny suns to celebrate the summer solstice, she had to force herself to eat slowly and not gulp it down in two mouthfuls.

'Here's to Aunt Miranda,' said Lee, raising the plastic wine glass.

'To Mum,' said Caitlin. 'Thank you for this Lee. You're an angel.'

'Poppy would probably disagree,' he said, wryly.

'Have you heard from her?' asked Caitlin.

'No, not since I ended our engagement.'

'Do you regret it?'

'Honestly, no,' he said, picking up a sandwich and taking a huge bite. 'When she was offered the job in Australia and insisted on taking it, the decision was made for me. She was desperate to go, but for me, it felt wrong. We tried to work out a compromise, but, eventually, I had to face some hard truths.'

'Which were?'

'Did I love Poppy?'

'And how did you know?'

'I realised, if I truly loved her, I'd do everything possible to support her dream and make her happy. We could both have converted our qualifications to work in Sydney and have a great life, but the thought of leaving Mum and Dad felt like physical pain. The idea of being on the other side of the planet, thousands and thousands of miles from Goldenwych and everyone I loved, made me realise I cared more for them than my fiancée. No matter how much I pretended things could work with Poppy, I knew in my heart, they never would. I loved Poppy, she's a wonderful person, but she wasn't a part of my soul. Real love is soul deep and my feelings for her were head and heart deep. She deserved better.'

Caitlin sighed, she understood Lee's dilemma more than she dared to admit. Was her love for Stan soul deep? Was his for her? There were days when she wondered if it was even heart deep.

'You could have stayed in London,' she said, pushing her concerns about her relationship with Stan away.

'Yes,' he agreed, 'but I wanted a new start, even if it was in a familiar place. I'd been accepted onto the GP training programme, which felt more my thing than working in a huge hospital. When Dad told me his partner was retiring from the GP practice, it felt as though fate was telling me to apply for the position. Now all I need is to find somewhere to live and I'll feel as though I'm properly home. It's a shame my offer on the cottage three doors down from yours fell through, otherwise we would have been neighbours again like when we were children.'

'Best friends forever,' she said and they clinked glasses.

They ate in silence and Caitlin felt the tension that had arisen when she had thought about her fiancé leaving her body. The food, the wine and the warm embrace of the starry night were helping her to think clearly. The evening had been frightening with the unexpected collapse of her father, especially on the night when the emotions of the three sisters were heightened – the second anniversary of their mother's death from lung cancer.

'Lee, can I ask you a question?' Caitlin asked, sipping her wine.

'Of course.'

'When you found me asleep in the hospital, was there anyone else in the room?'

'No,' he replied.

'Did you pass anyone dressed strangely in the corridor before you found me?'

'Not that I remember,' he said. 'I'd gone to fetch us bottles of water and I assumed the others would stay with you, rather than have a mass trip to the car park.'

'Alan wanted to stay,' she said, 'but the others were determined to find someone "senior" to discuss Dad's condition on their way and insisted they went together.'

Lee gave a sigh of frustration.

'When I came in, you were slumped across the bed and you were so pale, I thought you were dead,' he said.

'I'm sorry...' she began, but he shook his head.

'Don't apologise, I'm a doctor, I should have been more objective. After all, how could you be dead – you were the wrong colour for a corpse.'

Caitlin laughed. 'You're rubbish,' she said, lapsing back into their childhood exchanges when 'rubbish' was the highest insult they could throw at each other.

'Why did you ask though? Did you see someone? When you came around, you mentioned a woman in a costume, a forest and a castle.'

Caitlin bit her lip, a sign of nervousness.

'Promise not to laugh,' she said.

Lee nodded, drawing a cross over his heart.

'Before I fell asleep, or whatever it was that happened,' she explained, 'a woman appeared in the room. One minute she wasn't there and the next, she was, but she was dressed in the most extraordinary outfit. A long white robe embroidered with the Celtic triskele in a bright yellow thread, a head-dress of antlers, a heavily patterned belt and a necklace with a dark purple pendant, maybe an amethyst...'

'Could she have been part of your dream?' asked Lee, but Caitlin shook her head.

'No, because she bumped into Dad's bed and I could smell her perfume, it was familiar: floral but with a hint of woodsmoke and warm honey, like one of Mum's teas. It was intoxicating. We stared at each other, then suddenly we were in a forest...'

'Go on,' Lee said.

'There were three of us,' she began, then described the dream in detail. Lee listened in silence until she had finished. 'The strange thing is, the woman I saw in the hospital... she was me,' she said.

'What do you mean?'

'We were identical. I also know I've seen her before, but the memory is hazy.'

'Moon, you've been under a lot of stress this evening—'

'Don't patronise me, please,' she snapped. 'Anyway, it wasn't a dream. It was more intense, it felt real, as real as this does now.' She waved her hand around the stone circle.

'I'd never patronise you,' Lee said, 'but this could be your sleeping mind sorting through things – anxiety, wedding nerves maybe. Not to mention the anniversary of your mum's death and the feud with your sisters.'

'I haven't been sleeping well,' she admitted. 'Perhaps you're right and I was overwhelmed.'

'Have you told Stan?'

'About what?'

'Not sleeping.'

'No, not this time. I mentioned it in passing a few months ago and he suggested I pray last thing at night,' she said. 'When I lit a lavender candle, he gave me a lecture on the ridiculousness of folklore and mythology. He disapproves of superstition or symbols – outside his own religion, of course.'

Caitlin did not see the flicker of anger in Lee's eyes.

'Stan can't have realised it was a serious problem,' Lee said, with a hint of contempt in his voice.

'Stan, who hasn't even bothered to reply,' she sighed.

Lee pulled the rucksack behind them, covering it with a blanket so it was like a pillow. He opened his arm for Caitlin to cuddle against him, a position they had adopted since they were children.

'He'll call when he hears your message,' Lee said in an attempt to reassure her. 'Let's stay here and wait for the sunrise.'

'We should clear away the food,' she murmured, her eyes suddenly heavy.

'We'll do it later,' Lee replied, yawning. He pulled the other blanket over them and moments later they had both drifted into sleep, with Caitlin falling into the deepest slumber she had experienced for months.

7

GOLDENWYCH, PRESENT DAY

Caitlin lowered her veil and glanced down to check she had everything she required: her smoker, J-shaped tool and spare gloves. *I must tell the bees,* she thought.

It was an ancient tradition to keep the bees informed of family news. One inspired by the belief that bees were a link between the physical and spiritual worlds. Not only could they carry messages to the other side, they also guided the lost spirits of the dead to other planes. To Caitlin, this made perfect sense; bees were, in her opinion, the wisest and most magical creatures on the planet. Despite Lee's reassurances, she knew her unease about her father's condition would remain until she had completed this ritual.

When she and Lee had been awoken by the first fingers of sunlight rising between the Three Sisters at the stone circle earlier that morning, they had watched in awe as the sky had turned a kaleidoscope of colours, wispy with morning mist and dew. Exhausted but elated by the wonderful display played out by nature, they had basked in its beauty before, eventually, gathering the remains of their picnic and driving back to the village.

'Try to get some sleep,' Lee had said as he dropped Caitlin at her cottage.

'You too. Are you working today?'

'Not until later,' he replied.

Her phone had bleeped and she had expected to see a message from Stan, but it was Sindy.

How's your dad? I'll open up the café. Mum is
going to help me, don't worry about a thing.

'Stan?' Lee had asked.

'No, Sindy,' she had replied and when Lee had made a noise of disapproval for once, she did not defend her fiancé's behaviour. 'She and Vicki are going to open up.'

'What about the hair salon?'

Vicki Simmons was Sindy's mother. A single parent who had raised Sindy alone, she ran a busy hairdressing salon in the village. For years, Vicki had cared for her own mother, dividing her time between the flat above the salon where she and Sindy lived and her mother's home. After the old woman had died, Vicki had inherited her cottage, which was a few doors down from Caitlin. When Sindy's marriage to Ricky Mansell had collapsed a year earlier, Sindy and her daughter Rosalind – who only answered to Rosie – had moved in with Vicki. Sindy had suggested she rent the flat above the salon from her mother, but Rosie's asthma had made it impossible. The hairspray and other chemicals had triggered multiple attacks before Vicki insisted they live together.

'There's plenty of room,' she had said, 'and you're three doors away from Caitlin.'

'She didn't say,' Caitlin had said to Lee with a pang of guilt, 'but knowing Vicki, she'll have organised cover. She's a dynamo. It's good of her to step in at such short notice.'

'It really is,' Lee had agreed. 'Right, I'd better head off. Sweet dreams.'

He'd hugged Caitlin tightly before driving away.

Caitlin had not expected to sleep but, to her surprise, as soon as she'd laid on the bed, she was unconscious.

'The bees,' she had murmured when she awoke several hours later. 'Mum would want me to keep them informed.'

* * *

Now, showered and dressed in her beekeeping suit, she made her way down the long but narrow garden to the small orchard at the end. The two beehives were positioned near the trees, but not under them, and beside a natural stream that cut across her garden before disappearing underground. Her mother had always claimed it was the source of a sacred well.

'How could you possibly know?' Caitlin had asked in amusement when her mother had accompanied her on her first viewing before buying the cottage several years earlier.

'I know these things,' Miranda had replied, and despite the fact they were laughing, Caitlin had a strange sense that her mother did see and know more than most people.

'Hello, bees,' she said as she passed the row of lavender bushes that surrounded her hives.

She puffed a small amount of smoke into the entrance and waited for the bees to calm.

'I need to check all is well with you,' she said in a quiet voice, 'and also to tell you Dad is ill, but we're hopeful he'll make a full recovery.'

The steady hum seemed to momentarily intensify, then three bees flew around her head. They paused in front of her veiled face before flying in a figure of eight and heading upwards and away.

'Tell the others,' Caitlin murmured as she watched their tiny shapes disappear.

She removed the lid from the calm hive and lifted off the metal queen excluder before gently wiggling the dummy frame from its position at one end of the super – the box which held the honey frames. Using the metal tool with the J-shaped end, she loosened one of the frames to examine the honeycomb. The oblong frame hung vertically in the super and as she lifted it out, she smiled; it was oozing with golden honey.

'Soon,' she whispered to the bees as she continued her inspection, 'it's nearly time.'

With great care, she checked both hives and, content they were healthy, she stepped away, listening to the gentle buzz of their song. As the hum enveloped her, she gazed at the stream, watching the ripples, the rush of the water over the stones, and as she did, the rest of the conversation she had shared with her mother drifted into her mind.

'Tell me then, Mum,' she had teased. 'How do you know this is a sacred spring?'

'The *genius loci* is standing over there and she's nodding her approval.'

'The *genius loci*?'

'The deity of the water.'

'What does she look like?' Caitlin had asked. She had always been intrigued by her mother's uncanny nature and her ability to glimpse things that were invisible to others.

'Tall, slender, long dark hair and with a headdress of antlers,' Miranda had replied.

'A headdress of antlers,' gasped Caitlin now as a cold shiver ran down her spine.

The calm created by spending time with the bees dissipated, but not wishing to startle her apian friends, she walked slowly away from the hives. However, once past the lavender bushes, she raced through the garden and back into the cottage.

'*Genius loci*,' she muttered as she hurried into the bright sunny kitchen, removing her heavy beekeeping suit as she went, kicking off her shoes and running barefoot through the house into her study where she kept her mother's notebooks.

An avid journal keeper, Miranda King's writings were numerous and Caitlin had them lovingly arranged on an antique bookcase. The colourful books contained Miranda's recipes, sketches, anecdotes and poems. Caitlin had inherited these along with her mother's café. When she had offered Gillian and Rachel the choice of any they had wanted, both had refused.

'They're yours,' Gillian had snapped.

'We don't want them,' Rachel had said. 'They'll only gather dust.'

Even though Caitlin had been wounded by her sisters' words, there was part of her which had exhaled in relief. She had always cherished the books and was unsure whether Gillian or Rachel would have treated them with the same reverence.

'*Genius loci*, the presiding deity or spirit of a place, this is the one,' she muttered as she ran her finger along the spines, her dark hair crackling with energy.

She pulled a leather-bound navy-blue notebook from one end of the shelf and flicked through the pages. Her mother's handwriting and her exquisite drawings filled every page, each one a memory for Caitlin, bittersweet with love and grief. Today, she skimmed past the images until she found the sketch of the vision her mother had seen when they had viewed the cottage.

Caitlin stared at the line drawing in wonder. The woman was identically dressed to the one she had seen in the hospital and, even more startling, this image bore a close resemblance to herself. She wondered why she had never noticed before, perhaps she had never looked closely enough in the past.

'Who are you?' she whispered. 'You're not the goddess of the spring or you would never have been able to travel to the hospital. You'd be rooted here.'

Caitlin studied the page properly for the first time, reading the comments her mother had added over the years.

One was dated from many years earlier when Caitlin had been in her teens:

She spoke last night but I couldn't hear her message, it's frustrating. I think she said, 'Everywhen'. I've looked up the term and it's a spiritual plane where the ancestors are supposed to reside.

Another dated a week later:

Tonight she said, 'The third daughter of the third daughter'???

and then underneath:

Henbane tea?

It was then Caitlin noticed the date her mother had written beside the original image. She had presumed it would have been at the time she had bought the cottage, but the date recorded in tiny digits was three days after her birth.

'No...' she whispered, but the buzzing of her phone with Stan's ringtone distracted her.

'You poor darling,' he exclaimed as she answered. 'I rang as soon as I heard the message.'

'Stan, it's midday. I left the message at seven o'clock last night.'

'You know what these conferences are like,' he said. 'Busy, busy, busy, like your bees, darling. How's your father?'

'Doing well, it was a TIA, a—'

'I'm aware of what it is,' he interrupted. 'Most people make a full recovery, but until then, no matter what he needs, we'll ensure he has the best care available.'

Caitlin bit back her irritation, this was not a decision for Stan. It was for her and her sisters, Larry was their father and his care would be decided by them, no one else.

'The staff at the hospital said he should be fine, Lee checked his charts and—'

'What was *he* doing there?' snapped Stan, his sympathetic tone disappearing.

'He drove me to the hospital,' said Caitlin, then continued, even though she knew she did not have to justify her movements. 'I bumped into him in the church car park after visiting Mum, the call came through while we were talking.'

'*Your mother's grave*, you were visiting her grave, not your mum,' said Stan.

It was a point of contention between him and his parishioners, whenever anyone claimed they had been visiting a relative, he corrected them, stating they were visiting the grave. Caitlin found she spent a lot of time apologising to people whom Stan had upset, usually giving them a free cake in the café when they poured out their woes.

'Are you coming home?' she asked, quelling her irritation created by his correction of her words. She lacked the energy to have the usual pointless argument which would ensue if she commented.

'Why?'

'To support me,' she replied, wondering if he really could be so insensitive.

'But you said your father is recovering,' he said. 'I'm very busy here, there are a number of high-profile bishops and it could be very damaging to my future prospects if I were to leave.'

'*Your* future?' she said before she could stop herself. 'I thought it was *our* future?'

'Don't be pedantic,' he replied. 'You're upset, Caity, we'll talk when I'm home in a few days. Love you.'

Caitlin was about to reply when she realised he had hung up.

'How dare you?' she said to the handset.

A recklessness filled her and her eyes went back to the word, *henbane*. She knew it could be poisonous, but the plant was more well known among herbalists for its hallucinogenic properties rather than its lethal edge. She had never seen a recipe for henbane tea in her mother's notebooks, but turning to peruse the shelves, she wondered where, if it existed, such a recipe might be found.

On the second shelf down, in the middle, was an old school exercise book which she knew held Miranda's early experiments with herbal teas. It was these speciality blends that had made the café so successful. Miranda had been a herbalist, but she had no interest in creating her own range of cosmetics or skincare products, for her, herbs were practical magic. They were for everyday use in food and drinks, designed by nature to keep all the creatures of the planet healthy. Miranda had spent years experimenting with a variety of plants and had begun brewing the teas for herself and her family and friends. Word had soon spread and with Larry's financial backing she had created a range of blends designed to help with a gamut of problems, from insomnia to a broken heart.

The café began as a hub for villagers seeking help but word of mouth caused the demand for her potent brews to grow until the café began selling Miranda's teas online. They supplied several other local businesses but Miranda had refused Larry's offer to help her grow the business into a global brand.

'I don't want the teas to lose their integrity,' she had explained and Larry had eventually ceased his pestering.

'If you'd been alive in the Middle Ages, you'd have been burned as a witch,' Lee's mother, Suki, had once said to Miranda. 'Your thyme and honey tea has cured my cough even though the GP's prescribed medicines never touched it.'

The café was a hub of herbalist knowledge, too. The decorations around the ochre-toned walls included an array of delicately painted pictures of herbs and flowers with descriptions of their healing properties written alongside them. Large windows flooded the café with light even on cloudy days and, in Miranda's day, plants had jostled for position on the wide windowsills. The day her mother had died, so had the plants and Caitlin had never replaced them, instead she ordered deep cushions for the windows, turning them into extra seating in a bespoke fabric embroidered with images of the lost plants.

As Caitlin reached for the book, her front doorbell rang, and with a pang of disappointment at being halted from her purpose, she walked along her hallway to admit her brother-in-law, Alan.

'Hello, Moon,' he said, leaning forward to kiss her cheek, 'how are you feeling today?'

'Not bad,' she replied.

'I was worried because you haven't replied to any of the messages on the family WhatsApp,' he said, following her into the kitchen.

Caitlin glanced at her phone and saw forty-six messages.

'You've all been very chatty,' she said.

Alan gave her a rueful smile. 'Shouty, rather than chatty. I've organised a visiting rota, as it seemed pointless for us all to go to the hospital at the same time. Much better to use our resources wisely and take an hour or so each.'

'This is why you're the managing director,' said Caitlin.

'Unfortunately, it's upset Rachel and Pete,' he admitted, folding his arms across his expanding middle, 'and because I hadn't heard from you, it occurred to me you might have thought I'd overstepped the mark too.'

'Everything upsets Rachel and Pete,' replied Caitlin, 'taking offence is their super-power. I'm relieved you've taken charge.'

Alan boomed with laughter. 'You always manage to make me feel better,' he said, then with a sad sigh added, 'I wish you could make Gilly-Bean smile.'

'Is she very upset about Dad?'

'Yes, she hardly slept last night,' he said. 'When she went downstairs, I heard her crying, but it felt the wrong moment to intrude.'

'You did the right thing,' said Caitlin. 'Bean has never been good at expressing her emotions in front of people, especially those she loves. It's as though she thinks she's letting us down or being weak by showing she's upset.'

'You're very astute,' he said. 'I still don't understand what happened between you all. You were always so close.'

'Things changed after Mum died,' she replied, not in the mood for soul-searching.

'Gilly-Bean.' He murmured her name as though it were a prayer. 'She's very unhappy. What can I do to help her?'

'In the short term, sit her down to watch the film *Practical Magic* starring Sandra Bullock and Nicole Kidman,' said Caitlin. 'You know Alice Hoffman's book, which it was based on, was Mum's favourite and she named Gilly after one of the characters, it's where her nickname came from. Gilly loves it.'

'Of course, I'd forgotten.'

'Then feed her a Hawaiian pizza.'

'Hawaiian pizza?' Alan looked horrified.

'Beneath her sophistication and hauteur, Gilly loves a ham and pineapple pizza.' Caitlin grinned with affection. 'Give her a Malibu and pineapple too and she'll explode with joy, even if at first she does pretend to be above such things.'

'How do I not know this?' he asked.

Caitlin shrugged. 'Are you telling me she's stopped scoffing pineapple chunks out of the tin with every meal?' she said with a smile. 'When we were younger, she couldn't eat without a bowl of pineapple being present.'

'No, never,' said Alan in astonishment.

'Poor Gilly-Bean,' said Caitlin. 'She does feel a need to punish herself.'

'For what?'

'I don't know,' replied Caitlin, quickly. 'Gilly changed when she was fifteen, she was always the one who helped Dad with the Players. The two of them were always watching musicals and quoting them to each other or singing the songs. Quite often, they'd make up new lyrics to the old tune and sing entire conversations before collapsing into laughter. Their favourite tunes were from *Seven Brides for Seven Brothers*.'

'The 1954 film starring Howard Keel and Jane Powell?' asked Alan.

'Yes, it's possibly not the most politically correct film. Did you know it was based on the tale by the Roman historian Livy of the rape of the Sabine women, where the Romans staged a mass of abduction of young women?'

'But the film is much gentler,' said Alan.

'Yes, of course, it's a romantic comedy,' said Caitlin. 'The scene near the end where the girls have all fallen in love with the brothers and sing about being brides-to-be was one Gilly re-enacted, singing and dancing brilliantly, a few months before she left the Players for good. She was amazing, good enough to turn professional, then one day she refused to take part again.'

The silence grew between them as they contemplated Gillian and her withdrawal from the creativity of the Players.

'And you say pineapple will cheer her up?' said Alan.

'Yes, Rachel and I bought her a gold pineapple pendant and matching earrings for her sixteenth birthday, but she doesn't wear them any more. She's probably thrown them away,' said Caitlin with a pang.

She remembered how hard she and Rachel had saved, catching the bus into nearby Hereford to buy the present. Even more, she remembered Gillian's delight when she had opened it.

'She hasn't,' said Alan. 'The pendant's in her jewellery box, but it's broken. She was looking at it last week.'

Caitlin felt a small surge of hope.

A timer buzzed on Alan's watch.

'Sorry, must dash, but thank you,' he said, hugging her. 'You're an absolute angel. Before I forget,' he reached into his jacket pocket, 'I've printed out the rota for you, I hope that's all right.'

'Of course.'

'Now, my mission is to buy pineapple and sugary 1980s drinks,' he said. 'On the morrow, fair maiden.'

He bowed as Caitlin waved him off, making her giggle. Alan always made her smile.

Closing the door, she looked down at the rota. It was a work of art, each member of the family had been colour coded and slotted into a spreadsheet. She was turquoise and, running her finger along the column, saw she was scheduled to relieve Gillian in half an hour. It was only as she walked down to the church to collect her car from where she had left it the previous evening she realised Alan had not included Stan.

8

THE TALE OF THE THREE SISTERS

As night fell, The Queen, The Baroness and The Princess were welcomed to the formal banquet in the great hall. They were well-rested and dressed in the gifts of finery laid out in the bedchambers. The Lord Chamberlain ushered them to seats, side by side, in a position of great honour high above the salt. Golden goblets of honey-drenched mead were placed before them, the smell as intoxicating and welcoming as a summer's day.

The assembled courtiers listened with rapt attention as they encouraged The Queen, The Baroness and The Princess to recount the tales of their adventures.

'We are sisters,' said The Queen.

'Alone in the world, except for each other,' continued The Baroness.

'Determined to do good,' added The Princess. 'We travel far and wide, but not, as we often suggest, at the behest of our husbands. Our journeys manifest because we feel compelled to move ever forward, as though we're searching for an answer to a question we do not know.'

She placed her hand over her mouth, horrified by her own words. The Queen and The Baroness did not react and The Princess felt a thrill of unease. She would never ordinarily reveal this secret. The wanderlust in their souls had been with them since childhood, but they never spoke of it; to do so would be a betrayal of their bond of blood. She waited for a reproachful look, but it was as though her sisters had not heard her words.

'Will you know when you find it?' asked a tall man who stood alone, nonchalantly leaning against a pillar carved with images of dragons, his face hidden in shadows.

'The question?' asked The Queen.

'Or the answer?' said The Baroness.

'Both,' said the man, stepping forward into the light.

As he did, the three sisters gasped. For each saw their tormentor in the face of this man.

'We will,' said The Princess, her voice cracking with horror but compelled to respond. 'We will recognise both and then our journey will be over.'

'And what if you never find them?' said the man, his features flickering, his face altering with each turn of his head.

'Our journey will never end,' replied The Queen.

'And we will never return home,' finished The Baroness.

The Princess stared at her sisters in shock. When she turned back to address the man, he was gone and the banquet continued as though nothing unusual had been discussed.

9

GOLDEN VALLEY, DOBVNNI, 862 BCE

The sun was high, beaming down from a flawless sky on to Cordelia, Regan and Goneril as they gathered on the flat ground near the unusual green stones in the circle known as the Three Sisters. They had promised to teach the eager suitors the basic steps of the dance they had performed on the night of the solstice and as the lessons began, the noisy group attracted a great deal of amused attention from the rest of the encampment as the men variously stumbled or excelled.

Maglaurus proved to have natural rhythm, slipping into the dance with ease. Goneril was enjoying every opportunity to take his hand or insist he wrap his arm around her slender waist as she demonstrated the steps. Regan was teasing Henwinus, dividing her attention between him and Ebraucus. Both young men were showing more enthusiasm than skill in their desire to impress her. Cordelia was laughing as Aganippus tried to master the complicated series of steps they used when crossing in front of each other, before swirling around and spinning back to the starting position.

'Like this,' Cordelia said, her mouth twitching with suppressed laughter as Aganippus lost his balance. 'Careful.' She reached out to steady him.

'I'm no dancer,' he said, resting his hand in hers as Goneril and Maglaurus spun past in perfect unison.

'You're improving,' said Cordelia, but when she caught his eye, he looked sceptical and they both giggled. 'We'll try one more time.'

She placed her hand on his forearm, instructing him to look at her feet as she demonstrated the steps again. She found it hard to concentrate, his nearness and the thrill of his hand on her skin sent shivers through her. The swooping feeling of excitement deep within her soul, in her heart and between her legs was one she had never before experienced. Once again, she felt a pang of regret that her path was to remain at the hill fort as the tribe's shaman, rather than marry this man and spend her days teaching him to dance.

'Try again,' she said and wound her arm around his waist, guiding him.

A crease appeared between his eyebrows as he concentrated, but as he followed her deft feet, he relaxed and the manoeuvre was completed in one swift, perfect motion. A huge cheer went up as they finished and he grabbed Cordelia, spinning her around in delight. She laughed as their eyes met, an intensity passing between them. She was savouring the moment when a keening shout of despair ripped through the camp, shattering the carefree mood.

'Come! Quick!' Ivor's voice roared as he ran towards them, his tunic stained with fresh blood. 'Cordelia, come, you must come...'

Locrinus, the male healer and Ivor's father, hurried from his round-house. 'What's happened? Are we under attack?'

'There's been an accident. Fa, bring your potions!' shouted Ivor before his green eyes fixed on Cordelia, his voice tense with urgency. 'Cordelia, you must come. It's your father, he's...'

He did not finish the sentence, instead he turned and ran back to the main gates that marked the entrance to the settlement, where a group of men were staggering towards the largest roundhouse.

'Fa,' she said, all the laughter draining from her as she ran after Ivor, 'what's happened...?'

The end of her question was lost as she saw Dardan, her father's steward, drenched in blood, his face whiter than the winter snows as he directed the three men carrying a stretcher-bound Lear towards the chieftain's round-house. The crowd parted as the men moved as quickly as they dared, and as they passed, people reacted with terror and revulsion. Cordelia heard someone vomit and turned to see who was afflicted. The noise acted as a catalyst on her sisters. Goneril and Regan had been standing as though entranced, silent, watchful, but the dreadful wet, squelching sound shook them from their horror and they both screamed in anguish.

'Fa!' howled Goneril dashing towards their father, Regan a heartbeat behind.

Cordelia swallowed hard, her own stomach churning with nausea and shock as she saw the full extent of the damage her father had incurred. Lear lay unmoving, drenched in blood, a broken wooden spike protruded from the top of his head. It had entered through his left cheek, passing at an angle behind his eye. Cordelia's gaze travelled to her father's chest and she saw shallow movement. He was alive, but she did not know for how much longer.

'He was inspecting the works when he slipped...' Dardan began before his voice stuck in his throat.

All day, the men had been placing sharpened stakes around the perimeter of the hill fort as extra protection from raiders and wandering tribes.

'Come, you must bring your herbs. You are the only one who can save him,' he said.

Cordelia's years of training had taught her to resist fear, to put aside feelings of hopelessness, despair and uncertainty, to channel her healing spirits and ask for their help in making her herbal potions more potent. As dread rose inside her, she forced herself to breathe in a controlled manner, to focus on what was important: healing the esteemed leader of her tribe but also the man she loved more than any other in the world.

She ran across the compound towards the temple to gather all she would need, but Becuma met her halfway, one of the priestess's white willow healing baskets in her hands.

'Here,' said Becuma, 'there is witch hazel and rose to staunch the blood. Wild garlic for his wounds, with honey and goldenseal to keep it clean. We'll follow with more but this will be enough to start your father's recovery.'

Cordelia looked down, checking the contents of the basket. It was lined with the softest of down gathered from the hedgerows where the sheep's wool had snagged on thorns. Inside were stoppered clay jars containing tinctures, small parcels of premixed cures, bunches of herbs, a bottle of vegetable oil and a flagon of the distilled ale they used in ceremonies.

'Thank you,' she said.

Cordelia stumbled across the compound, the bright sunshine blinding her, the basket banging against her legs as she hurried across the stubbly, dry summer grass to her father's roundhouse, the largest in the oppidum. He was the leader of their settlement, he ruled with wisdom and kindness. *He has no sons, if he were to die, who will succeed him?* she thought. Her mind flickered towards her uncle, Kamber, the younger brother of her father, who was chieftain of Credenhill, the settlement that bordered their own. Would he take over the hill fort of the Golden Dobvnni or would there be a battle for supremacy? The line of succession did not always follow the trail of family blood.

Then she scolded herself. 'He will live,' she said aloud as she ducked into the shade of the roundhouse.

For a moment, she was blinded, blinking away the dazzle of the sun in the gloom of the interior, but as her sight adjusted, she saw her two sisters waiting, their arms around each other, both ashen-faced. They had slipped inside in the few minutes it had taken Cordelia to converse with Becuma.

'Cordelia,' Goneril exclaimed. 'He is...' Her voice tailed away into sobs.

'You must use your powers to save him,' said Regan, before her voice cracked and halted as tears streamed down her face. Regan pushed Cordelia towards the private rooms at the rear of the building.

When she entered, her father lay motionless on his bed. His face was grey with pain, but he was alive. Locrinus kneeled beside Lear, inspecting the wound. He turned when he heard Cordelia's footstep.

'We must combine our skills,' he said, drawing her close. 'I've given your father poppy seed, willow bark and camomile in mead to ease his pain, but we must remove the stake or he will never heal.'

'Remove it?' she whispered.

'Wait outside, Lagon will help me.'

'No, I...' began Cordelia but the rustle of the curtain and Lagon's appearance in a long clean robe halted her.

'We don't doubt your healing abilities,' Lagon said, 'but he is your father and it will be too distressing for you to watch. Let us use our skills to take the spike from the wound, then you can use your powers to heal him and ensure he does not journey too far into the Everywhen.'

Angarad and Becuma entered the room behind Lagon, carrying a steaming pot of water and a leather bag containing bowls, spoons, knives, spatulas and linen bandages, bleached white in the sun.

'They're correct, Cordelia,' said Angarad, who had heard the final part of Lagon's entreaty. 'Your skills are better employed mixing the balms to speed his healing. Becuma will accompany you while we prepare your father for treatment.'

Cordelia stared down at her father, his face waxy, his breath shallow and forced her racing heart to calm. He needed her strength as a shaman and healer, not the tears of his youngest daughter. With great reluctance, she allowed Becuma to lead her away to a small antechamber.

The murmur of voices surrounded them like a spell as, with trembling fingers, Cordelia mixed her potions. She knew her measuring and combining of the correct ingredients had never been more important. Many of the plants she used could be poisonous if incorrectly prepared and she could not afford to make a mistake.

In silence, Becuma passed her each herb or flower, their joint knowledge blending seamlessly as Cordelia mixed the strongest remedies of their tribe.

From the other side of the curtain dividing them from the bedroom, there was an unearthly sucking noise and a cry of distress from her father.

'Fa,' Cordelia whispered, biting her lip to prevent herself from sobbing.

'The stake is out,' said Angarad, pulling the curtain aside. 'Let us clean the wound before you look, Cordelia.'

There was silence as they worked, then Angarad said, 'The honey and wild garlic, please, Cordelia.'

Cordelia stepped forward, ready with the healing herbs, her wits gathered once more as she helped the healers, her friends, to aid her father. Angarad knelt beside Lear, a smoothly polished spatula in her hand as she anointed the wound on his cheek with the salve.

'His head,' said Lagon. 'We must cover the wound.'

On the bed, Lear twitched, then his eyes opened and, with a rush, he leaned over the side of the bed and vomited. Blood and brain spattered from the wound across Locrinus's face. Nobody moved, then Lear spoke.

'Sorry, old friend,' he said, reaching a trembling hand towards Locrinus. 'You look a mess.'

Lear lay back on his bed and stared at the ceiling before closing his eyes and falling into a deep sleep.

Locrinus stared down at Lear, then said, 'My work here is done, the fate of our leader is in the hands of the goddesses and the gods.'

He touched his forehead and, after one last look at the prone figure in the bed, disappeared outside, tears streaming down his face.

'Go with him, Lagon,' instructed Angarad. 'He's in shock, he'll need care too. They've been friends since boyhood, like brothers. Brew him a blend of poppy seed, willow bark and mead and encourage him to rest.'

'Leave him with me,' said Lagon and hurried after his father.

'And we will do all we can to ease the Chieftain's pain,' said Angarad.

After an hour, Lear was clean, comfortable and breathing more easily.

'We must go to the temple,' said Cordelia.

'Are you sure?' asked Angarad.

'I am the shaman. If it were anyone else, you would not question the next stage of the healing process. This is my role. We have done all we can to heal the body, now I must speak with his soul and encourage him to stay on this plane.'

'No, Cordelia,' said Angarad. 'We must let the salves do their work. Then, when you have recovered from your own shock at your father's injury, we will speak with his soul.'

Cordelia knew Angarad spoke sense, but she was desperate to reach out to her father, to heal him in the best way she knew, but then images from her visions flashed across her mind, his anger, his hatred, his cruelty, all opposed to the kind, wise man who lay sleeping, his head and face swathed in bandages.

'Very well,' she said. 'But if he worsens, I shall journey to the Everywhen.'

Language of the Stones

10

GOLDEN VALLEY, DOBVNNI, 862 BCE

The summer passed in a haze of concern. Each day, the high priestesses prayed, while Locrinus and Angarad trained more people to help care for their leader. He was never alone and, with the dutiful tending and devotional prayers from the temple, Lear Bladudsunu began to heal. Cordelia had taken henbane and travelled to the Everywhen but had been unable to converse with her father's soul.

'He was shaded,' she told Angarad afterwards. 'Whenever I tried to make contact, he stepped into the shadows as though he didn't recognise me.'

His spirit animal, the brown bear who paced beside her father in the Everywhen, had not challenged her, but he had been blurred around the edges as though he too was confused. The other troubling part of her walks into the dreamworld had been more glimpses of the woman with her face.

'Why haven't you spoken?' asked Becuma when Cordelia confided in her. 'Do you think she's a shade?'

'No, her light is clear and pure, a shimmering amethyst similar to my pendant.' Her hand strayed to the necklace that had once been her mother's.

'Perhaps she's a new guide,' Becuma suggested.

'It's possible,' Cordelia replied, 'but the time doesn't feel right to speak yet. We'll both know when to communicate.'

What she did not confide to Becuma was the way her trips to the Everywhen had begun to blur with a recurring and confusing dream. She would find herself in a strange building made from stone, inhabited by people wearing clothes she had never seen before, her consciousness shifting from her own mind into that of the other shadowed woman, who, like her, watched from a distance. Each time she dreamed about her, Cordelia awoke with the sound of lazy summer bees buzzing in her ears. The hives had always been the domain of the bee maidens, Becuma and Oudar, but each day she was drawn to them more and more, watching Oudar in particular, who seemed to communicate with the insects as though she could speak their language. Cordelia had begun offering to help gather the honey and, whenever she did, she felt a sense of intense peace.

Her father continued to make good progress. After the first terrifying days, when the entire settlement had prayed to the gods and goddesses, he began to show signs of recovery. Each day, his dressings were changed and, despite not having spoken since his apology to Locrinus, as the wound healed, he began to speak again. Although these were monosyllables rather than recognisable words, Locrinus believed this was a good sign.

'He knows us,' Locrinus said, after another day of smearing honey and witch hazel on Lear's wounds. 'Lagon and me, he said our names. His mind is returning from the Everywhen where it has been healing.'

There was a setback when Cordelia noticed a fungus growing on the two wounds. Her father's health sank to its lowest ebb and as the tribe prepared to hear the worst possible news, she prayed to the goddess to guide her as she cut away the growths, covering the wounds in the purest honey they possessed. She helped Oudar to gather it, whispering incantations as they scooped it from the combs, entreating the bees to add their healing powers. Three days later, her father spoke her name for the first time since his accident.

'Cordelia,' he whispered. 'Am I alive?'

'Yes, Fa,' she replied, tears of joy in her eyes.

'You are my favourite child,' he said. 'You would not lie. This is not one of your journeys?'

'No, Fa, we are in your roundhouse in the oppidum,' she answered, and with a smile he sank back into sleep.

It was when he awoke the next time, the trouble began.

* * *

The decree had been read by Dardan, Lear's chief steward and advisor.

'All members of the oppidum will gather in the meeting place tomorrow at the height of the sun to give thanks for the recovery of our great leader, Lear Bladudsunu,' he announced, and all around had cheered in relief and delight.

Now, as the sun reached its zenith in the cornflower blue sky, a party atmosphere pervaded. Cordelia made her way through the throng, laughing and joking with friends, acquaintances and cousins as she headed towards her sisters. Locrinus waved to her from the other side of the square, his sons, Lagon and Ivor, either side of him. Ivor's betrothed, Gael, was with them, while Lagon beckoned to Cordelia to join them, but she pointed to Goneril and Regan and blew him a kiss instead. The two women were smiling and chatting to Aganippus and Ebraucus, evidently relieved the danger to their father had passed.

The suitors had remained, at the request of Angarad, Dardan, Locrinus and the council of elders.

'Your father's weakened state could put the village in a vulnerable position,' Angarad had explained to Cordelia. 'There are always those, both inside and outside the oppidum, who might try to use your father's ill health to their advantage and attempt to seize power. The suitors have all sworn to protect the hill fort if this should happen. I believe the younger men remain hopeful of a match with one of your sisters and, as such, have offered to help with the administration of our home. These men represent powerful tribes, it is better to keep them as friends, rather than risk losing their goodwill and facing a coup within our own walls.'

Cordelia had found the conversation uncomfortable but had understood the reasoning behind the invitation for the men to stay. She did not trust Ebraucus, but she felt a sense of relief that Aganippus, with his wisdom and years of experience ruling his kingdom, was available should any squabbles or altercations erupt. Maglaurus and Henwinus had remained loyal and considerate too.

'Cordelia,' Goneril called, beckoning her over.

Goneril wore a headdress of pink harebells, while Regan's fair hair was adorned with deep purple loosestrife, and as Cordelia arrived, with much laughter, they adorned her head with a circlet of bright yellow marigolds and camomile flowers.

'These are beautiful,' she said, adjusting the willow frame on which the flora had been woven so it sat more comfortably.

'Regan made them,' said Goneril. 'We thought they were a suitable way to celebrate Fa's recovery.'

'Thank you, Regan,' Cordelia said, squeezing her sister's hand. 'You have such skill with flowers.'

Regan smiled in response, then turned as Ebraucus called her name. Cordelia felt her shoulders relaxing for the first time since her father's accident. The danger had passed and the world would return to normal.

Above her, a rook cawed and she sent it blessings, wondering if the shocking images of her father's violence had been a result of her fear for his recovery. The messages she encountered during her dream-walks were often difficult to interpret: had her terror at the thought of losing her father caused her to believe they were prophetic when they had in fact been a manifestation of her own emotions? It often made her doubt her abilities if she did not take the true meaning from her visions, but this time, she was delighted to have been mistaken.

The meeting place swarmed with people. It was a wide area in the centre of the hill fort and was the hub around which all activities revolved. A menhir marked the very centre and the tribe's history claimed this stone had been flown there by the Triple Bee Maidens – Corycia, Kleodora and Melaina. Legend said the bees had led their ancestors to the hillside and told them it was a safe and prosperous place to build their homes.

Cordelia watched as the children skipped around the menhir, garlanding it with flowers, laughing at their antics. All around, the tribe was celebrating, their happiness and excitement rippling through the air. Her emotions were heightened and she sensed Aganippus moving towards her even before he spoke in her ear.

'This is a joyous day,' he said and again Cordelia was unable to halt the shiver of excitement in her heart at the overwhelming intensity of his nearness.

'One I was scared we might not reach,' she admitted, trying to keep the tremble of desire from her voice.

'But you have the sight,' he said. 'You must have seen this…' He gestured with his hand towards the party.

'No,' she admitted, 'I was shown fear and despair. It scared me for the future, but I now believe they were warning me of my father's accident. Instead, I took them too literally, concerning myself that we would be forced into war and the poverty which inevitably follows a bloody siege.'

'Are you often wrong?' asked Aganippus.

'No,' she replied, 'but things have felt different this summer.'

'Different?' he said and held her gaze. 'How?'

Before she could reply, drums sounded and Dardan called for attention. As he waited for the crowd to quiet, with a sickening realisation Cordelia understood her inability to contact her father in the Everywhen. Her powers had dimmed because she had allowed her focus to be distracted by her unexpected feelings for Aganippus.

I am the shaman, she reminded herself. *Love is for others, my duty is to the tribe.* Whereas this status once filled her with joy, now she was suffused with sadness.

'Our leader, Lear Bladudsunu,' Dardan announced and, once again, there was a roar of appreciative noise, drawing Cordelia from her teeming thoughts.

* * *

The door to the central roundhouse was flung open and Lear appeared. His robes were light, flowing in the gentle breeze from the hillside, the delicacy of the fabric a contrast to his gnarled hand on the thick walking stick. Although Lear's eyes had not been damaged, the left eyelid now drooped and he had demanded a decorated patch as he did not like anyone to see this imperfection.

Cordelia felt tears well in her eyes, her father looked frail, stooped, a shadow of his former self and, although she knew he would eventually regain his strength, it made her realise he was fallible, an old man who would one day die and leave her.

Maglaurus and Henwinus, who had been helping to administer the hill fort since Lear's illness, stood either side of him, and when the immediate wave of cheering subsided, Lear banged his stick on the ground. Silence fell as the two men helped Lear to the ornately carved chair positioned beside the menhir. Goneril hurried forward to help settle him, arranging his robes and ensuring he was comfortable before he dismissed her with a wave.

'My people,' he called and there was a murmur of respect in response. 'My daughters,' he raised his hand to acknowledge them, 'these have been hard days and I thank you for your incantations.'

A ripple of affection and appreciation filled the meeting place. Cordelia heard Locrinus cheer in his hoarse, gravelly voice.

'As I lay recovering, it gave me time to think and I explored the possibility of what might have happened had I died. It haunted me.'

There were responding whispers and the rustling of clothes as the villagers, a few of the elders, men who had grown up with Lear, called encouragingly, acknowledging these fears had also been their own. With no strong leader, the oppidum had felt a frisson of danger.

'My son, my firstborn, died within a few days of his birth,' continued Lear, 'and since then, I have been given only daughters. It has long perplexed me. Why do I lack sons? Why is there no one to inherit my legacy?'

Again he gazed around, the sunlight glinting on the tiny amethysts sewn onto his eye patch. An uneasy quiet seeped through the assembly as he allowed the silence to grow, staring from person to person, before shifting in his seat to look towards Goneril, Regan and Cordelia.

'Yet,' he said and his voice sank to a low, angry growl as he gazed from Goneril to Regan to Cordelia, 'I have daughters. Women who could provide me with grandsons, heirs. A dynasty.'

Beside her, Cordelia felt Goneril twitch. She glanced at her sister's face, but it was impassive. Regan was in shadow, her expression unreadable, but Cordelia could see the tension in the set of her shoulders.

'My daughters, come forward,' Lear said.

'Fa...' they murmured, stepping towards his chair, bowing their respect.

'My girls. My loving children,' he murmured, but his voice had taken on a strange, dark timbre. 'How much do you love me?'

The three sisters exchanged a confused glance.

'Goneril, you are my eldest, tell me, how much do you love me?'

Goneril stared around her in desperation. Cordelia reached for her older sister's hand and squeezed it, Regan took Goneril's other hand.

'Hurry, child,' said Lear. 'I have no patience for your feminine dullness.'

The unease of the watching crowd expanded and Cordelia started as the rook cawed again. Its voice loud, urgent, a warning.

'Fa, you know how much I love you,' said Goneril, stammering slightly. 'My love for you is greater than the sky above, than the sun that ripens our crops, than the rain that nourishes the land. I love you beyond all of nature's bounty. As much as any child can love a father.'

'And you, Regan?'

'As much as Goneril and more,' she said, confusion in her voice.

'Tell me.'

'I love you as much as the gold in our strongbox, more than the salt from our mines, more than the spices from our trades with our neighbours, more than the animals in our oppidum that give us food. I love you more than my heart.'

Regan's shoulders relaxed as her words caused a smile to flicker across their father's face.

Lear turned his attention to Cordelia.

'And Cordelia?'

All three sisters continued to grasp each other's hands, to show their support for each other as their father humiliated them in front of their people.

'What is this, Fa?' Cordelia asked in a soft voice. 'Why do you question our love? You know you are our world.'

'Am I?' he said. 'So why were you dancing when I fell? Why were you not at my side but were entertaining men.'

A stunned silence swept across the tribe like a wave. No one had ever heard Lear speak in such a manner, especially to his beloved daughters.

'Lear, stop,' came Locrinus's voice, but Lear held up a hand to silence his old friend.

'Tell me, Cordelia, how much do you love me?'

They stared at each other, the glowering man and his youngest child.

'You know how much I love you,' she replied.

'Stubborn,' said Lear and there was a cold smile on his lips. 'Do you think you are above my rule? With your trances and your prophecies, your ridiculous shows of madness that mean no more than the jarring caw of the rook in the tree. You are no daughter of mine.'

'Fa, what are you saying?' said Cordelia in horror. 'I love you.'

'Do you, faithless creature? What will you do to prove it?'

'Nothing,' she replied. 'I will do nothing, because love is not something that can be measured like grain or gold or salt. Love is a thousand small gestures, a smile, a kindness, a lifetime of caring. No two people love in the same way, no one can define the true meaning of love because it is as different as each person here. My love for you is that of a daughter for her father, the deepest respect and regard, but also the joy of knowing I am loved in return.'

'You are loved in return?' sneered Lear. 'What makes you think I would waste my love on a foolish wretch like you? Your sisters have told me of their love, why won't you?'

Cordelia stared at her father, but she did not respond, holding his gaze until he looked away with a derisive snort. He beckoned to Dardan, who walked forward with an ornately decorated tablet. The large square of wood was covered in a layer of wax and it was used for declarations and important announcements within the tribe.

'Listen and listen well,' declared Dardan as he did before every binding decree from Lear, but whereas this was usually followed by a cheer of enthusiasm, the crowd remained quiet.

Lear handed his stick to Dardan and held the wax tablet aloft.

'I, Lear Bladudsunu, King of Britain, chieftain of the tribe of the Golden Valley in the region of Dobvnni, do decree that in order for my daughters, Goneril, Regan and Cordelia, to inherit my lands, they must prove their love,' he read. 'Tomorrow, at the highest point of the sun, Goneril will marry Maglaurus of the Albany tribe; Regan will be bride to Henwinus of the Dvmnonii people and Cordelia will marry Ebraucus of the Brigantes tribe. All three will be given dowries of gold worth a third of my kingdom and whomever gives me a son first will rule this land when I am dead—'

'But I'm a high priestess, your shaman,' Cordelia protested, approaching her father's chair. 'I have taken an oath never to marry—'

'Do you refuse my request?' thundered Lear, handing the wax tablet to Dardan and wrenching his stick back into his hands.

'Yes,' she replied, leaning towards him, supplicating. 'You're confused, Fa. You know my words to the goddess are sacred and can't be broken—'

The blow from her father's calloused hand halted her words and sent her flying to the ground, where the red earth of the meeting place was dry with dust, unyielding and unforgiving as stone. Cordelia did not scream, she was too stunned to respond, instead she remained where she fell, breathing deeply as she tried to control her tears. Behind her, Goneril and Regan gasped in dismay, while the crowd murmured in dissent. Whether the people's anger was aimed towards her or her father, Cordelia was unsure.

A shadow loomed over her. Lear had risen from his throne and glowered down at her.

'Unnatural and ungrateful child,' he hissed, his one eye narrowed. 'For this outburst, you shall have no dowry.'

'Then I refuse to marry her,' said Ebraucus, who smirked. He appeared to be amused, rather than horrified, by the day's events. 'I want a wife who will obey me without question. This woman has too high an opinion of herself. With a dowry, her looks would have made up for the strangeness, which no doubt could have been whipped out of her, but with nothing to compensate me, then I refuse.'

Lear spat at Cordelia's feet and raised his walking stick above her head.

'No!' shouted several voices, including Lagon and Locrinus, who had run forward to intercept Lear.

Cordelia sprang to her feet, putting distance between herself and her father, preparing to defend herself. She would not allow him to lay hands on her again.

'What use are you without a husband?' sneered Lear. 'Perhaps we should burn you at the next solstice instead of a straw man? It might make the gods show me favour. Your goddesses have never helped further my male line. You are nothing but a useless mouth to feed. Your histrionics as shaman are worth less than nothing, so what shall I do with you? Lock you in the oubliette with the grain? Or perhaps throw you down the old well?'

'Fa, you're ill, you don't know what you're saying,' said Cordelia, but she could feel the sweat of fear trickling down her back.

Her father raised his hand, beckoning two of their tallest warriors.

'Take her to the tomb on the east side of the oppidum and block the entrance, let her ask the ancients for help until I decide what to do with her...'

'I will wed her,' said Aganippus, his voice cold, cutting across Lear's diatribe like a winter storm.

'Why would you shackle yourself to her?' said Lear. 'She has no dowry.'

'I have no need of gold.'

Cordelia saw Aganippus's eyes flash with anger, but she knew his fury was not aimed at her.

'Very well,' said Lear dismissively. 'You will wed Cordelia and take her from my sight.'

Cordelia opened her mouth to protest, but both Aganippus and Locrinus shook their heads, warning her to remain quiet.

'I shall also wed,' Lear announced and the crowd radiated deep unease. 'Perhaps I shall win the race of the heirs and then my useless daughters will be left with nothing. My son shall be showered with gold.'

'Old friend,' said Locrinus, his tone gentle, 'what jest is this? You plan to marry again when you swore you would never take another to wife after the death of Estrildis? Who do you intend to honour as your queen?'

There was a scream and two men whom Cordelia did not recognise emerged from the temple, dragging Angarad between them. Three more emerged: one grasped Becuma's arm, another held onto the twins, Gloigin and Ignogin, while the final man pushed Oudar in front of him.

'As from this moment, the temple will no longer be a haven of female worship!' bellowed Lear. 'The Matronae and her Bee Maidens are no more, instead my new priests' – he swept his hand to include the men who were dragging the priestesses forward and a group of ten more who emerged from the shadows behind the stone circle – 'will lead worship to Neit, the god of war. I shall marry Angarad and show her who holds the balance of power in this tribe.'

He indicated to the two men who held Angarad to throw her at his feet.

'You will be my wife and you will provide an heir or you will be sacrificed at the next summer solstice,' he declared, before beckoning to the men to help him return to his roundhouse.

Maglaurus and Henwinus had taken their places beside Goneril and Regan, all four shocked and pale. Aganippus and Lagon were either side of Cordelia, with Locrinus a few steps away. There was silence as the two men supported Lear as he stumbled to his roundhouse.

He paused in the doorway and roared, 'Tomorrow, we will wed and soon I shall have my heir!'

The curtain over the entrance was dropped into place and he was hidden from view.

11

GOLDEN VALLEY, DOBVNNI, 862 BCE

'He can't do this to us.'

Goneril stood in the centre of the temple vibrating with fury. Her voice rebounding off the walls.

'He can and he has,' replied Regan, who was white-faced and tearful.

'Pack up what you wish to keep,' the leader of Lear's new warriors ordered with a dismissive sneer. 'After tomorrow, this place will be stripped of your women's trappings in order to be recreated in Morrigan's image. Anything remaining will be burned.'

He left, his cold laughter echoing back at them as the women stared at each other in horror.

After Lear had made his dramatic exit, the women had been dragged into the temple by the men Lear claimed were his new priests. Cordelia did not believe this statement, these people were mercenaries, accepting her father's gold in exchange for the power of violence he offered.

Cordelia turned to Angarad, the Mother of the Temple, who stood beside their altar, her eyes wide with both determination and despair.

'The goddesses will not allow such destruction,' said Angarad. 'The Matronae and the Bee Maidens will show us the way. I shall travel to my guides for wisdom while you clear the temple. We must appear to be complying.'

The women stared at her until Cordelia broke the silence. She bowed low, as was tradition with priestesses and the Mother of the Temple.

'Yes, Módor,' said Cordelia using Angarad's official title. It was only ever used during ceremonies, but the gravity of their situation was such that it felt natural to her lips. 'We shall follow your wisdom.'

'May the Triple Goddesses guide your path,' the other priestesses intoned.

Angarad bowed her head in response, then disappeared through the curtain that divided the main temple from the sacred inner sanctum.

Cordelia gazed around her, the large space was one of peace and serenity, but now it felt tainted. Goneril and Regan moved further inside before collapsing to the floor, sitting hunched together near the altar. Becuma and Oudar bustled about, sorting herbs into piles, organising candles, wax votives and other temple paraphernalia into baskets, bags and urns. Gloigin and Ignogin concentrated on stripping the woven hangings from the walls, folding them with care, revealing the close woven strands of the wattle walls.

'This is a roundhouse,' Gloigin said to Cordelia, 'it doesn't matter if your father has chosen to change its use. We are high priestesses, all we need are our hearts to create a sanctuary.'

'Yes,' she murmured. 'It's a roundhouse, we are the temple makers.'

Re-energised by Gloigin's words, Cordelia reached up to the shelves where the tools she used as shaman were stored, before turning to the tablets and scrolls containing their prayers and recipes. She placed it all with care into a series of leather bags. It was as she lifted her antler headdress that the enormity of the situation hit her fully and an involuntary sob escaped from her lips.

'Cordelia, you must reach within yourself and find your path too,' said Gloigin, her voice firm but kind. 'You're to be married to a kind man, maybe this was always the intention of the goddesses, for you to be a wife, a mother, a warrior—' She stopped, her hand over her mouth in surprise at her final word.

'A warrior?' said Cordelia. 'Did you see? Is this a premonition?'

'No,' replied Gloigin, 'I saw no images, but the words came from my heart, rising without effort. You must prepare for what is to come and do not be afraid when you are asked for help.'

Again, Gloigin stopped, looking horrified.

'Cordelia, I'm sorry, it's not my place—'

Cordelia reached over and hugged her friend, halting the remainder of the sentence, but Gloigin's unexpected confusion over her prediction had brought her to her senses.

'You're correct, Gloigin,' she said, feeling her usual serenity return, 'this is a new path for us all and there must have been a reason why we weren't shown what has transpired. The goddesses don't always reveal events, there are many we must navigate alone. Let's clear this space and wait for Angarad to return. She will have answers.'

The women continued their packing in silence, wrapping delicate vases, jars and the heavy pithoi, the storage jars in the corners of the storeroom, in protective wool.

'How will we carry the pithoi?' asked Becuma.

'You can't,' said Regan, from where she sat by the altar. 'They're too heavy. When we're able, Goneril and I will have them moved to our round-houses for safekeeping. We'll ensure the pithoi remain safe.'

'But the men said they would destroy anything left inside,' said Oudar.

'Then we'll have to try to take them out through the back entrance and leave them in the stone circle,' said Goneril and together she and Regan rose, rolling the jars between them as the others continued with their tasks.

Cordelia felt her heart burst with pride for her sisters and their determination to take charge, even if in a small way.

'Will you remain at the oppidum, Gloigin?' asked Goneril, as she and Regan returned for another pithoi.

'No, we shall vanish into the darkness this night,' Ignogin replied, answering for her sister, pausing in her packing of three leather satchels.

'The guards will catch you,' said Cordelia in concern.

'We are in the dark of the moon,' said Gloigin. 'Oudar is preparing jugs of our strongest mead laced with valerian root. We wondered if Goneril and Regan would be prepared to offer it to the guards? If it came from Lear's daughters, we think they are more likely to accept and drink it. Valerian is a potent sleeping draught and when they are in the depths of slumber, we will be shadows in the night.'

'Where will you go?' asked Cordelia.

'To Credenhill, the home of Kamber Bladudsunu, your uncle,' Gloigin replied. 'It's the home of our mother's people too. We shall be welcomed there and Oudar will be safe because she is our companion.'

'We'll do whatever is necessary to help,' said Regan as they gathered the final jar. 'Would it be possible to give the guards such a powerful dose of valerian they never awake?'

'And face charges of treason with its death penalty?' asked Oudar. 'No, it's enough they'll fall into an unnatural torpor and suffer dreams from Dubnos, the dark underworld.'

'I pray to the goddess their night is full of torment,' hissed Regan, bitterness in her voice. 'Would you like me to take the drink now?'

'The herbs must steep, we shall deliver our gift as the first stars appear. The longer the valerian swims in the mead, the more wicked her power will become as it whispers through their blood.'

The women exchanged looks of complicity.

'And you, Becuma?' asked Goneril.

'It is written, my fate is tied to Cordelia's,' she said. 'Our paths are entwined, we have known this since childhood when your mother assigned me to the temple.'

'I am to marry Aganippus though,' said Cordelia.

'Who will no doubt allow you an entourage of your own, or at least a woman to accompany you,' said Becuma. 'I shall be by your side.'

'Thank you, my friend,' said Cordelia.

'And what will become of us?' wailed Goneril.

'You will survive,' said Angarad. Her voice was low and calm as she reappeared through the curtain, her face remaining in shadow. 'Do not fear, Goneril. However, to survive you must leave this place; the oppidum is no longer safe for you.'

'Leave?' said Goneril in surprise.

'Yes, both of you. If you stay, the pathway will be different,' said Angarad.

'Módor, what did you see?' Cordelia asked, unnerved by the flatness of Angarad's voice.

'Darkness,' she replied. 'A strange place of mists and unformed sorrows. My pathway will change all our lives,' she replied.

'Please, Módor,' said Regan, echoing Cordelia's formal address to Angarad. 'Tell us how we can best protect each other and our tribe.'

'I cannot,' Angarad responded. 'The goddesses have shown me how this ends and it is my burden to bear.'

'Flee with the others,' said Cordelia, as icy tremors flooded her. 'Don't let my father force you into marriage. You swore to serve the goddess, you must remain true to your oath.'

'You are young, Cordelia, I see a path of happiness for you with the potential for healing. However, mine is different. The goddesses have never yet been wrong and I shall follow their words.'

'But your vows,' said Cordelia.

'They shall remain unbroken,' Angarad replied.

She took a deep shuddering breath and Cordelia felt fear run down her spine.

'Sisters, you have done well,' said Angarad to the women, her voice more like her usual self. 'Cordelia, Becuma, Goneril, Regan and I will finish packing away our treasures. Gloigin, Ignogin, Oudar, you must rest, you will need your strength for your night walk. Your paths will be winding, but you will reach your destination, and one day, this hurt will be healed.'

Angarad radiated a quiet power and the other women followed her instructions, busying themselves with tidying and cleaning the temple, an unspoken decision reached by them all to leave the place stripped clean of the goddesses, to leave no trace and allow no one to sully their years of worship. Food was delivered, shoved through the curtained entrance, and Angarad advised them all to eat.

'We must stay strong for ourselves, for no one else,' she said and, again, the women did as they were bid.

* * *

When the day began to fade, Oudar roused herself from her slumbers to drain the mead and sweeten it with extra honey in order to disguise any lingering bitterness from the valerian. Goneril and Regan twisted each other's hair into plaits, which Cordelia adorned with flowers and feathers from their trove of ingredients.

'Here,' said Oudar, handing them a heavy jug each, 'I'll follow with the beakers.'

Cordelia waited inside, relieved to hear the faux giggles of her sisters as they engaged their best flirting techniques with the guards.

'Pig-headed fools,' she murmured to Angarad. 'They are arrogant enough to believe my beautiful sisters would stoop to their level. None of them are good enough to lick the mud from Goneril and Regan's boots.'

'They'll soon be in Dubnos,' said Angarad. 'But, for now, we must wait.'

At the zenith of the dark moon, as the guards snored and twitched, Gloigin, Ignogin and Oudar dressed in dark cloaks, bade their farewells and merged into the shadows. Each carried a bag filled with herbs, a skin of water and food. Angarad blessed them as they left.

'We shall meet again,' she said, but Cordelia could sense the sadness in her lie.

12

GOLDEN VALLEY, DOBVNNI, 862 BCE

'Wake up, you useless scum.'

As the sun rose, the man's rough voice outside the temple entrance felt as though it came from another realm.

'Is he speaking to us?' murmured Regan from where she was curled up asleep next to Cordelia.

'No, he must be talking to the guards,' she replied. 'Oudar gave them a huge dose of valerian, I doubt any of them will wake properly until evening.'

The commotion continued outside the temple, with drowsy-voiced men protesting against what sounded like slaps and kicks from their compatriots. At last, the curtain was pulled back and a group of wives from the oppidum, laden with baskets, hurried inside.

'We are here to help you prepare,' said Sadiald, the wife of Dardan.

She and the other women looked wary and one had a swollen eye.

'What's happening outside?' asked Cordelia.

'Your father has been in his roundhouse with Dardan, Aganippus, Maglaurus, Henwinus and the leader of the new men, who I think is called Caradoc. He claims to be a priest, but he is like no holy man I've ever seen.'

'What of Locrinus and his sons?' asked Angarad.

'Locrinus has been banished to his roundhouse after he tried to reason with Lear, questioning the chief's decision,' said Sadiald. 'He attempted to persuade him to stop the marriages, but Lear refused. When the new guards threw him from Lear's dwelling, Lagon ran to his aid and he was beaten.'

'No,' gasped Cordelia, 'is he...?'

'He lives,' said Sadiald, 'but he has sustained injuries. When the other men saw what had happened to him, they retreated.'

'Cowards,' said Goneril in contempt.

'Not to hide but to work on a strategy,' retorted Sadiald. 'Lear has always taught us to search for weaknesses in our adversaries and this is what the men are doing. They know Lear is a good man and this madness can't last, they want to help him return to himself.'

'He won't,' replied Regan. 'He is no longer our Fa. The gods have sent a changeling in his place.'

'I fear Regan is correct,' said Cordelia. 'We don't know this man.'

Angarad sat in silence as two of the older wives plaited her hair, winding coloured thread through the intricate style.

'You will be queen,' one of the women whispered, trying to raise the mood.

'I shall not,' replied Angarad, but her tone was kind. 'There will be no queen and there will be no male heirs.'

Cordelia was unable to turn to look at her friend as Gael, Ivor's betrothed, was applying delicate swirling patterns of blue woad to her cheeks, but the way she spoke felt unreal, as though it were Angarad, and not Lear, who was possessed.

'The suitors came prepared,' said Goneril as she was laced into a dress of forest green embroidered with leaves provided by Maglaurus.

'They were told to bring bridal chests,' said Regan. 'They knew they would marry us, it was why they accepted Fa's invitation.'

Cordelia glanced over, Regan was looking down at the gown supplied by Henwinus in dismay. It was a periwinkle blue and far too big for her petite frame, two of the other women were intent on shortening it and tightening the bodice.

'We usually have more time to fit the bridal attire,' said one, near to tears.

'You're doing your best and I'm grateful,' said Regan and the woman gave a sob.

'Here, Cordelia.' Gael held up a gown of pale ivory.

It was unlike any clothing Cordelia had ever seen, the fabric was soft and pliable with a sheen all of its own. When it was lowered over her head, it rustled, cool and supple against her skin. The sleeves whispered down her arms and, as they did, she noticed more of the strange silver lines had appeared, swirling around her wrists.

'Aganippus said it's called silk,' explained Gael, drawing Cordelia's attention away from the marks on her skin. 'He bought it from a merchant who had travelled east. He told me his mother had worn a similar dress when she married his father and he wanted a version of his own for his future wife.'

'It bears the triskele,' remarked Cordelia, looking at the sleeves where the Celtic symbol was embroidered in blue.

'He asked me to sew those last night,' said Gael. 'I'm sorry they're so hurried.'

'They're beautiful,' said Cordelia and for a moment she forgot the horror of the previous day and allowed her thoughts to roam to Aganippus and what marriage to him would entail.

'The sun is nearly at its highest,' came a male voice from outside and all the women except Angarad jumped, their nerves taut. 'Everyone but the brides must leave.'

'Where are Gloigin, Ignogin and Oudar?' whispered Gael to Cordelia as she gathered together the trappings and cast-offs of the bridal preparations.

'They fled in the night,' she replied. 'We'll have to pretend they left without anyone seeing them and are somewhere in the oppidum.'

'I shall say I saw them on the other side of the fort,' whispered Gael, 'and will ask the other women to do the same; we'll be able to keep their disappearance secret for a while at least.'

'Thank you,' said Cordelia.

Gael smiled, then hurried after the other women.

There was a tramping of feet and Lagon's voice reached them through the curtained entrance.

'You are summoned to your handfasting ceremonies,' he stated. 'I am to be your chaperone.'

'Thank you,' said Angarad, but her voice was once again flat and dull.

Goneril squared her shoulders, her eyes swimming with tears. Regan scowled and Cordelia raised her chin, thinking of her mother and how she would have reacted to such treatment. *She would have fought back*, she thought, *and so shall I*, as courage surged through her.

'Our new high priest, Caradoc, will perform the ceremony,' Lagon said as the women walked into the bright sunlight.

Lagon was surrounded by a phalanx of soldiers, his right eye was swollen shut and his lip split. Cordelia felt her hope falter, until Lagon turned to look at her and the defiance in his eyes bolstered her resolve.

We are women, she thought, as she followed her sisters, *we have been forced into marriages with strangers for centuries.*

She remembered her mother, Estrildis Loegriadohtor, had been the third daughter of a third daughter like Cordelia and the youngest princess of a tribe on the other side of the Golden Valley. Her home had been in Castell Dinas on the borders of the territory of Demetae.

'Your father and I met on our wedding day,' she had told Cordelia. 'It was frightening, but your father is a good man. There are many good men.'

Aganippus is a good man, Cordelia reminded herself.

'Follow me,' said Lagon.

Angarad and Goneril fell into step behind him, walking side by side, clutching each other's hands for comfort. Cordelia and Regan followed, with the soldiers at the rear ensuring the women reached their destination with no interruptions from the sullen crowd who lined the way to the centre of the oppidum.

* * *

As was tradition with the tribe of the Golden Dobvnni, a marriage altar had been built overnight around the menhir at the heart of their meeting place. There was a sweeping archway made from oak branches decorated with flowers standing at the entrance of a walkway of colourfully woven mats. These were loaned by each of the family groups within the hill fort and the majority were heirlooms, passed down through the years. Nearest to the standing stone was the most elaborate of all, the carpet belonging to the Bladud family, the longest line of leaders of the tribe. On this was a wooden table draped in linen where four elaborately woven cords, each a different colour, waited for the handfasting ceremony.

A tall, thin man stood behind the makeshift altar and Cordelia surmised this must be Caradoc, her father's new high priest. He wore the white robes of a Druid, but a scar ran the length of his right cheek and his shoulders were broad as though he might once have wielded a weapon. Cordelia could see unease in his eyes, but, despite Sadiald's comments, she sensed Caradoc was a genuine wise man, although perhaps not a Druid. She wondered what lies he had been told to bring him here, what promises had been made to keep him onside with her father's new regime.

On the table in front him, near the handfasting cords, was the Weddian Scroll of the Golden Dobvnni. Each tribe owned such a document, where the marriages, births and deaths for each year were recorded. A new scroll was created with the coming of Alban Arthuran, the Yuletide celebrations of the winter solstice, and these lists were considered to be the history of their people. As each new scroll was created, a ceremony would be held as the old one was retired into the inner sanctum of the temple.

Alas, now, they are piled into the boxes and chests, thought Cordelia as Caradoc began to speak. *Will they ever be given the proper reverence or consideration again or will they be used to light fires now the temple has been defiled?*

Lagon halted at the entrance to the walkway and the soldiers fanned out, making their way to the edges of the crowd, a wall of potential violence holding the Golden Dobvnni people in the meeting place. The bridegrooms waited beside the oak arch, each in clothing which matched the dresses of the women. Lear was seated, his bejewelled eye-patch once again glinting with other-worldly light in the sun, his other eye closed, whether in contemplation, sleep or pain, Cordelia could not decide.

Aganippus stepped forward, taking first Cordelia's hand, then Angarad's, leading them through the arch onto the walkway.

'I apologise,' he whispered to Angarad, 'your betrothed has not the strength to stand throughout the other ceremonies and he asked me to be your chaperone.'

Angarad did not reply but gave a small nod, then stood beside Cordelia.

Maglaurus led Goneril to the opposite side of the walkway, followed by Henwinus and Regan.

'Goneril and Maglaurus, step forward,' said Caradoc.

Cordelia noticed he did not bother to introduce himself. *Was he ashamed?* she wondered. *Or was this another of her father's directives? Remain aloof, explain nothing, cause tension and fear.* The image of Regan with her head shaved, Goneril being brutalised by their father flashed through her mind. She felt the ground lurch beneath her, but a strong hand gripped her, holding her upright.

'I'm here,' said a low voice and she felt a rush of gratitude towards Aganippus.

There was a rustle of fabric and Goneril stepped forward, taking her place beside the menhir.

'There is a word my people use,' said Angarad in a low voice to Cordelia. '"Wĕding", it is not dissimilar to your tribe's words, "wedd" and "weddian" which both mean to engage, to pledge oneself, to marry, but our word has a very different meaning.'

'What does it mean in your language?'

'Madness.'

As though at a distance, Cordelia heard Goneril and Maglaurus repeat the words of the ancient handfasting ceremony, promising devotion and honesty, fruitfulness and support, love and family. They joined hands and the first cord was draped across their wrists, knots were tied to seal their bond as the high priest intoned the Druidic prayers of love, fecundity and steadfastness. Regan and Henwinus followed, tears rolling down her cheeks as she repeated her vows and the knots were tied. Then, feeling as though she were in a trance, Aganippus led Cordelia forward.

Cordelia stood beside the menhir, it felt both familiar and strange, while Aganippus took his position opposite her. She had watched many hand-fasting ceremonies but had never considered she would one day participate. Her unfamiliar dress rustled in the breeze and as Caradoc said her name, she stared up at Aganippus.

'Shall you offer your body and your spirit to this man?' asked the high priest.

'I shall,' she said.

'Shall you care for and adore this man?'

'I shall.'

'Shall you obey this man?'

She hesitated and a small movement at his side caught her eye, he had crossed his fingers, she shot him a confused look, then she understood. This was the old wives' tale that if you cross your fingers a promise did not count, she crossed her fingers too and he gave a small, approving nod, as she said, 'I shall.'

'You now, Aganippus,' said Caradoc, and while he offered his own troth, Cordelia wondered again about this man to whom she was bound. Why would he release her from the command to obey?

'Join hands,' ordered Caradoc.

Aganippus's palm was dry and strong against her own, she could feel callouses from his years of riding and hunting, but beneath its strength she felt gentleness. These hands held no cruelty and for this she was grateful. The cord to bind them was as blue as her eyes, a silken skein dyed in woad and decorated with white flowers. She knotted the cord, Aganippus added his knot and the priest combined the two. They unclasped their grip and the priest slipped the woven fabric from their wrists. He laid the knotted cord on the table beside those of her sisters and indicated for them to take their place with the other couples to the side of the menhir. They were married. It was a situation she could not fully comprehend.

'And now, our final ceremony,' the high priest announced. 'I, Caradoc, of the Druidstone of the Blackwood, do hereby join Lear Bladudsunu, Chief of the Golden Dobvnni in the Druidstone of Dobvnni, with Angarad Hrocdo-htor, the Chosen Maiden of the Druidstone of Halliggye.'

Lear was helped to his feet by Dardan and his son, Cangu. Cordelia watched as Angarad followed her father to the standing stone. Lear glared down at her, but Angarad's eyes remained strangely blank.

'I, Lear Bladudsunu, leader of the Tribe of the Golden Dobvnni, welcome you, Angarad Hrocdohtor.'

Caradoc turned to Angarad and stated the words for her to repeat. There was silence, she remained motionless and gave no indication she had even heard the high priest speak. Caradoc looked at Lear, who took Angarad's limp hand.

'Answer, woman,' he commanded.

Angarad wrenched her hand from Lear's, her eyes suddenly wild and feverish. She moved closer to him, then opened her mouth and emitted an eldritch howl. Her eyes rolled and she turned to look at Cordelia, then swung back to Lear, focusing all her energy and power upon him.

'I, Angarad Hrocdohtor, Chosen Maiden and High Priestess of the Temple of the Matronae Melissae, do curse you, Lear Bladudsunu!' she roared and above them a huge cloud covered the sun, a gust of wind rattled the leaves of the trees and in the distance dogs barked and wolves howled. Her voice was wild, unearthly, gaining in volume and strength as she continued, 'You trade your daughters as though they are cattle. You defile our sanctuary for your male vanity.

'You shall never bear sons. Your daughters shall never bear sons. All shall have three girls. Three by three by three by three by three until one shall come, a youngest child of a youngest child of a youngest child who shall have the power to heal this curse. One becomes two; two becomes three; and out of the third comes the fourth, the One.

'The triple goddess of the bees curses you. In the glory of the goddess, your line will remain ever female. No sons shall be born to the House of Lear until the day the Charmed One heals the pain of the past, present and future. As punishment for your disrespect of the feminine, you will bear the greatest of all pain, one of such magnitude your mind will shatter into dust for all eternity!'

Screaming in triumph, Angarad pulled a bottle from her sleeve and drank its contents in one gulp.

'No!' shouted Cordelia, lunging forward, but she knew it was too late because she recognised the small vial. It contained their purest, most deadly hemlock.

Angarad was dead before she hit the floor and as screams and howls of terror filled the air, hail poured from the huge cloud, bouncing off the ground with icy viciousness. Cordelia cradled her friend's head in her lap and allowed her tears to fall.

13

THE TALE OF THE THREE SISTERS

After the banquet and the dancing, the three sisters lay in their comfortable beds in their adjoining rooms. As the darkness pressed against the castle, leaning heavily on the windows, wrapping the night around them like a curse, each woman lay awake. Unseen behind the ornate hangings and curtains, each face illuminated by the flickering, heady scented candlelight, the sisters thought of the man who had questioned them.

The Queen knew the man. He was the one who sent her on the path towards cruelty. A life away from all she held dear, leaving her alone and scared in a place of hardships, fear and dread.

The Baroness knew the man. He was the one who had humiliated her, belittling and taunting her throughout their marriage, punishing her for loving another. As his face hung in her mind's eye, she wondered why had they revealed the truth of their quest to this man? Her unease intensified and she resolved, at first light, they must leave the castle. They were not safe here.

The Princess knew the man. He was the one whom she had once loved, but she knew this man to be long dead. If this was the case, the creature who had spoken this evening was a spectre.

Beside her, the candle guttered and, as it did, The Princess was overwhelmed by an unexpected truth.

'We have lived this before,' she murmured, yet she did not understand because the castle was unknown to them. They had travelled there for the first time that day.

Or had they?

A pain pierced her heart and confusion filled her soul.

All night, the women were haunted by their thoughts. Finally, moments before dawn, the sisters fell into restless, dreamless slumbers, awaking several hours later, more exhausted than when they had retired the previous evening.

A platoon of liveried servants arrived, carrying a sumptuous breakfast, displaying the finest hospitality from their unknown host.

'There is fine hunting,' said the Lord Chamberlain, 'or, if you prefer, a large tiltyard in which to practise. We have a vast library and by our lake, in our orchard of cherry blossom trees, is a troupe of entertainers composing music. Whatever you desire, we will provide.'

As the Lord Chamberlain finished speaking, the women looked at each other.

'We must leave...' began The Baroness, the remnants of her night-time thoughts melting on her tongue because she could no longer remember the reason why and it would be the height of rudeness to dismiss the hospitality offered by the Lord Chamberlain.

'We must thank...' began The Queen, but her voice faltered as the rest of her sentence vanished from her mind. To whom should they offer their gratitude?

'We must find the man from last night,' said The Princess and, as she spoke, her sisters' expressions cleared and they stared at her in surprise.

'Why?' asked The Queen.

'I don't know,' admitted The Princess, all thoughts and remembrances of the previous day stolen by her brief but heavy slumber, 'but I think he might hold an answer for us.'

'The cause of our quest?' asked The Baroness.

'Perhaps,' said The Queen. 'We must each use our particular skill to discover him and if we have not found him by nightfall, we shall leave.'

'A plan, at last,' said The Baroness. 'I shall visit the stables and the tilt-yard. While I am there, I will ensure our horses are ready to depart at any moment.'

'I shall visit the musicians at the cherry orchard,' said The Queen. 'My skill is playing the lute; musicians often hear things the nobility do not, they might know more about the man.'

'And I shall visit the library,' said The Princess. 'Books will always offer an answer, even if it is not the one for which we search.'

With a smile, the Lord Chamberlain clapped his hands to summon servants to help the women dress. They returned to their rooms, re-energised by their tasks.

The Princess sat at the huge oval looking glass and picked up the silver-backed hairbrush, ready to attend to her long dark hair. It was then, she saw them.

Two women, one on either side of her. Behind her left shoulder, the woman wore a headdress of antlers, her face painted with intricate blue patterns, her eyes wide with confusion; behind her right shoulder, the woman's hair was loose and her dress was fitted, flaring out at her waist, her arms heavy with bracelets and a necklace with a bee pendant around her neck. All three faces were identical.

'Who are you?' shouted The Princess, leaping from the chair, turning to face them, but the women had vanished.

14

GOLDENWYCH, PRESENT DAY

Caitlin parked in her usual place. Stan was in the middle of a conversation on his mobile phone and shrugged apologetically as she switched off the engine. Caitlin did not mind; she was still on edge after her strange and vivid dream of the previous night. Stan's preoccupation with church business meant she could continue to try to make sense of it. She could not understand why she and the woman with the antler headdress, the *genius loci* of the stream in her garden, had been watching a third woman brushing her hair in a mirror. Another woman who looked exactly like them.

When she had awoken with a start, Caitlin had rummaged through her bookcase for her books on King Arthur and Arthurian legend because this was what the castle and the clothes resembled, but she could not find a story about three women on a quest. It was the men who traversed the highways and byways searching for the Holy Grail and doing good deeds as they swept from town to village to hamlet. Even more disturbing, when she was in the shower, she noticed a series of silver lines around the delicate Celtic tattoos on her arms. These had appeared overnight and reminded her of a long-healed scar.

With her eighteenth birthday money, she had travelled with some trepidation to a tattoo artist near Ross-on-Wye who had been recommended by a friend, but as soon as she had walked into the studio, all her nerves had disappeared. A small woman with cherry-red hair in a 1950s-style quiff and high ponytail introduced herself as Misty. She wore black jeans, a black T-shirt and bright red, high-heeled Mary Janes, her arms were swathed in tattoo sleeves of roses, rooks and magical creatures and in her ears were multiple crystals that shimmered as they caught the light, casting a rainbow around her as she walked. What had made Caitlin happiest, though, were the many Celtic patterns around the wall that were delicate rather than brutal and conveyed the mysticism of the past.

It had taken several sessions, but by the time they were finished Caitlin had a small but intricate Celtic triskele decorated with flowers on the inside of both forearms in the crook of her elbow. The third triskele was at the base of her spine; this was larger, more elaborate and encircled by flames. As the last tattoo healed, she had felt a strange sense of completion, as though these images had made her whole. She had never regretted her ink, but the change in their appearance concerned her.

Leaving Stan to his call, she climbed out of the car and walked around to the boot. As she flipped it open, she thought, *Dreams and tattoos are things I must resolve later, there are family issues to be dealt with first.* She picked up the large cool box and sent a silent thank you to Sindy, who had excelled herself in creating a vast picnic lunch for the King family.

Caitlin carried the box to the door and as she slotted her key in, Stan finished his call and struggled out, his foot catching in the seat belt.

'Sorry,' he said, righting himself and hurrying over to join her as she locked the car with a click of her key fob. 'The diocese is being difficult, they're pushing me to balance the financial deficit. As I keep explaining, my parishioners give as much money as they're able, I can't make funds appear out of thin air. I'll have to pray about it.'

His narrow eyes strayed towards the impressive King family home, but Caitlin shook her head.

'Dad has enough to worry about without you asking for another donation from the foundation set up in Mum's name,' she said, shoving the cool box into his hands.

'Which you help him administer,' said Stan.

'He was very generous when you asked him to help with the Sunday School fund, but the foundation isn't your private bank to prop up the church,' she reminded him. 'It's to help the whole village. Anyway, Dad needs to focus on recovering. If you begin discussing money, it might cause him undue stress.'

'Credit me with a certain amount of sensitivity,' Stan said. 'I visit sick people most days in the course of my work. I'm aware of the correct time to choose my moment.'

Yes, thought Cordelia as she shut the front door behind them, *you're very clever at pouncing when someone is in a vulnerable position and turning it to your advantage.*

As soon as the words flashed across her mind, she felt ashamed of herself. It was unlike her to be judgemental and it was unfair on Stan. Yes, there were times when he could be pompous, but his true nature was kind and considerate. No doubt her tetchy feelings were due to stress over her father and tiredness from her troubled night.

Pull yourself together, she thought as she dropped her keys into the wide uneven dark brown bowl where the family always placed their keys. It had been made by Rachel during her pottery obsession in her teens and despite its wonky shape, her parents had always given it pride of place.

The familiar scent of home enveloped Caitlin as she walked through the vast Arts and Crafts property, with its steep gables, intricate art nouveau woodwork and large bay windows. On one of the quieter roads in the village, the house was set in the middle of its plot and had a long driveway with a parking area to the front. To the rear of the house was a vast open-plan kitchen and living space and Caitlin felt her shoulders relax as she entered, soothed by being back in the room where the family had spent the majority of their time.

When it was first built in the 1990s, Larry and Miranda's friends had been surprised by the design.

'It'll be hard to heat,' their aunt, Larry's elder sister, Primrose had stated.

'Never mind,' Miranda had replied. 'We love it.'

As the years passed, an open-plan family room had become a commonplace feature, but Caitlin had always been proud of her parents for leading the way.

Her memories of growing up involved her father covering the diningroom table with scripts as he wrote, edited and annotated plays for the Goldenwych Players. The scent of her mother's cooking was the perfume of their world as she experimented with ingredients, each recipe carefully catalogued in her array of notebooks, while the three girls had lounged on sofas watching television, puzzled over their homework, played in the garden or rehearsed with their father.

The garden wrapped around the house and there were tables and chairs dotted in positions chosen with care to capture the sun's rays at different times of the day. Mature trees marked the perimeter, while a small orchard of apple, pear and plum trees stood in a sunny corner. It was on one of the meandering pathways to the orchard where Miranda's bees had lived. When she had died, Caitlin and the local beekeeping club had moved the hives to her garden. A criss-cross of paths wandered through the garden leading to various planting areas which created hidden, private nooks behind neat, clipped yew hedges.

Caitlin had always thought of the house as magical and her favourite part of the garden was in a small dell near the front where three large stones lay as though toppled by a giant. As a child, she believed the fairies had flown the stones there from the circle on the edge of the village – a smaller version of the Three Sisters for her and her sisters. She would take her dolls there and whisper spells to them in the hope they might speak to her in return.

One day, the shoe of her favourite doll had disappeared down the gap between the stones. Despite her best efforts from poking sticks into the void to try to feel for it, and even after she had enlisted the help of the entire family, the shoe, they realised, was lost forever.

'There must be a hole under the stones,' her father had said as they had dinner later. 'Perhaps a passageway?'

Caitlin, Gillian and Rachel had been wide-eyed with excitement.

'Shall we look for it tomorrow?' Rachel had asked.

'No,' their mother had said, but there was amusement in her voice, 'the stones weigh a huge amount, and even if we did have the necessary equipment to move them, we wouldn't.'

'Why not?' Gillian had asked.

'Because the stones have been there for thousands of years.'

'How do you know, Mum?' Caitlin had asked.

'Many, many years ago, when Auntie Helena, Auntie Bea and I were little, Granddad Jeeves told us about an archaeological dig that had taken place when his father was a boy, which was in Victorian times. They excavated the stone circle and part of the land that is now our garden.'

The girls had stared at their mother in wonder.

'Did they find anything?' Caitlin had asked.

'Yes, they found several skeletons' – the girls had squealed – 'and with one there was an amethyst set in gold which they think had been a woman's pendant,' Miranda had said. 'It's in a museum in London now because it was so valuable. There were other finds too and the archaeologists have said there was a hill fort where the village now stands that can be traced back to the Iron Age.'

'Is that before the Romans?' Rachel, who had been studying the Romans at school, had asked.

'Yes,' Larry had responded. 'The Romans invaded in August 55 BCE and the Iron Age ran from 1300 to 900 BCE.'

The rest of the evening had been spent in sillier and sillier speculation about the people who had lived in the hill fort, ending with Larry and Gillian making up a song and dance routine called *The Iron Age was full of Sage* which had caused Caitlin, Rachel and Miranda to cry with laughter.

The house triggered an abundance of happy memories for Caitlin, it was her safe place, the family hub where they all belonged, while for Stan, it held a different appeal. When he had first seen the property, his eyes had lit up and Caitlin knew he was impressed. Her father had given lavishly to the church over the years, the donations increasing when Caitlin and Stan had become engaged, but she was irritated Stan would mention the ongoing financial woes of his parish when they were awaiting Larry's return from hospital.

'Would you put the cool box on the counter, please,' she said, turning to open the bifold doors and let in the summer sunshine. 'Dad's going to be tense enough having been away from the factory for a few weeks, so the family has agreed not to mention work today.'

'It might have been pleasant to be included in this instruction,' said Stan, depositing the box with undue force.

'It's on the family WhatsApp,' she said. 'You were the only one who didn't reply.'

Stan scowled as he scrolled through his messages. He was a good-looking man with well-defined features and thick dark hair which he wore in an old-fashioned 1940s-style modelled on his idol the actor Cary Grant. His clothes were of a similar ilk and were mildly eccentric, but, when out of his dog collar, his unusual style made him appear non-threatening and easy to approach. He was well-loved by his parishioners and villagers alike. Easy to laugh and with the ability to charm people, he was tipped to rise high in the Church of England.

In recent months, however, Caitlin had become aware of another side to her fiancé. He could be secretive, then patronising when questioned about his behaviour. He was also a sulker, refusing to speak if he felt he had been slighted or challenged in his opinions. At first, Caitlin had laughed about it, but as time passed, she found his moodiness exhausting. She understood couples disagreed and, while she was ready to find a solution to suit them both, Stan would often refuse to discuss problems, preferring to remain silent until, in frustration, she bent her views to mirror his own.

His phone rang again and he gave an apologetic shrug before answering in a booming hearty voice, 'Hello, Daphne, what can I do for you this morning?'

Caitlin began unpacking the cool box, depositing the neatly wrapped packages of sandwiches, salads and pies in the fridge, before laying out the cakes on a series of decorative plates. She filled the kettle and was sorting out cups and plates when she heard Stan say: 'Goodbye, then.'

He walked over to the counter and took a square of brownie before continuing as though there had been no interruption. 'Who's collecting your dad?'

'Uncle George and Lee,' she replied. 'We all offered, but he insisted on what he called his "medical escort".'

'Why do you call him Uncle George?' said Stan irritably. 'He's not a relation.'

'We've always done it,' replied Caitlin. 'Uncle George and Aunt Suki were a huge part of our life growing up. It was polite as children to give them the honorary title of uncle and aunt.'

'But you're a grown woman now, you could drop the "uncle" and "aunt" tag.' He said the words in a childish lisp. 'It's very juvenile.'

Caitlin was saved the bother of responding as voices filled the hallway.

'Moon, you're here,' said Gillian, bustling in. 'Hello, Stan, good to have you home.'

Her tone was polite, but there was no warmth. She glanced at the food Caitlin was laying out and her eyes narrowed in distaste.

Alan followed her in and beamed, before hugging Caitlin. 'Hello, Moonbeam,' he said, releasing her. 'How are you bearing up?'

'I'm fine now we know he's going to recover,' she said.

'It's a relief,' Alan agreed. 'Can I have a brownie?'

He took one of the cakes with a naughty grin. Alan was ten years older than Gillian, balding and with an expanding girth, but there was a warmth and likeability about him. Gillian and Alan had met when they had worked together. Gillian had left university with a first-class business studies degree and had managed to secure a prestigious placement at a London bank. Although very junior at first, she had shown huge aptitude and was quickly promoted. Alan had been her team leader. For him, he claimed it was love at first sight; for Gillian, the attraction had been slower to grow.

When their father had offered Gillian a role in the family business, a position she had refused upon first leaving education as she had wanted to prove herself, she decided to accept. When she gave three months' notice, Alan was devastated and, unbeknown to Gillian, applied for a job at her father's company. Larry had been surprised by the application as there were no vacancies, so he had rung Alan, and in his usual self-effacing style, Alan had explained his feelings for Gillian and her growing fondness of him.

'She's determined to put her career first,' he had explained. 'She wants to prove herself to you.'

'There's no need for her to impress me,' Larry had replied, appalled. 'My heart explodes with pride every time I think about her.'

After the conversation, Larry had created a role especially for Alan, determined to do his best to foster the romance. Gillian had been stunned when she had arrived for her first day at King's Factories to discover Alan seated in the office opposite her. He had told no one except his immediate superiors he was leaving in order to keep it a surprise for Gillian.

'Isn't it a bit like stalking?' Rachel had said when Gillian confided in her sisters that evening.

'Or it's incredibly romantic,' Caitlin had suggested.

'Do you love him, Bean?' Rachel had asked and Gillian's deep blush had been all the answer they needed. 'Then I concede to Moon, it's romantic.'

They had married a year later, with Caitlin and Rachel as their bridesmaids.

Gillian walked out into the garden, shaking her dark auburn hair away from her pretty heart-shaped face, a haunted look in her amber eyes. A wide terrace spread the entire width of the house, with a large table and chairs in the centre. She leaned across the table and opened the umbrella before walking over to the summer house and gathering the cushions for the garden furniture. When she had arranged everything to her liking, she took a seat as far away as possible from the house.

'Don't mind her,' said Alan. 'She's struggling.'

'I'll talk to her,' said Stan and followed Gillian out before either Caitlin or Alan could advise against it.

'By the way, Moon, thank you for the info on the pineapples and witches,' Alan said in an undertone. 'When I surprised her, she burst into tears but assured me they were happy tears; we had a fabulous evening. We've become rather partial to piña coladas.'

'Wonderful news,' she said.

Moments later, Stan returned looking flustered.

'Perhaps she's better on her own,' he said and wandered off, phone in hand, checking his messages.

Caitlin and Alan exchanged an amused look; both had been on the receiving end of Gillian's sharp tongue many times when she had not wanted to be disturbed. The entire family had learned to read the signs of when to back away from Gillian and give her space to regain her equilibrium. Stan, with his self-righteous belief he knew better than everyone, was yet to learn when to leave her in peace.

Another key grated in the lock, followed by footsteps, and Rachel paused in the doorway. Tall and slim, her highlighted blonde hair was styled into casual-looking waves which Caitlin knew took hours to perfect. Pete put his hands on her waist and propelled her into the room.

'This is a surprise,' he said. 'I didn't realise there was a reception committee.'

'Larry insisted,' said Alan.

'Who'd like a drink?' asked Caitlin. 'I've put the kettle on.'

'I'll help,' said Alan.

Rachel walked past her and outside, where she took a seat a few spaces away from Gillian. Pete followed, wandering around the garden admiring the plants. It was beautifully landscaped and with a gardener tending it twice a week, it was as immaculate as when Larry was at home.

'There's pineapple cake here if you want to take Bean a slice,' said Caitlin as she poured water into the teapot and the cafetière.

She placed them on the tray and, as Alan reached over to lift it, she added the plate of cakes.

'You're a star,' Alan said.

'I'll be out in a moment,' said Caitlin and Alan gave an understanding smile as he set off with his cargo.

Caitlin sipped her tea and watched as Stan, having finished checking his messages, joined the rest of her family. He picked up the teapot and began pouring.

Go out there and talk to them, she told herself, but her stomach knotted at the idea.

She loved her older sisters, but there was no one on earth who could injure her with such cruelty and precision as Gillian and Rachel. She could do the same in return, but she had no desire to drive the wedge any further between them; she was desperate for it to heal. Yet, she knew she had to take responsibility for her part in the rift. She had spoken, not out of malice but astonishment, and this had led to the fallout.

The tea she sipped was one of her mother's herbal brews and was supposed to bring about calm and strength, but it was not helping. Stan had turned to beckon her outside, but to her relief as he did, the doorbell rang.

'I'll go,' she called, although none of the others appeared to have heard it.

To her surprise, her father's long-standing personal assistant, Heather Blackstone, was on the doorstep with an attaché case on wheels.

'Hello, Caitlin, love,' said Heather in a soft Yorkshire accent. 'I'm sorry to intrude, but your father left me a message asking me to pop by; he wanted this paperwork.'

'Thank you, Heather,' said Caitlin, stepping back to let the woman pass. 'He's his own worst enemy. He's supposed to be resting.'

'Your father will never stop,' Heather replied. 'He also asked if I'd wait for him to arrive home as he wants me to witness a document.'

'What document?'

'I've no idea, love.'

'You'd better go through,' said Caitlin, but before she could follow, Lee's car swept up the drive. 'Dad's here,' she called to the others, then hurried outside to meet her father.

'Darling,' exclaimed Larry as George helped him out of the car, 'it's so wonderful to see you.'

Caitlin felt her father's arms around her as he hugged her tightly, but despite his best efforts, his grip was less than half its usual strength.

'Dad, you're home...'

'Dad, let me help you...'

There was a surge of people as Gillian, Rachel, Alan, Pete and Stan hurried out.

'Careful, everyone,' said George. 'Don't knock him over in your enthusiasm.'

'Stop fussing, you lot,' Larry said, but Caitlin knew her father was enjoying being the centre of attention.

'How are you feeling today?' Lee asked her as he entered last, carrying Larry's bag.

'Bearing up,' she replied, pointing for him to put the bag at the foot of the stairs.

'No, I'll take it up,' he said and hurried away.

Caitlin followed the others through to the garden where Larry was already ensconced in his favourite chair in the shade. Rachel was pouring him tea and Gillian was helping him to choose a cake.

'My girls,' he said. As Caitlin joined them, he added with a beaming smile, 'My baby.'

Gillian and Rachel exchanged a sour look but said nothing. Instead they took seats either side of their father, while Caitlin settled next to Stan.

'And Heather, you're here,' said Larry, reaching out to grasp her hand.

* * *

For the next half an hour, they chatted, then Caitlin suggested lunch and the food from the café was laid out, then demolished with enthusiasm. The chatter and noise was resonant of any family group but Caitlin knew it was surface deep. Each of them was relieved to have Larry home but the ties that had once bound them remained severed and with each forced laugh and retold tale of reminiscence, she felt scars grow on her heart.

Oh Mum, she thought, *if you were here, we'd have resolved this tension by now.*

'Where's Lee?' asked her father, interrupting her thoughts.

'He went inside...' began Pete, but Lee had returned, pushing his phone into his back pocket.

'Good, you're back,' said Larry and tapped his teaspoon on the side of his cup in a request for silence. 'I don't want anyone to miss my announcement.'

'Announcement?' said Alan, taking another cake. 'Have you fallen in love with one of the nurses and are planning to elope?'

'He's still got the looks,' riposted George to a ripple of laughter.

'No, nothing so exciting,' Larry said. 'But, lying in my hospital bed, terrified I might never recover made me reconsider many things.'

He sipped his tea, his blue eyes serious.

'What's going on?' asked Gillian.

'I asked Heather here to enable her to witness some documents.'

'Did the doctors discover something else?' said Rachel anxiously.

Larry beamed but he would not meet any of their gazes. 'No, Rabbit, I'm on the mend,' he assured them, 'but I've made a decision, I'm retiring from King's Factories and rather than wait until I die to divide up my business empire, I'm going to do it today.'

15

GOLDENWYCH, PRESENT DAY

A tense silence enveloped the table.

'But, Dad,' said Caitlin, unsure if she had heard correctly, 'you love the business. You're its heart. Why would you choose to walk away?'

'This is madness,' said Gillian. 'Why not have a holiday and we can discuss shortening your hours—'

'Caity's right,' interrupted Rachel, 'you *are* the business, its soul. When you feel better, you'll realise and will want to return.'

Larry smiled but did not respond to his daughters' comments, instead he held up his hand to halt them. Caitlin saw a strange expression enter his eyes, as though a cloud had passed over the sun on a summer's day. She nudged Lee who was beside her, wondering if her father was about to collapse again. Lee glanced over and, as he did, she felt his fingers on her arm tracing the silver lines around her tattoos. She shook her head, her focus was on her father, she could discuss the anomaly of the unexpected scarring another time.

When he spoke, Larry's voice was quiet, firm and detached; he caught no one's eye, instead he gazed out across his manicured garden as though he could see something they could not. 'From today, Gillian and Alan will be responsible for the day-to-day running of the factory,' he said. 'Rachel and Pete will take on full responsibility for the distribution and haulage wing.

And you, Caitlin, will continue to administer the foundation I set up in your late mother's memory. There are other bequests, too, but these will wait until my demise. Whereas I once oversaw you all, you are all responsible—'

'Dad, no...' began Gillian, who was white-faced with shock, but Larry shook his head.

'This health scare has woken me from my midnight slumber to *express our darker purpose*,' he said, his voice taking on a theatrical edge. '*Nothing comes from nothing* and the realisation there are fewer years ahead of me than behind has given me the courage to change my life. You stare at me, your eyes wide with confusion, and wonder at my deeds, but this is an opportunity for me to do great things, to recreate my mortal toil, to roam and venture through my twilight years with freedom and courage.'

Caitlin wondered whether the others had noticed the Shakespearean quotes dotting her father's words. A suspicion was beginning to steal over her. She glanced at Stan, who was holding his phone, a schoolboy smirk on his face, uninterested in the family conversation, instead he began surreptitiously texting under the table, his cheeks pink. Rachel and Gillian looked discomfited, Pete was twitching with irritation, but Alan, George and Lee exchanged surprised looks.

'What do you intend to do, Dad?' asked Caitlin.

'Tomorrow, the house will be put on the market; it's too big for me to live in alone—'

'Sell the house?' exclaimed Rachel in horror. 'But it's our home.'

'It hasn't been your home for many years, Snow Rabbit,' said Larry, but her words drew him from his reverie. He looked around at their surprised faces and gave a wry smile. 'Girls, you all knew this day would come; I couldn't live here forever. Your mother and I had been discussing downsizing before she became ill. This is a family home and I'm an aging man. It's time to move forward.'

Caitlin knew there was sense in his words but his announcement felt like another betrayal of her mother and her memory.

'Will you buy a retirement home in the new development on the other side of the village?' asked Stan who had obviously been half-listening while he texted. He placed his phone face down on the table and helped himself to a slice of lemon drizzle cake, oblivious to the tension around him.

'No, not immediately.'

'Where will you go?' asked Caitlin. 'Will you rent a property?'

Larry sipped his tea and Caitlin again had the feeling he was giving a performance. When they had been growing up, if ever there had been difficulties or awkward situations, he had often retreated into this other-worldly version of himself, quoting famous writers and poets, declaiming and posturing, while her mother had tried to bring calm and reason to events.

'Illness clears your head,' he said. 'Lying in my hospital bed with the beeping of the monitors playing their tunes of despair, ideas came to me. Wonderful images, thoughts and dreams.'

'Are you going to go travelling?' asked Pete.

'No, nothing like that,' said Larry, 'but being forced to remain motionless, even for a week, made me realise how much I missed charging about at one hundred miles an hour all the time.'

Caitlin looked at Gillian and Rachel, and for once the three shared a united look; this was a complaint their mother had often made about their father. He would dash from place to place, idea to idea, scheme to scheme, with varying amounts of success, always leaving a trail of good-natured chaos in his wake. George was usually by his side, egging him on, while their two wives would roll their eyes and indulge their spouses as though they were children.

'Waiting to be released from the confines of my room, your mother's words came back to me, "Family is the most important thing",' continued Larry, 'which is why I've decided that instead of buying a new home, I shall divide my time between you, my three wonderful daughters.'

'What?' snapped Rachel. 'Move in with us? What about the children? Emelia and Porcelain have a very strict regime, they'd become anxious if it was disrupted.'

'They'll be able to spend quality time with their grandfather,' Larry replied with a serene smile. 'You've often mentioned the importance of "quality family time".'

Caitlin glanced at Lee and swallowed her giggle. Rachel used the phrase often, usually as a reason to avoid doing things she did not like.

'But what about if my parents come to stay?' spluttered Pete.

'You have three spare bedrooms and a granny annexe,' said Alan. 'How many rooms do your parents require?'

Pete glared at him and Rachel folded her arms defensively.

'You're welcome at my cottage for as long as you need, Dad,' offered Caitlin. 'The bedroom downstairs has an en suite, which will probably be the most suitable.'

'Thank you, Moonbeam,' Larry said.

'And, of course, you'll be welcome at the vicarage when Caitlin finally packs up her cottage, rents it out and moves in with me,' added Stan with a touch of acerbity.

'I thought you said it didn't set a good impression having Caitlin move in before the wedding,' commented Alan mildly.

'Quite right,' Stan replied, 'but there isn't long to go and plans must be made.'

'You're very thoughtful, Stan,' said Larry, 'but it feels fair to do this in age order.'

Larry beamed at Gillian, who looked startled.

'You want to move in with me and Alan?' she said. 'When?'

'Not immediately but soon,' he replied.

'Larry, we'd be delighted,' exclaimed Alan. 'Depending on how long it takes to sell this place, we could convert the old stables into a self-contained apartment for you. It's a project we've been considering for a while—'

'Alan, stop,' interrupted Gillian. 'Dad, this is preposterous. These are big decisions, they're not things to decide in the aftermath of a frightening medical scare. What if you change your mind and regret selling the house?'

'No,' he said with a calm certainty, 'I won't. These are possibilities I've long been considering. My TIA brought things into bright clarity. *"As flies to wanton boys are we to th' gods, they kill us for their sport"*. It's time for change.'

Caitlin recognised the quotation and again glanced at Lee, who raised his eyebrows at her in bemusement.

'But what will you do?' asked Gillian. 'You love being busy.'

'Gillian has a point,' said George, who had remained silent, watching his old friend with a hint of concern. 'When your strength returns, you'll be bored. What will you do?'

'I shall write the play that has been forever waiting in my heart,' Larry declaimed.

'You're retiring to write a play?' asked Caitlin, but for some reason this comment caused her heart to flutter with anxiety.

'This isn't any play, Moonbeam, it's my masterpiece, and it'll be performed this Christmas by the Goldenwych Players.'

Caitlin glanced over at George who shook his head, indicating he had no idea either.

'The rest of the creative board will have to approve it, Larry,' he said and Caitlin could tell he was trying to inject sense and calm into the increasingly fraught atmosphere. 'You might be the founding member of the Players but we're a democracy.'

'The creative board will love it, George,' said Larry, waving off his friend's concern. 'This play will go down in the Players' history as our finest hour.'

Rachel stood up, her handbag looped over her shoulder. 'Enough of this, Dad,' she said. 'When you're ready to speak sense, I'll listen, but Bean's right, you shouldn't rush decisions like this, you need to calm down.'

'Sit down, Rachel,' ordered Larry in a voice of thunder. 'I have another announcement. It's why I summoned you all here today.'

'Dad, we're adults, you have no authority to dictate our behaviour,' she said, but her querulous tone faltered under his steely gaze.

'You claim to be an adult, yet you continue to accept your allowance every month, on top of the "wage" you earn for running the haulage department even though you visit the office just twice a month for a few hours,' said Larry, glaring at Rachel, who squirmed as though she were a teenager again. 'Sit down if you wish to continue to fund your lavish lifestyle from King's Factories.'

Rachel sank back into her seat, her cheeks flaming.

'In order to benefit from the changes I'm suggesting, with the increased salaries and bonuses on top of your allowances,' said Larry, 'there is a condition to which you must all agree and sign. If you do not, then your allowances will be stopped with immediate effect.'

'But, Dad—' interrupted Gillian.

'What condition?' Caitlin asked, unable to shake her growing feeling of unease.

'You will all star in my new play. All of you – Alan, Pete, Stan, you too,' Larry said. 'It'll give us time together to work out our differences, heal the rift—'

'The rift you created,' snapped Rachel in fury.

'And what if we refuse to take part in this ridiculous scheme?' Stan asked, placing his phone face down on the table again and finally giving his full attention to the discussion.

Larry's eyes narrowed. 'You will no longer be welcome as a member of this family and I shall refuse to allow my daughter to marry you.'

'Dad!' exclaimed Caitlin, her temper rising. 'You can't choose who I marry.'

'I can disinherit you,' he snarled.

'Keep your money,' Caitlin spat back. 'I can earn a living from the café.'

'I'm an optician, a respected member of the community,' interjected Pete. 'You can't order me to take over your haulage department and then make a fool of myself starring in your amateur dramatics group's Christmas panto.'

'But I can cut Rachel's wage as well as her allowance,' said Larry. 'Half of which is logged as your contribution to the family business.'

'You said that was a wedding present to welcome me to the family,' said Pete.

Larry shrugged dismissively and a long silence grew.

Lee shifted uncomfortably in his position beside Caitlin and his father, as though taking this as a cue, said in a voice of would-be calm, 'It's an interesting idea, Larry, but as the girls, Alan, Pete and Stan aren't members, they'd have to audition like everyone else. You know the rules; we wrote them together.'

'No, they won't, George,' said Larry, his voice cold, his eyes once again taking on the shadowed appearance. 'They have no choice, nor do the Players, because if you and the committee refuses, I'll withdraw the funding and the Players will have to close.'

George looked as though Larry had hit him.

Larry signalled to Heather, who wheeled the attaché case to his side.

'While I was in hospital, I rang Muldoon Solicitors and had them draw up these contracts,' he said as Heather distributed them, looking horrified.

Caitlin stared down at the sheaf of paper. Her name was written on top and she began flicking through the pages but she could not take it in.

'Dad,' she said, 'I can't do this. You know I can't—'

'There will be no exceptions,' Larry declared, cutting her off, and Caitlin recoiled at the coldness in his voice.

Gillian shook her head, her disbelief turning into anger as she too read the contract. Rachel left hers, unopened, on the table.

'What's the play, Larry?' said Alan. 'What kind of performance could you possibly write to give everyone a starring role and heal the damage you've caused to your daughters?'

Larry's eyes gleamed.

'My masterpiece: *King Lear – The Musical.*'

16

GOLDENWYCH, PRESENT DAY

The Hill Fort Café was positioned at one end of a small row of shops on the narrow road leading to the church. Its terrace overlooked the village green and to one side was a small car park. As Caitlin cleared one of the outdoor tables, she thought about Stan. When he had first moved to the village, his daily run had taken him past the café. He would flash by in a blur of black Lycra but would pause on his return, buying a coffee to take back to the vicarage that stood beside the church.

It was how we met, thought Caitlin, as she wiped away the final crumbs and threw them over the small wooden balcony for the birds. His gentle flirting, his nervous enquiry if she would like to have a drink one evening and her acceptance. When he had bought her a gin and tonic, she had never imagined it would lead to marriage.

Engagement, she corrected herself. *We aren't married yet.*

The rush of panic she always experienced at the thought of the following year's spring wedding overwhelmed her once again. She pushed the emotion aside, convincing herself it was because she was tired and stressed over the huge family row that had erupted at her father's house two weeks earlier.

No one can hold grudges with such determination as my family, she thought as she turned to go inside.

After her father's revelation, Gillian and Rachel had stormed out, followed by their spouses, Stan had vanished, claiming a problem with a nearby parishioner, leaving Caitlin, Lee, George and Heather to clear away the food and try to reason with Larry. Her father had been unrepentant.

'This show will be a triumph,' he had declared as Heather had packed away the unsigned documents and closed her attaché case. 'The girls will soon come around to the idea and they'll understand.'

'Dad, you have to stop this,' Caitlin had insisted, but Larry had shaken his head.

'It's time you girls realised I'm head of this family and my word is law,' he had responded.

'Larry, it isn't,' George had said. 'The girls are adults, you have no authority to force them to do anything.'

'Watch me,' he had snarled in response before asking Lee to help him up the stairs because he was tired.

Caitlin had cleared away the food, appalled by her father's behaviour, trying to make sense of his baffling demands that the family perform in his new play. She stacked the dishwasher, leaving the two Doctors Glossop to attend to Larry before loading her car and driving away. She had not spoken to or heard from her father since.

'Morning, love, your dad's looking better, isn't he?' said a woman's voice, interrupting her thoughts.

'Hello, Annie,' said Caitlin, leaning forward to accept the woman's kiss on her cheek. 'Yes, he's recovering well and very relieved to be home.'

'He was on top form last night, we couldn't stop laughing at his antics,' said Annie.

'Last night?' queried Caitlin.

'At his place, a top-secret meeting about the new show.' She made a locking motion over her mouth. 'Don't ask because my lips are sealed but it's going to be spectacular. Is this table free?'

She pointed to the place Caitlin had finished clearing.

'All ready for you,' Caitlin said, pulling out a chair. 'Would you like to order or wait for Barbara?'

'I'll wait,' Annie replied. 'We've a huge amount to finalise before the announcement tonight. We'll need another seat, Daphne will be with us today.'

Caitlin forced a smile and fitted a chair into the corner by the balcony before walking back inside, wondering what 'antics' her father had demonstrated to his cohorts. Annie Jefferson and Barbara Orchard were two of her parents' oldest friends. They had all grown up in Goldenwych and were founder members of the Goldenwych Players. Annie's husband, Paul, had died three years earlier from cancer. Barbara's husband, Linus, was foreman at King's Ball Bearings Factory and was also a member of the Players. Every Friday, Annie and Barbara met for breakfast at the Hill Fort Café.

On occasions, Daphne Hawthorne joined them. Caitlin had never warmed to Daphne, who had moved to the village ten years earlier when her husband had retired from his job in the City. His death shortly afterwards had been a surprise but her husband's will had left her a wealthy widow and Daphne had decided to remain in Goldenwych. She had joined the Players as soon as she had moved to the village and had thrown herself into every production, even if her skills were not quite as good as she believed. Her delivery of the line, 'What's that on the road? A head?' rather than 'What's that on the road ahead?' had gone down in King family folklore.

When the three women met, the conversations ranged from local gossip to family updates and, without fail, a discussion about the Players, whether it was the current rehearsals or more specific chat about particular members. On the days Daphne Hawthorne joined them, the comments were even more caustic. Caitlin and Sindy had long learned to turn a deaf ear as the women's whispered confidences to each other were not always kind.

* * *

Inside, the café was suffused with the usual heady aroma of coffee and chocolate cake, but the base note permeating all these was the deep scent of the herbs her mother had used to make the herbal teas. It was a scent that lifted Caitlin's spirits, no matter her mood.

Caitlin always found comfort and peace at the Hill Fort Café and today was no exception. As children, Caitlin and her sisters would hurry to the café's warm and inviting interior after school to join their mother. When the weather was cold, Caitlin had loved doing her homework on one of the tables near the fire, while in warmer months she had sat on the small terrace overlooking the village green. For her, the café was an extension of her mother and their home.

When she had inherited it, Caitlin had considered long and hard whether to make any changes. She did not want the café to become a shrine to her mother, so she decided to make enough alterations to show her own taste but to keep the pieces she knew her mother had always loved. This included an old oak sideboard that was used to display the home-made cakes baked to Miranda King's secret recipes and the counter: an expanse of wood that had once been a table.

On the walls, Caitlin had commissioned a local artist, Ella Kerr, to update the images of herbs and wildflowers and had written the explanations of their use beside the delicate pictures. She had also shown photographs of the carvings from the stone circle to Ella and she had included these in the images. The window seat was new, but the mismatched wooden tables and chairs which her mother had adored remained. Caitlin had repositioned the tables at careful angles in order to give distance from other diners and had decorated them with Celtic patterns, including the triskele.

In one corner, she had added a bookcase, where there was a regular exchange of second-hand books, while on top were daily and local newspapers alongside leaflets of what to do in the area. The fireplace was now flanked by two worn leather armchairs and a two-seater sofa, rather than the two small tables her mother had preferred. Caitlin felt the easy chairs gave a homely feel.

The café was quiet; the early-morning rush of people grabbing coffees on their way to the station for their commute to work and the parents on their way to and from the village school were a distant memory. The lull in customers was a chance for Caitlin and Sindy to restock, clear the tables and prepare for the mid-morning coffee and cake brigade, as well as the brunchers and early lunchers.

'Hello, lovely girl,' said Barbara Orchard as she bustled inside. 'I thought it would be easier for me to bring our order to you.'

'Thank you, that's kind. Your usual?' said Caitlin before reeling off, 'two egg sandwiches, one on white, one on brown, a pot of breakfast tea and two slices of lemon drizzle.'

'You know us too well,' said Barbara with a smile. 'Daphne's asked for smashed avocado on wholewheat toast and a slice of carrot cake. I also wanted to check everything was going smoothly for the food this evening; we're expecting a large turnout.'

'All sorted, Barbara,' called Sindy from behind the counter. 'I'm baking the last batches of brownies now. Everything will be ready for Caitlin to take to the theatre by 5 p.m.'

'You girls are wonderful,' Barbara said. 'Will you and Rosie be joining your mum there tonight, Sindy?'

'Yes, Rosie is determined to take part this year, but I'll either be backstage with Caitlin or in the audience,' she replied.

'It's a shame. You have a wonderful singing voice; we really miss you,' said Barbara.

Barbara smiled and returned to Annie, who had pulled a folder from her bag, and Daphne, who was settling into her seat. Annie opened the folder and the three women were immediately absorbed in conversation.

Sindy stood behind the counter, her blonde hair pulled into a messy bun, her dark roots showing several months of growth, already slicing the cake in preparation.

'Are they having their usual?' Sindy asked as Caitlin placed the dirty plates she was carrying in the dishwasher.

'Yes, egg sandwiches and smashed avo on wholewheat toast with carrot cake.'

'Daphne didn't ask for fresh blood then?' said Sindy with an exaggerated shudder.

Caitlin laughed. 'She's not that bad.'

'Caity, she's a self-satisfied nightmare,' retorted Sindy. 'Mum said that the word in the hairdresser's is that Daphne is having a clandestine fling with a younger man.'

'Poor bloke,' said Caitlin. 'Want me to cook their order?'

'No, I'll do it,' Sindy replied and disappeared into the kitchen at the rear of the café. 'It'll keep me out the back, away from Daphne.'

'She can be hard work,' Caitlin admitted as she took one of their locally made teapots from the shelf and spooned in the loose-leaf tea they always served. 'Barbara's right, though, you do have a fabulous singing voice. Do you remember when you and Gilly sang "Lady Marmalade" in Dad's adaptation of *Cinderella*? It was incredible, but it was the last show either of you were in.'

'It was fun, but we were both in our mid-teens and boys were more interesting than singing,' she said.

'You started going out with Ricky around then, didn't you?' mused Caitlin.

'Yes, and Gilly left the Players,' said Sindy as an alarm buzzed. 'The brownies are ready.'

Sindy disappeared into the kitchen and Caitlin glanced at the clock. She estimated there was perhaps half an hour before the café became busy. Once she had delivered Annie, Barbara and Daphne's brunch, she would have time to begin wrapping up and organising the food for the evening ahead. There was always a buffet at the end of rehearsals and everyone took it in turns to provide the refreshments, although the bulk of the catering usually fell to her and Sindy, helped by Suki Glossop.

Caitlin hummed 'Lady Marmalade' to herself as she headed towards the three women on the terrace who were deep in conversation.

'Thanks, love,' said Annie as Caitlin placed the tray on the table.

'You're looking lovely today, Caitlin,' said Daphne.

'Thanks,' Caitlin replied. Daphne was wearing skinny jeans and a sequinned top slipping artfully from one shoulder to reveal her intense fake tan.

'Not everyone can pull off that shade of— er— what would you call it? Greige?'

'Sindy will be out with the sandwiches in a minute,' Caitlin said, ignoring the jibe, but before she could retreat inside, she heard Rachel calling her name.

'Moon, we need to talk to you,' her sister snapped and Caitlin froze as first Rachel, then Gillian bounded up the shallow steps towards her.

'What's happened?' she asked. 'Is it Dad?'

'Yes, but not what you think,' said Gillian, taking her arm and steering her inside. 'Can we use the back room?'

'Of course,' Caitlin replied.

Sindy appeared in the doorway of the kitchen, Rachel ignored her as she marched behind the counter, while Gillian gave her a stiff smile before following Caitlin down the short flight of steps that led to a large room at the rear. This space had always been used as an office and a place to relax during quiet periods and Caitlin had updated it when she had inherited the café. She had discarded all the ancient office furniture, wobbly tables and sagging chairs, replacing them with a large desk, which looked out over the small yard and a series of custom-built bookshelves. On these were folders in a range of bright colours containing recipes, accounts and other miscellaneous paperwork. On the other side was a sofa and small armchair grouped around a low coffee table where there was a television set, CD player and radio.

'Tell me,' said Caitlin as her two sisters halted.

'Dad's cut off our allowances,' said Rachel. 'Have you checked to see if he's paid yours? Neither mine nor Gilly's have arrived in our bank accounts this morning and whenever we try to call Grace in finance we're diverted to her voicemail.'

Caitlin pulled her phone from her back pocket. Her allowance from her father, a monthly sum paid to all three women alongside their salaries, went directly into a savings account. She did not need it and regularly suggested to her father he keep it – her money from the café was enough to live on – but he insisted it was her due.

'No,' she said, checking the balance and the recent transactions. 'Nothing.'

'Damn him,' snarled Rachel. 'He really is serious about this stupid play, isn't he?'

'It appears so,' said Gillian.

'I need to speak to Pete,' said Rachel and hurried out, her phone clamped to her ear.

'Bye, Rache,' murmured Caitlin. 'Come again.'

Gillian laughed.

'Her manners are worse than ever,' said Gillian.

'Rachel first and always, remember,' stated Caitlin.

'Ever since we were teenagers,' agreed Gillian. She ran a hand through her hair and pulled her phone from her bag. 'There's something else too,' she continued and navigated to the webpage of the local estate agent. 'The house has been sold. I spoke to Lacey who was dealing with it and she said it had barely been put on their website when a cash buyer came forward and offered the asking price. They want a quick sale, so Dad's hoping to move in with Alan and me at the end of the month.'

'The house has been sold already? But what about our stuff? Mum's things?'

'No doubt we'll receive a summons to collect anything we want before Dad disposes of the rest,' said Gillian. 'He's awful when he's in one of these moods. Do you remember when he redecorated the dining room one weekend when we'd gone away with Mum and Grandma to visit Auntie Bea?'

'He threw out all Mum's china and carved up the dining table and chairs for firewood,' said Caitlin. 'Mum was furious.'

'He replaced that beautiful oak table with the awful round glass one and those uncomfortable stools,' added Gillian.

'Mum salvaged a chunk of the table to use as the counter in here.'

'True, it was a relief when the leg fell off the new table and Mum replaced them all again.'

They shared a smile of remembrance and Caitlin felt a glimmer of hope, but almost as soon as the thought had entered her mind, Gillian's friendly smile vanished.

'If I'm not able to reach Dad on the phone, I'll probably go to the Players meeting tonight. Will you be there?'

'Yes,' she replied. 'I'm doing the food.'

'See you later then,' she said and marched away.

* * *

Caitlin opened the boot of her SUV and reached inside to pick up two of the large containers.

'Moon, let me help you.'

'Hey, Woody,' she said as Lee appeared at her side and reached in to take the remaining two cool boxes.

'I'll come back for the crate of drinks,' he said.

Caitlin opened her mouth to protest.

'Doctor's orders,' he finished and gave her a cheeky grin.

'Fine,' she retorted in a mock huff and turned to walk towards the theatre, but as she did, a window was flung open on the side closest to where she was standing and she heard music. 'What the...?' she asked, panic rising like bile as a song from her childhood flashed across the summer evening.

It was a tune she had not heard for years: a mouse wearing clogs. As quickly as the tune interrupted the balmy evening, it stopped.

'What's the matter?' asked Lee.

'Nothing,' murmured Caitlin but she was unnerved. 'Let's get these inside before everyone arrives.'

'How are things?' Lee asked as they made their way inside.

'Weird,' said Caitlin as the familiar scent of beeswax polish mingled with an underlying hint of mustiness enveloped her. 'Dad won't take any of our calls and Stan's dropping deep dark hints that he has a surprise for me.'

'Your dad sulking isn't great,' said Lee, 'but Stan's news is exciting.'

'Is it?' she said. 'I don't like surprises, they're rarely good even when that's the intention. Anyway, he won't be able to tell me for a while, he's away.'

'Where?'

'London, interviewing potential new curates,' she replied.

'He's away a lot,' said Lee.

'Yes, he said it's because he's being noticed by important people within the Church hierarchy. It's the reason he's requested a curate, to ensure there's constant cover to maintain the wellbeing of his flock when he's called to other duties.'

'Did he say "wellbeing of his flock"?' asked Lee.

'I might have embellished,' said Caitlin and they grinned.

'It makes sense, though,' continued Lee and Caitlin could tell he was attempting to minimise the sarcasm, 'Stan being given help. After all, one day a week is a tough gig. You hardly see each other at the moment.'

'I know you and Stan have never really clicked, but he means well.'

Lee shrugged and Caitlin laughed.

'Woody, you're so stubborn,' she said.

'I like your new ink by the way,' Lee said and she knew he had deliberately changed the subject. 'I noticed it when we were at your dad's.'

'My what?'

'The silver lines around the triskele.'

'They're not a tattoo,' she admitted. 'In fact, I've been meaning to make an appointment to see you in your professional capacity. The lines appeared overnight and, well, look...'

She put down the containers she was carrying and rolled up the loose cotton sleeves of her dress; Lee's eyes widened in surprise. The lines which had begun around the triskele had spread, winding silver trails along the inside of Caitlin's arms.

'Do they hurt?' asked Lee, following suit and putting his own boxes on the floor.

'No,' she replied.

He hovered his hand above her arm as though asking permission to touch her. She gave a quick nod and he ran a gentle finger along the scar. She shivered as he turned her arm over to inspect the skin on the other side.

'This one's the same,' she said, rolling up her other sleeve.

'I've never seen anything like this,' he said. 'Do you mind if I take some pictures and send them to Poppy? We might have split up, but she's still the best dermatological specialist I know.'

'Of course,' said Caitlin but she felt a stab of irritation.

Lee pulled his phone from his pocket and took a series of images, asking questions as he clicked away.

'Thanks,' he said, when he had finished. 'I'm sure there's a simple explanation, maybe an allergy.'

'Probably,' said Caitlin, but she doubted it. The lines were strange and yet they held a sinuous beauty, tracing curves and whorls across her skin in a mysterious and deliberate pattern.

'Actually,' said Lee, bending down to pick up the cool boxes before changing his mind and straightening up again. 'I arrived early because I wanted to talk to you. I didn't want you to hear it from another source and misunderstand.'

'What's happened?' Caitlin asked, staring up into Lee's uncharacteristically serious expression.

'Please don't be upset or think I'm being a crazy stalker but there's no easy way to break this to you...'

'Just tell me,' she said as a sharp stab of panic ran through her.

'I've bought your mum and dad's house.'

'What?' she exclaimed, wondering if she had heard correctly.

'You know how long I've been looking for a property and, being at the surgery, I hear a lot of rumours. One of the guys from the new estate is a property developer and I overheard his wife saying the plot he's always wanted is your dad's house because he thinks he could build at least five houses or a block of flats on the land. I was determined to stop him, so I asked Lacey at the estate agent to let me know when your dad put it on the market. She called to say they were listing it this week, I offered the asking price and your dad accepted.'

'But, Lee, it's a five-bedroomed house, why do you need so much space?'

'I don't at the moment,' he agreed, 'but Poppy and I made a lot of money from the house we sold in Fulham and I've made some good investments over the years, thanks to Slick's advice. Nothing else has come up for sale in the old part of the village, which was why I decided to go for it.'

Caitlin was unsure how she felt about Lee's announcement. It was strange to think of him living in their home, changing the décor to suit his taste, perhaps altering the garden.

Another, darker thought filled her mind, was he planning a family? Had he met someone else since his relationship with Poppy had ended? The idea of an unknown woman, Lee's future wife, cooking in their kitchen was horrifying.

For some reason, she also did not feel he was being entirely truthful, the only good thing he had said was that he had thwarted a property developer from demolishing their beautiful home.

'Thank you for saving it from being flattened,' she said. 'It's going to take time to adjust to the idea of it being your house and not ours, though.'

'For me, too,' he admitted. 'You're welcome any time. I can leave your teenage bedroom as it is if you like, with the My Little Ponies and crystal mobiles.'

'I never had My Little Ponies,' she said, bending down to pick up the cool boxes, 'but I will concede to the crystal mobiles.'

17

GOLDENWYCH, PRESENT DAY

The theatre doubled as a church hall and community centre, but the presence of the Goldenwych Players was dominant. The name hung over the door leading into the main auditorium in large red and gold letters, while the walls of the square entrance lobby were covered with photographs from former shows. A few images were dedicated to the dance school, one to the flower arranging club and another to the judo team. A noticeboard took up one wall, advertising upcoming events for the multitude of other clubs who used the space.

Caitlin led the way along the corridor to the kitchen area, which was made of several rooms at the back of the hall. At the front was a large space with sinks, worktops and a vast hob with a serving hatch opening into the auditorium. Two smaller rectangular rooms led off this; one acted as a food storage and preparation area, while in the other were several cookers, adjustable worktops and a demonstration area for the cookery classes. Tonight it would be used for the refreshments.

'Hi, Aunt Suki,' said Caitlin as a short woman with dark hair shot through with moon-bright silver strands entered from the warren of small interlinking rooms that made up the remainder of the kitchen.

'Caitlin, Lee, you're here.' She hugged one, then the other.

'Hi, Mum,' said Lee. 'Where's Dad?'

'He's backstage with Larry and Judy,' she replied. 'I think Annie, Barbara and Linus are with them, too.'

'I smell a dance routine,' groaned Lee.

'Probably, but I have no idea what's been planned. You know what your dads are like,' said Suki, including Caitlin in the comment, 'they behave as though the details of each new production are a state secret.'

'Unless you're a member of the inner circle,' said Caitlin.

'Exactly,' replied Lee, 'and we are but lowly underlings on the outside.'

The two women laughed but Caitlin felt awkward. Not only did she and Lee know exactly what Larry would propose tonight – which she sensed would cause a huge amount of upset – she was still reeling from the news that Lee had bought their family home. She wondered how Gillian and Rachel would react when they heard.

Caitlin took a deep breath and decided to push this information aside for the present, there was nothing she could do about it and worrying was a waste of energy. The most important thing this evening was limiting the damage her father might unleash on the local community. All she could hope was that George and the committee had persuaded her father away from his crazy idea.

She checked her banking app again, but there was still no deposit. Whatever her father was doing, he was determined to try to control them through money.

How dare he? she thought. *He's behaving as though we're children who need to be taught a lesson, rather than adults.*

'Will you two be doing your usual double act of stage manager and assistant stage manager?' asked Suki, interrupting her angry thoughts.

'Unless Dad wants to try someone new,' replied Caitlin, attempting to keep her voice level.

'Why would he?' said Suki. 'He always says you two are the dream team. It's been your job since Junior Players.'

Lee placed the cool boxes on the table before heading back towards the door to fetch the drinks.

'Sindy and Vicki are bringing Rosie,' said Caitlin. 'Rosie is hoping to be involved in the play, which means Sindy might like to be stage manager to be here too.'

'Are you bored with it?' Suki asked as they began unloading the food.

Caitlin was about to reply when, to her relief, a woman's voice interrupted their conversation.

'Hello, ladies.'

'Hi, Judy,' called Caitlin as a petite, blonde woman in flowing pink dance dress appeared in the open serving hatch.

Judy Pelham ran the local dance school and choreographed the shows performed by the Goldenwych Players.

'How were the Junior Tappers?' asked Suki.

'Not bad,' Judy replied. 'Do you think you should put the chairs out? People will be arriving soon.'

Caitlin bristled at Judy's authoritative tone but Suki put her hand on her arm to stop her retorting.

'Lee's bringing a few more things in from the car for us, then he'll start on the chairs,' said Suki. 'You're very welcome to help, Judy.'

'I would but I'm far too busy backstage,' said Judy with a dismissive wave. 'This evening is going to be more spectacular than ever. It's important everyone is in their seats on time.' She gave them a knowing wink, then bustled away.

Caitlin's unease notched up another level. What exactly was her father planning? She found it hard to believe he truly intended to force her, Rachel, Gillian, Alan, Pete and Stan to participate against their wills. It was preposterous, and yet, there was no denying he had been true to his word about the money. For the first time, Caitlin wondered whether the TIA had affected her father more than they had realised. He had always been impulsive but his behaviour at present was alarming.

'Do you have any idea what they're planning?' asked Suki.

'None,' Caitlin lied, crossing her fingers under the table to absolve herself.

Lee returned with the crate of drinks. He placed it on one of the tables and handed Caitlin back her car keys.

'Let's do what we usually do,' he said in a low voice, 'keep our heads down, dole out sandwiches and cakes, pour drinks and then run away to the pub.'

A shiver ran down Caitlin's spine and a strange image of a man who bore a resemblance to her father but older, brandishing a sword, flashed across her mind like a dragonfly across water. As it did, a thought occurred to her. Lee was medically trained, he might know.

'Can I ask you something? It's a bit odd,' she said.

'Anything,' he replied.

'Could someone survive if a stake pierced their skull?'

Lee stared at her in astonishment. 'What's prompted this?'

'Something I heard on a podcast,' Caitlin improvised, not wishing to explain she had seen it in a vivid and terrifying dream or why this snapshot of an image in her mind had triggered the memory.

'It sounds like Phineas Gage,' said Lee.

'Who?' asked Caitlin.

'It's known as the "American Crowbar Case",' Lee explained. 'Phineas Gage was a railway engineer who was involved in an accident on site in the nineteenth century. During a controlled explosion, an iron tamping bar went through Gage's cheek and out of his head.'

Caitlin shuddered, the description was identical to what she had seen in her dream.

'Did it kill him?' she asked.

'No, Gage recovered, but it affected his personality,' said Lee. 'He changed from being a responsible, hard-working, sensible man to one who was irrational, irascible and prone to violent rages.'

'Violence,' murmured Caitlin and she heard the slicing sound of metal through the air.

'Are you all right?'

'Yes, fine,' she said, forcing a smile onto her face. 'How do you know about Gage? Was it part of your neurology training?'

'Partly, but, if you remember, my original plan was to be a psychiatrist,' Lee said. 'It was while I was studying the mind I first came across the Phineas Gage case.'

'Minds,' said Caitlin and her usual sense of humour reasserted itself. 'You should have stuck with it, you'd have made a fortune in this village, unscrambling everyone's minds.'

Before Lee could reply, Suki called from the kitchen requesting their help. Caitlin followed Lee into the kitchen, yet despite his calm and measured answers to her questions, she could not shift her concerns about the strange images she had dreamt about.

* * *

An hour later, the hall had been transformed. The burgundy and gold velvet curtains were drawn across the stage and the rows of chairs were filling up with eager members of the Players and those hoping to join or offer other services like costume making or scenery painting. The blackout blinds had been dropped over alternate windows to block out the majority of the bright summer evening, giving an other-worldly feel to the otherwise mundane space. There was a buzz of anticipation as Caitlin and Lee took their favourite seats in the back row. Suki made her way a few rows further forward to sit with her friends.

Lee's phone pinged and, with an apologetic grimace, he flicked open the message.

'Are you on call?' asked Caitlin.

'No, but I thought I should check in case there was an emergency.'

'Is there?'

'No, it's the rotas for next week,' he said, then, with an exaggerated sigh, finished, 'I'll have to stay.'

'Never mind,' she said, patting his arm patronisingly as Lee became engrossed in the information on his phone.

Caitlin waved to Sindy, who had arrived with her mother and daughter, then leaned forward to chat to her cousin, Kayleigh, who was in the row in front. Kayleigh was the daughter of Larry's older sister Primrose. Kayleigh's wife, Gail, was beside her with their ten-year-old daughter, Honey.

'What do you think it's going to be this year?' asked Kayleigh.

'It was *Sleeping Beauty* last year,' said Gail, 'so we think it'll be a Shakespeare this time. You know how rigidly they stick to their schedule. Panto, Shakespeare, Wilde, West End musical, panto, Shakespeare, Wilde, West End musical...'

The two women laughed, then Kayleigh murmured, 'Hey, look, since when have the Glamorous Olds attended Players meetings in recent years?'

Caitlin, Lee and Gail glanced towards the doors. This was the nickname Kayleigh had bestowed upon Caitlin's and Lee's elder siblings when they were teenagers.

'Astonishing,' whispered Gail. 'I don't remember the last time Gillian graced us with her presence. Perhaps Alan's persuaded her; you know he's always been desperate to join.'

'He does have, *"a most pleasing baritone",*' said Caitlin, trying to behave as she usually would, and did an uncanny impression of her brother-in-law.

'As he tells your dad regularly,' said Lee.

'Do you think Brandon and Candy will come?' said Gail, referring to Kayleigh's elder brother and his wife.

'No, they're out tonight, Mum and Dad are babysitting Jayden and India, it's why they're not here. Uncle Larry was furious when Mum told him.'

Caitlin watched Gillian, wondering how she would react to the meeting. Her sister had left the Junior Players when she was fifteen years old and had refused to take part in any form of performance ever since. The one exception was when she sang at their mother's funeral.

It's a shame, thought Caitlin, *because Gillian is the most talented of us all and could have made acting her career.* It had been her ambition when she was younger, but when she stormed out of rehearsal one night, she dropped all her interest in anything to do with theatre and threw herself into her studies, determined instead to follow her father into the world of business.

As though sensing Caitlin's eyes upon her, Gillian turned and acknowledged Caitlin with a nod. In her tailored, dark-rose-coloured dress with matching jacket, which was thrown over her arm, and her stiletto heels, she looked out of place among the casual summer clothes of the other villagers. Alan's lightweight blue suit and white shirt were more informal and he smiled and waved at a few people as he ushered Gillian towards two vacant seats in the front row. Gillian's lips were pressed into a thin line as she allowed herself to be swept along by her husband. It was not until he turned to hang his jacket on the back of the chair that he saw Caitlin and Lee. He blew a kiss to Caitlin and saluted Lee, then waved to Kayleigh and Gail, but there was strain around his eyes. Gillian sat rigid in her seat, facing the stage.

'What's going on?' whispered Kayleigh. 'Rachel and Pete are here too.'

Rachel looked neither left nor right as she walked down the centre aisle, dropping into a seat several rows behind Gillian, glaring at the back of her sister's head. Pete said hello to a few people and sat beside Rachel, both looked unnerved.

On the other side of the auditorium, Kayleigh and Gail looked at Caitlin and Lee, bemused.

'Did you know they were coming?' asked Kayleigh.

'Yes,' Caitlin admitted, then, trying to lighten her tone, added, 'although if Edward arrives, we'll know there's dark magic in the air.'

'Surprise,' murmured Lee as a tall, good-looking man wearing sunglasses, dark jeans and a blue shirt entered.

'You are kidding me,' giggled Gail.

'What's going on?' whispered Caitlin to Lee.

'Dad insisted he come for moral support,' said Lee.

'For whom?'

'Not sure,' Lee admitted. 'Slick's not known for his reassuring manner.'

Edward removed his Ray-Bans and stared around the hall. Caitlin noticed a number of the women giving him an appraising glance. She had always been immune to his charms, preferring Lee's gentler, less flashy good looks to those of his older brother, but she could understand why women were drawn to Edward's charisma. He saw them in the back row, raised a hand in greeting and began shuffling along to take the empty seat beside Lee. Kayleigh winked before she and Gail turned to face the front again, their shoulders shaking with suppressed giggles.

'Hey,' Edward said to Lee as acknowledgement. 'Caitlin, you're looking as gorgeous as ever. Why are the dynamic businesswoman Gillian and the beauteous Rachel lowering themselves to attend a meeting of the Golden-wych Players? Neither of them has been anywhere near this place for years.'

'Dad's orders,' said Caitlin. 'You're not exactly a regular yourself.'

Edward put his hand on his heart as though her comment had wounded him. 'Harsh,' he said. 'Dad asked me to pop in. Where's the vicar?'

'He's away, interviewing potential curates,' she replied.

'It must be a tough life working one day a week,' said Edward, echoing Lee's snide comment from earlier.

When Lee had said it, Caitlin had found it faintly amusing, but Edward's delivery was offensive. However, before Caitlin could verbally swipe back, the lights dimmed and the low hum of chatter faded away. She shot Edward a filthy look as the room fell silent. Aware of her irritation, Lee nudged her with his shoulder and offered her a Fruit Pastille from the packet he had pulled out of his pocket. It was what they had done since childhood and she allowed her annoyance with Edward to float away as Lee unwrapped the tube until he found her an orange sweet, which was her favourite. She whispered her thanks as she popped it in her mouth.

There was a swishing sound and the curtains opened. A spotlight picked out a man, centre stage, with his back to the audience. He was dressed in the full motley of a playing-card Joker, complete with Elizabethan ruff and belled stick. He hummed 'Greensleeves' before, with great theatricality, turning to face the audience. His exaggerated double-take at finding people there elicited a ripple of laughter.

'Dad,' groaned Edward as he and Lee exchanged a pained look.

Dr George Glossop, the Jester, capered around, accompanying himself in a dance to his continued la-ing of 'Greensleeves' and the tinkle of bells. He finished to the right of the stage and bowed, waiting for the last ripples of laughter to die away.

'My lords, ladies, and gentlemen,' he said, shaking the belled stick as though it was a drum roll and bowing from the waist. 'I give you: The King.'

There was a crackle of static, then music began to play.

'Elvis Presley?' whispered Lee.

'This is one of Dad's favourites – "It's Now or Never",' said Caitlin. 'Oh no...'

Larry was rising through a trapdoor in the centre of the stage wearing a white spangled Elizabethan doublet and hose with a gold crown perched at a jaunty angle on his head. Caitlin thought he looked thin but his usual excitement at being on stage radiated from him.

The audience erupted into laughter as, from the wings, Larry and George were joined by Annie, Barbara and Linus. They were also dressed in the sparkling, Elvis-inspired, faux-Mediaeval attire, and as Larry sang, the others shimmied their way around the stage in a low-key rumba.

Despite themselves, Caitlin and Lee looked at each other and began to laugh; Edward had his head in his hands, his shoulders shaking. When she glanced at her sisters, Caitlin saw they both remained rigid in their seats: Gillian had her eyes tight shut, while Rachel and Pete looked appalled. In contrast, Alan was entering into the spirit of the performance and was cheering along with the rest of the audience.

As the number ended to tumultuous applause, Larry stepped down from his podium.

'Thank you very much,' he said, curling his lip and wriggling his hips, then his eyes swept the audience, pausing on each of his daughters. Caitlin was about to wave at him, but there was a strange expression on her father's face which she could not read. He held her gaze a few seconds more, then turned away and with great deliberation said, '"*Meantime we shall express our darker purpose...*"'

A gasp fluttered through the auditorium and those who recognised the line, whispered, '*King Lear,*' to each other until the words hummed around the audience like bees.

On stage, Larry waited for the muttering to desist. He was flanked by George and Linus, with Barbara and Annie on the outside. The five friends gazed out and Caitlin had a flash of an image as they had been when they were teenagers with a shared love of performing, the five who had created the Goldenwych Players.

'*King Lear!*' boomed Larry from the stage. 'Yes, my friends, this year, we are returning to the Bard. The man himself, the great writer from Stratford-upon-Avon, Mr William Shakespeare and one of his finest works.'

A few people clapped but Larry held up his hand for silence.

'The time has come for the Goldenwych Players to finally be acknowledged for the brilliance of its extraordinary performers and this is the production I believe will put us on the map. The combining of a classic work of literature with a classic stage genre. Using music selected from across the years, bringing to life the *Tragedy of King Lear* in a unique way. A magnificent production of beautiful words, superb music, song and dance – my masterpiece: *King Lear – The Musical.*'

There was a stunned silence.

'But first,' said Barbara, stepping forward with a radiant smile, 'we have a performance from the Junior Players and Judy's Signet Tappers.'

She ushered the others off stage and as the clapping faded, to Caitlin's surprise, Annie Jefferson appeared at her elbow.

'Caitlin, love, could you come with me a moment, please?' she whispered.

'Of course,' Caitlin replied.

'Leave your stuff,' said Lee. 'I'll look after it.'

Caitlin followed Annie around the edge of the auditorium and through the side door that led backstage.

'Is there something wrong?' she asked.

'No, your dad asked me to fetch you. Barbara and George are collecting Gillian and Rachel...'

And then, Caitlin heard it. The music from earlier, the song.

'No,' she said.

Three little girls ran onto the stage in pink dresses with large white Peter Pan collars, mouse ears on their heads and whiskers painted on their cheeks. The room rang with applause from the audience as Caitlin stared across the stage to where Gillian and Rachel stood in the wings opposite her. Horror filled all their faces as a very old song began: 'A Windmill in Old Amsterdam' by Ronnie Hilton. It had been their grandfather Reggie King's favourite and he had played it whenever they visited.

One year, the three girls, who had all been in the Junior Players, as well as learning tap, ballet and modern, had asked if, as a birthday surprise, they could work out a routine for the song to perform for him. As the eldest and possessing the best voice, it was Gillian who had taken the lead vocal, singing about the mouse and his growing family in the windmill in old Amsterdam, while Rachel and Caitlin, both enthusiastic and talented dancers, had worked on a complicated tap routine.

'*A little mouse with clogs on...*' Gillian had sung in her clear, powerful voice while Rachel and Caitlin danced.

A musical break was introduced for Caitlin to perform her show-stopping turning triple-time step, but on the day of the performance, tragedy had struck and, afterwards, Caitlin had never danced or performed again. Even hearing the music was causing her to panic.

'No,' she said to Annie, struggling to push past the older woman, to escape. 'Why is he doing this?'

'Please, Caitlin,' said Annie, her eyes wide with surprise at Caitlin's reaction, 'stay with me, your dad wants to make an announcement.'

'No, you don't understand, I know what this is about, I have to leave.'

Caitlin reached into her pocket and withdrew her asthma inhaler. She turned away, the blue plastic to her lips as she puffed it, her breathlessness retreating, even as her panic remained.

To her surprise, Gillian appeared at her side, having made her way around the back of the stage. 'Moon, are you OK?' she asked and Caitlin shook her head, surprised at the concern on Gillian's face. Despite their rift, the horror of hearing this song seemed to have bridged the gap between them.

'Why's he doing this to us?' she said.

'What the actual...?' said Rachel, appearing beside them, her face ashen. 'Has Dad finally lost it? Why are those kids singing our song and doing our dance?'

'Surely they won't do the turning triple?' said Gillian, but as she spoke, the music changed and the three sisters stared at each other in disbelief.

The youngest girl stepped forward and began to dance, her feet flying as she re-enacted Caitlin's former routine.

'I'm leaving,' whispered Caitlin.

'No, you're not,' said a deep voice and the three women turned to see their father standing in the shadows. 'You're all staying and you will all do as I command.'

His voice sounded different, thought Caitlin, sadder, rougher, and there was an edge of harshness.

Before any of them could reply, the music stopped to excitable applause and several minutes of clapping for the dancers.

Larry strode on stage, leaving the three women silent and shocked.

'My daughters. My three beautiful daughters,' he said and there was an awkward silence from the audience. 'They're here,' said Larry, beckoning them forward. 'Gillian, my eldest, my brilliant businesswoman; Rachel, my middle daughter who has given me two beautiful granddaughters; and Caitlin, my baby, my special child. Please, my darlings, join me...'

The atmosphere shifted as the audience looked around for the three sisters. Many faces registered amusement, others annoyance and yet more – confusion. The announcement of the new play was usually followed by a short performance, as they had seen, then people were invited to give their views, suggest ideas and discuss its suitability. There had never before been an invitation on stage for women who no longer acted in the Goldenwych Players productions.

'Come on, girls,' Larry demanded, beckoning to them. 'Gilly-Bean, Snow-Rabbit, Moonbeam, on stage, now.' His tone was abrupt, as though he were addressing recalcitrant children.

Caitlin looked at her sisters and, to her surprise, Gillian stepped forward, followed by Rachel, anger evident in every movement. Annie took

Caitlin's arm and gave a gentle tug as they both stepped onto the stage. Caitlin stumbled, causing a titter of laugher from the crowd. Scarlet in the face, she stood as far apart from her sisters as possible. On the opposite side, Barbara and Linus had also returned to the limelight, with George beside Larry.

'Are you sure this is a good idea, Larry?' Caitlin heard George whisper.

'Yes,' her father replied before lapsing into silence and staring at the back wall of the theatre.

'It's ludicrous,' hissed Linus and Barbara scowled at him. 'He can't do this—'

'We have another announcement,' said George, stepping forward and speaking over Linus's protests.

Barbara's eyes were fixed on Larry. Her husband, Linus, looked upset and Annie stepped back, remaining on stage but no longer in the spotlight, her expression one of confusion. Caitlin stared around in panic.

'The reason Larry has requested his daughters join him on stage,' continued George, 'is because this will be his last show.'

Larry stepped forward, present again, his vagueness gone.

'Today,' declared Larry, 'I'm doing more than telling you all the name of the Christmas spectacular, I'm also announcing my retirement from King's Ball Bearings.'

The audience gasped.

'And as this will be my grand finale, I am inviting my daughters and their spouses to star in this adaptation.'

'But they're not members,' said Linus. 'They'd have to audition like everyone else.'

Larry's face hardened. 'No, they won't. They'll be in it. They have no choice, and neither do the Players, because if you and George refuse, I'll withdraw the funding, and the Players will have to close.'

The auditorium erupted in fury. As people shouted and George, Barbara and Linus fielded questions, Larry stood silently in the centre of the stage, once again staring at the back wall, oblivious to the chaos around him.

Caitlin turned to flee the stage, her heart pounding, when Gillian grabbed her arm.

'Stay with us, we need to sort this out,' she said.

Gillian beckoned to Annie, whispered in her ear and, a few moments later, the older woman had produced three radio mics before she hurried to the piano at the back of the stage.

'Join in where you can, Moon,' whispered Gillian. 'Rabbit, are you ready?'

'What are we doing?' Rachel asked.

'Hold Caitlin's hand, we're singing Mum's song. It's the only thing that might make Dad see sense.'

Tears welled up in Caitlin's eyes, but it felt good for the three of them to be united again, even it was against their father.

A movement in the wings caught her eye and she saw Lee, ashen-faced, his doctor's bag in his hand, and a wave of relief washed over her. He gave her a thumbs-up and she smiled gratefully.

'Ready?' Annie called and Rachel raised her hand in response.

The trembling opening chord cut across the increasing chaos in the hall but, as the people both on stage and in the auditorium acknowledged what was happening, silence fell and all eyes turned to the three sisters. Annie was playing the lilting tune of 'Moon River', from the film *Breakfast at Tiffany's*. She went through the introduction twice, ensuring the auditorium was quiet, then she cued Gillian and, into the muttering and dissent, Gillian began to sing.

Caitlin felt goosebumps rise on her arms as her sister's voice rose pure and clear, filling the small theatre. Rachel took a deep breath and added her own, deeper alto voice to Gillian's soprano as they sang the piece they had performed at their mother's funeral. Then, as they reached the middle of the song, both turned to Caitlin, who swallowed hard and, even as terrified as she felt, added her own soprano voice, harmonising above Gillian and Rachel's ranges.

As the three sisters sang, there was silence. Caitlin stopped first, allowing her voice to fade, Rachel followed a few bars later, leaving Gillian to finish in her astonishing voice. The final chord died away with the audience held spellbound before thunderous applause wrapped itself around them and rose into the ancient rafters.

The three women turned to their father and Caitlin knew they were all hoping he would smile, laugh and open his arms to them, but instead he gave a curt nod and stalked off the stage.

18

THE TALE OF THE THREE SISTERS

The Princess gazed around the octagonal room. It rose twenty storeys high and each level was lined from floor to ceiling with books. Never had there been such a monument to the written word. Volumes as big as gravestones stood sentinel beside folios smaller than a thumbnail; there were thick books, slim books, some bound in the softest, supplest leather, others in ancient carved wood stained black with age and wisdom. Books in languages she did not recognise; there were funny stories, sad stories, stories about love, adventure and life. Factual books bulging with knowledge, rustling their pages as they craned forward, desperate to impart their information about the world.

The Princess was humbled by the towers of learning, but she feared, if she let them, they would overwhelm her mind. The desire to read each book crept through her like a spell, but if she tried to absorb each of their tales, teachings and ideas into her fragile mortal mind, madness would ensue. Tears flowed from her eyes as she contemplated the treasure trove of literature. She loved to read, to tell tales, but she had been taunted, told this would drive her to insanity by the prince who was her husband. In her heart, she knew this was untrue, but his words haunted her because this was her most desperate fear: to lose her mind, her sense of self, her soul.

'You are moved?' said a male voice from the shadows with a hint of a sneer.

The Princess started; she had thought herself alone but he stood before her, his face the man of one she knew to be dead.

'I am humbled,' she replied, moving her leg, feeling the knife wedged in her boot, assuring herself she was armed and prepared.

The man stepped into the jewel-bright light cast by the eight stained-glass oriel windows. Each was positioned to mark the very centre of the library and the colours they cast were like nothing she had ever seen before. The man's russet hair glowed with a million dancing lights as he bowed.

'Are you afraid?' he asked, the coldness of his tone making her skin prickle with unease.

'No,' she replied, but her voice was small, like the child she had once been when this man was her friend. 'I must leave.'

'No, you shall stay,' said the man and pulled a book from a shelf, flicking casually through the pages.

The Princess tried to move, to turn away from the man, but she was rooted to the spot.

'Are there tales of this kingdom within these books?' asked The Princess.

'There are many,' replied the man. 'They tell of the peace that has reigned here for many generations, handed down from father to son, father to son.'

'Father to son,' she echoed.

'Father to son, for generations, until the line was polluted by endless daughters.'

'I am the third daughter of a third daughter,' she replied. 'My betrothal to the prince was arranged when I was a child. I was sent away from all I knew and from my best friend who loved me, whom I loved.'

'From me?' he said with a sneer. 'You were a snivelling child, it wasn't love, I forgot you as soon as you were gone.'

'No,' she whispered to herself.

'Yet now you travel with your sisters,' he said. 'Three women together, each bearing a title, you seek adventure and accolades, but you never settle.'

'My eldest sister, The Queen, is a widow; when her reign ended, she was sent to her dower palace. My next sister, The Baroness, was married to a cruel man and she sought refuge with The Queen.'

'And you?'

'My husband has many lovers,' she said. 'I left one dark, rain-tossed night and went to my sisters. We have been travelling ever since.'

'He is dead,' said the man with a cold smile.

'Dead? Are you sure?'

'Perhaps you no longer need to flee, Princess,' he said. 'What about your parents?'

'We don't remember them,' she replied.

The man smiled and The Princess stared at him in confusion. These truths she had told were the secrets she and her sisters guarded most fiercely. Even between themselves, they were discussed in hushed tones, at the midnight hour when the candle guttered and there were no other ears to listen.

'Who are you?' asked The Princess.

'I am the question and the answer,' he replied.

'To what?'

'To everything you've ever wondered and all you dare to seek,' he said, and with a shimmer of eerie blue light, he vanished.

19

GOLDEN VALLEY, DOBVNNI, 862 BCE

Cordelia sat astride the chestnut mare her husband had assured her was worthy of the new queen of Gallia. She wore robes he had presented and, while they were beautiful, she was no longer her own woman; these lavish gifts marked her as belonging to Aganippus. The fabric of her gown fell in soft folds either side of her saddle. Her dress was a cool, finely woven cream linen with a blue flower printed on the hem, over this was a long sleeveless tunic in the unusual silk which had made up her wedding gown but in a colour she had never before seen in clothing. Cordelia had been dazzled by the shimmering green-blue fabric.

'The colour is called blæhæwen-wæter,' Aganippus had explained. 'It's named after a stone found in many places to the east.'

He had then placed a golden ring set with a glinting green-blue blæhæwen-wæter stone onto the third finger of her left hand. It caught the light and made her think of water made solid but without the freezing pain of ice; this stone was summer captured by nature.

'Why do you ask me to wear it here?' she had said.

'A line runs from this finger, under your skin, to your heart,' he had replied. 'In Egypt, it's a custom for spouses to each wear one to indicate their devotion.'

'I have nothing to give you in return,' she had said.

'When you're ready, you'll find the correct present,' he had replied enigmatically and once again she had wondered about this man, her husband.

My husband, she thought as the mare clopped forward, jolting her back to the present. The words felt unfamiliar in both her mouth and her mind.

Becuma rode beside her on a smaller pony, several of the bags holding the treasures they had rescued from the temple were tied to her saddle. Cordelia glanced at her friend, it was strange to see her dressed in the clothes of their tribe rather than the white robes of a priestess. Becuma's long, light brown hair was captured in a plait that snaked down her back, her face was relaxed but determined as she concentrated on guiding her pony. This was the first time Becuma had ridden any distance and Cordelia knew she was nervous. When she had mentioned this to Aganippus, he had enlisted his second-in-command, Buel, to ride near Becuma to ensure her safety.

Cordelia gazed around, the hill fort was already changing, the people no longer smiled and laughed spontaneously, instead they were wary, nervous of the new men who strode around, shouting instructions and bristling with aggression. The villagers moved aside as Aganippus, who headed the procession, led them towards the gates. As they passed, the women touched their foreheads to Cordelia and Becuma, who responded in kind from their position in the centre of the Gallian men.

When they left the hill fort, Cordelia did not look back. Goneril and Maglaurus remained to assist their father, while Regan and Henwinus had travelled to his tribal lands in Dvmnonii the previous day.

This is no longer home, she thought and an unexpected wave of gratitude to be leaving swept through her.

As they made their way down the well-worn paths through the fields, she saw a man waiting at the bottom of the hill. It was Lagon. Although they were a short distance from him, when he raised a hand to touch his forehead, both she and Becuma returned the blessing. A moment later, Aganippus drew level with Lagon and paused to speak. Cordelia could not hear the conversation, but she watched their faces and saw friendship and respect. They clasped hands in a gesture of brotherhood, then Lagon stepped back. She wondered what had passed between them.

* * *

It was three days since the humiliation and horror of the wedding day. The tribe had erupted in fury and shock at Angarad's violent death, swarming towards both her and Lear with shouts and screams, whether to offer solace and help or to challenge their chief's rule was uncertain. Lear had screamed abuse at them all, standing behind his new soldiers, whom he had instructed to rebuff the villagers with unnecessary violence and force.

'Move her body!' Lear had yelled and the women had run forward to gather Angarad to them, taking her to the nearest roundhouse, where they refused entry to any man.

'It is a woman's duty to prepare another for the path to the Everywhen,' Sadiald had said, blocking the entrance.

Lear had ignored the fury of the mob, leaving it to the soldiers to quell the reaction of the villagers, instead he had shouted to his daughters and their husbands, 'Go now! Your roundhouses are waiting. I need heirs.'

'Fa, what are you saying?' Goneril had gasped.

'No consummation, no wedding feast,' he had growled.

'You think we want a wedding feast—?' Cordelia had begun, but Aganippus had grasped her hand and dragged her away.

'There is darkness in your father's mind,' he had said as he lowered the curtain and fastened the wooden panel used as a door. 'Don't try to reason with him.'

Cordelia was about to retort but Aganippus was unlacing his tunic and had pulled it over his head. She had backed away, her heart pounding in fear, but rather than turning to her, he had peeled away a small dressing on his side.

'I cut myself a few days ago,' he had said, worrying at the scab until it began to ooze droplets of fresh red blood. 'I'm trusting you will ensure this wound won't fester and kill me.'

He had smeared the blood he had encouraged from his cut onto a waiting white cloth, then turned to Cordelia.

'Would you redress my side, please?' Aganippus had said, nodding towards a table where dressings and balms lay waiting. 'Becuma gave them to me.'

Cordelia had stared at him. 'Don't you wish to consummate our marriage?' she had asked, annoyed with herself when her voice trembled. 'All men desire sons.'

'I have three sons and two daughters,' he had replied. 'My wife, Edra, died two winters past, but my children are strong and healthy. You needed protection and I wished to offer it. Your shamanic skills are of more interest to me than forcing myself upon an unwilling participant. We shall be married in name only. I will never expect access to your body. Should you ever wish to make our marriage more, then the decision will always remain yours.'

Cordelia had allowed the words to filter through her panicked mind; these were promises of calm and reason, but to her surprise, she felt the smallest stab of disappointment. A feeling she hastily quashed, instead busying herself with the application of the ointment made from honey and oats left by Becuma. She had smeared a scoop onto a soft, clean square of fabric before winding a bandage around Aganippus's middle to secure it in place. As she had worked, she had breathed in the scent of his skin, a musky smell, sweetened with the freshness of mint, and for a fleeting moment, she had longed to press her lips against his bare chest.

An hour later, during which time, they had discussed the horror of Angarad's death, they emerged from the tent and Aganippus had passed the blood-smeared cloth to Lear. Her father had given a coarse laugh, before demanding food for a feast. Angarad was not mentioned and her father gave no suggestion he had noticed anything unusual. A flushed Goneril and a furious Regan had followed after another hour. Maglaurus exuded smugness and satisfaction, but Henwinus was wary, staying as far from Regan as possible; Cordelia did not need her shamanic gift to understand things had not gone well.

For the rest of the evening, throughout the strange, tense celebrations, Cordelia had sat at her husband's side. It was a stark contrast to the light and joy of the night of the solstice. When Aganippus had stood, taking her hand and leading her to their quarters, the rook had cawed above her, and when she had looked over, it had bowed before taking flight. She knew it would never return.

The next few days had been the strangest Cordelia had ever experienced. Her father began stalking the hill fort, issuing commands, confiscating weapons and tools, ordering the farmers to train as soldiers and undoing the usual routines of the tribe which had made the settlement so successful. It was a relief when Aganippus had announced they were leaving.

'We shall travel to the Belgae tribe, not far from here, where we will stay for a while before continuing to the coast and sailing across the Dogger Sea to Gallia,' he had said. 'The journey will take many weeks, but with luck, the weather will be kind and we shall be home before the winter storms arrive.'

* * *

Now, as they made their way down the hill, away from the oppidum, Cordelia allowed her mind to empty, to brush away her fears of what the future held. In all her walks in the Everywhen, leaving her father's home was not a path that had ever been shown and she could not understand why such a huge change had been obscured.

What else have I missed? she thought. *Perhaps my skills are not so sharp as once they were, perhaps I need a new teacher and this quest will lead to enlightenment?*

Her eyes flickered forward to Aganippus. Was he the person intended to steer her along new avenues of discovery or was he the conduit? Her mind flickered towards the strange dreams she had been experiencing – of the three women and the unusual stone-built dwelling filled with many people.

'Why are we visiting the Belgae?' Becuma asked and Cordelia started, dragged from her thoughts.

'Aganippus has family there,' Cordelia replied. 'The Belgae have links with tribes in Gallia and Belgica. He is king of Gallia, perhaps they owe him fealty, too.'

Before Becuma could respond, Aganippus appeared at Cordelia's side.

'My lady, how fare you both in this heat?' he asked.

'We are well,' she said.

'In that case, it would be my honour if you would accompany me at the head of our procession,' he said. 'Buel will protect Becuma.'

'Of course, my lord,' she said.

They had spent almost no time alone together since the afternoon after their handfasting. Each night, Aganippus had slipped away, allowing Cordelia and Becuma to sleep in his roundhouse. Cordelia was impressed by his consideration, but she was also curious, imagining what might transpire if they were ever in a position where they were obliged to share sleeping quarters. *Would he be true to his word?* she thought, *and if he wasn't, how would I feel about succumbing to wifely duties?*

In the darkness, she had pondered how his kiss would feel, his touch, and in the heat of the summer night, her mind had wandered far and wide to wild places she had never before explored.

Aganippus smiled, waving to Buel, who trotted over to take the position at Becuma's side rather than behind her. Aganippus turned his horse and trotted to the head of his men, Cordelia followed.

'We shall halt soon,' he said as they took their positions, 'there is a settlement not far from here where I have family.'

'Do you have sisters who have been married to Belgae lords?' asked Cordelia, realising she knew nothing about this man.

'No,' he said with a wry smile, 'I have two younger half-brothers, but no sisters. It's my mother, Margan, who lives here.'

'Your mother?' said Cordelia.

'When my father died, she returned home to her tribe in Anglesey. As the youngest daughter, she was promised to a foreign prince – my father – and she had no choice but to leave behind her true love from her childhood, Kerin Goffarsunu. He was a distant cousin and a member of the Belgae. He, too, was promised to another. However, when my mother returned to her tribe a widow, news reached her that Kerin was also widowed. They were married and have kept a prosperous oppidum for many seasons.'

'Anglesey?' said Cordelia in surprise.

'Yes, she is descended from Druids,' he explained.

'But did she have no male relatives who wanted her to make a different political match? How was she able to marry Kerin Goffarsunu?'

'She is the youngest of three daughters, descended from a younger daughter, there were few men who were linked to them by blood. Instead, the matriarch of her family, her grandmother, promised her if she followed the tribe's needs for a foreign marriage for her first nuptials, if she were ever free, the second time, she could marry for love.'

'People do,' said Cordelia, 'although it's rare.'

'True,' he agreed. 'My parents arranged my marriage to Edra but my mother promised I could choose my next wife.'

'And you picked me?' said Cordelia.

'I did,' he said and his eyes twinkled. 'The reason I wanted to speak to you before we arrive is to tell you more about my mother.' A flicker of uncertainty clouded his face. 'It was on her instructions I accepted your father's invitation to attend the betrothal discussions.'

'Your mother sent you?' said Cordelia and did not understand why she found this unnerving.

'Yes, despite my reluctance, she was most insistent,' he replied. 'You must understand, Cordelia, although Edra and I married for duty, we found love with each other. It was unexpected but our union was a true meeting of souls. My belief was this would never be replicated and, at first, I resisted my mother's commands.'

'What changed your mind?'

'She claimed it was the most important thing I could do, not only for our people but for the Britons, too.'

'Does your mother have the sight?' asked Cordelia, her heart quickening.

'Yes,' he replied.

'She is a shaman?'

'No, she claims her skills are more mundane. She can see during trances but she doesn't have the ability to heal in the Everywhen or to alter the journeys of those in peril, all she can do is observe and interpret.'

Cordelia stared at him in surprise. 'She sees in the way Angarad saw.'

'Angarad was a distant cousin of my mother,' said Aganippus. 'Her determination to send me to the Golden Valley makes me wonder if she saw you during her walks in the Everywhen.'

He gave her a sideways glance but Cordelia did not meet his eyes. An intense cold was sweeping through her body, a tingling deep in her blood. She breathed into the sensation, concerned she would be snatched away to unconsciousness and an unasked-for vision. Instead, the cool dissipated and all around her she saw golden light, followed by her father's laughter. The momentary vision cleared and, to her relief, Aganippus did not seem to have noticed. Instead, he sounded rueful as he spoke.

'My mother is going to be unbearable when she discovers I have returned with a new wife. It will be Samhain before she ceases her boasting and teasing of us.'

He laughed, but Cordelia did not understand. She had few recollections of her own mother; Estrildis had died when Cordelia was young. She found it strange that Aganippus thought his mother would find their marriage amusing: to her it was a source of shame.

'Does your mother not respect the bond of handfasting?' she asked, her voice low as she tried to suppress the confusion of feelings pulsing through her. 'Will she think our union is unsound? A game? My life was ripped apart and you think your mother will laugh at my plight?'

'Cordelia, my love, you misunderstand,' said Aganippus and Cordelia blushed at the endearment. It was the first time he had referred to her in such an intimate manner and she felt an unexpected shiver of desire course through her, causing her cheeks to stain even more deeply. 'My mother upholds the traditions of the handfasting ceremony with great reverence. She will welcome you as a daughter and with all the dignity befitting a queen. However, she does enjoy being right and when we are alone, she may tease us. This is why I wanted to explain, I didn't want you to be offended or to fall out with my mother. You are both important women in my life and it would please me if you were friends.'

Cordelia realised she had shown her lack of worldly knowledge in her reaction to her husband's comments. As a high priestess and shaman, she was more accustomed to being admired and respected, this mistake did not sit well with her.

'My apologies, sir,' she murmured. 'We have been wed but three days, it will take me time to learn your ways and those of your family and your kingdom.'

'The apology is mine to make,' he replied. 'I've handled the situation badly and I'm sorry if you're offended. My mother will adore you and she will be in awe of your skills.'

Ahead, one of the forward scouting parties blew his horn.

'We have arrived,' Aganippus said and reached over to squeeze Cordelia's hand. 'Remember, you enter the Belgae hill fort as my bride and as Queen of Gallia.'

His words resonated with pride and Cordelia finally looked at him. A warmth shone from his eyes, she knew his words were true.

'You're correct, husband,' she said, squeezing his hand in return. 'I am your queen.'

She shook back her raven hair and straightened her shoulders. This was her new life and she would enter it with courage.

20

WOOLBURY RING HILL FORT, BELGAE, 862 BCE

'My liege,' said Kerin Goffarsunu as they entered the hill fort, 'we are honoured to welcome you and your new wife.'

Aganippus climbed smoothly down from his horse and helped Cordelia to dismount.

'The honour is ours,' he replied, clasping hands with his stepfather. 'This is Cordelia Leardohtor.'

Kerin bowed and Cordelia, unsure how to respond, bobbed a curtsy in return.

A woman hurried towards them through the eager crowd. She was tall and slender with an abundance of silver-white hair flowing down her back. Her dark brown eyes were alight with excitement, the fine wrinkles and laughter lines around them adding to, rather than diminishing, her beauty.

'My son,' she exclaimed, throwing herself into his arms. Aganippus spun her around as they hugged each other tightly.

Cordelia stood beside Kerin, watching this display of family affection, and felt her own father's betrayal sting a little deeper.

'My dreams were correct,' Margan said, releasing Aganippus and embracing Cordelia. 'My son has found a new wife, one fated with a great destiny of her own. You are welcome here with the Belgae, my daughter.'

As Margan's arms tightened around her, Cordelia's reserve almost cracked. She had not acknowledged that, throughout her journey, she had been banking up her emotions – her anger, her fear, her sadness – against her father and his behaviour. Margan's maternal hug, the first she remembered, nearly broke her.

'Come, my dear,' Margan said, 'let us find somewhere cool for you to recover while Aganippus and Kerin deal with the horses and baggage. You must tell me about your skills and I shall endeavour to learn all I can while you are my guest.'

Cordelia beckoned to Becuma, who stood watching this exchange and, together, the three women walked towards a large roundhouse.

* * *

Several hours later, Cordelia sat in an ornate chair as the official ceremony of welcome began. She had not expected their arrival to be greeted with such enthusiasm but Kerin and Margan had insisted upon it.

'Not only is Aganippus my son,' she had explained, 'he is the liege lord of the Belgae and, therefore, tribute and welcome must be made in full. Tonight, we shall celebrate your arrival with traditional honours.'

Cordelia adjusted the ornate dress she wore and glanced over to Becuma, who sat on a nearby bench beside Buel. Her friend blushed as Buel leaned over and whispered in her ear. She ran a hand over her dress and smiled. As the afternoon had progressed, Aganippus had shown Cordelia and Becuma to a separate roundhouse with a core of women to care for their every need. As they had washed away the dust of the road and were given an array of food and drink, another parcel of clothing had arrived, this time with robes for both women. Cordelia had seen the delight in Becuma's eyes when she had given her the vivid orange dress.

'I've never worn anything this beautiful,' Becuma had gasped as Cordelia laced her into it.

'Let me arrange your hair, too,' Cordelia had said. 'I think it might have been Buel who sent this rather than Aganippus.'

Becuma had blushed.

Now Cordelia watched as the Belgae took their place in the central hall of the oppidum. She had been surprised at its shape, it was square with wooden posts at each corner and was used as a central meeting place for the tribe. The walls were made of closely woven sticks covered in a form of red clay or mud. Aganippus had called it 'mud and stud' but said it was based on the Egyptian technique known as 'wattle and daub' or 'wattle and reed'. The roof was thatched and the interior was divided with screen walls made from more woven sticks, covered with animal skins and heavy fabrics.

'Are you comfortable, wife?' asked Aganippus, arriving by her side, a goblet of mead in each hand.

'Thank you, husband,' she replied, taking the drinking vessel he proffered. 'I'm most well. Will you be joining me?'

'Of course, we are guests of honour, and even if we weren't, the pleasure to sit beside you will always be mine.'

'You are too kind, sir,' she said as he took the large chair to her left.

He sipped his mead, then reached over to grasp her hand. Cordelia did not resist, she was his wife, it was her place to welcome his advances. However, she had noticed a growing and pleasurable tingle on her skin whenever Aganippus touched her; a feeling she was beginning to crave when they were apart for too long.

'My mother is delighted we have wed,' he said in a low voice. 'Did she say anything to you about her dreams?'

Cordelia shook her head. 'We spent very little time together. Your mother was very welcoming, but we were always surrounded by others. All she managed to whisper was a message that Becuma and I have yet to discuss or understand.'

'Which was?' asked Aganippus.

'She said, "You are the beginning, Cordelia, but you are also the end; great healing will come when your heart connects with the Charmed One".'

As she spoke the words, Cordelia felt again the cold rush of confirmation flash through her, a direct repetition of the afternoon.

'"Charmed one"?'

'Yes, these were the words Angarad used before she drank the hemlock,' said Cordelia, relieved to have finally shared this aloud.

'And this was all my mother said?'

'Yes, she had no further insight.'

Aganippus sipped his mead and Cordelia watched as his eyes narrowed in thought.

'What does Becuma make of my mother's comment?'

'She has yet to study the words in detail,' replied Cordelia.

Aganippus gave a slow nod, his face serious.

'Will you share her thoughts with me when she reveals them?' he asked. 'I would be most interested to discover more.'

'Of course,' said Cordelia, even though the idea of discussing prophecies with a man felt strange. As the tribe's shaman, she had divined the meaning of her walks with Angarad and the other priestesses before delivering the prophecies to her father and the elders. Her word had been accepted without question by the men; to hear Aganippus's request felt peculiar but not uncomfortable. She realised she was eager to hear his views and, again, she wondered at herself and these unexpected reactions and emotions to the man whom she had known for such a short time.

'As part of this evening's celebrations,' Aganippus continued, 'my mother has invited our favourite bard to tell us a tale. He travels far and wide but often winters with the tribe. He arrived two days ago and claims he was drawn back as there are a myriad of new stories rich in his mind which are desperate to be told. He is a wise man and I wonder whether he might have knowledge of this story weaving itself around us.'

'Perhaps,' said Cordelia with a sinking feeling in her heart. 'Do you know the name of the bard?'

Her father's hill fort had often hosted bards and there were numerous occasions when the yarns told had been based on mythical versions of herself and her sisters. She had never understood why they were of interest, but the stories always proved popular. Bards were notorious gossips and scandalmongers and she had no desire for her family to become a source of ridicule when news of her father's behaviour began to travel. In her heart, she continued to believe her father would regain his senses and send messengers with tidings of forgiveness and love, but she wondered whether this bard had arrived in order to try to discover more about the upheaval in Dobvnni.

'His name is Spaden the Gaul and he has been bard to our family for many years,' said Aganippus, 'although I believe he is from Brittany, rather than Gallia. He has adopted the name in order to appear more exotic.'

Cordelia had never heard of this man. She waited for her shamanic senses to offer advice on whether he might be friend or foe but, to her surprise, saw and felt nothing unusual. This confused her; ordinarily when someone new was presented, she had a flash of insight, but to experience no reaction was unnerving. She wondered if her shamanic skills had fled into the knot of the handfasting; as she became bound to Aganippus, perhaps her abilities had also been curtailed? It was a concerning thought, especially as the person to whom she would have turned for advice, Angarad, was dead.

'Here,' said Aganippus, taking a small bowl of food from a passing servant and handing it to Cordelia, 'relax and enjoy the entertainment. My mother has assured me the lore Spaden intends to tell is one of wonder.'

'Is it about my father?' Cordelia asked, no longer able to contain her fears.

'No, my love,' Aganippus replied, 'it is about a triple quest. He speaks often of the trinity of magic and its power to heal. Now, eat while the food is hot and let me look after you for a change.'

'What do you mean?' asked Cordelia, noticing again his use of the term of affection and having to suppress a smile of delight.

'When we were at the Golden Fort, I watched you and no matter the time of day you were always alert to the needs of others. You smoothed over countless issues between your villagers, halted a hundred potential feuds before they began, negotiated with traders, helped Angarad with the temple duties, yet you allowed your father to take the accolades for the management of the camp. Many will no doubt have noticed the change since you left.'

'You're mistaken,' she said. 'My input was minimal, my sisters and father always commented that my commitment was to the goddess rather than family.'

'Your father and sisters were wrong,' he replied.

Cordelia was about to defend them but was silenced as the loud beating of drums filled the air.

'My mother arrives,' said Aganippus with a grin that made him look years younger. 'She loves to make an entrance.'

Cordelia did not know how to respond. When she had been growing up, she and her sisters had teased each other, but to make such comments about a parent felt strange in the extreme. Yet even in the short space of time she had seen them together, Cordelia had seen the love, respect and affection flowing between mother and son.

'Should we stand to greet her?' asked Cordelia.

'No, my love, I am their king and, as my wife, you are their queen, they will first pay us fealty,' he said and she stared at him in surprise.

The huge wooden doors to the hall were thrown open and the sound of drumming increased, pipes played and bells jangled as Margan and Kerin processed the length of the large room, accompanied by the shouts and applause of the tribe. They halted in front of Cordelia and Aganippus and Margan and Kerin both knelt before them.

'We swear fealty to the King and Queen of Gallia,' they declared in unison and, to Cordelia's astonishment, the entire oppidum followed suit.

Aganippus raised his hand in acknowledgement. He stood, helping Cordelia to her feet.

'Thank you, good people of the Belgae,' he said. 'My wife, Queen Cordelia Leardohtor, and I bid you our thanks and wish you fortune, good harvests and prosperity. We are your honoured guests and I give blessings of the god Belenus.' He turned to Cordelia and whispered, 'Bless them with a goddess.'

She knew Belenus was the god of healing. Feeling the strength of his grip around her hand, his smile of encouragement, she allowed her shoulders to soften and let her shamanic power flow through her as she said, 'I, Queen Cordelia Leardohtor, wife of King Aganippus Epitussunu, give blessings of the Triple Bee Maidens, Corycia, Kleodora and Melaina, the goddesses of healing.'

Aganippus smiled at her.

'Rise, good people of the Belgae,' he said.

A cheer rippled around the hall as the villagers stood. Margan and Kerin took their positions beside Cordelia and Aganippus. Kerin clapped his hands and large tables were set up down the centre of the hall, followed by platters of food and jugs of mead.

* * *

Several hours later, the food had been cleared and the tables removed. People were seated in groups either on cushions or on wooden stools. Margan had already explained that the bard, Spaden, preferred to dine alone.

'He refuses to eat meat,' she had explained, 'and this can often draw comments. His wish is to eat alone and savour his meal uninterrupted.'

'A wise man,' Becuma had commented.

'Indeed,' Margan had responded. 'A bard but also a mystic. He is the brother of the High Chief Druid, which is why we welcome him. We won't tolerate the lower bards who spread mischief and falsehoods.'

'My father would welcome all bards,' said Cordelia. 'Many were tolerable, a few inspirational, but there were those who took liberties and based tales on my sisters and me.'

'I've heard this was the case,' said Margan. 'The beauty of the Leardohtors is legendary, yet the tales don't do you justice.'

Before Cordelia could even begin to think of response, a hush rippled across the room and all three women turned to see the doors of the hall standing ajar. Spaden the Gaul waited, surrounded by the fire of the setting sun.

'Good folk of the Belgae, please follow me, an auspicious sign has appeared in the sky,' he said, his voice was soft but it carried to the far corners of the room. Without waiting to see whether people had heard or even heeded his request, he turned and disappeared from view.

'Come,' said Margan, rising as Kerin, Aganippus and Buel joined them.

Cordelia glanced at Aganippus, who looked concerned.

'Is this how he begins?' she asked.

'No, I have never known him to request we follow him outside,' replied Aganippus. 'We shall soon understand, though. Do not fear, my love, you are well protected.'

'I'm not afraid, my love,' she replied truthfully and took his hand before he proffered it, causing him to send her a surprised but delighted grin.

They led the curious villagers out of the double doors and followed the path around the hall, where the height of the hill fort gave clear views over the fields and valleys below. Spaden stood gazing at the sky, his arms outstretched as he looked upwards, and as the tribe saw the solar phenomenon, there was a collective gasp of awe.

'The triple sun,' announced Spaden, 'a rare gift from the gods and goddesses. A sign of great change – whether for good or bad, only time will tell.'

Cordelia stared at the sun, hovering on the horizon, a fiery red ball of power, but on either side were two more suns, each angled away from the central orb, glowing with the same ethereal light. The sky was striped with pink clouds and the horizon was deepening to an indigo that bordered on purple. Then she felt it, the waves of a trance, and she was consumed with relief. She reached out to take Becuma's hand but it was Aganippus who responded, his arm around her waist.

'Don't move her,' came Becuma's voice. 'Hold her steady.'

Cordelia stared at the triple sun, pulsing with energy and the heat of life, potency and power. She allowed herself to relax into Aganippus's strong grip. Colours whirled around her, a rook cawed and then she saw her, the woman with her face, staring across the void. Tears ran down the woman's face, but as her vision cleared, she saw Cordelia. She reached out to her and Cordelia responded, their hands joining across time.

'Help me,' the woman gasped.

Cordelia stared down at the woman's hands and arms and saw silver lines on her skin, identical to the mysterious marks that had appeared on her own.

'Yes,' Cordelia whispered into the void. 'We shall help each other.'

The woman smiled, then she vanished.

21

THE TALE OF THE THREE SISTERS

The Baroness breathed in the freshness of the morning. The crisp air filled her with such completeness it was as though she had inhaled perfection. Every cell, every nerve, every fibre of her soul resonated and was revived by the cool, clear, vital atmosphere. Anticipation stoked her heart as she followed the directions given to her by the page.

The stables were on the far side of the castle and it was with relief she saw her steed, Valour, leaning out of his stall, welcoming her with a chirrup.

'I wish to practise jousting in the lists,' she called to the chief groom, waiting for the usual derogatory comments concerning women who wished to tilt. However, none came and, in an instant, the yard buzzed with activity.

The armourer and the blacksmith fitted her armour and two liveried squires brought a trolley with an assortment of lances. She tested the weight of each, selecting a simple painted weapon of perfect balance. Her armour shone and, as she moved, she noticed it fitted her better than it had since it was first forged in her own land.

'My lady, a number of our knights have requested the honour of a bout,' said the herald. 'They await in the lists should you wish to accept their challenge.'

'My lord, it would be both an honour and a pleasure,' replied The Baroness, delighted to have her skills treated with respect and accord. 'Come, Valour,' she said to her horse as she mounted, 'let's dance, you and I.'

With a whinny, the horse kicked his hooves and they rode into the lists. At first, they rode backwards and forwards, allowing both The Baroness and Valour to flex their muscles, to refocus their minds. The Baroness felt her blood coursing, her body taut, powerful, twanging with the intense excitement only combat could command. Valour shuddered, snorting eagerly, as keen as his mistress to show his skills.

The Baroness returned to her starting position, but before she could accept her lance from the squire, she saw him, the lone person in the empty stands. The man who had called her a freak, unnatural, an abomination. She blinked against the glare of the sun and he was gone.

'We shall follow your cue,' called the marshall to The Baroness.

With a last fearful glance towards the now empty stands, she nodded to the herald, who raised his flag and her first competitor rode into view. She pushed her visor over her eyes and bringing Valour around, watched for the flag to drop. A roar went up from the other knights, The Baroness touched Valour's side and they flew forward. Valour's hooves pounding across the soft ground, dust flying all around them, The Baroness lowered her lance into its cradle, braced herself and, with the roar of challenge, her lance found its mark.

She screamed in exultation as her competitor was unseated. Valour danced and bucked in delight, The Baroness raised her lance into the air, then with a whoop of victory she returned to her starting point and waited for the next challenger.

Knight after knight tilted against The Baroness and Valour. Each was bettered and, although The Baroness knew she had skill – she had not been beaten in the joust for many, many years – a drop of doubt entered her mind and she wondered whether the knights of the castle were pandering to her ego, diving rather than being truly vanquished. Would they wait until the end before the taunting and ridicule began? Fear rose in her heart like poison at the cruelness of men. She knew many were good, kind, careful with the hearts of others, but it had been her misfortune to know many with darkness in their souls.

All her life, her terror was being considered different. Her love of horses, the joust, the sword, the companionship of one woman. When she had been forced into marriage, her husband had whipped her twice a week, determined to beat her into submission. He had forced his sister to watch, laughing with cruel glee as he promised this, too, would be her fate if she did not succumb to his dictates. One day, The Baroness was told her sister-in-law had died of a fever in the night and, in despair, she had run for her life to her sister, The Queen, in her remote dower house.

A new challenger rode into the lists and both The Baroness and Valour felt a change in atmosphere. All around, the watching knights held a collective breath, an inhalation of such anticipation it even stilled the spring breeze.

The new opponent was clad in an armour of dazzling white. It shone with a clarity and purity, exuding an ethereal light. The visor of the White Knight's helmet was lowered, this antagonist's brilliant white horse pawed the ground, sparks emanating from its silver hooves. Even Valour paused, watching the stunning beast, his head tilted to one side with curiosity as though he had never encountered such a creature and doubted it was truly a horse.

The marshall called the riders to attention, the herald raised the flag and as The Baroness and Valour waited in the unnerving silence, she counted their thudding hearts – beating in time. The flag dropped as though in slow motion and, moving as one, Valour and The Baroness leaned into their tilt.

Even before it happened, The Baroness knew her fate. The lance of the White Knight connected with her breastplate, lifting her from Valour's saddle and tipping her backwards. She awaited the pain, the confusion, but there was none, instead she found herself turning in a perfect somersault; landing, miraculously, unharmed on her feet, as though she were a circus acrobat in a pre-rehearsed tumble.

The White Knight trotted towards her, the visor still in place.

'Good, Sir,' said The Baroness, bowing low. 'May I see the face of the champion who has such skill?'

'Of course,' the White Knight replied.

The White Knight pulled off her helmet, her light brown hair tumbling to her shoulders, her deep, dark eyes sparkling with mischief.

'You have done well,' said the woman who had long haunted The Baroness's dreams. The woman who had captured her heart when they were girls. The woman she had believed was dead. 'Once, you asked if our love would ever be worthy. Do you know the answer to this question yet?'

The Baroness stared at her in bewilderment, but before she could speak, the White Knight blew her a kiss, then turned her horse and rode away in a cloud of white dust.

From behind, The Baroness heard a cough and turned to see the man, her husband, the brother of the White Knight.

'Will you dare to follow?' he asked. 'You know the consequences will be severe.'

The Baroness hesitated, then, throwing the man a look of contempt, she vaulted back onto Valour, squeezed his sides and they cantered to the tent beside the tiltyard, where she knew without knowing, the White Knight awaited.

22

GOLDENWYCH, PRESENT DAY

'This is the last one,' said Lee, hefting the box onto the top of the pile in the corner of Caitlin's spare bedroom. 'Although, there was no need for you and your sisters to move everything. I told you I didn't mind buying it with things in situ.'

'Dad insisted,' said Caitlin, surveying the room.

It was of generous proportions and held a double bed, small armchair and dressing table, a wardrobe and chest of drawers, with a door leading to an en-suite bathroom. French doors opened out to a small patio with a path leading into the main garden. Caitlin loved the room and had considered using it herself when she had first moved in, but the master bedroom on the first floor had better views out over the fields surrounding Goldenwych, including glimpses of the stone circle.

The pale yellow walls were adorned with a number of prints: one was of the stone circle which had been painted by her mother, another was a detail of the carvings on the stones and the final was a charcoal sketch of the green slate monoliths known as The Three Sisters. The other two images Caitlin had bought at craft fairs and had been painted by local artists. When the sun set at night, the room glowed with golden light and Caitlin always felt there was a sense of peace and calm here which felt different from the remainder of the house.

'He threatened to throw everything into a skip if we didn't move it,'

Caitlin continued. 'The last few boxes are from the wardrobe in the spare room – they're more of Mum's notebooks, I couldn't risk him disposing of them.'

'It's a bit harsh though,' said Lee.

'True, but he was right, it's way past time for us to sort out our old bedrooms. I think we were all reluctant because it felt like destroying the final link with Mum and our life there as a family.'

'And how are you coping?' Lee asked with a hint of concern in his voice.

'I'm fine,' she said. 'It was time and, now it's all here, I can go through the boxes at my own pace and either sell stuff, donate it to charity, dump it or find a home for it in my cottage.'

'Don't you mean at the vicarage?' said Lee.

'I won't be selling this place,' she replied. 'Even though Stan keeps suggesting I should and make a huge donation to the church.'

'But it's your home,' said Lee in disgust.

'Exactly, but Stan doesn't seem to think that's important,' she said. 'He claims vicars aren't expected to own property because "God will provide". But the thought of having nowhere to call my own scares me. The cottage is in my name, which makes it my decision to do as I choose. My plan is to rent it out when I move into the vicarage after the wedding.'

Caitlin felt the usual overwhelming sense of claustrophobia as she thought about the changes that would follow her marriage to Stan.

Lee adjusted one of the piles of boxes, straightening the edges so they aligned.

'What?' she said, looking over at him.

'What do you mean, "what?"'

'We know each other too well, Lee, you always neaten things up when you're struggling to say something. Is it to do with my wedding?'

Lee sighed and sat down on the bed, holding her gaze.

'Tell me to mind my own business but is everything all right with you and Stan?'

'Why would you ask?' she said in surprise but her heart quickened. She thought she had kept her changing feelings for Stan hidden. *Wedding nerves,* she kept telling herself. *They'll disappear when we're married.*

'I didn't mean to pry,' he said, 'but, as you said, we know each other inside out and, as you can recognise my tells, yours are very clear to me.'

'My tells?'

'Yes, and whenever Stan or the wedding is mentioned, you clench your teeth. You've done it since we were children and it always means you're bottling up your true emotions.'

Caitlin stared into Lee's familiar face, the gentle blue eyes, and felt a lump rise in her throat wondering whether to spill her woes. A single tear slid down her cheek and she yearned for the relief of being able to share her fears. Once, she would have confided in her mother or her sisters, but after Miranda's death and the rift between the sisters, she felt there was no one. Sindy was her best friend, but, somehow, involving her felt wrong. Stan was the parish priest, a well-known and well-liked figure in the community, to discuss her doubts about him as a husband felt strangely disloyal. As a man of God, he should be above suspicion and gossip. And yet...

'Oh, Woody,' she said, sinking onto the bed beside him, 'I don't know what to do. Whenever I think about the wedding, it feels as though I'm about to step off a cliff.'

'Moon, no,' said Lee. 'How long have you been feeling this way?'

'A while,' she admitted.

'Have you spoken to Stan about it?' he asked.

'No,' she replied. 'During the past four months, I've hardly seen him and on the few occasions when I have, he's dismissive if I want to discuss the wedding. It sounds so lame, but he's become very argumentative recently and when we are together, it's a relief if we don't bicker, so my nerve fails me whenever I consider discussing my feelings.'

'You can tell me,' said Lee.

'Stan hates gossip,' she murmured.

'Discussing your feelings because you're unhappy isn't gossiping,' said Lee and Caitlin was surprised at the cold edge in his voice. 'If it helps, I promise not to mention it to Stan or gossip about him no matter the provocation, even if there's a lull in conversation during flower arranging in the church.'

Caitlin was unable to halt her snort of laughter at Lee's comment. Stan was unusually militant concerning the flowers in the church and would prowl the aisles as his 'ladies' arranged the weekly displays. The majority of the flowers were supplied by Caitlin's friend, Martha, who ran the village florist. She and her mother also made herbal remedies and Lee joked they were witches. Caitlin was aware their bouquets often incorporated flowers with distinct symbolism and hidden meanings. Lee suggested they were deliberately casting spells. Caitlin had decided never to mention her and Lee's amusement about his floral obsession to Stan.

'Stan is most particular about who is allowed to fiddle with his blooms,' she said, trying to hide behind humour to avoid the seriousness of the conversation. 'He'd never let you join the flower arranging rota anyway, he wouldn't be able to stand the competition from another good-looking man.'

Caitlin felt a faint blush stain her cheeks as she realised what she had said, while Lee looked flustered.

'Thank you for the compliment,' he said, 'but my dashing good looks aside, tell me about Stan. You met when he used to come into the café after his morning run, didn't you?'

'Yes,' she said, 'and, at first, he was funny, kind and he also held the allure of new blood.'

Lee rolled his eyes. It was an old joke between them all, the three King sisters and the two Glossop brothers. When they were teenagers, Edward had often compared the dating opportunities in the village to being 'similar to those after an apocalypse, but without the excitement of rebuilding the human race'.

'Do you blame me accepting his invitation for a drink when the other options were boys I've known since we were in junior school? Carter Jenkins and his amazing collection of worms or Abel Lester with his ferret obsession?'

'You forgot Parsley Hickson who asked you to marry him and move to the moon when you were four,' said Lee, trying not to laugh. 'We went to school with some very interesting people.'

'A diplomatic choice of words,' she said.

'I understand why you were attracted to Stan,' said Lee, his voice serious again. 'When I first met him, I thought he was charming, funny and, most importantly, he hung on your every word. Our dads were always singing his praises.'

Caitlin leaned into Lee and he put his arm around her.

'In the past few months, Stan has begun talking about his future.'

'Which is a good thing, surely?'

'You misunderstand, Woody – *his* future, not *our* future.'

'Ah, I see,' said Lee.

'Stan is very ambitious,' she continued. 'He views himself as a radical high-flyer within the Church and believes he has the temperament and skill to work his way up through the ranks to bishop or even archbishop. The trouble is, whenever he delivers one of his monologues about his meteoric rise, he never asks my opinion. He assumes I'll willingly follow him to whichever parish he's allotted without a backward glance. In other words, my life is no longer mine. He might be the vicar, but as his wife, I'd have to be involved too and do as the Church decrees.'

'The trouble is, he was a vicar when you met him,' said Lee. 'This was always a possibility.'

'Actually, it wasn't,' she replied. 'It was one of the first things I discussed with him when we realised our relationship was becoming serious. He promised me any decisions about moving parish would involve both our needs. I explained about the café and he said he'd never force me to choose between him and the Church or my family and my home.'

'It sounds as though he's changed his mind.'

'Yes, it does,' she said. 'Perhaps I was naïve to believe him. His job involves moving around, I should have been more mentally prepared for change.'

'Moon, he loves you,' said Lee. 'Talk to him, maybe he hasn't realised he's riding roughshod over you.'

'It's possible.'

Caitlin closed her eyes and breathed in Lee's familiar scent. For the first time in weeks, she felt her shoulders relaxing and unconsciously she began to stroke his arm where hers overlapped with his. In return, he gently played with her hair. A shiver ran up her spine and an involuntary desire to lift her head to kiss Lee overwhelmed her.

'By the way, how are the marks on your arms?' he asked, breaking the spell, and Caitlin moved her hand, freeing herself from their embrace.

'They're the same,' she said, flustered by her unexpected feelings. 'No more have appeared. Have you heard from Poppy about them?'

'Not yet...'

A key scraping in the door made Caitlin leap to her feet. She inwardly scolded herself for such a ridiculous reaction. Lee was like a brother and, once again, he had stepped in to help when Stan had been unavailable. On this occasion, Stan had called to say he was delayed on unexpected pastoral care on the other side of Hereford.

'Hello?' called Stan.

'In here,' Caitlin replied, then she turned to Lee, 'thank you.'

'Any time,' he said.

'Caitlin, I have news—' Stan began as he bounded through the door. He broke off when he saw Lee. 'Oh, hello, I didn't realise you were in the bedroom with my fiancée.'

Caitlin failed to squash her flash of irritation at Stan's insinuation.

'Lee helped me move the boxes when you were detained,' she said, walking out of the bedroom and into the kitchen, where she filled the kettle.

The two men followed.

'Tea?' she asked, but Lee shook his head.

'Thanks but no,' he said. 'I've promised Dad I'll test him on his lines.'

'The play,' said Stan with a broad grin. 'How's the masterpiece coming along? It's a shame my timetable won't allow me to join in with the fun.'

Caitlin scowled behind Stan's back. Despite her pleas, Stan refused to, as he claimed, 'lower himself to take part in such a debacle'. His continuing absence from rehearsals meant Larry refused to acknowledge Caitlin's presence, too. Her father also continued to withhold her monthly allowance. She was not worried about the money, but Stan was furious and would raise the subject whenever he saw any member of her family.

'It's beginning to take shape,' said Lee. 'The next rehearsal is tomorrow and Dad wants to run through his lines and his song.'

'Is it true your brother's taking part?' asked Stan, watching Caitlin as she arranged cups on the kitchen counter, poured the tea and added milk. 'I'll have a mug,' he said with a smirk as she pushed a cup and saucer towards him.

Caitlin stared at him and frowned. 'The mugs are over there,' she said and pointed to the cupboard behind Lee.

Stan raised his eyebrows as though Caitlin was being unreasonable.

'And in answer to your question, Stan, yes, Edward is in the play. He and I are playing the brothers, Edgar and Edmund, sons of the Earl of Gloucester. Dad is playing Gloucester.'

'Who's who?'

'I'm Edgar and Edward is Edmund.'

'In the real play, Edmund is the younger brother, he's illegitimate, too,' said Stan. 'I wonder why you've been cast the other way around. After all, you're the youngest, Lee.'

'And we both have the same parents,' replied Lee, pulling his car keys from his pocket. 'It's a play, we're cast into parts; it isn't real.'

Caitlin turned away, it was rare for Lee to lose his temper and his growing heavy sarcasm was a sure sign of his anger.

'Give me a call if you need any more help with the boxes, Moon.'

He raised his hand to Stan, who was sorting through the biscuit barrel and gave a vague smile in Lee's direction.

'I'll see you out,' said Caitlin.

They walked down the short corridor to the front door.

'Good luck with your dad,' she said.

'Thanks, I think we're all going to need it. Uncle Larry sent the list of songs over to Dad last night. Have you seen them?'

'No, why? He's usually fairly traditional, I was expecting endless variations on "Greensleeves" and anything he can find by Thomas Tallis. He loves Ralph Vaughan Williams's *Fantasia On A Theme by Tallis.*'

'You're in for a treat tomorrow then when your dad circulates the musical parts.'

'Tell me now,' she insisted.

'Dad has to sing "The Drugs Don't Work" by The Verve and, apparently, Slick and I will be asked to revive our performance of "Me and My Shadow" from our Junior Players days.'

'No way,' giggled Caitlin. 'Do you think he'll ask Rabbit to do "Ballroom Blitz"?'

'We can only hope,' said Lee. 'See you tomorrow.'

He dropped a kiss on the top of her head and hurried away down the path.

Lee makes me feel better, thought Caitlin as her skin tingled at his touch. *It's because we're friends.* But again she wondered what it would be like to kiss him and a liquid feeling of desire filled her.

Shocked at the wave of longing, she paused, taking long slow deep breaths.

This is Lee, she told herself. *My old friend. I have to pull myself together.*

She forced a neutral expression to her face and entered the kitchen, unaware she was humming the old Frank Sinatra and Sammy Davis Jr duet Lee and Edward would be performing. Stan was sitting on one of the high stools at the breakfast bar, the teapot and biscuit barrel in front of him, as with great deliberation he poured himself a mug of tea, his cup abandoned on one side of the kitchen counter, before turning to her. His face was furious.

'Are you and Lee having an affair?' he demanded.

'What?' Caitlin was so shocked, she took a step backwards and collided with the door frame, causing her to yelp in pain.

'You heard me,' he snarled. 'I come back here and find you together in the bedroom and now you walk back in here giggling like a schoolgirl. Are you sleeping with him?'

'No, I'm not,' she retorted, her own temper flaring. 'How dare you accuse me? Lee and I have grown up together, he's like a brother.'

'His behaviour towards you has never looked very fraternal,' said Stan. 'His eyes rove over you like the serpent in paradise, sinuous and full of treachery, preparing to lure you into temptation. I had been planning to say he moons over you, but I refuse to give credence to the stupid nicknames you all insist upon. "Moon", honestly, you're a grown woman.'

Caitlin stared at Stan in astonishment. 'What's wrong with you?' she asked.

'You don't think I have a right to be angry when I discover my fiancée in a bedroom with another man?'

'No,' she replied. 'This is the twenty-first century and it's fairly obvious Lee and I were stacking boxes, as well as being fully clothed.'

'Affairs aren't always carried out in bed,' Stan snapped. 'They're unnecessary distractions caused by predatory people who wish to disrupt steady relationships.'

'Lee and I have been friends since we were children,' she said.

'You can lie to me,' Stan said. 'You can lie to yourself, but you can't lie to God.'

'I don't believe in God,' she said.

They glared at each other.

'And there was me coming here to share my wonderful news with my caring fiancée but I find her in bed with another man.'

Caitlin was about to respond, then weariness overtook her. Stan was an expert at goading her, making her lose her temper with his ludicrous and untrue comments until she felt obliged to apologise when the entire crisis had been of his creation.

'What's your news?' she asked and took a certain pleasure at blindsiding him with her refusal to rise to his taunting.

'Very clever,' he sneered. 'You're trying to distract me, wanting to discuss my news, instead of resolving the issue of me catching you—'

'Catching me doing what?' she snarled. 'Chatting to an old friend? Calm down. Now, what's your news?'

Stan slammed the lid back on the biscuit barrel and stuffed a chocolate chip cookie from the café into his mouth. He reached over and sipped his tea.

'I've accepted a promotion,' he said.

'How wonderful, congratulations,' she said and realised her jaw was clenched.

'It's a new, bigger, more challenging parish,' he continued and there was a strange glint of satisfaction in his eye. 'In Newcastle.'

'What?' said Caitlin.

'It's a huge step up for me,' he continued. 'An inner-city church with a great deal of work.'

'When do you start?' she asked, dread filling her.

'We are scheduled to move there in three weeks' time, so there won't be any need to unpack your boxes.'

'But what about the wedding? We're booked into Goldenwych Church.'

'We can come back for the wedding,' said Stan. 'Just like in Shakespeare's *King Lear*, I am sweeping you away from all this madness to a kingdom of our own. You're welcome.' Stan beamed at her and Caitlin did not reply.

23

GOLDENWYCH, PRESENT DAY

'...And, of course, I'll pay for the damage to the ceiling rose in the dining room and the wisteria on the balcony.'

Caitlin dropped her shoulder bag onto a seat and glanced over at her sister. The theatre was filling with people for the first musical rehearsal and the revelation of soloists. With the nights drawing in, the room was becoming shadowy as only the wall lights had been turned on, but this did not stop the majority of the players casting interested looks towards Gillian and George Glossop, who stood in a gloomy corner near the stage. Lee was at his father's shoulder, his face in shadow.

Even from the distance she had placed between them, Caitlin could tell from Gillian's stance that her sister was irritated, but then she remembered Lee's comments about tells and looked more closely. Despite Gillian's folded arms, her foot was tapping, a sign her anger was superficial. She was making a point but Caitlin knew she was also battling to contain her amusement.

Her tell is her foot, thought Caitlin, *like mine is clenching my teeth.*

Her eyes wandered to Lee and she felt a swoop of attraction, which she squashed, refusing to acknowledge these strange new emotions. She turned hastily away before removing her sunglasses, hoping the make-up she had applied would disguise her red-rimmed eyes enough to halt anyone making sympathetic enquiries.

Gillian's voice floated back to her, her tone clipped, as Caitlin pulled her annotated copy of the script of *King Lear – The Musical* from her bag, along with a pen, notebook and tablet which she opened. She began scrolling through pages, half-listening to her sister's response.

'You're missing the point, Uncle George,' said Gillian. 'What was so upsetting was coming home after a tiring night resolving issues at the factory to find the house in such a terrible state. If it was the first time, I might have been more understanding but it's been every night this week...'

'Come on, Gilly-Bean,' said Alan in what Caitlin was sure he thought was a persuasive and conciliatory tone, 'your dad, George and I were working on the choreography for the musical swordfight in Act One, Scene Four. We cleared up.'

Lee suppressed a laugh, turning it into a cough when Gillian glared at him.

'Do men never grow up?' she said.

Without waiting for an answer, she stalked off to sit on her own, pulling out her phone.

Annie, Barbara and Daphne approached George, while Lee wandered over to Caitlin.

'What's happened now?' she asked.

'Dad, Alan and Uncle Larry were a bit too enthusiastic and trashed Gilly's living room.'

'Ouch,' she said. 'Gilly hates mess.'

'Red wine all over the white rug didn't help matters,' he said.

'Do you think she's all right?' asked Caitlin, looking over to her elder sister, who was hunched over her phone, engrossed.

As they watched, Gillian began typing rapidly, a closed, disappointed look on her face.

'Who knows with Bean?' sighed Lee. 'She was always the best actor and none of us have ever been able to tell when it was the real her or just acting a part.'

'True,' said Caitlin.

'What are you doing?' asked Lee, looking at the notes Caitlin had written on her script and in the open notebook. 'We're not stage managers this time, we don't have to make endless comments about cues and prompts.'

'They're neither,' replied Caitlin. 'We both know Dad's scripts are quite rambling in their first drafts but, usually, he and I work on them together...'

'You mean you rewrite them,' said Lee with a grin.

'We edit them,' she said and managed a smile, 'but this time, with Dad not talking to me, it's impossible for me to offer improvements. The story doesn't make sense and everyone else is either too polite or too worried he'll throw another hissy fit and threaten to withdraw funding if they challenge him. I've been doing some research and he's not only used the story from Shakespeare's version of *Lear*, he's also used some of Nahum Tate's, as well as *Holinshed's Chronicles* and Geoffrey of Monmouth and I think there are a few scenes from both *Hamlet* and *Macbeth* in there too, and another exchange that I think comes from *Mamma Mia*—'

'Slow down,' interrupted Lee. 'Who are all those other people?'

'Sorry. I've become so immersed in the *Lear* story, I keep forgetting how unimportant it is to most people.'

'It's important to me,' said Lee and Caitlin squeezed his hand in appreciation.

She was not yet ready to confide the other reasons for her research into the play, specifically Cordelia. Lee was always on her side, but even to her own ears, trying to explain the growing dreams and visions she was experiencing would sound peculiar and she did not want to worry him.

'Quick history lesson?' asked Caitlin and Lee nodded. 'Shakespeare made the legend of *Lear* famous when he wrote the play in either 1605 or 1606 – there's no definite date. He based it on a tale in a book called the *Holinshed's Chronicle*, which had been published in 1577, with a second version ten years later.'

'What was the *Holinshed's Chronicle*?'

'A series of folktales about early Briton and they were all drawn from Geoffrey of Monmouth's book, *The History of the Kings of Britain*, which was first published in 1135,' said Caitlin, her words tumbling out in her desire to share all she had discovered. 'Before this, British historians tended to begin the history of Britain with the Romans, but Geoffrey wrote a detailed document dating back to Brutus, the Trojan prince, who brought the first people to Albion, as Britain was called then. Geoffrey's was also one of the first known tellings of the King Arthur myth and it contained the origin of the story Shakespeare used for *King Lear*, which was set in the Iron Age.'

'Shakespeare's is set in an earlier time period too,' said Lee. 'It's why your dad wants us all to wear Viking costumes.'

'The Iron Age is much earlier than the Vikings,' explained Caitlin. 'The original would have been roughly 860 BCE.'

'That's a long time ago.'

'There's also a version of *King Lear* with a happy ending which has crept into Dad's play too,' continued Caitlin.

'You're joking,' said Lee.

'No, it's why Dad's put in a few romantic scenes between us as Cordelia and Edgar,' she said. 'There was a playwright called Nahum Tate who reworked *Lear* and gave it a love story between Cordelia and Edgar. It finished with a happy ending where Cordelia survives and marries Edgar. It was first performed in' – she checked her notes – '1681 and it was used until the Victorian era when the tragic ending was reinstated—'

A sudden burst of music caused them both to look up, followed by the house lights flickering on, illuminating the auditorium.

'Are you and Slick ready for your big number tonight?' asked Caitlin, stowing her notebook, tablet and pen back in her bag as there were general movements from the wandering crowd to indicate the rehearsal was about to begin.

'Don't,' sighed Lee. 'With Dad, we're the chosen ones who know the musical running order and your dad plans for us to open the rehearsal to put everyone in the mood for a song.'

'What else has he chosen?'

'Do you remember the Eminem song, "The Real Slim Shady"?'

'Yes.'

'Your dad's rewritten the opening to ask, *Would the real King Lear please stand up?*'

Caitlin giggled and Lee looked at her properly for the first time.

'What's happened?' he whispered, gripping her arm and moving her away from the enquiring looks of Annie, Barbara and Daphne, who had taken seats nearby.

'What do you mean?' she asked, shaking him off.

'Your eyes – you look as though you've been crying for hours,' said Lee.

Out of the corner of her eye, Caitlin saw Barbara leaning towards them trying to eavesdrop. Daphne was tapping urgently on her phone, looking unnerved.

'Come outside for a minute and I'll tell you,' she said, heading towards the exit, with Lee a step behind her.

'Hey, bro,' said Edward as he breezed past them in the doorway, his eyes searching the crowd and lighting on Rachel, who had appeared in the kitchen hatch, 'ready for our duet?'

'As I'll ever be,' Lee murmured. 'I'll be back in a minute.'

Caitlin led the way around the side of the theatre and into the adjoining graveyard, where a bench was hidden in a sheltered spot. It was a place they had congregated as teenagers.

Caitlin sat down and dropped her head into her hands, feeling her tears welling again.

'Stan happened,' she said.

'What's he done?'

'Accused you and me of having an affair.'

'What? How dare he?' Lee was furious.

'He dared and after he'd suggested we'd spent the afternoon in bed, he announced he's accepted a new position in an urban parish in Newcastle. He's starting in three weeks.'

'Are you going too?'

'No,' she said and held up her left hand. 'I ended the engagement.'

'But couldn't you work things out?' asked Lee.

'Not really,' she replied.

'Perhaps when you've calmed down?' Lee suggested.

'No,' continued Caitlin. 'While Stan was listing all the compliments the bishop had paid him when his new position was confirmed, I thought about a conversation Mum, Sindy and I had once. It was after Sindy's husband, Ricky, had done the same thing, accused her of having an affair. Sindy was devastated and told us she had no idea where the accusation had arisen. Mum, very wisely, suggested it sounded like projection. The uneasy conscience of a man who had either been unfaithful or was preparing to cheat. If the guilty person can find a cause or someone to blame, it allows them to justify their bad behaviour.'

'And had Ricky?' said Lee.

'Yes, it was why Sindy left him,' said Caitlin.

'I didn't know,' said Lee.

'You were living in London,' she explained. 'Anyway, Mum's words came back to me. Stan's accusation of us having an affair made me suspicious. He said affairs were "unnecessary distractions", which felt strange, so when he went to the loo, I checked his phone and there were four different WhatsApp chats called: "Unnecessary Distractions", each one was numbered. I looked at the messages from these individuals and they were all women.'

'Could they be parishioners and he's given them nicknames?'

'He hates nicknames, which was why this felt so odd.'

'What was in the messages?' asked Lee.

'Plans to meet, jokes, some eye-wateringly bad attempts at sexting,' she said, trying to make light of the pain of Stan's betrayal.

Lee hugged her into him as her tears erupted.

'Did you recognise any of the numbers?'

'Yes,' she whispered. 'You're never going to believe this, one of them is Daphne Hawthorne.'

'But she's at least thirty years older than Stan,' said Lee.

'And a wealthy widow,' Caitlin added. 'When I confronted him, he was furious I'd checked his phone but then he went on the defensive and claimed none of it meant anything; it was merely another way for him to do his pastoral duty to his flock and raise funds for the church. If it wasn't so tragic, it would be funny.'

'Oh, Moon, you must be devastated.'

'I've had better days,' she admitted.

With Lee's arms around, rocking her gently, Caitlin felt the first peace she had experienced since Stan's revelation. The harshest part had been when he had laughed and told her to grow up. He did not seem to be able to understand why she wanted to break off the engagement.

'It's up to you,' he had said, scooping up her ring where she had thrown it onto the kitchen counter and slipping it into the inside pocket of his tweed jacket. 'You'll come running back and I'll forgive you. It's what I do, you see: forgive people.'

He had walked away, a smirk playing around his lips, and had even had the audacity to blow her a kiss.

'Why did you bother coming to rehearsals?' asked Lee.

'I wanted to see you,' she said. 'To warn you that Stan might try to stir up trouble.'

'Don't worry about me,' he said. 'I've dealt with worse than Stan over the years.'

Caitlin did not reply, she could not imagine Lee ever becoming embroiled in messy affairs, but then, she thought, *What do I really know about him any more? I only have his version of what happened with Poppy; perhaps it was more complicated than he's said.* The pressure of his arms around her felt like a safe harbour and, again, she was overwhelmed by the desire to tilt her head back and kiss him.

'Have you told your family?'

'I've told Sindy,' she said, 'but why would Dad, Gillian or Rachel care, they consider me *persona non grata*.'

'This is so unfair, you're having a rotten time.'

'I'll survive,' she said and forced herself to leave the safety of Lee's arms. 'Come on, we'd better go inside.'

He put his arm around her shoulders as they made their way back to the theatre, and Caitlin, newly aware of her unexpected and disturbing feelings for Lee, slowed her pace, wanting the moment to last.

'How are your arms?' he asked.

'The same,' she said, surprised at the change of subject. 'Why do you ask?'

'Poppy messaged me.'

'And...?'

'This is really awkward, but I have to ask, especially as you're very upset at the moment and I wouldn't want anything else to happen—'

'What are you talking about?'

'Poppy said she's never seen anything like the marks on your arms but the closest she has experienced are healed scars from self-harm where the cuts haven't been too deep.'

'Are you suggesting I've done this to myself?' asked Caitlin, horrified, shaking off Lee's arm.

'No, of course not,' he said, 'but I'm sorry, I had to check. What sort of a friend or doctor would I be if I didn't at least ask?'

Caitlin stared into his familiar blue eyes and her wayward emotions, set into turmoil from the events of the past weeks, flared into anger. 'Why? Why would you *have* to ask?' she gasped, trying to hold back her tears. 'We've known each other all our lives, you know these marks are not self-inflicted.

They appeared after the solstice when we were all coping with Dad's TIA and it was a while before I even acknowledged them.'

'Forgive me?' he asked, looking stricken. 'It was clumsily done. Of course you didn't cause them. I'm sorry. Come on, let's go back inside.'

'Leave me alone,' she snapped.

'But the rehearsal...'

'Who cares? This is going to be as much of a disaster as all the other plays, with scenery falling over, costumes malfunctioning, everyone forgetting their lines, missing cues and children projectile vomiting from the stage into the audience. Every year, we all pretend we're rivalling the National Theatre with our productions, but they're terrible, embarrassing disasters and this one is going to be the worst of the lot.'

'You don't mean that—'

'Yes, I do!' she shouted. 'My father is trying to turn a play containing one of the biggest family tragedies ever written into a musical in a bid to save his own family. Perhaps if he told everyone the truth, we'd be able to resolve things; but even now, my sisters and I are bound by the promise Mum made us swear on her deathbed, the promise to continue to protect Dad and his shameful secret. A secret that actually isn't dreadful at all, except for the fact it would belittle Dad in the eyes of this village.'

'What secret?'

She pulled her keys from her handbag and stormed off towards her car, Lee running behind her. 'Ask your dad,' she snapped, climbing into her car. 'I bet he knows and your mum and all their friends, but I'm never saying it aloud again.'

'What are you talking about?'

'The reason none of my family wants to be near me is not because I inherited the café, that's just the story Bean and Rabbit created, it's because I'm the one who has already broken the promise we made to Mum and revealed Dad's secret to the person involved. I'm not sure I can sink any lower in their eyes.'

With a roar of the engine, she screeched out of the car park, leaving Lee standing alone while the moody chords of The Verve's 'The Drugs Don't Work' drifted from the open theatre door, filling the autumn air.

24

THE TALE OF THE THREE SISTERS

The Queen's heart lurched as she absorbed the beauty of the pastoral scene. For so long, she had existed alone in a city of ugly towers and narrow streets, yearning for the freedom of the natural world. When she had been widowed, it was her chance to escape, but her dower house had been surrounded by mountains, stark in their beauty but unforgiving in their glowering menace. When her sisters had joined her and their quest had begun, her heart had driven her to discover beauty, to relish the wonder of flora and fauna, yet nothing she had seen compared with the vista she now encountered.

An orchard of graceful trees stretched before her. The trunk of each shone with gentle golden and green light, the strong, supple branches reaching towards a soft blue sky edged with gossamer wisps of snowy white clouds. Wherever she turned, there were bouquets of cherry blossoms, changing in hue from the purest white to the deepest blush pink. A heady scent filled the air and The Queen smiled as she inhaled, her body relaxing as though she had imbibed the finest of wines.

With joyous steps, she wandered among the trees, her solitude a balm rather than a terror. Once upon a time, loneliness had been her companion. She would be locked away for weeks on end, her husband visiting with threats and violence. She feared she would die – lost, unmourned, her body thrown into the moat for the fish to eat. Today, these torments were far away and when she came to a clearing on the edge of a shimmering turquoise lake, the water was a solace, not a taunt.

It was the most unusual colour and she stared in awe at its magnificence. As she walked closer, she saw the brightly coloured tents and caravans of the troubadours, where a party atmosphere pervaded. On the lake were vibrant boats and pontoons where the players called merrily to one another as they rehearsed their many and diverse acts.

As The Queen walked forward, shy but desperate to join the merry band, two jugglers who were throwing jewelled batons to each other in a series of complicated movements, deftly caught them and called a cheery welcome.

'Madam,' said the first juggler, bowing low, 'we have long since heard of your skill with the lute. Legend has it your touch is of such lightness you create music that resonates with an ethereal clarity, the notes holding the purest and whitest of magicks. Would you do us the honour of playing?'

The Queen was overawed by this effusive greeting. She blushed as deeply pink as the blossom. For years, her talent had been diminished by her husband and his sons from his first marriage, her skills belittled and her desire for beauty in all things ridiculed.

'This is kind,' she said, 'but you're mistaken in these tales. I play most humbly.'

'But, Madam,' exclaimed the second juggler, taking her arm and leading her towards the edge of the lake, 'why such bashfulness? Come play your lute and let us all experience your magic.'

'My lute is with my belongings in the castle,' she protested, but with a flourish the first juggler produced the instrument.

'We heard you planned to visit and this was delivered a few moments before you appeared through the trees,' he said.

The Queen was surprised but delighted and for the first time in many years, her fingers tingled in anticipation. It was with a light heart and a joyous step she followed the merry jugglers to the nearest pontoon. They chattered and praised her as they led her to the large, flat, colourful barge in the middle of the lake, where the other troubadours tumbled and juggled, sang and played their instruments, warming up while waiting for the master jongleur to call them to order.

When they saw her, the troupe called out in great excitement and The

Queen found herself surrounded by the crowd of jewel-bright entertainers. Each wore a costume of gorgeous extravagance and she felt she was among a flock of exotic but friendly birds, all eager to make her acquaintance. Then from behind came the thunder of a drum roll.

The entertainers turned as one to greet their leader, Stefan. A muscular man of towering height, his hair was long and tawny, a lion's mane glinting in the midday sun. His skin was tanned, his warm golden-brown eyes sparkled and around his broad shoulders swung a long purple and green cloak embroidered with glittering mermaids and shimmering fish.

'Madam,' said Stefan to The Queen as he bowed deeply from the waist, 'would you do us the honour of playing your lute?'

The simplicity of the request calmed The Queen's nerves and, with a smile, she gave her assent. As she took her place on a golden stool in the centre of the barge, waves of warmth and friendship rippled towards her through the fragrant air. There was a hushed expectancy from the troubadours, an appreciative audience, understanding and encouraging a fellow artiste.

With well-practised fingers, she strummed her lute, adjusting the strings, making them sing in perfect harmony. She looked at the gathered crowd before raising her eyes to Stefan, who, with baton in hand, counted her in, and The Queen began to play.

The notes streamed from the instrument on her lap, a flow of liquid beauty enchanting and entrancing all around. No longer a woman and a musical instrument, they had merged to become a living, breathing organism creating the purest of sounds. As she played, words spiralled through The Queen's mind and, a moment later, she heard them being sung aloud by a haunting and ethereal voice of such clarity and tone-perfect pitch she felt as though she was drowning in sound.

Even if she had wanted to stop, she would not have been able. Instead, she played and played, allowing the words to unwind in her head like a fisherman untangling the iridescent catch from his net. As each phrase formed in her mind, the beautiful voice transformed it into song, tapping into her very soul as the music filled the air.

At last, her fingers and her heart were spent, the notes drew to a natural close. Silence followed as those around breathed again, the bewitchment of the song fading before they burst into rapturous applause. She lifted her face, wet with tears and stared around for the source of the voice that had accompanied her so unexpectedly, the person who was able to read her mind.

There on a small platform, standing alone, was the man. In a suit of harlequin silk, his hair dusted with tiny petals of cherry blossom from the orchard, he bowed from the waist. He was younger, smiling, but before her eyes, he transformed, his features twisting into the face she remembered, the man who had caused all their misery.

'I think, Madam,' he said, 'the time has come to show you the secret of this castle.'

And as he reached for her hand, everything went black.

25

GALLIA, 861 BCE

Cordelia stretched under the sheet and smiled.

'You're awake,' murmured a sleepy voice beside her.

'Yes, husband, the sun is already in the sky, yet we slumber,' she replied, feeling for Aganippus under the cool linen.

'I'm king,' he said, tracing his fingers across the silver lines on her arms before kissing her. 'I can do as I please.'

Cordelia laughed, succumbing to his embrace, wondering if she might soon be with child again.

It was a year since she had left her father's hill fort in the Golden Valley and a great deal had changed. Upon arrival at Aganippus's kingdom, he had introduced her to the tribe. Cordelia had believed the hill fort where she had grown up to be large, but Gallia was a vast country with hundreds of settlements, all under the auspices of Aganippus. The oppidum Aganippus used as his main home was on the coast in the settlement of Venelli, within the region of Aremoria.

She had stared in awe at the seemingly endless number of roundhouses stretching across the high ridge of the settlement looking out to sea. Other buildings were interspersed, which she later discovered were for storage for each family group. A huge square hall, similar to the one at the Belgae fort, dominated the central area of the oppidum. A short walk from its vast carved entrance doors was a menhir, similar to the stone at her father's fort, and for a moment, she had been overwhelmed by homesickness. The stone was tall and carved with the names of the kings and queens of the tribe.

'Your name will be added,' Aganippus had told her as he had shown her around her new home. A thrill of excitement had coursed through her as she realised again the importance of this man, her husband, and her elevated position as his queen. 'One day, I'll take you to the furthest-flung reaches of my kingdom, but for the present, I feel remaining near the coast of Britain is wise.'

'Why?' she had enquired.

'Your father is a powerful man and it concerns me what might transpire as he lets loose his new reign of terror,' Aganippus had replied. 'With Maglaurus and Henwinus as his allies, his potential reach is vast and dangerous.'

'My father is ill,' she had said. 'He doesn't have the strength of power or the support he believes. He also offered to split his kingdom to the first of my sisters to provide a son, this must weaken his position.'

'It will if either of them completes this task,' Aganippus had said. 'Babes take time to make and then grow, this will give your father a sizeable interval in which to gather his forces. We must be aware and protect ourselves and our people against his potential wrath.'

Cordelia had felt the grim reality in his words and promised herself she would do all possible to help both the men in her life – her husband and her father.

During her first months as Queen of Gallia, she had worked hard to earn the respect of Aganippus's people with her kindness and wisdom. Within a month of their arrival, Becuma had married Buel. Cordelia was delighted for her friend and admired the way she had adapted to this new and unexpected life.

It was after her vision at the night of the triple sun that Aganippus had invited Spaden the Gaul to travel with them as their honoured guest. Cordelia had separately requested that he might tutor her and he had accepted with alacrity.

'Our paths are meant to cross for a time,' he had announced with an enigmatic smile.

Since then, Cordelia had studied under the wisdom of Spaden. Never had she heard or read such tales as those he documented. They were on the rolls of parchments, guarded with honour by Aganippus's tribe, and kept in the great cavern of the dead on the edge of the settlement she now called home.

Each story was recorded in Spaden's neat handwriting in the ancient British tongue of her home. It told the history of Britain from its origins as Albion before it was renamed Britain after the arrival of the Trojan – Brutus. Even her grandfather Bladud's story was recorded, which made her dread how the annals would remember her father. She had no sense of being part of history herself, there were few women in the chronicles and this both irritated and surprised her. Would she and her sisters become part of the fabric of the past? A number of bards already used them as the basis for tales, would Spaden believe they were worthy of a place in his history or would they too vanish?

The biggest change was her relationship with Aganippus. On the first night at the Belgae hill fort, he had shown her into a roundhouse and apologised, 'My mother is unaware of our marital arrangements and has shown Becuma to the women's quarters. I shall sleep on the floor,' he had said and began gathering armfuls of fur rugs.

'No,' Cordelia had said, 'anyone might see you and we don't wish there to be any scandal. We shall sleep in the bed together.'

'Are you sure?'

'Yes.' She had dropped her gaze before admitting, 'I fear being alone tonight after the images I saw in my trance. Your arms would be a welcome solace.'

'Of course,' he had murmured.

Cordelia had blushed. While this statement was true, it was not the only reason. From her first meeting with Aganippus, she had felt the attraction between them, but she had denied her feelings. She believed her life was set on the path of shamanic ritual and goddess worship, her unexpected destiny towards marriage was not a route she had ever been shown during her wanderings in the Everywhen. *But*, she thought, *I never searched for answers for myself; whenever I entered the Everywhen, it was for the sake of others.* This thought had caused her great consternation as she wondered what else she had missed.

Ever since their handfasting, Cordelia had become more aware of Aganippus, as though on a subconscious level she had granted herself permission to notice him as a man, to feel desire as a woman, to shed her role as priestess, and with each passing day, her longing to touch him, to kiss him, to feel his skin against hers had been growing. He had been true to the promise he had made on their wedding day, he had been respectful, caring but distant. The marriage was new, but she knew she would have to follow his decree, any change in their current situation would have to be at her instigation. This thought both thrilled and terrified her.

They had prepared for bed and after Aganippus had wished her a goodnight, she had felt bereft as he rolled away, hunkering down beneath the sheet, leaving as large a gap as possible between them in the restricted space. His gentle snores found her through the heavy night and she felt a sense of loss. Cordelia had listened to her husband's breathing, her eyes adjusting to the depth of night allowing her to make out his shape, his face, his hands and she longed to feel his touch.

In the darkest hours, she had curled her body around his and dozed, but even through her sleep she was aware of him and when he rolled over and placed a tentative arm around her, she had kissed him. He had responded with gentleness at first, murmuring to her, asking her if this was what she desired, running his fingers over her body, exploring her skin, tracing a finger down the silver lines on her arms which had appeared after her father's accident. No longer able to resist the tantalising feel of his skin and the smell of his hair, she had kissed him in response and as their kisses deepened, her body had responded in a way she had never before experienced. She was powerless against her desire and as their passion intensified, he had whispered one last time before he possessed her entirely, 'Are you sure?'

'Yes, husband,' she had replied. 'I have never been more sure of anything.'

A daughter, Nest, was born nine months later to the day.

* * *

Ever since, Cordelia had believed their marriage had become more powerful. They understood each other, trusted and respected the judgement of the other, they were united and – she blushed whenever she thought it – in love. This emotion played across her mind as they lay, drowsy and sated, in each other's arms, talking and laughing about the day ahead when Buel knocked on the side of the roundhouse.

'My Lord,' he called, 'the watchtower has sent word. A messenger has arrived from the fort of Lear Bladudsunu. He claims to be a friend of the queen and gives his name as Lagon Locrinussunu.'

'Lagon?' gasped Claudia but Aganippus was already on his feet and pulling on his tunic and trousers.

'I'll send Becuma to help you dress,' he said as he hurried to the door, 'and a guard will be posted outside. I shall take no chances with the safety of you or Nest in case this man is an imposter.'

Cordelia was pouring water from the copper flask and sluicing away the heat of the night from her skin when Becuma hurried through the door carrying a dress of pale green linen.

'Is it true?' Becuma asked, handing Cordelia a cloth to dry herself. 'Buel says a man has arrived claiming to be Lagon.'

'Aganippus has gone to question him,' Cordelia said, slipping the dress over her head and sitting on the bed, while Becuma pulled a bone comb through her tangled hair. She tried not to wince as Becuma tackled a stubborn knot.

'If it is Lagon,' said Becuma, 'what could have brought him so far?'

'My fear is that he bears news of my father's death,' said Cordelia, voicing the words that had settled on her heart while she washed and dressed.

'Or a declaration of war?' suggested Becuma, braiding Cordelia's hair before inserting bejewelled combs.

'No, Lagon would never agree to such a task. If war was his intention, Fa would arrive at the head of an army.'

'Where is Nest?' asked Becuma as they hurried out into the summer sunshine, where a guard waited.

'With her nurse, Guardid,' said Cordelia, nodding towards the women's quarters.

A ring of men stood around the roundhouse, tools in their hands, ready to protect the women and children.

'Where is my husband?' she asked the guard.

'He's taken the messenger to the great hall,' the man replied.

'Then we shall also attend,' she said, setting off, the guard hurrying to keep up.

At the doors, Buel stood with several other loyal men.

'Aganippus said we were to accompany you,' he said, opening the huge doors and leading the way inside.

Cordelia pushed past him in impatience.

'Lagon?' she called, hurrying the length of the room to the raised dais, where Aganippus was talking to a dark-haired man. He was dressed in a rough, homespun tunic over tattered trousers, but his boots were sturdy. He had his back to Cordelia as she hurried forward. Her footsteps caused him to turn and Cordelia felt a rush of emotions at seeing her old friend. 'Lagon, it is you!' she exclaimed.

'Cordelia,' he said, hugging her tightly as she threw herself into his arms. 'You look radiant; being queen suits you.'

'Thank you,' she said, half-laughing, half-crying in delight at the sight of him. 'Why are you here?'

Aganippus beckoned her forward. 'Come, my dear,' he said, 'and you, Lagon, we shall retire to the quieter rooms and discuss your journey before we announce your presence to the rest of the oppidum.'

Cordelia led the way to the dividing wall, where there was a smaller room with chairs and rugs – a place where she and Aganippus would invite friends when the rowdiness of the hall became too much to bear. As the adrenaline rush of excitement at seeing her friend faded, panic was beginning to grip Cordelia. Lagon looked better than when she had last seen him as they had departed the hill fort, then he had been covered in bruises, his lip split after the altercations at the handfasting ceremony. He was thin but unharmed and he radiated a quiet confidence and determination.

Aganippus issued instructions to one of his men that they were not to be disturbed, then pulled the heavy curtain across the entrance. The light in the room dimmed with this action and Cordelia felt a strange intensity fill the space. Aganippus stood with his arms folded across his chest as Cordelia, turned to Lagon, indicating for him to sit beside her, her voice urgent.

'What brings you so far from home?' she said. 'This breaks my heart, but I must ask, do you bring news of my father's death?'

'No, Cordelia,' he said, grasping her hand in reassurance. 'Quite the opposite.'

'Lagon is here as your father's emissary,' said Aganippus. 'Lear Bladud-sunu was too ashamed to face us himself.'

'Ashamed?' said Cordelia. 'Tell me, Lagon, what's happened?'

'After you left, things became worse with the Golden Dobvnni. Your father handed the running of the hill fort to Maglaurus and the man he claimed was the high priest, Caradoc. The men who your father said were priests and new members of the community were paid mercenaries and it wasn't long before they turned on both your father and Caradoc.'

'Where was Goneril?' asked Cordelia.

'Your sister enjoyed the power of being married to a man who was behaving like a king in all but name and, unfortunately, it encouraged her darker side to show itself. We both know there is a venal side to Goneril, and with no one to challenge her, this hard-heartedness became more pronounced.'

Cordelia felt sadness washing through her. She loved her sister, but Lagon was correct. There was a ruthlessness to her eldest sister, which, when left unchecked, held a terrible cruelty.

'To whom was this viciousness directed?' asked Cordelia.

'Your Fa,' said Lagon and his voice caught as he continued, 'and mine.'

He was pale with anger as Aganippus finally moved from his standing position near the doorway to sit opposite Lagon. His face was closed, guarded, and Cordelia knew him well enough to understand he sensed Lagon's distress; Aganippus's move to sit with them was a show of solidarity and brotherhood.

'You're among friends here, Lagon,' Aganippus said. 'You're safe. Whatever you tell us will be treated with the utmost respect and consideration.'

'Thank you,' said Lagon. He swallowed, readying himself, then began to speak. 'Three months after you left, your Fa's senses seemed to right themselves. He banished the mercenaries and set about making amends with the villagers, but Maglaurus and Goneril had enjoyed running the oppidum. They plotted with Caradoc to imprison your father. He was much weakened, but with my father, he tried to plead for a return to the old ways, to when the fort was prosperous.

'Maglaurus is not a wise man. He believes he has knowledge above all others but he is lazy and stupid. He was easily duped by the leader of the mercenaries and, a week after your father had told them to leave, Maglaurus and Goneril welcomed them back. The first task was for them to imprison our fathers.'

'Locrinus was taken alongside Fa?' said Cordelia.

'Yes, Maglaurus believed him a troublemaker and Goneril didn't defend him.'

'Did Ivor protest?' asked Cordelia.

'Ivor and Gael left the fort shortly after you,' he said. 'There has been no word from either of them since.'

'I'm sorry, Lagon,' she whispered.

'It was a surprise when Regan and Henwinus arrived though,' he said. 'It transpires, Henwinus was more avaricious than we believed. They were halfway to his homestead of Dvmnonii when he decided to return to take advantage of Lear's madness. The Golden Dobvnni is a grand prize and he realised he had walked away from potential riches and power.'

'How was Regan?'

'Ill,' he said. 'She was with child and it sat heavily upon her.'

'Was the babe born?' asked Aganippus.

'Yes, a girl,' said Lagon, 'but she was ailing and she died within the day.'

Cordelia swallowed her sadness for her sister.

'And Regan?'

'Maddened by grief and determined to punish all who crossed her path.'

'This is a tragedy,' said Cordelia.

'There is worse to come,' he warned. 'Not only did Maglaurus imprison our fathers, when mine asked to see Goneril, to appeal to her better nature, Maglaurus not only refused his request, he ordered my father to be blinded so he could never "see" anyone ever again. His blindness, he said, would be a reminder to my father to respect the new regime.'

'No!' exclaimed Cordelia and Aganippus together in horror.

'And Goneril knew about this?' asked Cordelia.

Lagon shook his head. 'She was appalled when she discovered what had happened, but by then, there was nothing she could do, although, she did try to help my father.'

'How?' said Aganippus.

'She provided healing unguents which she had hoarded and, thanks to these, his wounds healed well,' said Lagon. 'It was Goneril who was instrumental in helping me to escape with our fathers.'

'She did?' said Cordelia and a small glow of hope filled her heart.

'Goneril provided us with clothes, money and a small donkey cart to enable us to leave under the cover of darkness,' he said. 'However, it's been a long and hazardous journey. Our fathers are lodged at a fort nearby, but neither wished to see you in their current state. Your father is deeply ashamed of his behaviour and begs your forgiveness. He wishes to put things right.'

'What are his intentions?' asked Aganippus.

'He wishes to raise an army and win back his land,' said Lagon.

There was a long silence, then Aganippus stood.

'You must rest, my friend,' he said. 'We shall discuss all you have told us and when we have reached our decision, you will be summoned.'

26

GALLIA, 861 BCE

Cordelia sat beside Aganippus on their ornate chairs. Carved from oak, each was decorated with a myriad of animal designs, patterns and the traditional triskele. They reminded Cordelia of the chair her father had used for important gatherings but these were more impressive. They were dressed in regal finery and Cordelia had been surprised when shortly before they took their places in the great hall, Aganippus had presented her with a heavy torc of twisted golden strands studded with amethysts and a matching circlet for her head.

'You are queen,' he had said as he placed the crown on her extravagantly braided hair, 'your father must remember your position.'

The great hall shimmered with light from a multitude of lamps, spotlessly clean and decorated with the finest hangings, rugs and throws loaned from villagers throughout the oppidum. The ranks of people who lined the long room in welcome were equally as impressive, dressed in an array of colours in fine fabrics with no workaday homespun clothing on show. This was a display of power as well as a diplomatic greeting. Cordelia burst with pride at the reception Aganippus had insisted upon for the official entry of her father.

'He's a great man,' Aganippus had said. 'Many have heard tales of his leadership; thankfully, fewer stories of his madness have circulated and he is still viewed with deference.'

The heartbeat thud of approaching drums caused a ripple of anticipation in the hall and, as the huge double doors were thrown open, pipes sounded, heralding the arrival of a visiting monarch. Lagon entered first, the emissary of peace bearing a sword with a garnet-encrusted handle, sheathed in a bejewelled scabbard. He held the blade flat across his outstretched hands in a gesture of fealty rather than as an act of aggression. Behind him were two more men from the Golden Dobvnni who Cordelia recognised as being loyal soldiers to her father in past skirmishes and walking alone, his eye covered in a golden patch, was Lear Bladudsunu.

He was dressed in the robes supplied by Cordelia and Aganippus, as were his entourage. After Lagon's visit, Cordelia had insisted her father be treated with dignity and respect. She had discussed her thoughts with Aganippus and he had agreed it was imperative to send money, food, clothes and horses to restore her father to his proper position. An official invitation was issued to Lear Bladudsunu, King of Britain and Chieftain of the Golden Dobvnni, and plans were made for his royal visit.

Lagon knelt before Aganippus, who indicated for Buel to take the sword offered as a gift. No one but the inner circle around Cordelia and Aganippus knew they had given the sword to Lagon. He moved aside and the two warriors knelt fealty before leaving a cloak of supple leather as another token of their respect, then Lear moved into position. Cordelia felt her heart clench; this close she could see the man beneath the expensive clothes and it was a shock. Her father always so strong, with powerful shoulders and muscular arms, was reduced to half his size. His arms and hands were wrinkled and wizened, his cheeks sunken and his mouth lined from the pain and suffering he had endured.

'King Aganippus of Gallia, Queen Cordelia of Gallia, I, King Lear Bladudsunu, come in a gesture of friendship, peace and to request your help,' he said and Cordelia wiped away a tear of sadness at the quaver in his once booming voice.

'We welcome you to our home,' said Aganippus. 'We offer you and your men the protection of beini, the age-old custom of hospitality and safety.'

He stood, helping the older man to a chair on his left, and as Lear settled on a vast cushion, his face grey with exhaustion, Buel led the traditional cheers of welcome. He and Becuma stepped forward, organising the arrival of the food and the arrangement of the long tables.

Cordelia leapt from her seat and hurried through the milling people to her father, her legs trembling, unsure if he had recognised her, wondering whether he continued to bear her ill will.

'Fa?' she said in a soft voice.

Lear turned and his lips trembled. 'Cordelia,' he said, 'my youngest daughter, my shaman. Can you ever forgive me for the pain I have caused you?'

Cordelia waved to Guardid, a small, dark-haired woman, who stood at the back of the hall in the shadows, an excited child in her arms.

'Of course, Fa,' she said. 'You were not yourself, but perhaps the path you forced me on to was the correct one. There is someone you should meet.'

She took the baby from Guardid and placed her on Lear's lap.

'This is your granddaughter, Nest Aganippusdohtor.'

'My granddaughter?' he murmured, looking down at the smiling child. 'A daughter...'

His voice tailed away and Cordelia stiffened, ready to snatch her little girl to safety in case her father's malady took control of his mind again.

'Daughters are precious,' Lear continued, stroking the baby's cheek, 'they are the strength and heart of this life. How was I foolish enough to lose my own daughters?'

Guardid stepped forward as Lear passed the child to Cordelia.

'I have failed you and your sisters,' he said. 'I failed Angarad. You deserved better.'

'Your injury took you from us but your senses have returned,' she said.

'Perhaps,' he replied, 'but at least you remain unchanged. Your sisters are no longer what they once were, they have become cold, cruel women and it is my fault.'

'The path could have been far darker, Fa.'

He narrowed his one eye at her. 'Did you see this?' he asked.

'What transpired was not as devastating as the potential,' she said. 'Angarad explained that often we are shown the worst possible outcome. With this knowledge, we are able to repair the damage before it happens.'

'Did you see an end to the curse? Did it die with Angarad?'

'Her death was the beginning, she sealed the curse with her final breath,' said Cordelia. 'At present, there is no end in sight.'

'Cursed,' he lamented. 'The fault was mine, I violated her vows. Her

Druid magic was strong and she used it in revenge for my stupidity. Tell me, what else did you see?'

'It no longer matters, Fa,' she said.

'Tell me what you saw,' he begged, his withered hand shooting out with unexpected speed and determination, clasping her wrist in a desperate, vice-like grip.

She winced, struggling to release herself.

'All that matters is that you are well and we shall restore you to your kingdom.'

'Even if it means fighting your sisters?'

'If we must,' she replied and he loosened his grip, a sad smile on his lips, 'but let us hope this will be unnecessary.'

'I shall be king,' he said in a low voice, as though he was speaking to himself, 'but will it be a hollow crown? Will any bow fealty to me again after my cruel transgressions? I do not deserve their compassion or forgiveness.'

Before Cordelia could reply, Aganippus called for Lear to join him in the antechamber while the food was laid out. No one else knew Locrinus was secreted there, with Becuma checking the injuries inflicted by Maglaurus's commands.

Cordelia stared down at the red marks on her wrist left by her father and saw them, the silver lines, swirling up her skin, around the patterns of the triskele on her inner arms.

An unexpected shiver ran down her spine and she remembered Gloigin's words as they had cleared the temple, *'This was always the intention of the goddesses, for you to be a wife, a mother, a warrior... You must prepare for what is to come and do not be afraid when you are asked for help.'*

The image of her father wielding a sword over her prone body flashed across her mind and she felt a sting in the words of her friend's prophecy. How much help would the goddess desire in repayment for the gifts she had bestowed upon her? Unable to help herself, Cordelia shuddered in fear.

* * *

The following night, Cordelia and Becuma stood inside the cavern of the dead, waiting for the singing moon to rise. It was Alban Elued, the autumn equinox, and Spaden, who had visited the settlement many times before on his travels, had told them of the magical light that suffused the inner cavern when the full moon struck the walls.

'This cavern worships both birth and death,' he had explained to Cordelia and Becuma not long after their arrival as he had led them through the winding tunnels. 'This gallery' – he indicated the lavishly decorated pillars – 'is aligned to face the southerly moonrise of the Alban Elued, while this opening draws the light of the Alban Arthuran sunrise – the point of midwinter where Yule is celebrated and the darkness begins its slow retreat. This white pillar of quartz is the point where the lines of the sun and moon cross, it is our most sacred place.'

'Do you recognise the spring and summer rites?' Becuma had asked.

'We do, but they are welcomed in the stone circle to the west of the oppidum,' he had said. 'This is the tomb of the ancestors and they prefer the shadowy days of the autumn and winter, its silver light echoes the realm of Dubnos, the underworld, where they dwell. The stone circle is a place of light, a celebration of Albios, the home of our benevolent goddesses and gods, while we mortals scurry hither and thither in this mortal plane of Bitu. These are sacred places and we must be mindful of their power.'

'Are you sure this is wise?' asked Becuma now as she gazed around.

'Yes,' Cordelia replied. 'At the feast of welcome, a shade overwhelmed my father and his words changed from those of sorrow and respect to destruction and war. We must know if he speaks true when he requests our armies to save the Golden Dobvnni or whether he is possessed by the evil of his madness.'

'It's been many moons since you walked in the Everywhen,' said Becuma.

'Yes, my dearest friend, which is why you're the one person I trust to remain here and bring me home if necessary,' she said. 'I'm sorry to lay this burden upon your shoulders, especially when we have both been forced away from our pathways of worship. It's imperative I understand the visions flashing into my mind, otherwise it's possible both Aganippus and Buel could be in terrible danger.'

'Very well,' said Becuma and from the leather satchel at her feet she unpacked the treasures she had brought with her from the temple at the Golden Dobvnni. The girdle flashed with its autumn colours, while the amethyst pendant lay heavy and familiar in Cordelia's hand when Becuma passed it to her.

'Here is woad,' said Becuma, 'and these – although they are no longer joined to the leather bindings which made them secure.'

Cordelia stared in surprise at the two delicate antlers that had once formed her headdress. 'You saved everything,' she said.

'There was time to pack,' she replied. 'I followed my instincts, my path was entwined with yours, these are the items necessary for you to walk, along with the henbane, which I have since cultivated here – although far from my hives. I shall prepare the woad while you dress yourself. There are not enough of us for the full ritual, but your powers are strong enough to walk anywhere – even these trappings are, perhaps, unnecessary.'

'Becuma, your wisdom is beyond that even of Angarad,' Cordelia said and hugged her friend before they set to work on their preparations.

* * *

When the moon rose an hour later, Cordelia was ready. Becuma had painted the swirls and patterns of the dreaming spells in woad across Cordelia's face, including the triskele in the centre of her forehead. They had created an altar in front of the quartz pillar and placed a shallow copper bowl upon it, filling it with small spills of wood and lighting it from the flame of one of the candles they had placed around them.

The white willow baskets of the Golden Dobvnni Temple had long been lost, but instead Becuma has used one of the darker reed baskets common in the Gallian oppidum, filling it with five small, round wax tablets and a bunch of herbs. Cordelia had beamed in delight when Becuma had revealed another treasure she had saved: the golden flask engraved with images of bees and its matching goblet. Once again, they glinted in the firelight, giving the impression the bees were moving.

The two women were checking the final details required for Cordelia's walk when an unearthly beam of the purest silver light filled the tomb.

'The singing moon has risen,' said Becuma. 'Are you ready?'

'Yes,' said Cordelia and took her place by the altar.

'Good luck, my friend,' whispered Becuma, gripping Cordelia's hand.

'Thank you,' she murmured, her heart beating in anticipation.

Becuma bowed low and in a voice of calm authority began the ancient ritual. 'May the Goddess hear your words.'

'Your wishes have been heard,' replied Cordelia.

Becuma stepped back into the shadows but Cordelia could sense her friend's eyes upon her, watching, waiting, ready to pull her to safety. This was Cordelia's first walk in the Everywhen since she had become a mother and she wondered if this would change her pathway, whether she would see differently. She poured wine from the flask into her goblet, before adding a libation to the flames. It sizzled as the tiny red drops evaporated in the heat, spreading a burnt vinegary smell into the glowing white light of the cavern of the dead.

'Matronae, mother goddess, I invoke thee for protection,' Cordelia said in a low voice and, as she did, she felt a release of tension in her shoulders. 'Hecate, my sister moon, I invoke thee for my safe return. Aine, sister of the sun, I invoke thee to shine a light on my path as I heal our past and future.'

Her heartbeat slowed, steady, sure, pounding in her ears as her body relaxed, preparing for the Everywhen. The fire spluttered as she dropped in two of the small wax tablets. The flames flared purple and the familiar sweet scent of the honey from the beeswax filled the silver air. She was home, this was her place, the shaman, the wise woman who protected the multitudes. The confidence in her voice grew as the words of the ritual rose effortlessly to the surface of her mind.

'Corycia, Kleodora, Melaina, the Bee Maidens Three, show me the way to the truth,' she invoked as she crumbled herbs into her drink. 'Help me to repair our wounds and return our strength and wisdom. Show me the path as I ask for the veracity of my father's intentions.'

Cordelia swallowed the wine in one gulp, wincing from the bitterness of the herbs. She closed her eyes as she waited for the hallucinogenic properties of the henbane to whisper through her blood, her breath slowing. With a rush, there was a spark of light behind her eyelids, followed by a tumbling, sinking feeling as though the soul of the earth itself were rocking beneath her feet. She groaned, throwing back her head, her eyes widening; rolling uncontrollably as she sank to her knees, her arms outstretched.

'Adsagsona, goddess of magic, walk with me,' she implored, her voice eldritch in the eerie light.

A wolf howled and on her shoulder she felt the claws of her spirit guide, her rook, as Cordelia stepped into the Everywhen.

Daughter of the Storm

A wolf howled and on her shoulder she felt the claws of her spirit guide,
her rook, as Cordelia stepped into the Everywhere.

27

THE TALE OF THE THREE SISTERS

The three women stood in a row, The Queen, The Baroness and The Princess, their hands clasped. The man stood before them, his edges blurring as he prowled, his face in shadow, his expression unreadable.

'You are on a quest,' he stated.

'Yes,' replied The Queen.

'We search for answers,' said The Baroness.

'But we do not know the question,' said The Princess.

'Then I shall tell you both,' said the man, his voice low; cruel laughter twinkling in his words. 'You search, you quest, yet you never leave this castle.'

'What do you mean?'

'When the adventure ends, you ride the white path again, you return, you repeat. You're not free, you don't travel, you are here for eternity.'

'No,' said the sisters together.

'Yes,' he replied. 'You are bound to me forever because of your fears.'

Behind him was a door, aged and solid, with heavy iron studs and hinges. He turned the huge key in the lock and opened it to reveal a stone staircase, spiralling upwards, out of view.

'Come,' he said. 'Do you dare break the pattern?'

He sneered, before running up the stairs on silent feet and disappearing from view.

'Shall we?' asked The Queen.

'No,' said The Baroness, fearful of the man.

They turned to The Princess and as the word 'no' began to form, she saw them again, the two women. They were either side of the doorway and they beckoned her forward before vanishing.

'Yes,' said The Princess. 'Or we shall never know.'

The women felt the ground shift under their feet, as though thunder had roared underground. They reached for each other and, with a nervous glance, the three sisters mounted the stairs.

The man was waiting as they rounded the final bend of the steep tower and when he saw them, his smile of contempt transformed to incandescent rage.

'You have dared to follow?' he hissed. 'You dare to challenge my game?'

The three sisters stood resolute, their hands clasped.

'Very well,' said the man through gritted teeth. 'You have chosen to challenge me, then behold.'

He clapped his hands and a raised dais appeared in the centre of the room. It held a vast four-poster bed with heavy lawn curtains drawn all around it, hiding the figure within.

Masked attendants, their faces obscured but their voices clear as they chanted, moved in an endless trudging circle around the bed. 'One becomes two; two becomes three; and out of the third comes the fourth, the One. The fourth is the Charmed One who will heal the curse.'

'The trinity,' said the man, pointing to the three women. 'The triple-aspect goddess, the triple-aspect god, the power of the triskele. Three is known by wise men to be the perfect number. The number of harmony, wisdom and understanding. The number of time – past, present, future; of birth, life, death; the beginning, the middle and the end. It is the number of the divine.

'The triple goddess of the bees cursed your line with pain. Three by three by three by three by three, the third daughter of the third daughter of the third daughter from the time of shadows and fear, until one shall come, a youngest child of a youngest child of a youngest child who is both third and fourth. She shall have the power to heal this curse.'

The women did not speak, they barely breathed.

'Come forward, my dears,' said the man, pulling back the curtains. 'Meet your father and understand the depth of your trouble.'

28

GOLDENWYCH, PRESENT DAY

Caitlin breathed in the scent of the herbs: sage, rosemary and henbane, combined with honey from her hives. A brew created from her mother's recipe, but, for the first time, she was apprehensive about ingesting one of Miranda's teas. Henbane was not a plant she had used before in her blends. She knew it was a hallucinogenic and, in certain quantities, it could be poisonous. Until an hour earlier, she had considered cancelling the ritual but a text from Stan asking if she required his forgiveness yet followed by a laughing emoji had put her in a reckless mood. She had felt a rush of heat and fury, solidifying her desperate desire to escape her present misery and it had pushed her onwards in her endeavours.

When she had returned to the cottage two weeks earlier after her row with Lee, she had poured herself an enormous glass of wine, sat on the bed in the spare room and pulled the two boxes of her mother's notebooks beside her. She had tumbled the volumes onto the bed before sorting them into colour, then size order, enjoying the variations of clarity: some were bright and reasonably new, while others were ancient, faded to shadows of their former glory.

She had decided to work through them in rainbow order – red, orange, yellow, green, blue, indigo, violet – for no reason other than this was the way she had arranged them on the bed. Many of the books contained recipes for cakes, tea blends and the delicious quiches and pies her mother had made for the café. Others were sketchbooks, a myriad of images of Caitlin, Gillian and Rachel as children. In others were drawings of her father, several self-portraits of her mother and numerous faces of their friends from when they were younger. There were animals, too, alongside swirling designs and patterns, inspired by Celtic imagery. In one book, a series of images of women gazed at her. All wore robes and their faces were uncannily familiar, even in their strange aloofness they held echoes of herself, Gillian and Rachel. As she studied them, Caitlin felt a cold shiver as she realised these were the women from her strange, quest-like dreams, faces that appeared not only in her sleeping hours but in moments of distraction when they would flash into her mind. As she had turned the pages, she had gasped in surprise, staring at the detailed pictures depicting scenes from her dreams, images of the castle, the lake, the tiltyard and even the horse, Valour.

How is this possible? she had thought.

She had been halfway down the bottle of white wine, but it was losing its appeal, the crisp iciness from the fridge was fading and with it the flavour had soured. She had put it to one side, then spent a long time studying the drawings, flicking backwards and forwards through the scenes from her dreams that had been captured by her mother many years earlier.

The final pile of books looked old-fashioned, the deep violet covers were padded and the pages edged in gold. They were more formal than the other books, which ranged from school-style exercise jotters to brightly patterned spiralbound volumes. The violet books seemed out of place among the exuberant colours of their fellows.

'What have we here?' Caitlin had murmured.

She had piled the cushions behind her and pulled the five notebooks onto her lap. Her mother's writing was as familiar to Caitlin as her own and when she had opened one, on the first page was a tea recipe she had never seen before:

Henbane infusion – for problems (shamanic).

A shiver had run down her spine.

When she had turned the page, she had felt another unexpected lurch.

Copied by Miranda King from the diaries of Esther Maydman, 1687:

These are my dreams, the story I visit every night, the sisters and their quest, again and again. My plan is to capture it on this page and hope to free my heart and mind. The third daughter of the third daughter, forever caught in the cycle of three, over and over, this is my story...

Who was Esther Maydman? she had wondered.

She had flicked through, reading the headings of each new section:

Copied by Miranda King from the diaries of Margaret Valentine, 1730

Copied from the diaries of Alice Farringdon, 1763

more names followed, coming up to the present day with first her grandmother, using her maiden name, Dolly Jeeves, and her mother, Miranda Tempest, using her maiden name, too.

As Caitlin had read each tale, she had realised they were all the story of three women on a quest. With each page, Caitlin had become more confused, each of the writers had claimed she was a third daughter of a third daughter, the same as her grandmother, the same as her mother, the same as her. Each had experienced the same convoluted dream, but none had ever reached its conclusion. The entries ended along similar lines:

There have been no dreams for several months now, not since The Queen entered the cherry blossom orchard and was offered the secrets of the castle...

It was this that had made Caitlin slam the books shut and shove them back in the box because the previous night, she had dreamed of the cherry blossom orchard.

Her mother's final words had read:

My dreams are more than a coincidence, there is a pattern here. The henbane recipe has been passed down through the centuries, I wonder if this holds the key. One day, I shall share these books with my little Caitlin Moonbeam and perhaps we can unravel their meaning together. She might be the one to solve this riddle.

Underneath was a small line sketch of the woman from her mother's earlier notebooks, the *genius loci* of the stream, followed by:

I've just remembered, she was wearing an amethyst necklace – the dig Granddad mentioned? Could it be the one?

Caitlin had felt a shiver run down her spine as she thought about the day she had lost the doll's shoe. Pulling out her phone, she had typed in:

Amethyst necklace, Goldenwych, archaeological dig

An image of the jewel had appeared, with several academic papers explaining its significance, as well as blog pieces and newspaper features. Caitlin's breath had caught in her throat: she had seen this necklace around the throat of the woman in her dreams, the woman with the antler head-dress and the silver marks on her arms. The necklace found in Goldenwych hundreds of years ago that now resided in the British Museum.

Caitlin's asthma, which was usually under control, had taken her unawares as she had stared at the pictures of the pendant and she had been forced to call Lee for help.

'You haven't had an attack this bad for years,' George Glossop had said, concern in his eyes when he had arrived with Lee. They had both attended because Lee was staying with his parents while his new home was being redecorated and George would not let him go alone.

'It's probably the dust from moving all the boxes,' she had wheezed.

'Or stress,' Lee had suggested.

'What's happened?' asked George.

'Stan's been having an affair,' Lee had said before Caitlin could stop him. 'Caitlin's ended their engagement.'

George had looked at Caitlin, who confirmed Lee's statement with a sharp nod.

'I'd prefer it if someone could stay with you.'

'Who?' she had said.

'One of your sisters, perhaps.'

She had shaken her head.

'I'll be fine,' she had replied and insisted they leave.

* * *

'Are you sure about this?' asked Sindy, bringing her back to the present.

It was dusk, the purple shadows of night were claiming the edges of the world, drawing it down into the blackness of the velvet night. The sky's glorious display of gold and red, pink and silver was fading as the darkening line on the horizon swallowed the day. They were in the stone circle and Caitlin was laying out candles and wreaths of autumn leaves around the Three Sisters.

'We've never done a ritual at the autumn equinox before,' said Sindy. 'What's prompted this?'

'A passage I read in one of Mum's diaries,' Caitlin replied as she placed an ornate, stoppered glass bottle in the centre of the circle she had created.

'And this new tea,' Sindy said, sniffing the flask Caitlin had placed to one side, 'what's in it? It smells heady.'

'It's a recipe for meditation,' she said. 'Mum used it, now I'm going to use it to go into a trance.'

'What?' Sindy was shocked. 'Caity, is this wise? You've been very poorly.'

'I'm fine,' snapped Caitlin, then softened her tone when she saw Sindy's surprised look. 'Sorry, Sind. My asthma attack was a two weeks ago and it was because of the dust.'

Sindy gave her a long look and raised her eyebrows. 'Whatever you say.'

'Please, not you too,' Caitlin sighed. 'The rest of the family give me constant grief about nearly everything I do, challenging my decisions and treating me as though I'm incapable of rational choices because of my asthma. I'm the one who's had it since childhood, the medication works and attacks are few and far between—'

'But, they do come,' Sindy interrupted. 'The night you collapsed after the dance for your grandfather, we all thought you were dead. It was the most terrifying thing I've ever seen and no one who was there will ever forget it. George was doing CPR on you for twenty minutes before the ambulance arrived.'

Caitlin dropped her head forward so her hair covered her face, biting back her frustration. Back then, no one had realised the wheeze she had developed was anything serious, but the exertion of the performance to the song 'A Windmill in Old Amsterdam', including her show-stopping turning triple-time step had been the catalyst that had changed her life. Once she had recovered and a treatment regime had been issued, her parents had told her, with as much gentleness as possible, she could no longer dance and it might be safer for her to step away from performing too.

'Why?' she had sobbed.

'It's too dangerous, Moonbeam,' Miranda had said, hugging her, and Caitlin was banished backstage, where, with Lee, she had gradually worked her way up to stage manager.

'Tell me what this is really about,' said Sindy. 'We've done summer and winter solstice rituals before but never the equinoxes.'

Caitlin sat beside her and stared out over the Golden Valley as it disappeared into the shadows of the autumn twilight. A breeze rustled the remaining leaves on the trees further down the hill, lifting her hair as it danced past, a hint of summer remaining in its breath.

'This is going to sound very strange...' she began.

'We've known each other most of our lives, nothing you say will seem strange,' Sindy replied. 'We've always been odd, it's why we're friends.'

'True,' said Caitlin. 'The Odd Squad – wasn't that what Gilly and Rache called us?'

'Yes, although that's nothing to what we called them,' she replied and they shared a grin of remembrance.

'For the past few months, I've been having intense dreams,' Caitlin confessed, and in a low voice, she described all she had seen of the quest of the three sisters, 'but even more peculiar, in Mum's last boxes of notebooks, which I found shoved in a wardrobe in the spare room when we were clearing Dad's house, there was a story, copied out in Mum's writing, which told the dream in detail.'

'The same dream?' said Sindy.

'Yes, the three sisters on a quest, but with a few variations.'

'You and your mum have shared a dream?' said Sindy but she was curious rather than disbelieving.

'Grandma, too, and women whose names date back to the seventeenth century. I joined a genealogy website and each of these women are my ancestors through Mum's side.'

'That's mad,' said Sindy. 'What do you think it means?'

'I don't know, but that isn't all,' she said.

The first stars twinkled overhead as Caitlin told Sindy about her visions of the woman with the antler headdress, of the way she kept appearing in the dream of the three sisters and of the drawing in Miranda's notebook dated a few days after Caitlin's birth.

'I think I'm being told the same story that has been passed down through the women in my family for centuries but my dreams have taken me further than any of the accounts in Mum's journal.'

'What do you mean?'

'All the other dreams stop in the cherry orchard, but last night, I travelled further,' Caitlin said and described the room and the chanting.

'Can you remember what they said?' asked Sindy.

'Yes, I wrote it down as soon as I woke up.' Reaching into the rucksack she had brought with her, she pulled out a new notebook, which she handed to Sindy.

'"One becomes two; two becomes three; and out of the third comes the fourth, the One. The fourth is the Charmed One who will heal the curse",' Sindy read. '"The triple goddess of the bees cursed you. Three by three by three by three by three, the third daughter of the third daughter of the third daughter from the time of shadows and fear, until one shall come, a youngest child of a youngest child of a youngest child who is both third and fourth. She shall have the power to heal this curse."'

'What do you think it means?' asked Caitlin.

'I have no idea,' she replied. 'Is this why you want to use the henbane?'

'Yes, Mum's notes said it was shamanic and the other woman who I've seen – the one with the headdress – she was a shaman,' said Caitlin.

'Caity, this is dangerous,' warned Sindy. 'Who knows what this tea might do to you. Why are you so determined?'

'From the way the diaries were written, it looks as though the henbane tea recipe has been handed down for centuries,' said Caitlin. 'Mum copied it for a reason and she even wrote about the two of us solving this puzzle together. I believe the women of my family are connected to this curse. In the past few years, my family has fallen apart and I want to repair it. This might be the way to heal thousands of years of pain, to break the curse and to stop my family tearing itself apart any further. Please, Sindy, you have to help me.' Caitlin's voice quavered as she finished speaking, her eyes wide with despair.

Sindy stared out over the valley, it had disappeared into the creeping night, with only lights from houses and cars on the distant road flashing like fairy magic in the blackness.

'There is one condition,' Sindy said.

'What?'

'We call Lee,' Sindy replied. 'If you're planning to put yourself in a trance, I want a doctor nearby in case I can't revive you. Otherwise, I'm going home.'

With great reluctance, Caitlin nodded and Sindy reached into her pocket for her phone.

29

GOLDENWYCH, PRESENT DAY

The moon had risen – *the singing moon*, thought Caitlin – by the time Lee arrived. Caitlin glared at him when he said, 'Are you sure this is safe?'

'Mum used it,' she replied.

'Did she?' he asked.

'There was no warning not to use it,' Caitlin retorted.

The hurt in Lee's eyes made her feel wretched but she would not allow anything to stop her. Ever since her argument with Lee, she had felt twitchy, unsettled. A feeling that was exacerbated when, earlier in the evening, Stan had sent her a picture of himself wearing a Newcastle United scarf and not much else. She had blocked him but with her confusing and heightened emotions towards both men overwhelming her, she felt as though the world was closing in and she needed to escape.

'There's a tiny amount of henbane,' Caitlin said in a conciliatory tone. 'It can't be dangerous.'

'Nothing we say could dissuade you?' asked Lee, pointing between himself and Sindy.

Caitlin shook her head.

'Come on then,' he said in a resigned tone. 'Let's do this. Do I have to wear robes and chant?'

Caitlin smiled, despite herself. Lee's joke meant their row was forgiven and forgotten.

'It's your choice, as is painting yourself blue with woad,' she said.

'Wasn't it emulsion we daubed ourselves with when we were children?' asked Sindy.

'Yes, and our mothers weren't sure whether to laugh or be angry,' he said.

Caitlin looked at her two best friends. 'Thank you,' she said. 'I'll light the candles.'

They flickered in the gentle breeze as Caitlin stood in the centre of the circle she had created in front of the Three Sisters. The stones bore silent witness as she bowed first to them, then to the west, where she placed an aquamarine.

'This is to expose spiritual truths and increase psychic powers during the dream-state,' she intoned, before turning to bow again, this time to the east. 'I place amethyst for protection and spiritual healing. To the south, I place citrine to protect against nightmares, and to the north, I place tiger's eye to create order and harmony.'

She sat cross-legged in the centre of the circle and Sindy stepped forward with a pottery goblet that Miranda had owned since the 1980s.

'Good luck,' she whispered.

'It might be a tea, nothing more,' Caitlin replied, wondering whether she was reassuring herself or her friends.

'Travel safely,' said Lee, his face more serious than Caitlin had ever seen. 'I have a defibrillator and oxygen in the car.'

Unsure whether he meant this, she did not know how to respond. Instead, she focused on the goblet, pushing away Lee's obvious agitation. She lifted the vessel to her lips and inhaled. The scent of honey pervaded but underneath were the earthy notes of sage and rosemary and a sweeter smell: the henbane. Caitlin closed her eyes and swallowed the draught in one gulp. She placed the cup on the floor, put her hands on her knees with her palms upwards as she had learned when she had once attended yoga classes and waited.

Nothing's happening, she thought, as she listened to the wind, the rustling of the trees, the gentle sounds of the equinox, flooded with disappointment. *It's a tea, nothing more.*

Above her, a rook cawed, then she felt a heaviness on her shoulder and the pincer-like grip of its claws as the bird landed. It crowed again and, with a rush, opened its broad wings, lifting her into the darkness.

Caitlin felt weightless as they flew upwards towards the stars. She opened her eyes and saw colours streaming past, every shade imaginable and thousands more, sparkling with light, passing through her, around her, she was the colour, they were her, as the rook lifted her higher and higher. The desire to scream in elation was impossible to resist, to laugh, to shout. She felt connected to everything, her body dissolving into light as she flew at supernatural speeds, twirling, tumbling, flashing past stars, planets, galaxy after galaxy until she realised they were slowing and, in a rush of brilliant white light, they landed.

She was standing in an Iron Age hill fort, the stone circle she knew so well in its tumbled form lay a few metres away, pristine and complete, but the rook squeezed her shoulder, turning her towards the centre of the oppidum. An altar had been built and a woman with long white-blonde hair was shrieking a devastating curse. Caitlin screamed along with the surrounding crowd as the woman swallowed poison and fell dead to the ground, rushing forward to help, but as she moved, the rook whirled her away.

They travelled on again and again as the snippets, the flashes and the shadowy glimpses of the woman with the antler headdress formed into a full and coherent story. She heard the woman's name at last and those of her sisters, but what shocked her was the resemblance of Goneril to Gillian and Regan to Rachel as Cordelia was her double.

Finally, they stopped and all around her was brilliant sparkling light, then her chest constricted and she struggled to breathe. Colours whirled around her, the rook cawed and then she saw her – Cordelia Leardohtor – staring at her across the void. Tears ran down the woman's face but Caitlin's vision cleared. She reached out to Cordelia, who took her outstretched hands, joining them across time.

'Help me,' Caitlin gasped.

Cordelia stared down at the woman's hands and arms and saw the silver lines.

'Yes,' she whispered. 'We shall help each other. Breathe with me, breathe.'

Caitlin's lungs released and she was able to take gulps of fresh clean air.

'Where are we?' Caitlin asked.

'We're in the Everywhen,' Cordelia replied. 'Your shamanic powers must be strong, I have seen you here many times.'

'Are you Cordelia Leardohtor?' asked Caitlin.

'Yes, what's your name?'

'Caitlin Kingdohtor,' she replied, unsure why she had changed her surname, yet it felt right.

Cordelia considered her, then a wise smile spread across her face.

'You are the Charmed One,' said Cordelia. 'I see it with such clear vision, the truth is blinding in its brilliance. You are the third and the fourth, the Charmed One to save us all.'

Cordelia smiled again and vanished.

30

GOLDENWYCH, PRESENT DAY

'King Lear, king of the Britons,' she murmured as she awoke.

'What?' Lee's voice was incredulous, there was also a tremble of anger, which Caitlin knew was disguising his fear.

'King Lear, it's why Dad wanted to call me Cordelia,' she said, her voice slurred.

'Lee, what's wrong with her?' said Sindy.

Caitlin heard the caw of the rook and saw herself bowing to the bird, who gave a nod in return before he flew away. As the bird vanished, her eyes sprang open and she was back in the stone circle with Lee and Sindy on either side of her, torches directed at her face.

'Stop it,' she said, holding up her hand to deflect the glare. 'This is like being interrogated.'

'You were talking during your trance,' said Sindy, white-faced and terrified.

'King Lear,' said Caitlin again.

She was beaming and felt as though she had been imbued with a huge blast of energy.

'Come on,' she urged, springing to her feet and collecting the four crystals. 'Let's clear up and then we'll go back to mine, I have so much to tell you.'

'How do you feel?' asked Lee, reaching for her arm to take her pulse.

'Amazing,' she said, laughing with delight as she shook him off. 'Truly, I've never felt better. I want to sing, dance, shout with joy.'

'Is this the henbane?' she heard Sindy ask Lee as Caitlin blew out the candles.

'Perhaps,' he replied. 'I don't know anything about the effects of henbane.'

'Do you think it's addictive?'

'Will the two of you stop panicking?' called Caitlin. 'I feel great.'

* * *

Half an hour later, they were in Caitlin's cottage and her euphoria had dimmed but her heart was at peace. As instructed by Lee, she was sitting in her favourite armchair while he made hot chocolate and toast. Sindy had offered to cook but he had despatched her to sit with Caitlin.

'Shout if her breathing changes,' he had said.

Caitlin scribbled in the notebook she had shown Sindy earlier, capturing all she could remember, hopeful the act of writing would help her to understand the things she had been shown. Sindy sat in silence, watching her. When Lee arrived with a tray, Caitlin could sense Sindy's relief at no longer being responsible. Caitlin continued to make notes but Lee forced a plate of toast into her hands.

'Eat this,' he said.

'I need to write it all down,' she protested.

Not of all it made sense yet, she did not understand where the dream of the three sisters slotted into the story but she knew this knowledge would come when it was necessary.

'Perhaps you could describe it and we could record it for you to transcribe later,' suggested Sindy.

'Excellent idea,' said Lee. 'Shall we use your phone or mine, Moon?'

Caitlin stared at the implacable faces of her friends. 'Mine,' she said. She placed it on the arm of her chair and opened the voice note app. 'It's difficult to know where to start,' Caitlin said, biting the buttery toast. 'Lee, you make the best toast.'

'Thank you,' he said, 'but don't change the subject. When you were coming out of the trance, you said, "King Lear, it's why Dad wanted to call me Cordelia".'

'He did, but Mum didn't like it,' mused Caitlin. 'She thought the name was cursed. Perhaps she was right to fear it.'

'Tell us,' said Lee. 'No matter how bizarre, tell us what you saw.'

Caitlin took another bite of her toast and sipped her hot chocolate. When she had been in the Everywhen with the rook and henbane to guide her, the images had seemed logical, normal, but trying to express the peculiarity of her experience, coupled with her utter certainty that all she had seen was true, made her realise the limitations of language; even as she framed the sentences in her own mind, they sounded odd, but she owed it to Lee and Sindy to at least try to give a coherent explanation. She took a deep breath and began.

'For the past few months, ever since Dad had his TIA, I've been having strange dreams about three women on a quest,' she said, 'but I've also been seeing another woman too. At the hospital, Lee, do you remember? You all assumed I'd fallen asleep and dreamed her but I was certain I hadn't and then I found this.'

She moved to her bookcase and withdrew Miranda's sketch of the *genius loci*.

'Look at the date,' she said to Lee, whose eyes widened in surprise. 'This was the woman I saw in the hospital, but Mum claims she saw her, too, a few days after I was born. Mum also said she saw her when we viewed the cottage for the first time.'

'It's certainly strange,' admitted Lee.

'Who do you think this woman is?' asked Sindy.

'I think she's the real Cordelia from the *King Lear* story,' said Caitlin, 'and that the women of my family have a connection to the sisters in the original legend.'

There was an uneasy silence and Caitlin realised how ludicrous it sounded. Nevertheless, in her soul, she knew it to be true.

'How is that possible?' said Sindy. 'It's a story written by William Shakespeare.'

'I know,' said Caitlin, 'but it's based on what I now know is a real story.'

She explained to Sindy all she had told Lee about her research into the origins of the Lear story.

'Geoffrey of Monmouth claimed his information about the early history of Britain had been supplied by his friend Walter, who was the archdeacon of Oxford,' she finished. 'He said Walter had given him "a certain very ancient book written in the British language". It had been brought to him from outside the country and Geoffrey translated it into Latin. It's thought this book originated in Brittany. Unfortunately, other scholars have dismissed the idea of the manuscript because it isn't cited by any other writer of this period.'

'You mean Geoffrey made it up?' said Lee.

'This is the assumption but I know differently,' she replied.

'How?' asked Sindy.

'I saw the book while I was in what Cordelia called the Everywhen,' Caitlin answered.

'The where?' said Sindy.

'It's a plane between worlds,' said Lee. 'Many ancient people believe shamans can access the Everywhen. It's the place where healing occurs. I read about it when I was at university. Healing takes place on many levels and I wanted to learn as much as I could about how to cure people.'

Caitlin and Sindy gave him a surprised look but he shrugged and crunched his toast noisily in defiant response. Caitlin and Sindy grinned.

'The henbane tea took me to the Everywhen tonight,' Caitlin continued, 'and as I travelled, I saw the book of history being given to Cordelia by her teacher, Spaden the Gaul. She commissioned a scribe to write the tale of her family when she helped her father retake his throne.'

'When would this have been?' asked Lee.

'The late Iron Age, the 800s BCE,' said Caitlin. 'I looked it all up a while ago.'

'But there was no writing back then,' said Sindy. 'How could there be books?'

'We don't have any remaining records of scrolls or words but there must have been some form of written communication. There are runes carved on stones from not much later and remember, Lee, what we saw at the Heraklion Museum last year?'

'When we went to stay with your friends Eloise and Claud in Crete for baby Alice's christening?' said Lee. 'You were godmother.'

'Yes, and in the museum, there's information and examples of two distinct styles of writing from the Minoan period – Linear A and Linear B. It isn't writing as we recognise it but it was a written form of record keeping.'

'Were the Minoans earlier than the Iron Age?' asked Sindy.

'Yes, they were Bronze Age, which is before the Iron Age,' said Caitlin. 'Egyptian hieroglyphics go back millennia and, despite the fact the Romans have always portrayed the ancient Britons as savages, there have been so many archaeological finds that dismiss the idea. In the Iron Age, people lived in organised homesteads, hill forts or oppida. They farmed, they were a structured society with religion and burial customs. There must have been some form of written word for all that to be possible. Who's to say the carvings on the stone circle aren't some form of ancient language?'

Sindy and Lee were quiet as they absorbed these ideas.

'When you put it like that, it's logical,' said Lee. 'Arthur Evans, the man who excavated in Crete and discovered the lost palace at Knossos, was of the same mind, remember? He didn't believe it was possible for the Minoans to achieve such success without some form of writing.'

'Yes, and it was his belief that led him to discover Linear A and Linear B,' Caitlin recalled. 'It's probable there was a similar writing system in Britain, too, which is how Spaden was able to give Cordelia the history book.'

Caitlin finished her toast and placed the plate on the coffee table. Lee held up the jug of hot chocolate and she passed her mug to be refilled, Sindy did the same, with Lee draining the final drops from the jug into his own cup.

'Caity, I'm not doubting you,' said Sindy, as she settled back into the cushions on the sofa, 'but why do you think the woman is the real Cordelia?'

'She told me her name,' replied Caitlin, 'and I saw her sisters, Goneril and Regan.'

'What?' said Lee. 'Where were they?'

'At the hill fort, which was near here in Goldenwych.'

'How can you possibly know?' asked Sindy.

'I recognised the stone circle with the Three Sister stones,' replied Caitlin and her excitement buzzed through her again. 'Even more eerie, Cordelia looks like me, Goneril is Gillian's double and Regan is like Rachel.'

'Did you know the "wych" part of Goldenwych is the Old English word for settlement?' mused Sindy.

'Really?' said Caitlin.

'Yes, Gran told me, so the village name means Golden Settlement,' said Sindy.

An astonished silence fell between the three friends.

'They were definitely here, then, where we are now,' said Caitlin in excitement. 'I saw it all: the sisters, the hill fort and even the moment when everything changed. In the past, Lear had a terrible accident. The tribe was reinforcing their security by placing sharpened sticks around the hill fort. They pointed outwards to deter raiders but Lear slipped and one sliced though his cheek and came out through the top of his head.'

'Gross,' said Sindy, wincing. 'Did it kill him?'

'No, but after he recovered, his personality had changed and this was when he forced his daughters to marry and promised to give a share of his kingdom to whichever one of them had a son first. It also explains the cause of his madness; I'd always thought it was dementia.'

'You diagnosed an illness to a character in a play?' said Lee in disbelief.

'Not consciously,' said Caitlin, 'but when I was reading the Monmouth version, I wondered what could have caused a previously reliable and trustworthy king to have such a change of direction.'

'Phineas Gage,' said Lee, and Caitlin nodded.

'Who?' asked Sindy.

Caitlin gazed at her mother's drawing of Cordelia, while Lee explained the American Crowbar case to Sindy.

'This is almost too much,' Sindy said when Lee had finished.

'You said you'd also been dreaming about three women on a quest too,' said Lee. 'Were they Goneril, Regan and Cordelia?'

'No,' replied Caitlin, looking away from the eerily accurate drawing, her focus back on her trip to the Everywhen. 'They're similar but the tale feels more Arthurian, there are castles, knights, armour and a macabre jester figure who's controlling events.'

Caitlin explained to Lee all she had told Sindy earlier about the diaries, showing them both her mother's sketches of the three women and their world. When she explained the story had been recorded in her mother's notebooks too by the women of her maternal line dating back to 1687, they were stunned.

'There isn't enough data to check each one definitively but from the information available over two-thirds of them are the third daughter of a third daughter.'

There was an uneasy silence.

'You heard a chant, didn't you?' said Sindy.

'Yes,' said Caitlin, turning to the first page of the notebook and reading aloud, '"One becomes two; two becomes three; and out of the third comes the fourth, the One. The fourth is the Charmed One who will heal the curse. The triple goddess of the bees cursed you. Three by three by three by three by three, the third daughter of the third daughter of the third daughter from the time of shadows and fear, until one shall come, a youngest child of a youngest child of a youngest child who is both third and fourth. She shall have the power to heal this curse."'

Lee stared at her in astonishment. 'Are you sure?' he said.

'Yes, why?'

'The first line is a well-known phrase from psychology and is known as the Axiom of Maria,' he said.

'The what?' asked Caitlin.

'I need a drink,' groaned Sindy. 'One that's stronger than hot chocolate.'

She walked into the kitchen and returned with a bottle of red wine and three glasses.

'Do you mind?' she asked Caitlin.

'Pour away,' Caitlin replied. 'Why do you know about the...?' She looked at Lee questioningly.

'The Axiom of Maria,' said Lee. 'You know my original plan was to become a psychiatrist, well, I came across it while I was studying. Let me find it online because it's quite complex and I want to make sure we know all the facts.' He opened his phone and after a few seconds tapping, he said, 'Here, it says this phrase was attributed to the third-century alchemist Maria Prophetissa, who is thought to be the sister of Moses.'

'I didn't know Moses had a sister,' said Sindy.

'It's because you never paid attention at Sunday school,' said Lee.

'It's because we never went,' replied Caitlin and they all laughed.

'I was interested in the work of Swiss psychiatrist, Carl Jung,' continued Lee, 'and there's an alternative version of the axiom written by Marie-Louise von Franz who worked with Jung.' Lee looked at his phone again. 'Here it is, it's a bit different,' he said and read, '"Out of the One comes Two, out of the

Two comes Three, and from the Third comes the One as the Fourth." Jung used the axiom as a metaphor for the process of individuation.'

'This is almost too much for me,' said Sindy, 'but I'm going to ask, what's individuation?'

'It's the process where an individual becomes distinct from other things,' Lee explained. 'The trinity, the number three, was always proposed by philosophers and psychologists as being the perfect number but Jung believed that rather than three being the most important number for the psychological development of Western humanity, it was four. He wrote an essay called *The Problem of the Fourth*. In it, he mentioned the works of Plato, who agreed with this theory and suggested the number four was vital to what he referred to as the "World-Soul".'

'The what?' asked Caitlin.

'Plato believed the World-Soul comprised the Same, the Different and the Mixture. It was the word mixture that intrigued Jung, so he suggested the psyche was in fact made up of thinking, sensing, feeling and intuiting. He believed each person has a dominant function, which is supported by two auxiliary functions, while the fourth function remains inferior and is often repressed. We think, sense and feel with intention, but the skill of intuition is less trusted by humans, therefore, it becomes the fourth, the shadow function.'

Lee drained his glass of wine.

'Jung said intuition is the most underdeveloped function?' said Caitlin, phrasing it as a question, her mind whirring, and Lee nodded. 'He was right. All I've seen and learned tonight is through intuition but even now we're unsure whether what I experienced was real or in my imagination because we don't trust the shadow function.'

'True,' said Lee. 'In your chant, there was also that line, "out of the third comes the fourth, the One", which points towards a theory called Quaternity, the square, rather than three, the trinity,' he continued and Sindy gave a small groan, squashing herself into the cushions and curling up on the sofa as though protecting herself from the verbal and mental onslaught.

Caitlin barely noticed, all her attention was focused on Lee. His words were helping her to untangle the web of stories.

'Did he say anything else about Quaternity?' she asked.

'I can't remember exactly,' said Lee. He fiddled with his phone again.

'Here it is, the definition of quaternity is a group of four things or people, with three males plus a female fourth or three females with a male fourth.'

Caitlin's eyes were wide with shock. 'Three females and a male,' she whispered. 'Like Lear and his daughters, like us.'

'Even more intriguing,' said Lee, turning his phone to show Caitlin an image of a red leather book, 'is a chapter in Jung's *The Red Book, Liber Novus*, which was an exploration of his own mental health and is entitled *The Castle in the Forest.*'

'Please don't tell me it was about three sisters,' said Caitlin, a feeling of dread swooping through her.

'No, it was about a traveller who stumbled across a castle in a dark forest and was given hospitality overnight by its scholarly owner. The daughter of the scholar visited Jung during the night asking for help as her father was holding her there. The Jung in the story fell in love with her. The remainder of the chapter discusses the meaning of this imagery.'

'And what did it mean?'

'It was about facing your own personal hell,' said Lee.

31

THE TALE OF THE THREE SISTERS

Every inch of his skin was covered in livid scars, ugly wheals and deep, purple-tinged pock marks. Red, suppurating sores glistened, following the silver scar lines which wound sinuously around his arms, flowing outwards and downwards to cover his entire body. The marks created a map of his pain, scored into his flesh over millennia, each a tribute to his punishment. The devastation wrought across his body, the extreme and terrible damage to his face, limbs and torso were of such cruel and heinous disfigurement, it was difficult to discern the possibility that this mound of flesh had once been a living, vital man. His eyes were closed but his chest fluttered; he was alive.

'What have you done to him?' said The Queen and there was an authority in her tone her sisters had long since forgotten.

'Me?' said the man. 'I have done nothing. You have caused this, you and every other person who has ever experienced love.'

'Love?' exclaimed The Baroness. 'This is not love. What do you know of love?'

'I know it takes many forms,' sneered the man. 'Where does your heart lead you, Baroness?'

'Love is the tale that defines us,' said The Princess, her calm, cold voice cutting across the conversation before the man could taunt her sisters any further. 'Love shapes our destiny, it sets us free, but its intensity can hold us as prisoners in the darkest parts of our mind.'

'Who would have thought you would be so wise, Princess?' said the man. 'Shall I tell you a tale?'

'No,' the voice from the bed was withered, grating, a rasping sound from the gates of Hell. 'Leave, do not listen to him. He is the lie.'

The three sisters moved a step closer together.

'Father?' said The Queen.

'Leave,' he implored.

'Or listen,' said the man, 'and discover the way to end your quest.'

The three women paused.

'Do you think he knows?' whispered The Queen.

'He might,' said The Baroness.

'He might not,' said The Princess.

They exchanged a confused look. Each woman remembered, they had experienced this before, thousands and thousands of times. One answer would free them, one would send them back around the white path to the gates.

A shimmer of light filled the room and, as it did, The Queen and The Baroness stepped forward, their eyes glazed. The Princess made to follow, then she saw the women, a fleeting blur as they spun around her, whispering the word 'No', imploring her, their eyes wide with compassion, before vanishing in a swirl of light. Her mind cleared and she felt the power and positivity of true love flow through her, giving her the strength to save them all.

'We shall hear your story,' said The Queen and The Baroness.

'You chose well,' said the man and clapped his hands in glee, 'and you, Princess?'

'No,' said The Princess.

'No?' The man turned to her in fury.

'No,' she said. 'We are the story, we are the tale and, if you begin, we shall be back on our horses, riding the white path to Hell.'

'Who told you this secret?' screamed the man, his face blurring to reveal his true and hideous visage.

'The women,' she whispered and, before he could speak again, The Princess pulled the blade from her boot.

It glinted, sharp, wicked, quicksilver in the flickering candlelight of the tower room and in an instant, the man lay dead at her feet.

'He is the Keeper of Hell,' she said before either of her sisters could speak. 'He has been spinning us around his maze of despair for thousands of years. His death was the only way to free ourselves.'

'And is this place Hell?' asked The Baroness.

'Not any more,' replied The Princess. 'This place is what we choose, it is where we take control and follow our true paths to love.'

'Do we want love if this is where it leads?' asked The Queen, her eyes upon the man in the bed.

'Love did not cause his agony,' said The Princess, turning to The Queen. 'It is the loss of love, the abuse of love, the denial of love that caused this torment. Love heals, it doesn't destroy.'

'Sorrow caused from a love that society says is forbidden is an incipient pain,' said The Baroness. 'It holds an intensity of despair of such strength, it will absorb the soul, the heart, the very essence of being and leave no room for reason. When denied, the loss of love is a darkness beyond all other, a well of pain so deep it feels like the sharpest blade across the heart. This creature has used our pain against us but called it love.'

They looked at the broken body of the man on the floor with no pity.

'He was the antithesis of love,' said The Queen. 'He was its dark twin, the cold night to the daylight of love. When I was alone, fearing death, convinced all love was lost; doom engulfed my senses, flooding every cell of my body with ice-sharp shards of hopelessness, loneliness, fear and regret. I was helpless, maddened by my belief that all happiness was lost forever. I was convinced I would never again feel joy or laughter, never feel the beauty of loving another, nor experience the alchemical reaction of love as it sends each soul soaring to the stars. Now, I feel hope again.'

'The scars caused by a broken heart have the longest memories of all,' said The Princess, her eyes drifting towards the figure on the bed as she spoke. 'They are an everlasting legacy because the wounds of the heart never forget how they came into being. The body appears to heal but the scars of love's betrayal, those gossamer lacerations, whisper outwards, infecting the mind, the soul. The slightest irritation, the tiniest disappoint-ment, an insignificant or thoughtless word causes these hibernating scars to glow, red and angry, smarting, splitting, rearing up, fearsome beasts, roaring with anger to weep blood forever.'

'He has absorbed eternity's pain,' said The Queen.

'Every broken heart has been his to endure,' said The Baroness.

'He has given away his hope,' said The Princess.

'What shall we do?' asked The Queen.

'We will save him,' answered The Baroness.

'How?' asked The Queen.

'With love,' replied The Princess. 'The answer is always love.'

32

BRITAIN, 861 BCE

The journey was long and arduous, but they rode abreast, Aganippus, Cordelia and Lear. Behind came Lagon and Locrinus, who had refused to remain in Gallia alone. Each day, they heard new rumours, stories of death, destruction and the never-ending malaise of the once prosperous land. Behind them snaked an army: men, horses, carts, cutting a swathe from Gallia to Dobvnni. At Belgae, they were welcomed by Kerin and Margan, they had heard of the destruction of Lear's lands by his son-in-law Maglaurus and agreed to join them.

'Once this land was united under your rule,' Kerin said to Lear. 'We will bring peace again by removing the tyrant who governs for no benefit other than his desire to wield power.'

As they travelled, more and more people attached themselves to the train, all wishing for a return to peace, to the thriving way of life they had enjoyed before the darkness of Lear's madness had cursed the land. Cordelia made no comment when the tales of cruelty and torture were delivered by eyewitnesses. She could not equate the monstrous behaviour with either of her sisters, yet the stories arrived on a daily basis.

'Queen Goneril presides over daily executions...'

'Lady Regan plots to remove her sister from power. They fight like she-wolves, torturing all who oppose them...'

'Henwinus has become cruel, punishing people for strange and mysterious

crimes, which he refuses to reveal. It is another way to terrify the Dobvnni into obeying his twisted laws...'

'Maglaurus has desecrated the stone circle, ordering men to topple the stones and destroy the power of the unbroken ring...'

The final story had roused anger in Cordelia. Stone circles were sacred, the protection of their magic was drawn from the completeness of the eternal boundary, to break this was to lose the favour of the goddesses and gods. It was an act of terrible destruction, the highest insult to the sanctity of the deities, and Cordelia knew there would be a reckoning.

'Has there not been enough damage committed?' she had murmured to Aganippus when they were curled up in the darkness. 'Why desecrate the circle?'

'Foolish men like Maglaurus believe this shows he has power beyond that of even the goddesses and god,' he had replied. 'When, in fact, it uncovers his weakness and fear.'

Each night, as she lay beside Aganippus, her eyes would become wet with grief as she relived her carefree childhood and its tragic loss. She saw them: herself, Goneril and Regan, the three daughters of Lear Bladudsunu, as they had been at the solstice during the last Litha celebrations, dancing with fire, flirting with the suitors, happy and excited about the adventures of life before them. She had hoped her dark visions had been wrong but the Everywhen had, once again, proven itself to be correct. There was darkness and despair and again the image of her father with his sword raised above her flashed across her mind making her shudder.

Angarad might have directed her curse at my father, thought Cordelia, *but we have all been equally damned.*

Finally, they arrived at Credenhill, the homestead of her uncle, Kamber Bladudsunu, her father's younger brother. His oppidum was further down the valley, but his land bordered the Golden Dobvnni settlement. The huge following army spread out across the landscape, encampments were set up and, as dusk fell, the glow of cooking fires twinkled in the gathering gloom, disappearing towards the horizon.

Cordelia shivered as she looked across the Golden Valley to the hill fort she had always called home. Beacons burned at regular positions along the fence, illuminating the fierce, sharpened wood that had been hammered into the ground as a defence, a bristling collar of pain around the walls where once it had been renowned as a place of safety.

'The bees,' Cordelia said to Aganippus as they entered her uncle's roundhouse. 'I wonder what happened to the bees.'

'Why would you ask such a question?' he said.

'The hives were an important part of our worship, as well as an integral part of our healing. Honey protects on many levels, as well as tasting delicious,' she said. 'I hope the bees survived the carnage or they, too, may add their contempt to Angarad's curse.'

'The bees are safe,' came a voice from the shadows at the edge of the central gathering space.

Cordelia spun around and uttered a cry of delight as Gloigin stepped forward, her arms wide with welcome.

'Gloigin!' Cordelia exclaimed, throwing her arms around the younger woman and hugging her tightly. 'You're safe. Ignogin and Oudar?'

'Both safe, too,' said Gloigin with shining eyes.

'May the goddess be praised,' said Cordelia. 'Tell me all. Your escape, was it smooth? Were you followed?'

'No, our journey was guided by the goddesses themselves, Corycia, Kleodora, Melaina, the Bee Maidens Three,' she said. 'Once we had left the fort, we hid in the woods for a week to ensure no trackers had been sent to force us to return. Oudar found wild honey for us along the way and the bees led us to Credenhill. Lord Kamber himself gave us beini and has made us part of the community.'

'This is wonderful news,' said Cordelia.

'How is Becuma?' asked Gloigin.

'Well and happy. She is married to Buel, the trusted second-in-command and friend of Aganippus. She is with child or she would have accompanied me,' said Cordelia. 'But the bees? Becuma will wish to know they are safe.'

'Kamber has been impressed by Oudar's healing skills and, at her request, he sent a raiding party to save the hives,' said Gloigin. 'We weren't convinced it would work. Oudar accompanied them and Ignogin and I believe the bees must have sensed her presence. They flew in a magnificent swarm to the camp in the woods where Kamber's men were based, then they followed Oudar here from the Golden Fort. It was astonishing to behold.'

'This is truly magical,' said Cordelia. 'May the goddesses be praised. What's your status here? Have you taken a place in their temple?'

'The temple here is led by Caius, a Druid of great learning, but he favours the rule of Taranis, the wielder of the thunderbolt and hammer, the father of the three gods of Dana. Goddess worship takes place in the women's quarters and we often participate, but there are no high priestesses in this oppidum,' she explained. 'Instead, I'm betrothed to the blacksmith, Rud. He's a kind man and when he proposed, my heart assured me this was the correct path.'

'Our futures haven't been as we imagined when we were high priestesses,' said Cordelia. 'I've found more happiness in my marriage than I expected and we have a daughter, Nest.'

The two women continued to exchange news while the men gathered around the fire to discuss strategies. When the drums sounded to summon them to eat, Cordelia took her place at the head of the benches, summoning the other women to join her. As Queen of Gallia, she was the highest-ranking woman in the hill fort, a position she was beginning to understand and use to its best advantage. She placed Margan, her mother-in-law, on one side, ensuring Gloigin was on her other. Oudar joined them and Cordelia thought she would burst with happiness and relief when she saw their smiling faces.

'Where is Ignogin?' asked Cordelia.

'She left after the Hunter's Moon,' said Oudar. 'She and two other women heard the call of the goddess and have departed for the Sanctuary of the Moon Sisters in Demetae. It's an all-female Druid encampment, they pray for peace to the moon and the stars, their desire is to spread love.'

Cordelia stared at Oudar in surprise. 'Of us all, I believed Ignogin was the least interested in the worship of the goddess,' she said. 'You must miss her, Gloigin.'

'We're twins,' said Gloigin. 'She is forever in my heart.'

Once the food was served and the conversation was loud enough to disguise her words, Cordelia whispered to Gloigin and Oudar, 'What news of Goneril and Regan? I have heard tales of darkness but struggle to believe my sisters could be guilty of such malefic crimes.'

Gloigin sipped her mead, her brown eyes clouding.

'There are many stories,' she said. 'Kamber has spies within the Golden

Dobvnni, including Rud's nephew, Sisillius, and Rud has told me of his discoveries. After Maglaurus blinded Locrinus, Goneril helped him and Lagon escape. I think this could have been a turning point for her, a return to reason and truth, but Regan and Henwinus returned and it wasn't long before she was lost.'

'What happened?' asked Cordelia.

'They had heard the stories of unrest under Maglaurus and Goneril's reign and Henwinus was determined to have Regan's share of wealth from the hill fort. For a short period, Maglaurus was generous and they ruled together, although they were disorganised. The summer was wet and, because of their mismanagement, the Dobvnni crops failed. Maglaurus blamed the gods but it was due to his refusal to allow the farmers to tend the fields, preferring instead to drill them as soldiers. When they were finally released, the plants had rotted in the ground.

'Our crop was good, perhaps not as bountiful as in other summers and Kamber gave them as much as we could spare. Soon after, smaller settlements in the area became victim to vicious raiding parties hunting for food. They were brutal, burning roundhouses, taking hostages and killing all who tried to stop them. Word came to us that Goneril and Regan were behind the plan.'

'They would know the strengths and weaknesses of the smaller forts,' said Cordelia, 'we visited them regularly when we were younger. Perhaps they gave the information to their husbands but it sickens me to think either of my sisters would be barbaric enough to authorise such bloodshed.'

'You have been gone a turn of the year, Cordelia, and much has altered. Goneril has yet to conceive a child and every moon when she fails, her bitterness increases. When Regan carried a baby, Goneril's spite and fury intensified but after Regan lost her daughter, her temperament became worse than Goneril's,' said Gloigin. 'She was pitiless. I believe they are under Angarad's curse.'

'Tell her the rest,' murmured Oudar.

'There is more?' said Cordelia, her heart sinking lower.

'Sisillius and his men have sent word that Regan has taken a lover,' said Gloigin and her voice was sorrowful. 'She flaunts him before Henwinus and has been heard saying she will raise her lover to the high position her husband holds. It is driving Henwinus to distraction and he has threatened to murder both Regan and her lover.'

'Who is the man?'

'Ivor Locrinussunu,' said Gloigin.

'Ivor!' Cordelia exclaimed, covering her mouth and looking around to see if her outburst had been overheard but no one was listening. 'Lagon said he and Gael had left and not returned.'

'They came here to Credenhill but after Gael died in childbirth, Ivor returned to Golden Dobvnni,' she said. 'By then, Lagon and Locrinus had escaped.'

'Why?' asked Cordelia.

'Gael's death maddened Ivor, then we heard of Goneril's punishment of Locrinus,' interjected Oudar. 'We believe he wished to revenge himself upon Goneril for her treatment of his father and he is using Regan to torment her.'

'What do you mean?'

'Cordelia, did you never notice? Goneril and Ivor had been lovers since they were sixteen summers old,' said Gloigin. 'He wanted to marry her but she refused; she wanted a rich husband.'

'How did I not know this?'

'You were young, your priority was the temple,' said Oudar. 'Once your powers showed, we tried to protect you from external influences. Angarad claimed it was important to keep you pure, this would enable you to inter- pret your visions with clear eyes, rather than those occluded with worldly woes.'

'Did Lagon know?' she asked.

'Of course but he was always too busy swooning after you to care,' Gloigin said.

'Lagon?' said Cordelia in astonishment.

'Even you in your innocence must have noticed,' said Ignogin.

'No,' admitted Cordelia. 'I had no idea.'

Gloigin laughed. 'Sweet Cordelia, you have always been the kindest of us.'

A draught caused the candle to flicker and a shadow fell across Gloigin's face. As it did, Cordelia had a vision of her friend when she was older, her features strong and more beautiful but with sun-lined skin, the bloom of youth replaced by the softness of middle age and, in a heartbeat, Cordelia understood. Gloigin, her twin sister, Ignogin, and Oudar, they were the shadow daughters of Lear. The dream of the three sisters' quest she had shared with the woman, Caitlin, was the world that might have been, the other path, the other daughters if she and her sisters had died while they were young. Understanding flooded her with such force, she pushed herself away from the table.

'Cordelia, are you well?' asked Gloigin.

'The man, he is Fa,' she said. 'In the Everywhen, you are his daughters, are you not?'

Gloigin stared at Cordelia in surprise.

'You are my sister?' Cordelia whispered, demanding confirmation with her tone.

'Yes,' replied Gloigin. 'It was after your mother died, leaving no living male heir, your father invoked the Golden Dobvnni creed of the Shadow Wives: a woman to share his bed for a year and a day in an attempt to bear a boy child. My mother, Anor, was sent from Kamber's court to your father's. She was the first Shadow Wife but when she gave birth to twin girls, she was sent home and we were raised in the temple by Angarad and the Mother of the Temple before her, Medlan.'

'And Oudar?'

'Her mother was your father's second Shadow Wife, Galaes,' said Gloigin. 'She died when Oudar was less than one summer old. After this, your father refused another Shadow Wife. Before his plan to wed Angarad, whenever marriage was suggested he said, he could not risk any more daughters.'

'Does he know you're his children?'

'Of course,' she said. 'It's why we were kept at the oppidum. We were there in case you or your sisters died. We were your shadows, to step forward into the light if we were required.'

Cordelia stared at Gloigin, shocked at her matter-of-fact tone.

'Did you resent me and my sisters?' she asked.

'No,' replied Gloigin. 'We were well treated, we were happy and, above all, while your father lived and was in his right mind, we were safe.'

'Angarad's curse, she claimed he would suffer all the pain from lost love.

I have seen you all in the Everywhen. You were the second part of the curse,' she said. 'You, Ignogin and Oudar were on an endless quest for love.'

'You have seen us in the Everywhen?' said Gloigin, her eyes alight with curiosity.

'Yes, but I didn't realise until now,' she said. 'You save Fa.'

'We do?'

The words of the chant returned. *The fourth is the Charmed One who will heal the curse.* 'You are the fourth daughter of Lear, perhaps you are the answer to the entire curse.'

'No, Cordelia,' said Gloigin, 'Angarad said the one who could break the curse was the third daughter of a third daughter. My mother is the eldest and has three brothers.'

'Does your mother have any other children?' asked Cordelia.

'No, we are her only offspring.'

Cordelia turned away, the belief she had solved the riddle fading. Angarad's words had been clear and the chanting in her dream had also proclaimed the third was also the fourth.

Perhaps we are doomed to carry this enchantment for eternity, thought Cordelia, then the image of Caitlin, the woman who bore the same silver lines on her skin, flashed through her mind and the small flame of hope burgeoned once again.

33

BRITAIN, 861 BCE

'We move at dawn,' announced Aganippus as he joined Cordelia in the roundhouse they had been allocated by Kamber.

'I shall accompany you,' she said in a tone of such fierceness, Aganippus took a step backwards.

'And if I were to forbid it?' he asked.

'I would ignore you,' she replied.

Aganippus looked anguished. 'The battle will be brutal and the wind is whipping up into a storm,' he said. 'How will I be able to protect you?'

'You won't,' she replied, 'but, equally, how will I protect you?'

'You can't,' he said. 'Cordelia, it will be wet and cold, people will die.'

'Exactly, it's a battle and I will ride beside my husband and my father,' she said. 'Fa trained us to bear arms, but if things become fiercer than my skills warrant, I shall retreat.'

'You promise?'

'Nest will not be an orphan,' she said.

Aganippus stared at her contemplatively. 'You're an extraordinary woman Cordelia Leardohtor.'

'Actually,' she replied, her eyes alight with mischief as she slipped her tunic from her shoulders, 'I am Queen of Gallia and deserve to be treated with the respect such a position deserves.'

He raised his eyebrows in surprise and began unlacing his own tunic before sweeping her into his arms and carrying her to their bed. 'Your majesty, I'll do my best to show you such respect,' he said as she giggled into his shoulder.

Cordelia was glad of the darkness and the distraction of her husband's touch because in her heart was fear at the potential devastation she believed would follow on the battlefield. Each day since they had left Gallia, the vision of her father standing above her, his face full of bloodlust, wielding a sword, had been intensifying. Was this her path? To die at her father's hands? The thought haunted her, but she had to know: were her visions and their interpretation correct or was there more?

Despite the horror of her father's madness, she did not believe he could kill her. Was this the catastrophe that led to the quest in the Everywhen, the terrible shadow path, the second part of Angarad's curse: *As punishment for your disrespect of the feminine, you will bear the greatest of all pain, one of such magnitude your mind will shatter into dust for all eternity.*

Were the souls of Gloigin, Ignogin and Oudar to wander the passages of the spirit plane while their father absorbed the pain of all lost love? Would her death be the beginning of the journey or the end? She was prepared to sacrifice herself if it were to free her sisters, all of them, and their father.

But, she thought, as she curled into Aganippus's arms, *what of Goneril and Regan?* Could they be saved from themselves, from the curse? She was unsure; both had displayed such violence, were they even the same women she remembered?

Cordelia breathed deeply as Angarad had taught her during her early days as a neophyte in the temple, calming her teeming mind, reaching for sleep, but as the darkness enfolded her, her mind slipping into unconsciousness, there was a panicked shout from outside.

'Lear! He's gone!'

The drumbeat echoed through the hill fort as the alarm was raised. Aganippus leapt out of bed, pulling on his tunic and trousers. Cordelia reached for the clothes she had laid out for the battle, a smaller version of the male tunic and trousers, with a heavy leather jerkin to protect her. She pulled on her boots and wound her hair into a plait as she raced after her husband. Voices and confusion rose above the sound of the drum, but when it stopped, the roar of the wind filled the void of silence.

Lagon stood in the centre of the oppidum, supporting his father. They spoke urgently to Kamber, gesticulating towards the narrow passage that led to the back entrance of the fort. People were emerging from roundhouses and the many animal-hide bivouacs scattered around the oppidum. As the crowd grew, each bringing more lights, they created a circle of fire with their flaming torches.

'What's happened?' demanded Aganippus, pushing his way through the gathering crowd towards Lagon and Kamber.

'We are undone!' howled Locrinus in misery. 'Lear's madness has returned.'

Cordelia felt a cold terror grip her heart.

'Tell us!' she demanded, taking Locrinus by the arm.

'We were sitting in the roundhouse, talking about our youth, our children, our loves, then the conversation turned and we ran through the plans for the battle tomorrow, discussing our strategy. We were about to prepare for sleep when he began to sing.'

'To sing?' said Cordelia in bemusement.

'Yes, the words, "Poor Lear, poor Lear, they have taken what is mine and I shall have it returned" over and over again in a low, flat monotone, faster and faster until the words no longer made sense. I tried to speak to him, to soothe his mind, but he became agitated, pacing around the room, then, suddenly, he announced he was tired. The bed creaked and he became quiet. I was relieved and hoped he had fallen asleep. A slumber overcame me, but I awoke with a start and realised there was no sound beside me of breathing. My hearing is more acute since my sight has been taken,' he explained. 'I called for Lagon but when he emerged from his quarters, he discovered our roundhouse was empty. When I believed Lear slept, he had tricked me, he had left.'

Above them, lightning forked the sky and thunder roared, the wind whipped through the trees, the branches rattling like bones and the storm broke over their heads, the rain lashing in icy torrents.

'We must find him!' shouted Cordelia. 'He is a danger to himself.'

Kamber began shouting instructions.

Cordelia caught Aganippus by the hand, called to Lagon and headed for the narrow back entrance to the fort.

'He must have used this exit,' she said. 'He's an old man, he can't have gone far.'

Above and below them, they saw the search parties spreading out in long lines, torches guttering in the deluge, calling his name, travelling further and further from the hill fort.

Cordelia walked the paths behind the hill fort with Aganippus and Lagon, their voices snatched by the cackling wind as they shouted for Lear.

'This is a madness all its own!' Cordelia shouted to her husband as she shook her wet hair from her eyes. 'He will have died from the cold before we find him. Let me reach him in the Everywhen and ask him to show me where he is in this plane.'

'Are you able?' said Aganippus.

'I can try,' she replied and looked around the unfamiliar landscape for a suitable place to enter the Everywhen. 'Over there, the oak tree will offer me sanctuary.'

Cordelia ran towards the small copse around the ancient tree. Its branches, nearly bare from the autumn storms, offered scant protection from the rain.

'What shall we do?' shouted Aganippus over the storm.

'Protect me while I'm walking,' she replied.

'I'll show you,' Lagon said to Aganippus, standing beside Cordelia, his arms outstretched but not touching her, ready to catch her if she fell.

As Cordelia faced the tree, Aganippus took up a position on her other side and Cordelia closed her eyes. She offered a prayer to the mother goddess and to the soul of the oak itself, asking for permission to use it as an entrance to another plane. A whisper of milder air surrounded her and she knew her prayers had been answered. With great reverence, she placed her hands on the roughened trunk.

'With thanks and rejoicing I ask you mighty oak to connect me to the earth. Matronae, the Mother Goddess, hear my prayer. Corycia, Kleodora, Melaina, the Bee Maidens Three, show me the path to my father so I may bring him home safely,' she intoned. 'Show me the way to heal these wounds and save my father and my sisters.'

The howling of the wind ceased and Cordelia saw her rook spirit guide standing before her. The creature blinked twice and bowed before flying down a twisted, wooded path. Cordelia followed and as she rounded a corner, she saw the tree where she stood in the mortal plane. A light glowed, illuminating a track through the woods. It sloped downwards to a clearing, where huge chalky white stones formed a natural ring. Her father strode around the circle, shouting, threatening, waving his sword aloft but Cordelia could see no other person: was her father talking to the stones as though they were people or were there movements in the shadows?

Above her, there was flash of lightning and Cordelia was back in the storm, her clothes sodden, her teeth chattering with cold but her heart determined.

'This way!' she shouted and Aganippus followed, while Lagon shouted to the other searchers.

'Fa!' screamed Cordelia through the storm, outstripping the men as she raced down the slope, swerving branches, jumping over rabbit holes, shouting her father's name, driven by a primal urge to protect, to save. 'Fa, can you hear me?'

All around her, men shouted his name, sheathed swords clanging against axes strung on belts as their owners ran in her wake, the noise resembling a battle.

'There!' Cordelia yelled as the glowing white of the natural stone ring appeared, 'Fa! King Lear!'

She raced into the circle, calling his name.

'Fa, I'm here!' she shouted and he turned, his eyes lucid but livid with fear at the sight of her.

'No!' he screeched. 'Not here, not you, not now! They will kill you.'

He raised his sword and as he did, she skidded, landing on her back in the mud.

'You shall not take her too!' her father screamed and as he raised his sword, she saw the truth.

Maglaurus had been in the shadows behind her and he was running towards her prone figure.

'She is mine!' screamed Lear in a frenzy as he brought down the sword again and again.

Cordelia curled into a ball, waiting for the pain, but none came. Instead, Maglaurus screamed and there was a heavy thud beside her before her father's fingers reached for her.

'Cordelia,' he gasped. 'You live, it is the chance which does redeem all sorrows.'

'Fa, watch out!' she screamed, pulling her father to one side as Henwinus, teeth bared, sword raised, ran from the other side of the stone circle, but before he could reach them, his legs buckled and a sword point erupted through his chest, spraying blood and sinew into the falling rain.

'Leave her!' screamed Aganippus, throwing his full force behind his sword as he cut Henwinus down. 'She is my wife and you will not have her.'

Cordelia pulled her father's trembling body into her arms, then the strong grip of her husband enveloped them both as Aganippus pulled her to her feet. Lagon supported Lear while Aganippus embraced Cordelia.

'My love, my love,' he whispered as he held her so tightly she thought he would squeeze the life from her.

A tentative hand touched her shoulder and Aganippus released her to the battered old man, her father.

'I'm sorry,' he said, tears mixing with blood, mud and rain on his cheeks. 'My love for you never wavered.'

'Nor mine for you,' she whispered as father and daughter embraced.

34

THE TALE OF THE THREE SISTERS

The Queen took charge. As the eldest, she knew it was time to wield her power. She called for servants and ordered them to remove the man's body.

'He is a scourge,' she said.

'He has held each of us in our own private hells for centuries,' said the Lord Chamberlain, looking at the man with contempt.

'His reign is over,' said The Baroness.

'I shall deal with his body,' said a familiar voice and the White Knight stood between The Baroness and the Lord Chamberlain. 'We shall burn him as the sun sets and destroy his power forever.'

'Who was he?' said The Princess.

'He was the personification of despair,' said a voice from the bed. 'He was inhuman, created alongside my curse, an aberration against nature, a shape-shifting creature of evil. He would choose his face to suit his malice.'

'For me, he was a tyrannical master from my past,' said the Lord Chamberlain.

'For me, he was my cruel brother who claimed I was an aberration against nature,' said the White Knight.

'For you, my daughters, he was all the hurt I caused you when I chose your loveless unions for my own gain: my eldest, for you he was me as a younger man when I should have known better, when compassion should have guided my choices. My sweet middle child, for you he was the husband you should never have been forced to marry, and for you, my youngest girl, he was the man you loved, the man I should have allowed you to marry rather than the man who was the richest suitor in the land but with the blackest heart.'

'He is dead, he can no longer spread desolation,' said The Baroness.

The White Knight and the Lord Chamberlain hefted the man from the ground and between them carried his lifeless form away.

'Is your curse ended, Father?' asked The Queen.

'Not quite,' he replied, 'but I am healing; look.'

The Three Sisters moved closer to the bed and saw him lift his thumb from the sheet, followed by each finger in turn until he could raise his arm.

'I haven't been able to move for hundreds of years,' he murmured.

'Your skin is repairing itself, too,' said The Princess. 'The redness is disappearing.'

As the sisters watched, the flesh which had been immobile lumps, wretched with open sores and wheals, scars and lacerations, was smoothing over, the blemishes disappearing before their eyes. The silver lines glowed with healing light before fading from his skin, the map of pain gone forever.

'Is our quest at an end?' asked The Baroness, with hope in her voice.

'If you so choose,' replied their father. 'You have displayed love towards me, even when I did not deserve your compassion. I abandoned each of you to despair and abuse, unhappiness and pain, but you have forgiven me with love.'

'Father, I shall remain here and help rule your kingdom while you recover,' said The Queen. 'It will be done with love.'

'When I die, which will be soon now I am free, as my eldest child, you will inherit my realm.'

'Father, I shall travel with my friend and companion, the White Knight,' said The Baroness. 'We shall return often to spend time with you but our lives and love shall be entwined in a future of our own choosing.'

'I shall await to hear of your adventures,' he said. Then he turned his head and gazed at his youngest daughter. 'To you, I was most cruel. I knew you loved a worthy man, yet for my own greed, I forced you to wed another.'

'My husband, the Prince, is dead,' she said and her two sisters looked at her in surprise.

'How do you know?' asked The Queen.

'The man told me,' she said. 'He believed it would hurt me to have this knowledge. Alas, the man I once loved is also dead.'

'What will you do?' asked The Baroness.

'I shall find love again.'

She smiled, an expression of radiance, hope and belief.

The three sisters joined hands, reaching out to include their father in their circle, and with a whisper on the breeze and the caw of a rook, the castle disappeared into a cloud of brilliant white light.

35

GOLDENWYCH, PRESENT DAY

The bees were preparing for winter. Caitlin used a soft brush to sweep away the tiny bodies of the remaining male bees as they died, their lives complete, their time over. In the past few days, the temperature had dropped and, recognising the signs, Caitlin knew her bees were beginning to cluster in the brood box. They did not hibernate, instead the colony formed a ball around the queen, using their combined body heat to keep her warm and safe. Caitlin remembered her mother saying, 'A cold bee is a dead bee,' when she had first begun helping with the hives.

'What do you mean?' Caitlin had asked.

'Bees are cold-blooded,' Miranda had explained, 'they have no ability to control their internal body temperature and are entirely dependent on the air around them. They survive the cold by clustering together and sharing warmth. To help them, I put extra honey in the hive for them to eat, make sure there's always water nearby so they can use it to dilute the honey and feed themselves. When they've clustered, I wish them goodnight and Merry Christmas and promise to see them in the spring with all the family news, then I close the hives and leave them in peace.'

When Caitlin had checked the hives a few days earlier, she had seen signs of clustering. Today, she planned to add extra honey to ensure the safety of the swarm through the cold weather before closing the hives for the winter. Her beekeeping suit was good protection against both the few drowsy insects who buzzed around her as she worked and the chilly wind creeping down from the north. The bitter snap was the first real taste of cold showing that they were over halfway through autumn and winter was waiting to steal across the land.

Caitlin checked the frames were straight and there were no holes in the supers that might cause a draught. It was delicate work but her years of experience meant she could allow her mind to wander as she ran through her list of tasks. As she finished the first hive, she thought about the rehearsal the previous evening. Despite her father's continuing anger towards her, she had decided to show she was willing and had learned her lines, as well as the songs she had been allocated. She had attended every rehearsal. However, despite her best intentions, whenever she stood on the stage, the words flew from her mind and panic overwhelmed her. On the few occasions her scenes as Cordelia had been rehearsed, her father had gazed at her with disappointment, refusing to acknowledge either her valiant attempts to please him or the obvious distress this caused his youngest child.

Gillian, Rachel, Alan and Pete were all in regular attendance, too. Alan had thrown himself into the production with enthusiasm. His natural friendliness, combined with his ability to organise people and situations in an unobtrusive manner, helped to calm numerous heated discussions or potential tantrums. Gillian was thawing towards the idea; Rachel had learned her lines but delivered them with a teenage huffiness that made Caitlin smile. Pete was struggling.

The previous evening had begun with Judy working with the chorus on a dance number in Act One, Scene Four. It came after Goneril had insulted her father, saying she would no longer tolerate his riotous knights destroying her home. The argument took the form of a duet to the tune of Perry Como's hit 'Papa Loves Mambo'. Larry had rewritten Shakespeare's words, with a few variations of his own, even managing to squeeze the words, *'How sharper than a serpent's tooth it is, to have a thankless child'* to the rhythm of the song.

When the duet finished, Lear and his entourage performed a spirited routine based on a cha-cha. This ended with the chorus, led by Lear, conga-ing off stage as the king declared he was going to stay with Regan instead. Among the chorus were Suki, Kayleigh, Gail, Vicki and her partner Ted, Caitlin's aunt and uncle, Primrose and Dale, and Martha the florist.

Caitlin had watched from the auditorium, biting her cheeks in order not to laugh, half-looking for Lee, even though she knew he was on call and might be late. As the routine ended, Larry, in his role as director, had stepped away, clapping his hands for attention.

'Well done, everyone,' he had called. 'The chorus scurries off stage left – not chased by a bear – leaving Regan and Cornwall on stage. Then, George, you and I, with our entourage of knights, enter stage right at the head of the conga line to take up residence with Rachel – I mean, Regan.'

As Larry had given his instructions, he and George had climbed the stairs at the front of the stage, taking their positions.

Larry's voice had suddenly taken on an edge of frustration. 'Why do you have your script, Pete?' he had shouted. 'You should know your part by now.' His irritation had been palpable as he turned to the rest of the Players. 'There should be no more need for scripts. After today, no scripts will be admitted to rehearsal.'

Pete had flushed with anger as he had snapped back, 'We've only had the complete scripts for a week. I'm running my own business, helping with your haulage company and looking after my family. I don't have time to learn this nonsense as well.'

Larry's eyes had blazed with fury. 'Nonsense? You dare—'

Rachel had stepped between them, trying to defuse the situation. 'Pete didn't mean it, Dad. Did you, Pete?'

Pete had looked even angrier and Larry had stalked towards his son-in-law in a menacing manner, when Alan had stepped between them.

'All artists are temperamental,' he had exclaimed in a jovial voice. 'Let's take it from the top, shall we? Larry, your first line is: "Good morrow to you..." No, my mistake, sorry, that's the original. Your new line is: "Hail, daughter, my beauty and grace, was I ever glad to see your face."'

Larry had taken his position, casting a furious glare at Rachel before beginning.

'Hail, daughter, my beauty and grace, was I ever glad to see your face. Your sister, the vulture, I've left behind. To stay with you won't be such a grind.'

'But, Father, dear, what say you now? Are you suggesting my sister's a...'

She left a beat before continuing, 'Not treating you with the love and devotion you crave?'

Alan had continued to mediate and as Caitlin considered the rest of the evening, which had passed without further mishap, she realised it was because Alan had taken over the directorial role.

The slow buzz of the bees drew her attention back to the hives and, with her checks complete, she replaced the lids.

'Sleep well, my darlings,' she whispered. 'I'll keep you updated on family news.'

Caitlin blew a kiss to each hive, before gathering her tools and walking back up the garden. She glanced at the spring as she passed but no ethereal figure hovered and she was relieved. The dream of the Three Sisters the previous evening had given her enough to consider.

Love, she thought, as she opened the back door and entered her kitchen, *the sisters claim it's always the answer. Where has the love in our family gone?*

Caitlin had woken from the dream feeling a mixture of emotions, horrified by the idea of one person bearing the pain of every broken heart in eternity, joy for the sisters and a deep sadness to have reached the end of the story, for she knew in her heart she would never see the sisters again. Was this part of the curse she had heard during her trip to the Everywhen? The three women and their Arthurian-esque tale were strangers to her, they were not the Goneril, Regan and Cordelia she had seen in her visions.

Shadows, a voice whispered in her mind. *A different path, different choices, the shadow daughters. We must all come together. The third is the fourth, she has the power, the Charmed One.*

Caitlin shook her head, ever since she had drunk the henbane tea these strange whispers appeared in her consciousness when she least expected it. Was it Cordelia? *No*, she thought, *it's impossible, if she was ever real she was alive thousands of years ago, how could she whisper to me across time?*

How did you travel to the Iron Age? came the whisper. *Trust your intuition, the Everywhen is a path to the truth.*

Her phone rang, Lee's name and picture flashing up. It was the day Lee was officially moving into the former King family home. Although he had collected the keys a few weeks earlier, he had hired a team of builders to make alterations, including updating the bathrooms and painting the interior. Caitlin had offered to help him settle into his new home, feeling she should reciprocate after he had stepped in when Stan had let her down.

'The sofa, armchairs and other large pieces of furniture have been in storage and are being delivered at lunchtime,' he had said. 'You could come over once they're in and help me arrange them or, if they're already in place, have a cup of tea, if it won't feel too odd.'

She had been grateful for his thoughtfulness but she had promised herself she would treat Lee's purchase of their old home as a new beginning for them all.

'Let me know when you're ready for me,' she had replied with determined cheerfulness.

'Hey, Woody,' she said now, glad of the distraction from her confusing thoughts about the past. 'How's the move going?'

'All fine, the furniture's arrived and in place,' he said but he sounded nervous. 'Are you able to come over?'

'Yes, of course. What's the matter?' she asked.

'I've found something of your dad's and...' He hesitated. 'It would be better if I showed you.'

Disconcerted, Caitlin began peeling off her beekeeping suit as she spoke. 'Ten minutes?' she asked.

'Perfect,' he replied and she could hear relief in his voice.

* * *

Caitlin rang the doorbell; the front door was a deep blue, it had been red when they had lived in the house.

Stop, she told herself.

Lee opened the door and as she crossed the threshold she could not help admiring the sleek, duck-egg blue paint that had replaced the violently orange, rag-rolled effect wallpaper her father had chosen for the hall in the early 1990s and never changed.

Lee hugged her in relief. 'Come in here,' he said, leading her through to the back of the house.

The kitchen had not been replaced but the doors had been painted in a series of pastel shades of yellow, orange and cream, with contrasting handles, and a wooden worktop had replaced the battered white marble her mother had chosen years earlier. A new pale wooden floor had been laid and the tri-fold doors updated. Lee's two large blue sofas dominated the living space, with a long pine dining table on the other side. On this was an old-fashioned biscuit tin and a battered leather briefcase.

'It looks great, Lee,' she said.

'Not too strange?' he asked.

'A bit,' she replied, 'but we all knew the house was desperate for an update and what I've seen so far looks amazing.'

'Thank you,' he said before walking to the table and pulling out a chair. Caitlin sat beside him. 'These are what I wanted to show you.'

'What are they?' she asked. 'The tin looks familiar, Dad used to have one, he kept important documents inside it – passports, birth certificates – until Alan explained they might be safer in a lockable box or safe and organised for one to be installed in their dressing room.'

'The safe is still there,' said Lee. 'These were in a hidden section of wall in your parents'— I mean, my bedroom.'

'What do you mean "a hidden section of wall"?'

'You know the corner where your mum's wingback armchair used to stand?' said Lee.

'Yes,' she nodded.

The armchair had been covered in a vibrant patchwork fabric and was a favourite with them all. Gillian had asked if she could keep it and the chair now sat in her open-plan kitchen, dining, living space that had been designed to be so similar to the one their parents had created.

'Did you know there was a cupboard behind it?'

'Vaguely,' she said. 'Dad wallpapered over it years ago by mistake and I assumed it had remained unreachable ever since.'

'No, it had been opened recently,' said Lee. 'The builder found these inside and I think your dad must have forgotten to take them when he moved. I wasn't prying, I opened them to see what was inside.'

'Of course, I would never think you were being nosy.'

'Did you know?' he asked. 'Is this what the row with your sisters is about?'

Caitlin swallowed nervously, wondering what Lee had discovered. 'Know what?'

Lee flipped open the biscuit tin and removed the contents, spreading it on the table. There were multiple leaflets from various sources – *Living with Alzheimer's Disease, Telling Your Loved Ones You Have Alzheimer's Disease, Next Steps for Living an Active Life with Alzheimer's Disease.*

'There was a diary in the briefcase,' explained Lee. 'There are appointments with a private GP dating from the beginning of the year. From April, there are details of his attendance at an Alzheimer's treatment centre.'

'No,' said Caitlin, tears welling in her eyes, she could feel panic and denial rising in her throat. 'Dad's only sixty-five. You must be wrong.'

'We have to ask him,' said Lee.

'Why didn't he discuss it with your dad?' Caitlin asked.

'Perhaps Uncle Larry couldn't face putting his best friend through something as awful as testing him for such a cruel condition,' replied Lee. 'Despite his occasional outburst, your dad usually tries to protect those he loves from being hurt.'

Caitlin stared at the leaflets, unable to process the enormity of Lee's discovery. Then she remembered the night she had sung 'Moon River' with Gillian and Rachel, the strangeness of her father's behaviour, the way his concentration had drifted and the announcement that it would be his grand finale.

'This is why Dad has said *King Lear* will be his last performance with the Players,' she said. 'I couldn't work it out. If he was retiring, he could have devoted his every waking minute to each production.' She looked at Lee, her eyes filled with distress. 'This must be the real reason he didn't want to buy another house either, why he wanted to be with one of us.'

'It's probably the reason he announced his retirement in the summer, too,' said Lee, wrapping his arm around her. 'The TIA was a good excuse and, having changed his will and updated his paperwork, it means everything is arranged before the Alzheimer's makes its presence felt even more deeply. I wonder if he might have arranged Lasting Power of Attorney too. Perhaps you could ask his assistant, Heather?'

'I have to tell Bean and Rabbit,' Caitlin said. 'We have to resolve this stupid argument and then we need to speak to Dad.'

'Would you like me to come?'

'No,' she said, 'thank you for offering but this is a conversation which has to be between the three of us.'

She leaned into Lee's side, taking comfort in his closeness, his familiarity, breathing in his aftershave. *Woody*, she thought, *a woody scent for Woody*. With his arm around her, she felt safe, protected, and without thinking she tilted her head, his mouth was millimetres away. Adrenaline coursed through her and the reckless feeling she had experienced the night she had taken the henbane tea overwhelmed her. She moved forward and felt his hesitation but when she leaned nearer, he bent to kiss her as though they had done it a million times before. Caitlin kissed him back with a passion that surprised her.

'Moon, are you sure?' whispered Lee, gently disentangling himself. 'You've had a shock.'

'This has nothing to do with shock,' she replied. 'Ever since the day you helped me move the boxes from here, I've wanted to kiss you.'

'Really?' he said.

'It was as though I suddenly saw you and realised I love—' She halted.

'You...?' he prompted.

'Love you as more than a brother,' she mumbled.

'At last,' he sighed and kissed her again. 'Trust me, I've never seen you as a surrogate little sister. My feelings for you were why I couldn't go to Australia with Poppy, the thought of being on the other side of the world from you broke my heart.'

'But I was engaged to Stan,' she said in surprise.

'Yes, but I could see you weren't happy and while I'd never wish what he did to you on my worst enemy, the fact you went white with panic whenever the wedding was mentioned gave me hope.'

'I had no idea,' she said as they kissed again.

'You were always a bit clueless,' he teased and she gave him a gentle shove.

When they drew apart, staring at each other in wonder, the bubble of their new-found feelings burst as the reality of the Alzheimer's leaflets blared from the table.

'I have to speak to my sisters,' Caitlin said, pulling her phone from the back pocket of her jeans. 'Then you and I need to talk, too.'

36

GOLDENWYCH, PRESENT DAY

Light blazed from Gillian's windows as Caitlin pulled onto the wide driveway. Gillian's Mercedes convertible was in one side of the double garage but Alan's Porsche Cayenne was missing. He was at extra dance classes with Larry and George as they worked on a three-part routine to 'Life on Mars' by David Bowie for the madness scene. Alan had placed a message on the family WhatsApp group saying he was unsure of this piece as he felt the contemporary dance element did not really suit them. He had suggested they change it to 'Wuthering Heights' by Kate Bush and allow the female members of the cast to excel instead; no one had yet responded.

As Caitlin cut her engine, Rachel swept up beside her. She looked tense and when Caitlin waved, her sister held up her phone to indicate she was in the middle of a conversation. Caitlin gave her a thumbs-up and walked to the front door, she had no desire to hang around waiting for her sister to finish talking.

'Hi, Moon,' said Gillian, opening the door. She peered out at Rachel's car.

'She's on the phone,' said Caitlin.

'I'll leave the keys in the door, she can let herself in when she's ready,' said Gillian, and to Caitlin's surprise, Gillian fished her door keys out of the wide unevenly shaped dark brown bowl Rachel had made for their parents.

'Didn't Rabbit want her dish?' asked Caitlin.

'No, it was in the skip,' said Gillian, shutting the door. 'I couldn't bear to see it there, so I picked it out when she wasn't looking.'

Caitlin was about to comment when the key grated and Rachel entered, her face white and her eyes red-rimmed. She threw Gillian's keys in the bowl without seeming to notice it was the one she had abandoned.

'Whatever this is about, can we be quick?' she said. 'Pete's kicking up a fuss about babysitting the girls.'

'You can't babysit your own children,' said Gillian. 'It's called parenting.'

'Not helpful,' muttered Rachel, hanging her jacket on the coat stand and stalking past her sister to the huge room at the back of the house where life was lived.

'Come through,' said Gillian, her voice heavy with sarcasm. She shook her head at Caitlin in mock despair, then led the way through the beautiful home she and Alan had created.

In happier times, Caitlin had always loved visiting Gillian and Alan, the house was warm, inviting and seemed to hug you as soon as you were over the threshold. Caitlin was unsure whether it was Gillian or Alan's interior décor skills that had created this ambiance but it held a memory of their family home when they were growing up, so she suspected it was her sister.

She followed Gillian into the large multi-functional space at the back of the house, where Rachel was texting, her back to her sisters. Tri-fold doors overlooked a long, beautifully maintained garden and Rachel's reflection was haggard as she wrote her message. Caitlin gazed out at the garden, trying not to allow shock to register over Rachel's appearance, instead letting her eyes follow the carefully placed lights which drew the eye down the lawn and through the flower beds, giving the outdoor space a magical glow.

A long, polished-wood table with velvet-covered seats in jewel colours stood to one side, while two sofas and several armchairs, including the patchwork wingback armchair that had once belonged to Miranda, were grouped around a modern log-burning stove. On the wall was a huge television and, below it, a vast array of musical equipment, including shelves containing hundreds of vinyl records and others crammed with CDs. Another shelf was lined with DVDs showing an eclectic mix of films, from black and white Westerns and early Hollywood musicals to modern French cinema. Caitlin noticed the white rug that had once been in the centre of the room had been replaced by one in a dark burnt orange.

'Tea, coffee, wine?' asked Gillian.

'Tea,' Caitlin and Rachel replied together.

Gillian pulled an old-fashioned caddy from the cupboard and both her sisters smiled. This, too, was an old family treasure and had belonged to their grandmother, then their mother.

Gillian placed the tea tray on the dining-room table and the three women sat, Gillian at the head, Rachel on her right, Caitlin on her left.

'What was so urgent it couldn't wait, Moon?' said Rachel, her phone face down on the table beside her. 'If you're trying to stage another intervention, you can forget it—'

'Will you stop it,' snapped Gillian. 'Perhaps it's time we discussed things and resolved them. Moon did what she thought was best.'

'But we promised Mum,' snapped Rachel and jumped as her phone pinged. She flipped it over and her eyes narrowed as she read the message.

Caitlin had heard Rachel's rambling argument about respecting their mother's last wishes before but ever since Lee's discovery she wondered whether they had misinterpreted her words. It was a huge assumption but once the possibility had lodged itself in her mind she had been unable to shake the idea.

'This isn't about Mum,' said Caitlin as Rachel slammed her phone back on the table. 'It's about Dad.'

'You're not planning to boycott the musical, are you?' asked Gillian. 'I admit, in your position, I'd be upset because Dad isn't being very encouraging but it's important we present a united front.'

Gillian poured the tea, pushing a cup towards each sister, followed by a plate of chocolate biscuits.

'No, this has nothing to do with the Players,' Caitlin said, sipping her tea, recognising the blend as her mother's, which Gillian had obviously bought from the café, purchasing it when Caitlin had been absent.

'What is it then?' barked Rachel.

'Do you remember the secret cupboard in Mum and Dad's bedroom?' Caitlin asked.

'Dad wallpapered over it,' said Rachel.

'No one's used it for years,' added Gillian.

'When Lee's builders were redecorating the bedroom, they discovered the door had been opened recently and these were inside, stowed in the old biscuit tin Dad used for valuables and the briefcase Mum gave him for his thirtieth birthday.'

She reached into her handbag and placed the diary and the Alzheimer's leaflets on the table. Gillian and Rachel stared at them in confusion.

Caitlin flipped open the diary to the dates of her father's appointments. 'Dad's been visiting a private doctor,' she said, 'and a few weeks before his TIA, he went for an appointment at a private clinic specialising in the care of people with Alzheimer's, dementia and other associated conditions. I suspect it's where he acquired these leaflets.'

Rachel pushed the leaflets away from her, as though they were contaminated, but Gillian began flipping through the diary, turning page after page, running her finger down the list of visits to the private doctor.

'But he's too young,' Rachel said, echoing Caitlin's words from her discussion with Lee.

'Lee said not,' she replied.

'Should Lee be discussing his patient with you?' snapped Gillian, looking up from the diary but Caitlin knew her sister's harsh tone was caused by fear.

'Lee and Uncle George knew nothing about it,' she said. 'Lee's meeting his dad after the dance class to tell him. Dad has been keeping this a secret from everyone.'

'First Mum and now Dad,' said Rachel and her voice broke into a sob.

Gillian closed the diary, then stood up, pacing the room, her face white with anguish.

'At the end of last year, Dad put the paperwork in place to give Alan and me Lasting Power of Attorney when the time was necessary,' Gillian said. 'We work with Dad, it seemed a sensible precaution, it never occurred to me there could be another reason.'

'How have we missed this?' said Rachel.

'No one would have guessed,' said Caitlin. 'Dad's always had moments where he has become fixated on an idea and refused to listen to reason. Whenever he does anything erratic, we all think, "Oh, it's Dad being Dad", why would we have suspected there was a different reason?'

Gillian sat down again, reaching for the biscuits.

'When Mum was dying, she asked us to protect Dad,' said Gillian. 'What if Mum had her suspicions Dad was ill?'

Caitlin felt all the stress she had been carrying since Lee had discovered the leaflets and diary dissipating. Gillian's keen analytical mind had drawn the same conclusion as her and the relief was immense. She could not fully explain why this release was so important except it meant she no longer bore the burden alone.

'How would she?' asked Rachel.

'She knew him better than anyone,' said Gillian. 'Don't you remember? On the night Mum died, Dad was with her for hours, then suddenly, she announced Dad was leaving, that he was going to collect George for a Players' meeting.'

'We were furious,' said Caitlin, 'but when Dad said goodbye, it was with such love – they knew they were saying their last farewell. It was after that, when we were alone with Mum, she told us the secret they'd been keeping and asked us to take care of Dad, to protect him from what was to come, to forgive him because he didn't always have control over his actions.'

'You're right,' said Rachel. 'Perhaps she had guessed.'

'Which means, the secret she wanted us to keep wasn't the one we thought,' said Gillian.

'What?' said Rachel.

'Perhaps Mum was trying to prepare us for what she feared lay ahead with Dad's health,' said Caitlin, 'and she wanted us to know we weren't alone.'

Rachel stared at her in horror as realisation dawned. 'Do you mean, all this time, we've been wrong about what Mum meant?'

'Yes,' said Caitlin. 'What do you think, Bean?'

Gillian took her sisters' hands, Caitlin leaned towards her, so their foreheads were nearly touching, Rachel mirrored her actions. The position was one they would adopt when they were growing up when they had made up after an argument – they called it the Triangle of Sisterhood.

'We have to tell our older sister,' said Gillian and there were tears in all their eyes.

37

GOLDENWYCH, PRESENT DAY

'Hi, Sindy,' said Gillian, when she opened the door twenty minutes later. 'Thank you for coming at such short notice, especially in this weather.'

The rain that had been threatening all day had begun falling in earnest an hour earlier.

'Caitlin said it was urgent and there was a problem,' said Sindy, handing her wet puffa jacket to Gillian, who hung it on the coat stand.

The two women walked through the house to Caitlin and Rachel who were sitting at the table where there was now a bottle of white wine in an ice bucket and four glasses. The diary was beside it but the leaflets were tucked carefully inside.

'Hi,' said Caitlin, rising to hug Sindy. 'Sorry to drag you out. Where's Rosie?'

'She's with Mum, they're practising their routine for your song, Caity, when you sing Katy Perry's "Roar" as you're about to return as Queen of France to England and save Lear.'

'It's street dance, isn't it?' said Rachel.

'Mum's got the moves,' said Sindy.

Despite the superficial lightness of the tone, there was an uncomfortable edge to the conversation.

'Wine?' asked Gillian, holding up the bottle.

'A small one, I'm driving,' she replied.

'Us too,' said Caitlin, pointing to her and Rachel. Then she patted the seat beside her, welcoming Sindy into the fold with a warm smile.

Sindy perched on the edge and accepted the glass from Gillian.

Caitlin looked at her sisters, who both sat mute, sipping their wine.

'I'll start then,' she said, and with no response from Gillian or Rachel, she turned to Sindy. 'Gillian and Rachel would like to apologise for their behaviour.'

Sindy's eyebrows shot up in surprise.

'Sindy, we're sorry,' said Gillian, her eyes downcast. 'We've treated you appallingly and we were entirely in the wrong.'

'Sorry,' echoed Rachel. 'I know there's a very wide mean streak in my nature and no one, least of all you, deserved the grief I've directed at you for the past few years.'

'Have you apologised to Caitlin?' asked Sindy.

'Yes,' said Gillian, 'we realise she was in the right. She's been gracious enough to forgive us because she knows we're a pair of nightmares. She's lived with us for thirty-one years. We don't have the right to ask the same from you because you were the innocent party in this situation.'

Sindy sipped her wine.

'Thank you, your apologies mean a lot,' she said after a few moments' consideration. 'It's been very hurtful.'

To the surprise of everyone, Rachel gave a sob and hurried around the table to hug Sindy. 'Sind, we're so sorry,' she said. 'When Mum was dying, she made us promise to protect Dad and we thought she meant keeping it a secret he was your father. After the funeral, when Caitlin told you we knew you were our half-sister, we felt as though she had betrayed Mum's final wishes.'

'But you didn't have to be so cruel to her,' Sindy said, disentangling herself from Rachel's embrace and there was real anger in her voice. Rachel sat back down looking devastated. 'To us both. Caitlin did what she thought was right for us all. Your behaviour was appalling.'

Gillian and Rachel hung their heads in shame, mumbling more apologies before picking up their wine glasses.

Silence bloomed.

Caitlin looked from one sister to another and was about to speak, to act as the peacemaker when Sindy said, 'But what Caity didn't know when she told me was that I already knew the truth; Mum and Miranda told me when Rosie was born.'

'They did?' asked Gillian in surprise.

'Yes, your dad was insistent on providing financially for Rosie, for us both, which was why Miranda's promise didn't make sense to me,' she said.

Caitlin, Gillian and Rachel exchanged a pained look, as though Sindy's words had confirmed their realisation about their father's illness and their mistake.

'What a mess,' said Gillian. 'You must have despaired about our behaviour.'

'I did,' agreed Sindy, 'but despite everything, I hoped one day we would be reconciled. Tell me though, why now?'

'We've discovered something,' admitted Caitlin. 'When he was clearing out our old house, Lee found a diary belonging to Dad, which has given us distressing information.'

'Which is?' said Sindy and there was a clipped tension in her voice as though she was bracing herself.

'We believe Dad has Alzheimer's disease and this is the real reason he's retired,' said Gillian, a break in her voice. 'For the same reason, we're certain it's why Dad announced *King Lear – The Musical* will be his final show for the Players and why he's insisted we all be in it.'

'But Caity said he told you it was because he wanted to heal the family rift,' said Sindy.

'To Dad, performing is the greatest source of happiness he can imagine. Perhaps he hoped the magic of the "biz" would mysteriously solve all our problems,' said Gillian.

Caitlin stared at Sindy, her friend, who was also her half-sister, waiting for a response.

'Who else knows about Larry?' asked Sindy as she gently turned the pages of the diary.

'Lee and George,' said Caitlin. 'Lee is going to suggest they talk to Dad and offer their support.'

'I see,' said Sindy. 'And when the truth about Larry's health is known, where will I fit in?'

'We'd like you and Rosie to be with us and spend as much time with him as possible,' said Gillian.

Caitlin sipped her wine, watching as Sindy absorbed the news. Her friend was a kind, caring woman, but, like all of them, she had an incandescent temper when roused.

'Do you mean tell people he's my father?' Sindy queried.

'Yes, and that you're our sister,' said Caitlin.

Sindy crossed her arms defensively. 'Do you know the full story?' she asked, and with reluctance, the three women shook their heads.

'When she was dying, Mum told us you were our half-sister and begged us to protect Dad.' Gillian's voice was apologetic. 'We thought she meant from the scandal of having another child but we wonder now if she'd guessed his behaviour was changing and he had early symptoms of dementia or Alzheimer's.'

'No doubt you've been imagining there was a sordid affair and I was a guilty secret to be hidden away,' said Sindy. She gave a derisive laugh. 'You weren't protecting Larry, you were ensuring you weren't the centre of gossip.'

The flush on Rachel's face was answer enough.

Caitlin waited, poised to leap into the breach and work as mediator if Sindy made a move to storm from the house, but instead, Sindy shook her head in mock despair.

'You two,' she pointed at Gillian and Rachel and gave a half-laugh as she said, 'are awful, but in the spirit of our newly admitted sisterhood, I forgive you and I'll tell you the whole story...'

A shiver ran down Caitlin's spine.

'You don't have to,' she interrupted.

'Don't worry, Caity, there was no scandal,' said Sindy, leaning over to squeeze her hand in reassurance. She released Caitlin and ran her hand through her newly dyed blonde hair.

For the first time, Caitlin saw the striking resemblance between Sindy and Gillian. The two women shared the same natural dark auburn hair but Sindy had been colouring hers for years, blurring the lines between their similarity.

'Back in the eighties, my mum, Ted, your – *our* – dad, your mum – Miranda, Suki, George, Barbara, Linus, Paul, Annie and a few others, were all friends. They loved amateur dramatics and, as they grew up, took over the ailing company that existed in Goldenwych, turning it into the Players.

'They were gradually pairing up; Annie and Paul were the first to announce their engagement, then George had a fling with a girl from medical school and your dad and my mum had a summer romance. At the same time, your mum was going out with a bloke called Greg who lived in the village for a while. My mum and Larry separated, Miranda dumped Greg and your parents began dating. It was a whirlwind romance, they became engaged and Gilly was conceived. Unfortunately, Mum had also discovered she was pregnant with me.'

Caitlin looked at Gillian and Rachel who were white-faced.

'Your – our – dad was in a tricky situation,' Sindy continued. 'My mum knew she didn't love him and it was obvious Miranda and Larry were head-over-heels. He insisted on taking financial responsibility but Mum decided to resolve the situation. For months, her aunt, who ran a hotel in Pembrokeshire, had been asking her to go and stay. Auntie Lorna and Mum had always been close, so Mum explained the situation and she was welcomed with open arms. The hotel was beside the sea and Mum said she had a wonderful time helping her aunt.

'After I was born, Mum did her hairdressing training, she met Phil and, eighteen months later, they married. No one expected him to die of cancer when he was so young. Mum couldn't bear to stay in Pembrokeshire and be reminded of him everywhere she looked and, as Gran was becoming weaker, we moved back to Goldenwych to be near her.

'Miranda and Larry were delighted to see Mum and insisted on including us in family events, parties, the Players and village life in general as often as possible. However, there was one condition: my mum insisted we should keep the truth about the real relationship between us all a secret.'

'Why?' asked Rachel.

'She thought the upheaval of losing Phil and moving house was enough for me to cope with, without suddenly being presented with a different father and three half-sisters,' Sindy replied dryly and Rachel flushed. 'At that point, I thought Phil was my biological father.'

'When did she tell you?' asked Gillian.

'I was fifteen,' said Sindy, 'and your dad had cast me as Wendy in the Players' version of *Peter Pan*. The part you wanted and deserved, Gilly. The part that caused the rift in our friendship, even though Larry didn't realise it.'

Gillian gave an involuntary sob and Caitlin reached over to take her sister's hand, but Gillian gently brushed her away, leaning forward and taking Sindy's instead.

'I'm sorry,' she said, tears brimming in her eyes. 'I hated you, Sindy, even though, deep down, I knew it wasn't your fault. It was Dad I loathed; it seemed that no matter what I did, nothing was ever good enough for him.'

Caitlin remembered the night when Gillian had stormed out of the rehearsal and had, ever since, refused to be in another production. They had all been there: Miranda was playing Peter Pan, the principal boy, as usual, and Larry was Captain Hook. Rachel was auditioning for Tinkerbell, which she won, and Gillian was trying out for Wendy. Caitlin had been backstage, helping her Aunt Primrose, who was stage manager. It was not long after Caitlin's dramatic collapse and George's medical advice had been for her to avoid the exertion of being on stage. Caitlin had been relieved; even then, the thought of performing again made her tremble with fear.

Gillian had finished her flawless rendition of 'Somewhere Over the Rainbow' from *The Wizard of Oz* and Rachel had been in the front row giving her a double thumbs-up, when Sindy had been called on stage.

'They're so alike,' Caitlin had heard Barbara whisper to Annie, who hastily shushed her.

Sindy had waited for Paul, Annie's husband, to begin playing, then she too had given a perfect rendition of her piece, 'The Deadwood Stage' from the Doris Day film *Calamity Jane*. Larry had walked on stage and announced Sindy was to play the part of Wendy. Gillian had broken down in tears and fled from the hall.

When they had returned home, Caitlin had heard Gillian's tirade against her father. At fifteen, she was self-righteous and terrible in her fury.

'You do this to me every year!' Gillian had shouted. 'You have never given me the lead, even though you constantly tell me I'm the best. No matter what I do, I AM NEVER GOOD ENOUGH FOR YOU. NEVER!'

She had stormed from the house and run to Suki and George, who lived a few doors away. Her friendship with Sindy – which until then had been good – fractured, and Caitlin alone had continued the relationship both Miranda and Vicki had encouraged.

'I asked Mum why Larry had favoured me over Gilly,' continued Sindy, 'and she finally told me the truth. My instinct was to run to your house and tell you all because I was so excited to know you were my sisters. Then

Miranda rang, asking if Gilly was with us, she was trying to track her down after she'd stormed out. Mum told Miranda she'd finally told me the secret but they decided it might be too incendiary to reveal all while Gilly was so upset. Mum and I agreed, then somehow time passed and nothing was ever said.'

'You must have hated us,' said Rachel.

'No, it wasn't your fault,' Sindy conceded. 'Mum explained that no one knew, not even their friends, and we'd all discuss it when the time was right.'

'I've always assumed Mum and Dad's friends knew,' said Caitlin, remembering Barbara's whispered comment. 'Our generation might not have known but I thought everyone in Mum and Dad's circle of friends either knew or would have guessed?'

'Perhaps,' said Sindy.

'How would you feel about the village knowing the truth?' Caitlin asked Sindy.

'As long as I have time to explain it to Rosie and she's fine with it...'

'And what about Emelia and Porcelain? They need to understand too,' snapped Rachel. 'Emelia is in the same class as your Rosie, they're friends – how do I explain to her they're cousins too?'

'Rache, this is the twenty-first century,' said Sindy. 'The kids are used to blended families. Who would care?'

'I would care!' shouted Rachel, her voice rising in panic. 'I hate being the centre of gossip. None of you understand the damage this could do to my family.'

'We are your family,' said Gillian.

'My family, my children, my marriage,' said Rachel and, to Caitlin's amazement, she burst into hysterical tears.

'What's going on?' said Caitlin, rushing around the table to hug Rachel.

'Nothing,' snapped Rachel but she allowed Caitlin to wrap her arms around her.

'Don't lie,' said Gillian, hurrying to Rachel's other side. 'You've been twitching with your phone all night and you look as though you haven't slept for weeks.'

Caitlin could feel Rachel trembling, tears were streaming down her face, all her usual elegance and poise crumbling around her.

'Pete wants a divorce,' she blurted out through her sobs.

'What?' gasped Gillian.

'Why?' asked Sindy.

'He's found out I've been having an affair and he's threatened to sue for custody of the girls unless I give him a huge lump sum. It's why I was so upset when Dad stopped our allowances. I'd been saving a chunk of it every month and my plan was to use it to pay Pete off.'

A stunned silence followed.

'Who with?' asked Gillian.

'Slick,' Rachel replied.

'You're sleeping with Edward Glossop?' exclaimed Sindy.

'Yes,' said Rachel, a faint blush stained her cheeks but there was a hint of her usual bravado too. 'It's more than a fling though; Edward wants to marry me.'

'Tell us,' said Gillian, her voice was gentle. 'I've wondered for a while if things have been difficult between you and Pete. As the eldest, I should have offered more support.'

Rachel's eyes welled with tears, while Caitlin stared at Gillian in surprise.

'What do you mean?' Caitlin asked.

'For the longest time, I've noticed that Pete's always picking Rachel up on things, humiliating her, undermining her confidence. I've often wanted to intervene, to defend Rabbit, but wasn't sure if it was my place. Every marriage is different...'

Her voice tailed away as Rachel hugged her.

'Our relationship has been over for years,' admitted Rachel. 'We tried counselling but it was a waste of time. When you've stopped loving someone, there's not much you can do except admit defeat and move on.'

'And you've stopped loving Pete?' asked Sindy.

'Now I have but he was the one who backed away first,' said Rachel. 'He told me after Porcelain was born he didn't love me any more, he said he'd stay for the girls. I suggested we separate but he refused, instead, he had several affairs. It was humiliating but I always forgave him and took him back because I was trying to protect Emelia and Porcelain. I think the real reason he stayed was because of Dad's money. Pete seemed to think the allowance Dad gives us was his own personal slush fund.'

Caitlin thought back through the many years of Rachel and Pete's relationship. Both were spiky personalities but as she considered the endless snide exchanges, the constant one-upmanship, she now realised all the antagonism had been led by Pete and she was angry with herself for not noticing sooner and offering help.

'How did things start with you and Slick?' asked Gillian.

'Eddie and I have always been friends on social media,' said Rachel. 'One evening, I'd posted a picture of a bottle of champagne and he made a comment offering to drink it with me, then he texted. I'd had a huge row with Pete and began to flirt with him. At first, he was resistant and I apologised for being forward but we couldn't stop texting and finally, we realised we'd always had feelings for each other.

'A few months ago, I suggested a trial separation to Pete, but he refused,' continued Rachel. 'A week later, he hired a private detective to have me followed. When he showed me the photos of Eddie and me in a hotel together, Pete said he would stay until after Christmas, then he intends to file for divorce. He's such a hypocrite because he's been sleeping with his practice nurse for over a year. Can you imagine how excruciating it's been during rehearsals?'

Caitlin, Gillian and Sindy stared at each other wordlessly.

Gillian was the first to recover and her words were driven by a fierce protectiveness for Rachel. 'How dare Pete threaten to steal Emelia and Porcelain when he's behaved so appallingly?' she said. 'Alan knows lots of good lawyers, we'll fight him every step of the way. Pete will soon learn never to cross the Kings.'

Rachel gave another sob and threw her arms around Gillian again.

When Rachel had calmed, Gillian and Caitlin sat back down.

Gillian straightened the diary in front of her. 'If we're finally onto Any Other Business,' she said and Caitlin gave a snort of laughter, which Gillian had intended as she smirked at the reaction. 'Another reason my moods have been stranger than usual recently is because Alan and I have been trying for a baby for over two years.'

Caitlin stared at Gillian, stunned by this information. She also knew her sister well enough to know what a huge leap of faith she had taken to tell them about what Caitlin was sure, Gillian saw, as her private failure. She always strived for perfection and, again, here was a challenge she had probably never anticipated.

'Three months ago, we began IVF,' she said. 'This was why I was upset about Dad stopping our allowances. I'd always thought of it as a safety net in case the IVF took a long time, especially as the first round failed. We have our second in a few weeks. It should have been sooner but the appointment was cancelled. It was disappointing because these things are a balancing act of hormones and injections; things are better now and we're trying again soon.'

'Did you receive the cancellation during rehearsal?' asked Caitlin.

'Yes, why?'

'I was watching you and you looked so sad. I wanted to give you a hug but was scared you'd brush me off.'

Gillian hugged Caitlin tightly. 'What a stupid mess this has been,' she said. 'I'm sorry about Stan, too. We should have comforted and supported you when you discovered he was being a cheating scumbag.'

'I'm sorry, too, Moon,' said Rachel.

'Thank you,' she said but her heart was singing as her sisters finally offered their love and care. 'Have you heard what's happened?'

'No,' said Gillian.

'It isn't common knowledge yet,' said Sindy as she and Caitlin exchanged a conspiratorial look.

'Stan's leaving Goldenwych in a few days and, from the rumours we've overheard in the café, apparently Daphne Hawthorne is going, too.'

'No!' gasped Rachel.

'Yes,' said Caitlin, 'and do you know what? It's a relief. Anyway, I snogged Lee.'

A scream of excitement greeted these words, followed by laughter and variations on: 'About time!' from each sister.

When they calmed down, Caitlin said, 'What are we going to do about Dad?'

'He has made mistakes,' Gillian said.

'Lots of mistakes,' Rachel added.

'We could forgive him,' suggested Caitlin. 'We could do it for Mum.'

Rachel shook her head. 'No, if we're going to do it, it must be for ourselves. We have to stop hiding behind Mum and blaming Dad.'

'He's the only parent we have left,' Caitlin said, 'and he needs us.' She reached for Sindy's hand. 'All of us, all his daughters.'

'All four of us,' said Sindy.

'This changes the hierarchy,' said Rachel with a grin.

'What do you mean?' asked Caitlin.

'Sindy is Dad's eldest daughter because she's six months older than Gilly-Bean. Bean is Mum's eldest daughter, but Dad's second child,' she said. 'I'm Mum's second child, but Dad's third and you, Moon, you're Mum's third daughter but you're also the fourth daughter of Dad.'

One becomes two; two becomes three; and out of the third comes the fourth, the One. The fourth is the Charmed One who will heal the curse, the words whispered through her mind. *Face your fears.*

Wasn't that what they had been doing this evening? What was her fear? The worry the rift between her and her sisters would remain forever? Yes, that was one, but the other, the fear of performing. She shuddered at the thought, even though she was desperate to return to her former confidence on stage, to be part of her father's play, to reconnect with him before it was too late.

Before she could fully comprehend the meaning or discuss it with her sisters, all their phones lit up and a cacophony of ringtones filled the room.

Caitlin saw Lee's number flash, Alan was calling Gillian, Edward was phoning Rachel and Vicki was trying Sindy.

'What's happened?' Caitlin asked, answering her mobile, fear coursing through her.

'It's your dad,' said Lee, his voice low. 'He stormed out of rehearsal a few hours ago and hasn't come back. Is he with you?'

38

GOLDENWYCH, PRESENT DAY

The four women burst into the auditorium of the theatre, causing the small group by the stage to turn in surprise. Suki, Vicki and Judy paused in their conversation; George and Lee hurried towards the women. Caitlin and Lee exchanged an understanding look and he moved towards his father, whispering in his ear.

The door creaked again and Edward entered, shaking water from his umbrella. 'I've checked the church and the graveyard again, there's still no sign of him out there,' he said. 'His car's in the car park, but it's locked.'

Rachel ran towards him and hugged him. Edward froze.

'They know and they're good with it,' she whispered.

'I told you they would be,' he said, kissing her.

Suki and George looked at their eldest son in shock.

'Not the moment to answer questions though,' said Gillian as Alan opened his mouth in astonishment. 'We'll explain later.'

'Have you heard from Dad since you called us?' asked Caitlin.

'No,' Lee replied. 'Dad's rung the pub and he isn't there either.'

'We didn't expect you all to be together,' said Alan, eyeing the sisters with interest.

'Caitlin called an intervention,' said Rachel. 'We had issues to resolve. We're friends again. All of us.' She included Sindy in her sweeping gaze.

Lee looked at Caitlin curiously, but before she could speak, George said,

'We know he's not at your house, Gilly, could he have gone elsewhere? Maybe to your cottage, Caity? It's the closest.'

'We checked my place on the way and Rachel rang Pete. He isn't at either of them,' Caitlin replied. 'Could he be at yours, Lee?'

'Why would he be there?' asked Vicki.

'He might have forgotten he's moved out,' said Sindy.

'What do you mean?' asked Judy.

The sisters exchanged a glance and Caitlin, deciding to follow Rachel's lead, slipped her hand into Lee's before saying, 'Lee found paperwork concerning Dad's health at his house. He may have told you, Uncle George.' The older man nodded. 'We think Dad has been diagnosed with Alzheimer's disease and this is why his behaviour has been even more erratic than usual.'

'Girls, no,' gasped Suki, walking forward to offer a maternal hug.

'If he's been gone for two hours and he's confused, we have to find him,' said Gillian, her voice cracking.

A flash of lightning cast an eerie blue light across the windows, followed by a roll of thunder.

'Give me ten minutes to check he hasn't gone back to mine,' said Lee.

'Ring as soon as you know,' said Alan. 'If he isn't there, I'll begin organising a search party. No one should be out in this weather, least of all a confused old man.'

* * *

Within half an hour of Alan posting messages on the Players' various social media accounts concerning Larry's disappearance, a small crowd began to gather in the theatre. They had agreed this was not the place to announce Larry's diagnosis, so Alan had phrased the message carefully, citing the intensifying storm as the reason for their concern. Gillian, Rachel, Caitlin and Sindy, the daughters of Larry King, stood in front of the stage, accompanied by Alan, Lee, Edward, Suki, George, Vicki and her partner Ted Littleton.

'Thank you all for responding to the message and for leaving the comfort of your homes on such a treacherous night,' said Alan, who had taken charge. 'Larry hasn't been missing for long but in this weather, we think it's best to search rather than wait for him to return in case he's had a fall or injured himself in some way. We've checked the pub and the homes of his family with no luck. His car is in the car park however he left his wallet and phone here, so he can't have called a cab. Therefore, we must assume he's on foot. Before we brave the tempest: has anyone else seen or heard from him?'

There were general murmurs in the negative and shakes of heads.

'It was worth asking,' said Alan. 'For those of you who are willing to risk the deluge on foot: George, Ted, Edward, Sindy and Gillian will lead teams; Caitlin, Lee, Rachel and Vicki will be driving. Suki, Judy, Barbara and Annie will remain here to co-ordinate. Those willing to walk, please go to the left, those preferring to drive to the right, please.'

There were nods and movement as people offered their services.

Lee hurried over to Caitlin, 'How are you?'

'Scared, for Dad,' she replied.

'I know but we'll find him. How did Bean and Rabbit take the news?'

'Shocked,' she said. 'We told Sindy, too.'

Lee's eyes widened. 'And you're all alive?'

Caitlin was grateful for the small spark of humour in such a bleak moment.

'We've discussed everything and, once we've explained it to Rosie, Emelia and Porcelain, we'll slowly let people know the truth about Sindy's parentage,' she said.

'What are you talking about?' said Lee.

Caitlin stared at him in surprise. 'I thought you'd know, that your parents would have told you. Sindy is our half-sister. She's Dad's daughter.'

'Sindy is your... what?'

'Lee, Caitlin, when you're ready,' called Alan, beckoning them over before she could reply. 'We've divided the village into routes so we can cover as much ground as efficiently as possible.'

'I'll tell you later,' she promised and, with Lee following in bemusement, hurried to take the photocopied map from Alan. It contained the list of roads and areas for her to search. Lee took his, murmuring something to his mother, who raised her eyebrows and nodded, a look of surprise on her face.

'Keep in touch,' said Alan. 'We'll put updates on the Players' Facebook and Insta pages every quarter of an hour.'

'Come on,' Lee said, his own map clutched in his hand as they headed out into the lashing rain.

When they stepped outside, Caitlin gasped. The car park was packed with people and cars, and two of the men from the Players were wearing the hi-viz jackets that were usually used on show nights to organise the car park. They were carrying huge torches and were calming frayed nerves as they guided the searchers in the cars out into the night.

'This is astonishing,' said Caitlin, staring at all the people who were willing to search for her father on such a terrible night.

As Martha and her mother passed, dressed from head-to-foot in wet weather gear, they hugged her with promises not to worry, they would find him, before they disappeared into the rain-sodden night.

'People love your dad,' Lee said, kissing her. 'Keep in touch.' And he ran towards his car.

Caitlin jumped into her SUV, slamming her door and shutting out the hubbub from the car park. She felt very alone as she glanced at the list of places she had been assigned to search.

'He's safe,' she murmured to herself as she clipped in her seatbelt. 'He's safe, he's safe. I'll find him.' She was ushered out into the lane, her wind-screen wipers on their fastest setting. 'Although how I'm going to see Dad in this weather is a mystery.'

The thunderstorm raged as Caitlin drove through the dark, rain-soaked streets of Goldenwych. Up and down she went, slowing to a crawl when she was able, sweeping her headlights as far as possible into dark corners but every road was empty of her father.

'Where are you, Dad?' she whispered, her knuckles white as her hands gripped the steering wheel.

Images of Larry lying alone, soaking wet, unable to call for help, flashed across her mind. Endless tragic scenarios played out as she turned into each new lane: Larry collapsed from another TIA or a full-blown stroke, huddled somewhere with a broken leg where he might have fallen, or confused and wandering onto a main road.

'No!' she shouted, scaring herself. 'He'll be fine. Any minute now, the phone will ring and he'll have been sulking at a friend's house all along.'

But her phone remained silent, and outside, the weather intensified. After another quarter of an hour, she stopped to check the apps hoping he had been found, but there were no sightings. She was about to turn back, to regroup at the theatre, when, to her delight, her phone rang.

'Alan,' she said, 'have you found him?'

'No,' her brother-in-law replied and her hopes plummeted, 'George has suggested we try the stone circle.'

'Why?' said Caitlin. 'The circle is quite a long walk out of the village, especially in this weather.'

'Apparently it was where your father proposed to your mother,' Alan said. 'George claims Larry was muttering, *"Our revels now are ended. These our actors, as I foretold were all spirits and are melted in air."* George didn't recognise it at first, but he's looked it up and it's from *The Tempest*.'

'Mum's play,' exclaimed Caitlin. 'Miranda, she was named after the female lead and her maiden name was Tempest. Of course. I'll head straight there now. Send a few others, too, it's a big area to search.'

She hung up, did a three-point turn and put her foot down as she sped towards the stone circle, certain her father would be waiting there.

* * *

'Dad!' Caitlin shouted as she made her way past the Three Sisters. The stones glistened black in the rain and the wind stole her cries for her father, tossing them high in the air, ridiculing her efforts to have dominion over the wilds of nature.

Above her, a streak of lightning flashed, illuminating the sky with an other-worldly silvery-white glow. She instinctively ducked, raising her hands protectively above her head, recoiling at the force of its energy. When, seconds later, the boom of thunder filled the air, it was so close she felt it reverberating through her solar plexus. Battling against the wind, she hung onto one of the Three Sisters and shone her torch into the pitch darkness. Despite the power of the light's beam, the density of the rain shortened its range and she realised it would be quicker to walk the perimeter of the circle to see if her father was sheltering against one of the stones.

'Dad!' she called every few steps, wiping the water from her eyes, searching with all her senses, listening intently in case he returned her cry.

Time lost all meaning as she continued on her slow campaign around the stones, checking each one thoroughly before moving on to the next. She wondered when the help Alan had promised would arrive. If her father was here, lost and wandering in the elemental storm, they needed to speed up the search or he might die from exposure. The stone circle, usually a place of familiarity and comfort, felt huge and menacing on this desperate night.

'Dad!' she shouted again as there was a lull in the wind. 'It's me, Caitlin, I've come to take you home.'

Behind her, there was a scuffling sound. She spun around and, as she did, a dark shape hurtled towards her, screaming in panic. Shouting for him to stop, Caitlin backed away, but the man ran at her, cannoning into her side so her torch flew in one direction and the small cross-body bag with her phone and inhaler caught on the sharp edge of one of the stones. The strap broke and the bag and its contents disappeared into the night. Caitlin sprawled on the ground, winded, struggling to catch her breath as her father shouted in eldritch tones, '"*So many horrid ghosts*",' before disappearing into the rain-soaked blackness.

'Dad,' she called, her voice muffled as she fought her way to her feet, 'it's me Caitlin. I won't hurt you. Let's go home.'

She stared into the darkness, her eyes adjusting enough for her to make out the edges of the stones. From behind one, her father's head appeared. To her relief, he was wearing his expensive weather-proof coat with the hood pulled up and fastened tightly, but as his jacket blended in with the night, his pale face shining through the gloom, seemingly unsupported, held a spectral quality.

'"*Who's there?*"' he called out, his voice filled with a mixture of fear and hope.

Caitlin had recognised the quote when her father had attacked her as being from *Henry V.* Was this question intentionally a line from *Hamlet* or was she beginning to see connections in coincidences?

'It's me, Dad,' she called, edging nearer, 'it's Caitlin.'

Larry shook his head as though trying to shake away a bothersome fly. 'Begone from me, demon. You're not real. You're dead.'

Caitlin hesitated, not wishing to scare her father but desperate to move nearer, to try to persuade him into the warmth and safety of her car.

'Who am I?' she asked.

'You're his wife,' said Larry.

'Whose wife?'

'Bill Shakespeare's wife,' he said. 'You're Anne Hathaway and I bet my Miranda sent you to talk sense into me. She always said she and Anne had a great deal in common, a playwright husband with too much enthusiasm for the stage and not enough for his home and his wonderful daughters.'

Unsure what to say, Caitlin decided to play along.

'You're right,' she said. 'I'm here to help you make sense of things.'

She moved a step closer.

'Sense,' Larry said and his voice was bitter. 'There is no sense. Not any more. All that I am, all that I was, all that I still hoped to become will be taken from me. Do you understand? Do you know how such treachery and despair feels? To have your sense of self, your very soul, stolen, while you are forced to live in an empty husk, waiting for death.'

Caitlin bit back her tears but did not attempt to reason with her father. Instead, she whispered, '"*Speak, I am bound to hear*"' – a line from *Hamlet*.

'Speak, you want me to speak?' he shouted. 'Very well, I shall tell you my tale, Mrs Shakespeare. My wife, Miranda, she was my true love. She gave me my three beautiful girls. All I wanted was to love and protect them, surround them with happiness, yet I failed. Miranda protected me from my own selfish ways, but when she died, my stupidity and carelessness glared at me from their eyes. I have lost my girls. My precious girls. All four... Did you have girls, Anne? Did your husband love them?'

Caitlin swallowed her gasp of surprise at his comment about all four of his daughters, but as she did, she coughed, her chest feeling suddenly tight and wheezy.

'We had two girls and my boy,' she said, but it was becoming difficult to speak. 'My husband claimed he lost them all after Hamnet's death.' The endless nights discussing Shakespeare and his life with her father allowed her to continue the conversation as though she were Anne Hathaway, wife of William Shakespeare.

'You had daughters?'

'Two. Susanna and Judith. And one boy, Hamnet. He died when he was eleven,' Caitlin said, trying to catch her breath. She reached for her bag and realised it was gone. Looking around frantically, she could feel her own panic rising.

'And your girls?' Larry asked.

'Married, both of them,' Caitlin replied, her voice rasping with the effort to keep her breathing regular. 'They were closer to me than Bill. He lamented he hardly knew them. Susanna, when she was older, became friendlier towards her father. She married a doctor. But Judith, no, they weren't close.'

'Doesn't it make you sad?'

'Haven't you read his plays, old man?' she said, wondering when the rest of the search party would arrive, her chest tightening painfully. 'The stories of fathers and daughters? The pain of loss between them? The loss of paternal love? His heart was broken.'

'I have three daughters – Goneril, Regan and Cordelia,' he said, then paused in confusion. 'No, there is a fourth, how can there be another? Lear has three daughters...' His voice trailed away and he wandered to one of the stones. 'Where is Cordelia?' he whispered.

'Dad,' Caitlin gasped, unable to continue the charade any longer. 'We have to go back to my car, I need my spare inhaler.' She was struggling to breathe.

'Cordelia will come for me,' he said.

Caitlin tried to inhale, to make her lungs work, but lights were popping all around her and the darkness at the corner of her eyes was more than the shadows of the night.

'Dad,' she gasped again as her knees buckled, no longer able to hold her up. 'Help me...'

Larry did not respond, instead he continued to speak to the standing stone.

'Not like this,' Caitlin said. 'Not alone.'

A hand reached out, grasping her wrist, and the woman stood before her. They stared at each other, their faces mirror images. The rain had stopped and they hovered in air of the softest blue. A rook circled above them and three bees danced around their heads.

'Cordelia,' Caitlin said. 'Am I dead?'

'No, Caitlin,' she replied. 'You're safe in the Everywhen, but you must breathe, you are the Charmed One, the one who will break the curse. Trust in the power of the Bee Maidens three, Corycia, Kleodora, Melaina, they will take you home and then you will tell my tale. The true tale will free us all from the curse of the past.'

Cordelia placed her finger on Caitlin's lips and, as she did, Caitlin felt a rush of relief as though the woman had given her the breath of life.

'Breathe,' Cordelia whispered as she faded away into the blue lights of the Everywhen.

"'Why should a dog, a horse, a rat have life, and thou no breath at all?'"

The words were distant, but she recognised her father's ranting voice as it drifted towards her. In the background were blue lights, the rain was easing and the cars parked near the stone circle were flooding the ancient stones with light. To Caitlin, it was hazy, strange – was she in her time or Cordelia's?

'Come on, Moon,' she heard Lee's anguished voice and in an instant she had returned to the present, 'breathe.'

She spluttered as the inhaler was placed to her lips, followed by the clammy plastic of an oxygen mask. The pain in her chest began to ease. Lee's white face was desperate, but the drugs were working and air was circulating her body, her mind, her heart.

'Lee,' she murmured, lifting the mask, 'thank you.'

'Where was your inhaler?' he asked, his fury driven by fear.

'Dad ran into me, I lost my bag,' she managed before a cough rendered her speechless.

Lee lost all control and pulled her into his arms, kissing the top of her head. 'Never do that to me again,' he sobbed.

'I promise,' she said, tears and laughter mingling. 'Where's Dad?'

'In the ambulance,' said Lee.

'How is he?'

'Confused, but he's safe,' he replied. 'If you're able to stand, I'd like them to check you too.'

Caitlin knew it would be pointless to argue and acquiesced with a nod.

'When we're home, I need your help,' she said as he helped her to her feet. 'I know what we have to do to save Dad.'

39

GOLDEN VALLEY, DOBVNNI, 860 BCE

Cordelia and Aganippus stood either side of Lear as the bodies of Goneril, Regan, Maglaurus and Henwinus were carried into the House of the Dead – the elaborate tomb on the edge of the hill fort. At Cordelia's request, Oudar had returned with them to take the role of Mother of the Temple. She had presided over the funerary rites and, as she led the procession, Cordelia wiped a tear from her cheek.

All around her, the battered and exhausted people who made up the remains of the once prosperous tribe of the Golden Dobvnni watched as the solemn rites were completed. Oudar poured the final libation to Corycia, Kleodora, Melaina, the Bee Maidens Three, at the entrance to the House of the Dead before Cordelia stepped forward, raising her hands in a request for silence.

'Today, we have laid to rest the daughters of Lear – my sisters, Goneril and Regan,' she said. 'A madness overwhelmed them but this does not excuse their tyrannical behaviour neither does it justify the cruelty of their husbands. To mark an end to this tragic era in our history, the House of the Dead will be sealed and a new burial ground created on the other side of the fort. Do not fear, even with the tomb sealed, our ancestors will not be abandoned. During the festival of Alban Arthuran, when the Cold Moon is full, Oudar and I will perform the sacred ritual of the dead to ensure our ancestors have a passage to the Everywhen. We will bless the three stones that have been toppled during the battles of the past year and create a conduit for the ancestors. They will remain connected to the land, to us, to those as yet unborn and to those who will one day join them in Albios, even if the burial ground is elsewhere.'

She pointed to the three standing stones that lay pushed against each other in a small dell and there was a ripple of approval.

'Remember the days when King Lear ruled and my sisters and I danced with fire,' she said and there was a respectful murmur from the gathered villagers. 'From tomorrow, we will begin again.'

* * *

After her father had saved her during the terrible storm, they had returned to Kamber's oppidum and, the following day, Lear had explained what had happened.

'A message came to me from Maglaurus,' he had said, 'stating he wished to negotiate terms. He refused to speak with any but me and told me where to wait. Once Locrinus was asleep, I followed the path from the back of the oppidum. When I arrived, he was waiting, but his suggestions were foolish, he claimed he was there on Goneril and Regan's command. It felt wrong.

'Then Ivor arrived, screaming his fury, claiming my girls were dead, murdered by the scoundrel Maglaurus. Ivor ran at him with his sword drawn and they fought, taking their battle beyond the circle. I knew this was a fool's errand and turned to leave, but Henwinus stepped out from behind one of the stones. He was quieter, calmer, trying to persuade me to side with him against Maglaurus, to make him my heir. He said if I refused, then he would hunt you down, Cordelia. He claimed he and Maglaurus would become renowned for killing the three daughters of Lear.'

He had paused, tears streaming down his face.

'I told them they would have to kill me first and Henwinus laughed, then we heard your voice and you ran to my aid. When you fell, I thought you were dead, but then I realised what had happened. You hadn't seen Maglaurus, he had returned from his fight with Ivor and was hiding in the shadows. I couldn't let him kill you, too, so I decided to do battle with him, no matter the outcome for me.'

There were tears in the one eye on show and he had turned to Cordelia, his face lined with age; defeated and full of regret.

'My madness has cost me dear,' he had said. 'From this day forward, I name you as my heir. I give to you and your brave husband, Aganippus, the charge of the hill fort of the Golden Dobvnni.'

Lear had broken down and Aganippus had commanded he be taken to his roundhouse and treated with kindness while he recovered.

Locrinus had asked after his son and Lagon had led a search party into the woods, but there was no trace of Ivor.

'We must assume he fled the fight,' Aganippus had said when Lagon returned.

'Should we search further, bring him to justice?' Lagon had asked.

'No,' Cordelia had interjected. 'There has been enough bloodshed; the time has come for peace, for a return to the life we lived before the madness of my father created havoc.'

Peace envoys were sent to the Golden Dobvnni with a decree from their new monarchs declaring an end to hostilities. Food was transported from Kamber's stores and a request was made for the bodies of Goneril and Regan to be treated with dignity.

When the envoys had returned, Sadiald, the wife of Dardan, Lear's former general, was with them.

'Dardan was murdered by the mercenaries not long after you left,' she had informed Cordelia and Aganippus.

'What happened to my sisters?'

'They changed,' Sadiald had said. 'Power does not always sit well on a person's heart. Goneril's dark side predominated, and when Regan watched her sister's cruelty, she too became imbued with evil. I believe they were bewitched by grief, power and shadow love.'

'What do you mean?' Cordelia had asked. It was not a term she had ever heard.

'Ivor returned,' Sadiald had confirmed. 'He and Goneril have long been lovers, but he also took Regan to his bed, then flaunted them to each other. The shadows that lurk at the edge of every love affair are deep with danger, love is a madness and when denied, the good can easily be subsumed by the despair and violence of thwarted emotions. When Maglaurus had them both murdered in their beds, Ivor lost his mind.'

Cordelia's devastation at the terrible fate of her sisters was all-consuming and she had excused herself from the roundhouse, hurrying to her and Aganippus's quarters for privacy. She had been aware of her sisters' darker natures, but she had hoped their goodness would prevail. Her tears had flowed, hot, desperate and full of loss, as she mourned the girls she had known and the happy, hopeful young women they had been the last night they had danced together.

'Will you visit them in the Everywhen?' Gloigin had asked her later that evening when, on Aganippus's command, she had taken Cordelia food and a goblet of mead infused with healing herbs.

'One day,' Cordelia had replied.

* * *

Now, as the winter sun threw its silver light over the funerary procession, Cordelia put aside the thoughts of the past and turned away from the House of the Dead and the three toppled stones. Lagon led Lear and Locrinus back to the central roundhouse, where a feast of tribute would be held for Goneril and Regan. Maglaurus and Henwinus would be quietly acknowledged, as was necessary for the favour of the gods, but there would be no celebrations of their lost lives. Tributes would be sent to the tribes of Albany and Dvmnonii to commemorate the loss of their heirs. The feast would be subdued and when it was over, the tribe would move forward.

'They must all be remembered,' Aganippus said as he and Cordelia made their way hand-in-hand from the House of the Dead towards the central roundhouse.

'Spaden the Gaul or one of his scribes will tell our tale,' she said.

'How will it end?'

'With daughters,' she said. 'Angarad's curse will remain for many generations.'

'How do you know?' he asked.

'I have seen how it ends,' she replied, 'and it is good.'

'Will you tell me?' he asked.

'No, but perhaps I shall tell our next daughter and she might whisper it to you when you're in your dotage.'

Aganippus looked at her in surprise. 'Another child?' he said and she smiled. 'It might be a son.'

'No,' said Cordelia. 'It will be a girl and we shall call her Caitlin.'

'It's a strange name,' said Aganippus, 'but you are queen and your wish is my command.'

Cordelia smiled up at her husband, then she took his hand and led him into the hall where the funerary feast awaited, where she could say goodbye to her sisters and wait for the day in the Everywhen when she was needed to save them all.

40

GOLDENWYCH, PRESENT DAY

Caitlin breathed in the familiar smell of the theatre. The faint mustiness no amount of beeswax polish could eliminate, the fresh paint of the scenery, the greasepaint and the mingled perfumes of the women who bustled around backstage. A buzz of excitement and anticipation filled the air, but there was an undercurrent of determination, a pride, a passionate desire that this would be the finest hour of the Goldenwych Players.

'Hey, Moon, are you ready?' asked Lee as he joined her in the wings.

'Yes,' she replied. 'Another hour, then curtain up at 7.30 p.m.'

'I have my doctor's bag,' he said, but she shook her head.

'You won't need it,' she said. 'Tonight will be magical.'

A shout from the other side of the stage for Lee's assistance with a poly-styrene standing stone caused him to shrug, drop a kiss on her lips and hurry away.

Annie walked past and gave Caitlin an exaggerated wink. 'I always hoped you two would find a happy ending,' she said.

Caitlin smiled. When she and her sisters had asked George Glossop and Annie Jefferson to call an extraordinary meeting of the Players and all cast members a week after Larry's disappearance during the storm, it was Caitlin who had taken the lead. She had stepped onto the stage, accompanied by Gillian, Rachel and Sindy, but she was the one with the microphone, deter-mined to overcome her fears of performing.

Waiting for the hum of conversation to fade away, gazing out at the auditorium, an unexpected electricity had flowed through her and for the first time since she was a child, she had felt the thrill of connecting with the audience. The rush of adrenaline and excitement of the live performance had suffused her and she understood her parents' endless joy at acting on this stage throughout their lives.

Familiar faces had gazed up at her and she had felt their love and concern.

'Thank you all for coming this evening,' she had begun and the last murmurs were silenced. 'Thank you, too, for helping to find our dad when he went missing. You'll all be relieved to know he is recovering well, he's home from hospital and has moved in with Gillian and Alan on a permanent basis.'

She had paused as there was a ripple of applause, which Alan had acknowledged with a wave.

'Dad, along with many of you, has been part of the driving force behind the Goldenwych Players since its inception,' Caitlin had continued. 'This place is more than a theatre to him, it's his second home. On occasions, Mum suggested he should make it his real home as he was here so often.' Caitlin had paused for the smattering of laughter, then she had taken a deep breath. 'My sisters, Gillian, Rachel, Sindy and I' – there was a gasp, but Caitlin had talked over it – 'have recently discovered that Dad has Alzheimer's disease. It's progressing faster than he expected and this is why his behaviour has been so erratic.'

Gillian, Rachel and Sindy had stepped forward, lining up on either side of her. Gillian had held out a tentative hand to take the microphone and Caitlin had passed it over, her throat thick with emotion.

'Dad suspected this might be his last show,' Gillian had said, 'and while we know he has upset a lot of people with his dictatorial manner, we hope you can find it in your hearts to forgive him now we know the reason.'

Rachel had then taken the microphone from Gillian.

'We're also aware the play is terrible,' she had said and there were murmurs of agreement in the audience. 'If you could be patient for a week or so, Caitlin has offered to rework the script to tell a different version of *King Lear*. Instead of the traditional line, following the king, she is going to adapt the play to be the story of his daughters. If we approach it from this angle, it takes the pressure off Lear – Dad – as the main character.'

'Is there another version?' a voice had called from the auditorium.

'Caitlin will be working the original history from Geoffrey of Monmouth,' Sindy had said. 'The first version of Lear.'

'What's the difference?' Ted had asked.

Caitlin had regained the microphone.

'In the original tale, Cordelia lives and helps Lear to win back his throne,' Caitlin had said. 'When Lear dies, Cordelia becomes the first Queen of the Britons.'

'Why did Shakespeare change it then?' another voice had called.

Caitlin had stepped forward again. 'It's possible it was for political reasons,' she had explained. 'Shakespeare's version of *King Lear* was written shortly after James I came to the throne. He was king following a period of female rule starting with Lady Jane Grey, Mary I, then Elizabeth I. In total, there had been a woman in charge for seventy years. There was also another potential queen who could challenge James's throne – the Lady Arbella Stuart. Shakespeare probably felt it was wise to make the king triumphant rather than end on another queen's rule.'

'We'll also endeavour for there to be no disasters on stage this year – no collapsing scenery, vomiting children or costume malfunctions,' said Sindy. 'So, we, the daughters of Larry King, the daughters of Goldenwych's King Lear, would like to ask for your help. Will you assist us in taking our dad's play – *King Lear – The Musical* – and creating the show he has always dreamed about performing?'

For a moment, there had been silence, then a murmur swelled, followed by clapping and shouts of, 'I will...' 'We're in...' 'We'll be there...'

'Alan should direct,' Barbara had called. 'He's been doing most of it anyway.'

There had been more shouts of approval.

'Please, if you're willing to help, a show of hands?' Rachel had said.

A forest of arms had shot into the air.

'Thank you,' Caitlin had said. 'Let's do this for Dad.'

The audience had responded with a cheer.

'For Larry!'

In the weeks that followed, the theatre had buzzed with activity. Caitlin had set up a base in the café, with members of the Players dropping by to help. Her own asthmatic collapse at the stone circle had shocked people, but her burgeoning romance with Lee was giving the village plenty to discuss. Her engagement to Stan had been a cause for much speculation when it was first announced, after they had separated and he had left with Daphne Hawthorne, the gossip level had risen ever further. Lee was a village boy, so his return and the ensuing romance was a story that was entertaining the inhabitants of Goldenwych for happy reasons.

'You might have told us about Lee first, dear,' Annie had said one Friday morning as she and Barbara ordered their usual.

'We're practically family, after all,' Barbara had said. Then, in a stage-whisper, 'And I promise we knew nothing about Daphne's carry-on with Stan. What a shocker! If we'd have had even an inkling, we'd have said.'

Caitlin had not replied, but as she turned to go, Annie had said with a kind smile, 'We always suspected Sindy was Larry's girl. She and Gillian are very alike. I'm glad you're all friends again.'

With the show scheduled for the week before Christmas, Caitlin's version of *Cordelia's Tale* had taken shape. She had felt as though her hand was being guided by generations of women. Cordelia appeared in her dreams at least twice a week and the detail of the story grew with each rehearsal. She had also noticed that since her final dream about the three sisters and their quest, the silver lines on her arms were fading, and in her dream the previous evening, Cordelia had held up her own arms to show the last of her strange marks had vanished too.

The Players practised with enthusiasm; dance routines were polished, scenery was built and costumes were fitted.

Alan had come home one evening to recount an incident to Larry, Caitlin and Gillian while Lee had squirmed with embarrassment.

'I was at the café, looking for Caitlin, and I let myself in the back room to find Annie kneeling in front of Lee, who was draped in red satin, while Barbara measured his bicep,' he had regaled roaring with laughter. 'It was quite a sight. Barbara turned around to me and said, "You're next, Alan, strip to your boxer shorts, please," and gave me a roguish wink. I ran for my life.'

'Coward,' Lee had snorted.

'Don't you find it strange that you're their GP now, even though you know both of them must have changed your nappies?' Gillian had added and Lee had buried his head in his hands to avoid the gales of laughter.

* * *

The week of the play had finally arrived and before she left for the theatre, Caitlin had visited the bees. She had whispered her father's diagnosis to them when she had awoken the dawn after the storm in the stone circle, but this morning she told them about the play.

'Please use your bee magic to ensure it's a success. Corycia, Kleodora, Melaina, the Bee Maidens Three, I ask for your blessing,' she had whispered.

A single bee had flown out of the hive, danced a figure of eight, then vanished back inside. Caitlin had felt the many layers of the story she had been drawn into were coming together in a harmonious and final ending.

Now, as she breathed in the silence of the theatre, enjoying the moment of respite before the noise and drama ahead, she wondered how the future would unfold. Was this play, the story of Cordelia's life, the charm to break Angarad's curse or had she convinced herself of this to make her sorrows easier to bear?

Her father's health was currently stable. When they had visited him in hospital the day after his breakdown in the stone circle, he had sobbed, apologising for not trusting them with his diagnosis sooner. He had agreed to try the experimental drugs he had been offered by the private clinic and, to the relief of the entire family, as well as Larry's friends and former employees, who held him in great fondness, these were helping. There were occasions when he became vague but they were less frequent than before he had begun his treatment.

'Will I be able to cope with playing Lear though?' he had asked Caitlin one evening when she had dropped in to see him at Gillian and Alan's.

'Yes,' she had replied, squeezing his hand tightly, 'because, everyone else has learned your part too and we can all prompt you. Not only that, but also Alan is playing Dardan, a new character, who was Lear's second-in-command, so he'll be beside you every step of the way.'

'But who's playing Albany?' Larry had asked. 'Husband of Goneril?'

'He's called Maglaurus in this version and Ted has stepped in,' Caitlin had replied. 'He's very good.'

Larry had been about to protest, then he considered Caitlin's words and gave a sharp nod of agreement. 'Yes, it's about time he stretched himself, instead of always scuffling about in the chorus.'

All around her, Caitlin could hear the bustle and panic of before-show nerves but she felt serene. In her heart, she knew the play would be a success and, if her father was well enough to take part in the following year's production, then it would be a bonus. She wondered if her mother was watching. If she was, then she would be relieved her daughters were friends again.

'What are you daydreaming about?' Lee said. He had changed into his Iron Age costume ready to play Aganippus, King of Gallia.

'Stories,' Caitlin sighed. 'Why do we tell them?'

'What do you mean?' asked Lee.

'My dad, your dad, the Players, everyone who has ever written a poem or a story, told a tale – why do we do it? What made the bards of old sit by the fireside and spin yarns?'

'Are you expecting an answer or is this rhetorical?' he asked, slipping his arms around her waist.

'We do it because it bonds us,' she said. 'It helps us to feel secure, to pass on shared history, to pull people together into a community. By telling stories, we're creating links with our past, with all the ancestors who have walked this planet before us. Our stories often flow from nowhere, as though they were already in our minds waiting to be accessed. What if it's because they're real, because we've lived them before?'

'It's possible,' said Lee, although he sounded sceptical.

'Do I really have to quote Shakespeare at you?' said Caitlin. '"There are more things in heaven and earth, Horatio, than are dreamt of in your philosophy."'

'Very funny and don't expect me to respond to the name Horatio,' he replied. 'What's brought on this bout of introspection?'

'Tonight, the telling of a tale we know is real, even if no one else understands,' she said.

'Moon, I know you think this will heal the curse cast by Angarad, but please don't raise your hopes that it might miraculously cure your dad,' he said.

'Is that why you think I'm doing this?' she said. 'Oh, Woody, you're the sweetest. I know the play won't heal Dad. I'm doing this for us, the King family, for Goldenwych, for Mum and for the real Cordelia – if she ever did exist – but not because I think it will heal Dad. One of his favourite quotes is from *As You Like It*: *"All the world's a stage, and all the men and women merely players: They have their exits and their entrances."* And Shakespeare was right, we're all playing parts, telling stories and acting on the stage of our lives; this is the new act or scene or even chapter in the drama of our life. The end of our family feud is enough – and the fact we're united in helping Dad as he faces the unknown.'

'I'll be there too,' Lee said.

'Of course you will, you're his doctor.'

'Not as his doctor, but I hope as his son-in-law,' Lee said and, to Caitlin's amazement, Lee went down on one knee and pulled a red ring box from underneath his costume. 'Caitlin Moonbeam Skylark King, will you do me the honour of being my wife? People may say it's fast, but we both know we've had a lifetime together already and I want to spend all the years of our present and future together too.'

Caitlin stared at him in astonishment, her eyes filling with tears as he opened the box to show her a gold ring set with a moonstone. 'Yes,' she said, her heart pounding. 'Yes, I will.'

Behind them, there was a huge roar of delight and as Lee slid the ring onto her finger, they were engulfed by the rest of the Players. Her father and sisters were the first to reach them, full of a sincerity and enthusiasm Caitlin had never felt they had shown towards Stan.

After a few moments of chaos, a whistle blew.

'Sorry to interrupt, but the front doors are opening!' Suki called, beaming at her son and Caitlin. 'Curtain up in twenty minutes. Beginners please.'

* * *

Caitlin stood in the wings, waiting for her cue. From the moment her father and Alan had walked on stage, the play had been perfect. Every song and dance number had been completed with aplomb, all lines had been remembered and even Pete's no-show had been covered by one of the other members. Rachel had fretted about it at first, but with Edward beside her, she had eventually thrown herself into her part, forgetting her troubles.

And now, thought Caitlin, *is the moment of truth.*

Her heart fluttered with nerves, but this extra, secret routine, had been at her suggestion. When she had mooted the idea to George and the rest of the cast, there had been some concern, but Gillian, Rachel and Caitlin had been determined.

'There will be two doctors there,' Caitlin had said and, eventually, the secret rehearsals had begun.

'Ready, Moon?' said Gillian, coming up beside her, holding the hand of Sindy's daughter, Rosie.

Sindy followed a few seconds later, zipping up her costume after a quick change.

'Yes. You two?' she replied and Sindy nodded.

'As I'll ever be,' Gillian replied, reaching up to adjust the neck of her costume. As she did, Caitlin saw a flash of gold as the pineapple pendant she and Rachel had bought Gillian all those years ago caught the light.

'Your necklace,' she whispered.

'Alan had it repaired and the earrings, although I didn't think they were suitable for my costume,' she said. 'I tucked the pendant inside during the play. He gave them to me when it was confirmed I was pregnant.'

'What?' Caitlin and Sindy gasped in delight.

'Don't tell anyone yet,' she said, but she was beaming.

'Of course. Does Rabbit know?'

'I told her a few minutes ago.'

They waved to Rachel, who was in the wings on the opposite side of the stage with her daughters, Emelia and Porcelain. Rachel gave a double thumbs-up.

Lee and George left the stage as their scene finished and the lights dimmed.

Rosie, Emelia and Porcelain ran on stage, their tap shoes loud in the silence.

'Ready?' whispered Gillian.

'Ready,' said Sindy.

'Ready,' Caitlin said and they joined hands.

The music began, the old story of the mouse in a windmill in old

Amsterdam, and the four King sisters ran on stage to stand behind their nieces and daughters, the routine reworked to include them all.

In the wings, Caitlin saw George, Suki, Edward and Lee surrounding Larry, who had tears of joy in his eyes. Annie, Barbara, Saul, Vicki and Ted watched from the other side.

The younger girls began to sing, then Gillian's voice filled the theatre, followed by Rachel, Sindy and Caitlin. Her heart pounding, Caitlin waited for the change in music, and as the beat sped up, she stepped forward and began to dance her turning triple-time step. A roar of excitement from the audience filled the small theatre and as she finished with a flourish, her father, with Lee and George running behind him, flung himself into her arms.

'Family,' he said as his four daughters and three granddaughters hugged him and the audience cheered. 'There is nothing more beautiful than the love of your family.'

The lights dimmed and the entire cast assembled on stage for the final number, the end of Lear's troubles, the reuniting of Goneril, Regan and Cordelia, the happy ending never written for Lear but hoped for throughout every tale ever told. As the bars of Sister Sledge's 'We Are Family' boomed out, Caitlin saw a gold light at the back of the auditorium and, in a flash, the real women from the past flickered into being, the inspiration for all the stories of their lives, and Caitlin knew, whatever they were facing with her father's illness, they would face it together and with love.

Cordelia and her sisters bowed to her and she bowed in return.

The golden light faded and, as Lee took her hand, a peace settled in her heart as, with her family, she began to sing.

EPILOGUE

GOLDENWYCH, TWO YEARS LATER

'Would you wait a moment, please,' said the nurse as she guided the scanner over Caitlin's swollen stomach. 'I'm going to fetch a colleague. There's nothing to worry about.'

She smiled reassuringly and left the room.

Caitlin and Lee stared at each other in surprise. Caitlin's pregnancy had been progressing smoothly so far.

'Have a look while she's out of the room,' Caitlin whispered.

'No,' Lee replied.

'You're a doctor,' she said, her voice tense. 'You'll be able to tell if there's something wrong.'

'I probably could tell, but this isn't my area of expertise,' he replied.

Caitlin lay back and waited. Ever since the triumph of *Cordelia's Tale*, life had taken on a magical quality and she had been convinced this was thanks to the breaking of the curse.

'The curse that probably didn't ever exist,' Rachel had laughed one day when Caitlin had mentioned this theory.

Gillian's pregnancy had gone without a hitch, delivering a multiple birth of three girls. Both she and Alan had been overwhelmed but delighted.

Rachel's divorce from Pete, while not friendly, had not hit anything other than the usual snags and Larry had insisted on paying Pete a lump sum if it would ensure Rachel, Emelia and Porcelain were protected. Pete had recently moved to Spain with his new girlfriend, but he spoke to his daughters twice a week. Edward had been true to his word and as soon as Rachel's divorce was final, he had proposed. They had opted for a quiet register office wedding and been blissfully happy ever since.

Sindy, Rosie and Vicki had been absorbed seamlessly into the King family and there were days when Caitlin forgot it had not always been this way.

Caitlin and Lee's marriage had taken place in Goldenwych Church with a reception in the theatre afterwards. Larry had walked her down the aisle and had managed to make a speech at the wedding breakfast afterwards. His condition had continued to deteriorate, but at a slower pace, thanks to the drugs. Caitlin hoped he would be able to understand and enjoy the birth of her and Lee's first child.

'Why do you need to find out the gender?' Rachel had said with a laugh when Caitlin and Lee had set off for the scan. 'It'll be a girl. It's always a girl. We only have girls.'

'It'll be good to have it confirmed,' Caitlin had replied.

The door opened and another nurse entered. She smiled at Caitlin.

Caitlin gripped Lee's hand as the nurse examined the screen.

'Perfect,' she said. 'My colleague was correct, but it's always good to confirm these things.'

'There's nothing wrong, is there?' asked Lee.

'Absolutely not,' said the nurse. 'Two happy and healthy babies, twins.'

'Twins?' said Caitlin in surprise.

'Do you want to know? Boy or girl?'

'Yes,' said Lee.

'Congratulations, it's one of each, a baby boy and a baby girl.'

Outside the window, a rook cawed, before disappearing off into the brilliant summer sky and the Everywhen.

* * *

MORE FROM ALEXANDRA WALSH

Another book from Alexandra Walsh, is available to order now here:
https://mybook.to/AlexandraBackAD

ACKNOWLEDGEMENTS

Thank you for reading *Daughter of the Stones*. I hope you enjoyed meeting Caitlin, Lee, Cordelia, Aganippus and their friends and families as they found a way to heal their pasts.

This is a book I have wanted to write for a long time, so I hope you've enjoyed it. The present-day section began life as a film script, a comedy, but somehow I was never able to make it work, probably because the subject matter was not actually very funny. Once this penny dropped, I revisited Caitlin, Gillian, Rachel and Larry and realised they needed to link with the original version of the *King Lear* story as told by Geoffrey of Monmouth in *The History of the Kings of Britain*. *The Tale of the Three Sisters* was a legend I created long ago but was never able to use, then it managed to work itself into this story. The connection to Carl Jung came from a random thought one day and after checking a few references, I understood why my unexpected Arthurian-style legend had pushed its way into this story.

A book is never the work of one person, it's a collaborative effort. Thank you, as always, to my wonderful agent, Sara Keane, with her kindness, humour and understanding. Thank you to Sarah Ritherdon and Francesca Best for their constant support and brilliant editing. A huge thank you to the wider team at Boldwood Books too: Amanda, Wendy, Marcela, Mills, Ben, Hayley and the marvellous team responsible for the cover, copyediting, proofreading and marketing.

Thank you to all the people who are always there to offer support, advice and wine. Mum and Unc, Deborah Black, Gemma Turner, Alison, Katy (God-daughter extraordinaire), Martha and Richard Miles, Shaun Rose, Kathryn, Simon, Daisy and Nelly Bennett, Ian Connell, Emma Gregory, Jo Walker, Viv Bishton, Suzi Judd, Kate Richardson, Colena Abosh, Jane Cable, Carol McGrath, Sarah Bennett and Bijou Mgbojikwe.

Most importantly, thank you to you for reading this book, without you, none of this would be possible.

THE REAL CORDELIA

My inspiration for this story came when I first read William Shakespeare's *King Lear* many, many years ago. I was struck by the strength of the female characters, even though by the end they had sunk into stereotypical female roles: women turning on each other because of a man's manipulation and the death of the innocent. However, it inspired me to write a contemporary version, exploring the roles of the three sisters.

A great deal of rewriting and refinement has brought this original story into the book as the present-day section. In its first draft, the story of Caitlin, Larry, Gillian, Rachel et al was a film script. However, despite numerous rewrites and interest from film producers, I never felt the story was right and put it to one side. The story remained with me though, and I soon realised the reason it hadn't worked was because it needed an historical timeline. In order to do the women in the tale justice, my quest began for the origins of the *King Lear* story – and what a journey it became. Here is what I discovered.

There are two versions of *King Lear* from Shakespeare's time: the Quarto (1608) and the Folio (1623). The texts vary; the Quarto is missing 100 lines that are in the Folio and there are 300 different lines in the Folio that are not in the Quarto. Shakespeare scholars believe these differing lines are complementary to each other and the story. All very interesting, but digging deeper it was quickly clear Shakespeare had taken his inspiration from an older folktale.

In 1577, the *Holinshed's Chronicle* was published. This was a collaborative work featuring the old legends of Britain. A second version was republished ten years later and it's believed this was what encouraged Shakespeare to write not only *King Lear* but also *Macbeth*, *Cymbeline* and perhaps nudged him towards the history plays. However, the *King Lear* tale in the *Holinshed's Chronicle* was based on a much older manuscript: the words of the cleric, Geoffrey of Monmouth.

Geoffrey of Monmouth's book, *Historia Regnum Britanniae*, translated as *The History of the Kings of Britain*, was first published in 1135. Prior to this, British historians tended to begin the history of Britain with the Roman invasion in 55 BCE. Geoffrey was to change this when he wrote a detailed account of Britain's history dating back to Brutus the Trojan prince who brought the first people to Albion – Britain's original name – followed by pages and pages of previously unheard stories, including one of the earliest versions of the King Arthur myth.

In the book *Britain Begins* (Oxford University Press, Oxford, 2012), author Barry Cunliffe writes, 'How did Geoffrey learn all of this? His reply was simply that his friend Walter, the archdeacon of Oxford, gave him "a certain very ancient book written in the British language" which he had brought from "outside the country".' Geoffrey claims he translated this text into straightforward Latin, shortening a few stories, adding some details of his own and creating the *Historia*.

Unfortunately, no other contemporary scholars ever viewed this book and the general consensus has been that Geoffrey created the entire history. If he did, then he was a brilliant writer because his stories continue to be used as a basis for folklore and storytelling today.

It was from Geoffrey I took my main inspiration for the Iron Age section of the book. Using various clues within the text, I estimated the Lear story was set in approximately 862 BCE. The Iron Age ran from 1300 BCE to 900 BCE, followed by the era known as Classical Antiquity, which overlapped with the Iron Age and saw the rise of the ancient Greek and Roman empires. The Romans invaded Britain in August 55 BCE.

The first challenge was creating a viable world in the Iron Age, then linking it to Caitlin in the present day. There are no written records from this period but there have been many archaeological digs and the lives of people from this period have become well-documented from the goods they left behind. This includes the outlines of roundhouses, cooking utensils, seeds, food waste and weapons, which have given incredible information on everything from warfare to daily food. Stone circles, statues of deities and funeral goods have given suggestions of religious rituals and beliefs.

I am also lucky enough to live near Castell Henllys, a recreation of a real Iron Age village. A visit here is truly a portal to another time and it helped me to visualise the hill fort and surrounding areas. At Castell Henllys, the roundhouses are built on the footprints of postholes discovered during the archaeological dig that has been ongoing for over twenty-five years. It's a fascinating place and its staff and volunteers are very knowledgeable. I was even able to sample Iron Age recipes and have my face painted with intricate blue woad patterns while we watched a straw man burn.

It was with these experiences in mind that I returned to *The History of the Kings of Britain*. In the original, Geoffrey used the spelling 'Leir', but I decided to go with the more familiar Lear. All the other main character names featured are from this original version, while the supporting cast have been given names from stories either side of Lear, to ensure they were contemporary.

The *King Lear* of Shakespeare's time follows the majority of Geoffrey's version: Lear plans to divide his country between his three daughters, Goneril, Regan and Cordelia, once they have publicly declared their love for him. Cordelia refuses and when Lear disinherits her, the first suitor, Ebraucus, Duke of Burgundy, rejects her. However, Aganippus, King of Gallia, agrees to marry her even with no dowry and the fact she has been banished from the family. Goneril marries Maglaurus, Duke of Albany, and Regan weds Henwinus, Duke of Cornwall. In Geoffrey's tale, Goneril and Maglaurus have a son, Marganus. Regan and Henwinus also have a boy, Cunedagius. This was obviously part of the story I changed.

As time passes, the two sisters become aggravated with their father as he moves his huge entourage into their homes and creates havoc. The two husbands decide to take over Lear's territories and, in despair, Lear and a small entourage flee to Gallia (France) where Cordelia and Aganippus take pity upon him. They agree to help him recover his land and the trio return at the head of an army.

Maglaurus and Henwinus are killed in the ensuing battle, although Monmouth gives no information about what happens to Goneril and Regan. All he states is they 'disappeared' when their father was no longer prepared to bestow gifts upon them. Aganippus, Cordelia and Lear are successful and Lear regains his kingdom as King of Britain.

This is where the *Holinshed's Chronicle* tale ends but Geoffrey continued the story. Lear reigned for another three years, then both he and Aganippus died, leaving Cordelia to reign, effectively making her the first queen of Britain. She ruled for five years until her nephews rebelled against having a woman on the throne. There was a bloody battle and Cordelia was eventually overthrown. She was imprisoned and, according to Geoffrey, was in such despair, she hanged herself.

Perhaps Shakespeare had access to a copy of *Historia Regnum Britanniae* and took his inspiration for his own tragic ending for Cordelia from there. In Geoffrey's version, there was no subplot concerning Edgar and Edward, the sons of Lear's great friend, the Earl of Gloucester, as there was in Shakespeare's version, although I have included them as Locrinus, Lagon and Ivor.

There was also no mention of Cordelia as a shaman, but in order for her to be able to connect with Caitlin in the present day, I needed a means. Druids, shamanism and the tradition of talking to the ancestors in the Everywhen are ancient practices and this felt the easiest way to have my two heroines communicate. In Alice Roberts's book, *Ancestors, The Prehistory of Britain in Seven Burials*, she discusses the use of henbane as a potential hallucinogen that could have been used as part of religious rituals. As henbane is a plant native to the UK, I realised I had found my way for both Cordelia and Caitlin to enter the Everywhen.

The women in the temple with Cordelia are my own invention, but the idea of giving women seniority over religion was inspired by the multitude of goddess figurines and female deities discovered throughout hundreds of years of archaeological digs. It also felt important to give Cordelia a power-base that was exclusively feminine, a feeling of women working together for survival, as well as being part of the wider community. As both a princess and high priestess/shaman, Cordelia would have been a significant and respected figure in the village.

Whether Cordelia was ever real or simply a creation of Geoffrey of Monmouth's imagination, we shall never know, but *Daughter of the Stones* challenged me to enhance and evolve the tale of *King Lear* in order to create a more realistic role for the women of the story. Whenever I write, I try to give back the voices to the women of the past and Cordelia, with her sisters, Goneril and Regan, are no different. They are as important as the women who came centuries later but whose lives have been lost to the shadows. This is my tribute to Cordelia, the first Queen of Britain.

SELECT BIBLIOGRAPHY

If you're interested in discovering more about this period of history, literature and folklore, then some of the books I found useful were:

Airey, Raje; Greenwood, Susan, *The Illustrated Encyclopedia of Witchcraft and Practical Magic* (Lorenz Books, London, 2007)

Beck, Martha, *Finding Your Way in a Wild New World* (Hachette, London, 2012)

Burl, Aubrey, *Prehistoric Astronomy and Ritual* (Shire Publications, Oxford, 1983)

Clark Hall, J. R., *A Concise Anglo-Saxon Dictionary* (Cambridge University Press, Canada, 2004)

Cowan, Tom, *Fire in the Head, Shamanism and The Celtic Spirit* (Harper Collins, San Francisco, 1993)

Cunliffe, Barry, *Britain Begins* (Oxford University Press, Oxford, 2012)

Davies, Andrew, *Beekeeping: Inspiration and practical advice for would-be smallholders* (Anova Books, London, 2007) and cotswoldbees.co.uk

Dixon-Kennedy, Mike, *A Companion to Arthurian and Celtic Myths and Legends* (Sutton Publishing, London, 2004)

Eason, Cassandra, *Cassandra Eason's Complete Book of Natural Magick* (Quantum Books, Slough, 2006)

Ferguson, Diana, *Tales of the Plumed Serpent, Aztec, Inca and Mayan Myths* (Collins and Brown, London, 2000)

Fox, Margalit, *The Riddle of the Labyrinth* (Profile Books, 2013)

Hoffman, David, *Welsh Herbal Medicine* (Abercastle Publications, Ceredigion, 1978)

Horwitz, Sylvia L., *The Find of a Lifetime: Sir Arthur Evans and the Discovery of Knossos* (The Viking Press, New York, 1981)

Jung, Carl Gustav, *The Red Book: Liber Novus, A Reader's Edition* (W.W. Norton & Company, China, 1962)

Kruta, Venceslas, *Celts: History and Civilization* (Hachette Illustrated UK, London, 2004)

Lawrence, Sandra, *Witch's Forest: Trees in Magic, Folklore and Traditional Remedies* (Welbeck, London, 2023)

Mansell, Chris, *Ancient British Rock Art: A Guide to Indigenous Stone Carvings* (Wooden Books, Glastonbury, 2007)

Ordnance Survey Historical Maps, Ancient Britain (Ordnance Survey, Southampton, 2016)

Parr, Kevin, *The Quiet Moon, Pathways to an Ancient Way of Being* (Flint Books (imprint of The History Press), Gloucestershire, 2023)

Rhys, Ernest (Editor), *Holinshed's Chronicle* (The Temple Press, Letchworth, 1943)

Roberts, Alice, *Ancestors: The Prehistory of Britain in Seven Burials* (Simon and Schuster UK, London, 2021)

Roberts, Alice, *The Celts, Search for a Civilization* (Heron Books, London, 2015)

Ruden, Sarah (Translation), Murnaghan, Sheila (Introduction), *Homeric Hymns* (Hackett Publishing Company, USA, 2005)

Shakespeare, William, *King Lear, The Arden Shakespeare* (Thomson Learning, London, 2004)

Shakespeare, William, *The Complete Works* (Oxford University Press, Oxford, 1984)

Tate, Nahum, *The History of King Lear, Regents Restoration Drama Series* (Edward Arnold Publishers Ltd, London, 1976)

Thorpe, Lewis (Translation), Monmouth, Geoffrey of, *The History of the Kings of Britain* (Penguin Books, London, 1966)

Wohlleben, Pete, *The Hidden Life of Trees: What they Feel, How they Communicate, Discoveries from a Secret World* (William Collins, London, 2007)

ABOUT THE AUTHOR

Alexandra Walsh is the bestselling author of dual timeline historical mysteries. Her books range from the fifteenth century to the Victorian era and are inspired by the hidden voices of women that have been lost over the centuries. Formerly a journalist, writing for national newspapers, magazines and TV.

Download your exclusive bonus content from Alexandra Walsh here:

Visit Alexandra's website: http://www.alexandrawalsh.com/

Follow Alexandra on social media:

facebook.com/themarquesshousetrilogy

x.com/purplemermaid25

instagram.com/purplemermaid25

tiktok.com/@alexandracwalsh

ALSO BY ALEXANDRA WALSH

Letters from
the past

Discover page-turning
historical novels from
your favourite authors
and be transported
back in time

Join our book club
Facebook group

https://bit.ly/SixpenceGroup

Sign up to our
newsletter

https://bit.ly/LettersFrom
PastNews

Boldwood

Boldwood Books is an award-winning fiction publishing company seeking out the best stories from around the world.

Find out more at www.boldwoodbooks.com

Join our reader community for brilliant books, competitions and offers!

Follow us
@BoldwoodBooks
@TheBoldBookClub

Sign up to our weekly deals newsletter

https://bit.ly/BoldwoodBNewsletter

www.ingramcontent.com/pod-product-compliance
Ingram Content Group UK Ltd.
Pitfield, Milton Keynes, MK11 3LW, UK
UKHW041049201025
8482UKWH00007B/53